Praise for
the New York Times bestselling
Belador series

DRAGON KING OF TREOIR

"Once again, Dianna Love gives us another fantastic story that keeps us glued to our seat, unable to put the book down."~~The Reading Café

"…an ongoing fantasy series, and definitely not the end, nor is it a cliff hanger. I loved the ending and can't wait for the next book to come out."
~~ Madison Fairbanks, Amazon

"As much as I am impatient for each installment these stories are so worth the wait." ~~ Rosemary, Amazon

"Dianna Love has created an extremely diverse group for her Belador series, and seeing if they can overcome challenging issues makes her stories continuously riveting." ~~ Always Reviewing

"What a ride!!! This series keeps getting better and better." ~~ Gaby, Amazon

ROGUE BELADOR

"When it comes to urban fantasy stories, Dianna Love is a master." ~~A. Richards, Always Reviewing

"This adventure win or lose is going to change things for Evalle and her friends. Brava Ms. Love for another fantastic ride." ~~ In My Humble Opinion

"It was worth every day of waiting." ~~ J. Cazares, Amazon

"As always, Dianna Love delivers another sensational story that will blow your mind," ~~ Barb, The Reading Café

"Keep them coming and I will keep reading. Thank you for another awesome adventure." ~~ Candi, Amazon

WITCHLOCK

"Fans of Rachel Caine's Weather Warden series will enjoy this series. I surely do." ~~D. Antonio, In My Humble Opinion

"Every scene in WITCHLOCK is absolutely spellbinding...This remarkable author repeatedly leaves you wondering if there truly are happenings on earth of which we are not aware..." ~~Amelia, SingleTitles.com

"I LOVE THESE BOOKS! I wait impatiently for every book to come out and have never been disappointed." ~~Elizabeth, Reader

DEMON STORM

"..non-stop tense action, filled with twists, betrayals, danger, and a beautiful sensual romance. As always with Dianna Love, I was on the edge of my seat, unable to pull myself away."~~Barb, The Reading Cafe

"There is so much action in this book I feel like I've burned calories just reading it."~~D Antonio, Goodreads

"...I have to thank Dianna for keeping this series true to the wonderful world, witty dialogue and compelling characters that I have loved since the first book." ~~Chris, Goodreads

RISE OF THE GRYPHON

"...It's been a very long time since I've felt this passionate about getting the next installment in a series. Even J. K. Rowling's Harry Potter books. It's a story you don't want to end and when it does, you can't help but scream out 'No! NO THEY DID NOT JUST DO THIS TO ME!! NO!!!!'" ~~Bryonna Nobles, Demons, Dreams and Dragon Wings

"...shocking developments and a whopper of an ending... and I may have exclaimed aloud more than once...Bottom line: I really kind of loved it." ~~Jen, Amazon Top 500 Reviewer

"I want more Feenix. I loved this book so much...If you have not read this series, once again, what are you waiting for?" ~~Barb, The Reading Cafe

THE CURSE

"The Beladors series is beloved and intricate. It's surprising that such a diverse and incredible world has only three books out." ~~ USA Today, Happy Ever After

"The precarious action and genuine emotion in THE CURSE will continuously leave the reader breathless..." ~~Amelia Richards, Single Titles

"If you're looking for a series with an epic scope and intricate, bold characters, look no further than the Belador series...This new addition provides all the action and intrigue that readers have come to expect...a series to be savored by urban fantasy and paranormal romance fans alike." ~~Bridget, The Romance Reviews

ALTERANT

"There are SO many things in this series that I want to learn more about; there's no way I could list them all... have me on tenterhooks waiting for the third BELADOR book. As Evalle would say, 'Bring it on.'" ~~Lily, Romance Junkies Reviews

"An incredible heart-jolting roller-coaster ride ... An action-packed adventure with an engrossing story line and characters you will grow to love." ~~ Mother/Gamer/Writer

"An intriguing series that has plenty of fascinating characters to ponder." ~~ Night Owl Reviews

BLOOD TRINITY

"BLOOD TRINITY is an ingenious urban fantasy with imaginative magical scenarios, characters who grab your every thought and more than a few unpredictable turns ... The meticulous storyline of Book One in the Belador series will enthrall you during every compellingly entertaining scene." ~~Amelia Richard, Single Titles

"BLOOD TRINITY is a fantastic start to a new Urban Fantasy series. The VIPER organization and the world built ... are intriguing, but the characters populating that world are irresistible. I am finding it difficult to wait for the next book to find out what happens next in their lives." ~~Diana Trodahl, Fresh Fiction

"BLOOD TRINITY is without a doubt one of the best books I've read this year... a tale that shows just how awesome urban fantasy really can be, particularly as the genre is flooded with so many choices. Brilliantly done and highly recommended." ~~ Debbie, CK2s Kwips & Kritiques

BELADOR COSAINT

BOOK NINE

THE
BELADOR
SERIES

DIANNA LOVE

The Belador series is an ongoing story line, and this is the reading order:

Dedication

Thank you to the Dianna Love Reader Community group on Facebook who brighten my days. I appreciate all the love of reading and time you share with me.

CHAPTER 1

Quinn moved with stealth toward a rusty railroad trestle ten feet high, which spanned a narrow creek feeding straight into the Chattahoochee River on Atlanta's west side. The trickle of water barely qualified it as a creek.

He held up a hand for Devon, the Belador warrior following him, to wait a moment. His other teammates, Evalle and Tristan, were approaching along the river from the other side of the railway. He had to give credit to the murdering trolls.

They'd chosen well for a hideout.

They'd have remained hidden, too, if they hadn't started killing adults and kidnapping children.

Giving Devon a hand signal, Quinn continued on, preparing to insert his team and rescue kidnapped human teenagers from dangerous preternaturals.

It would be simpler if Quinn and his people didn't have to hide whatever happened from humans in the area.

Rush hour traffic had started hours ago, but still slogged along the interstate fifty yards away where six lanes crossed the river.

At least now it was dark. Between that and today being Monday, he had less chance of his team getting seen by some sporting enthusiast floating down the Hooch, as this part of the river was known locally. On the other hand, the city was enjoying warm temperatures for early April. Some adventuresome spring breaker might decide to get wet.

Eyeing the trestle ahead, Quinn shook his head. What had triggered this insane action?

The local trolls had to be out of their minds to harm *any* human, but to go after families of Belador warriors was suicidal.

Beladors had even stopped a preternatural who'd been *killing* trolls last year.

Relations had been pretty decent, until now.

In the latest attack at a midtown home, a mother had been found dead, mangled, and her two teenagers missing. That made five attacks in two days.

Three dead and a total of eight teenagers taken.

So far.

Those two words twisted his gut. No child should fear being kidnapped.

What about my child? Who is watching over her?

Quinn's chest tightened with pain. Weeks of searching for a child he'd learned of only recently, and he'd turned up nothing. He had a duty to save these teenagers first, then he'd go right back to hunting Phoedra.

Devon tapped his shoulder.

Quinn turned to see what the Cajun wanted.

Evalle and Tristan were Alterants, mixed-blood Beladors, with bright green eyes they hid behind dark sunglasses, but they had natural night vision.

Like Quinn, Devon was a full-blooded Belador with supernatural powers, but they had to utilize night vision monoculars. Quinn looked down to where Devon had located four-toed footprints heading toward the dark underpass. Each toe had a deep claw mark.

That confirmed the intel.

Nodding, he turned to move ahead. He and his team had finally gotten a break on today's heinous crime, which led them to this location.

Good thing since Storm wouldn't be back until later this evening. Evalle's Skinwalker mate could track any scent, even a preternatural one, in his human form or as a black jaguar. He'd been in Roanoke, Virginia, for the last twenty-four hours helping a short-handed Belador team dealing with similar attacks there.

Six hours had passed since a Belador father here in Atlanta, just off patrol, had walked into his house expecting to find his family getting ready for a spring break trip.

Instead, the Belador had found food scattered around the kitchen island, his wife ripped into pieces and his two children missing.

Quinn continued moving slowly toward the underpass.

His team was exceptional, but they were also friends he didn't want to see harmed. As their Belador Maistir, he ordered people into danger all the time, but everything about these attacks said this was not a normal situation.

He did a mental eye roll at that thought.

Talk about an oxymoron.

Everything Beladors confronted fell under the heading of abnormal.

Reaching the spot where he and Devon were to watch for Evalle and Tristan, Quinn dropped into a crouch behind a small bush to scan the area. From the other side of the narrow rail bridge, Evalle removed her dark sunglasses, exposing her glowing green eyes. She blinked twice at Quinn to signal that she and Tristan were in place.

Quinn gave a hand signal of confirmation, then looked over his shoulder at Devon, who crouched close behind him. Quinn gave the signal to move out. Devon had limited telepathic ability, but the Cajun could move in this environment as silently as a lizard.

Speaking mind-to-mind would be simpler, but Quinn had been the one to caution against using telepathy unless they had no other choice.

Until recently, no one besides other Beladors or their Treoir rulers could communicate with a Belador telepathically. The one exception to this rule being select Beladors who could reach the VIPER liaison, Sen. But the Laochra Fola, an enemy group related to Beladors, had appeared in Atlanta recently with the ability to pick up their telepathic messages.

As if trolls weren't enough to contend with?

Quinn opened his senses wide as he picked his way over rutted ground that deteriorated further every time foul weather drove the water hard through here.

He smelled rotting foliage, but no trash.

Another sign this had to be the right place.

Trolls kept the area leading to their nest free of human debris.

Dirt had been piled against one shoulder of the underpass.

Using his telekinetic ability, Quinn pushed gently at the loose earth. The dirt shifted aside easily, meaning it hadn't been in that spot very long.

As he used his power to quietly clear dirt out of the way, a rough-cut, wooden covering five feet across and six feet tall came into view.

No hinges.

It should lift away, but what waited on the other side?

Cutting his eyes around, he signaled Evalle and Tristan to watch their backs.

Quinn motioned Devon into position on the opposite side of the wood covering.

Devon moved with Belador hyper-speed.

Since they were somewhat hidden, humans shouldn't see anything unusual that happened down here unless this turned into a battle of power and majik that exploded in bright bursts.

Letting out a slow breath, Quinn lifted his hands and nodded at Devon, who mirrored his moves.

They each raised one side of the wood hatch by using kinetic power, and moved it an inch at a time until Devon took control of the cover and slipped it softly to the ground.

No one came flying out with a mouthful of sharp teeth, but trolls wouldn't need to when they could wait in the perfect ambush spot.

Quinn squatted to look inside.

Stone stairs went down, disappearing into a black hole.

That could lead to a simple, large room if the trolls hadn't been here long, or if they'd had more time, to a maze of tunnels.

He hated tunnels. Only one way in and one way out unless you had inside information.

The trolls would have an exit plan, but they'd also keep it well hidden, which made for a perfect trap if someone was crazy enough to break into a troll nest.

Schedule me for a psych eval as soon as this is over.

Quinn ducked his tall frame into the hole, glad he'd worn cargo pants for ease of movement. They were all outfitted in similar black clothing from neck to toe.

The air had a damp, sour odor to it the deeper he went, but he had no complaint about the solid rock steps.

No squeaking noises.

No sound at all.

His skin crawled with warning.

Trolls had never been a docile group, but for the most part the local ones kept to themselves. There had been one instance when Svart Trolls from another country invaded Atlanta with plans to take over the city. Other than that, the trolls tended to be good about policing their own community to avoid VIPER stepping in to do that for them. The VIPER coalition acted as a governmental body over all preternaturals in the human world.

With the exception of a select few, humans never knew what happened in the supernatural underbellies of cities across the country because VIPER *did* police its own. But trolls attacking the human families of Beladors threatened to expose the preternatural world if they didn't put a stop to it.

Once humans discovered just what lived among them, it would be chaos.

Twenty steps down, Quinn moved aside to allow Devon to join him. Tristan followed with Evalle taking up the rear.

Quinn gave them a sign to wait, then stepped away to figure out what lay ahead of them. The area opened up into a wide hallway fifteen feet across and an easy eight feet tall, but maybe forty or fifty feet deep.

A light glowed way down at the other end, which outlined an arched opening into another room.

Giving a hand signal to move out, but be alert, Quinn led them forward.

Halfway to the end of the tunnel, Quinn sniffed. Ah, the putrid stench of troll.

He looked around at Evalle, Tristan and Devon who all pinched their noses to let him know, yes, they smelled the nasty beings.

Quinn would have liked for Storm to be here, since the Skinwalker could discern just how many trolls they were going up against.

Devon touched Quinn's shoulder. When he looked back, Devon pointed at Evalle, who tapped her ear.

Quinn listened, and the faint sound of a child crying reached him. Shit.

He nodded and moved ahead.

At the end of the tunnel, he peered ahead into a cavernous area with a higher ceiling. Ripped roots dangled from where the trolls had hollowed out earth for their hideout. The barren space held two wooden tables and four beat-up chairs suitable for the dump. Two torches were mounted on each side of a room sixty feet across.

Quinn couldn't determine the depth.

The room fell away into blackness.

The child's whimpers were louder now. Was it real?

His instincts screamed *trap*.

Troll stench permeated the air. He was not leaving until he knew for sure whether the children were here or not.

He took it all in, trying to figure out what he couldn't see. There had to be some kind of strong glamour hiding the true interior of this place and the number of people actually inside here.

A child whimpered again.

Stepping inside the room, he moved quickly to the right, leaving enough space for Devon to follow his lead and stand with his back to the wall as well.

Evalle and Tristan did the same on the other side of the archway.

Tristan leaned forward and gave Quinn a signal that he had an idea.

Oh, hell. Quinn's disconcertment must have shown because Tristan sent him an irritated look.

A bonus of being half-blood Beladors meant Tristan and Evalle could shift into gryphons. This would be the worst place for them to shift, though, with limited room for movement.

What else could Tristan be thinking? He sucked at hand signals.

Then it hit Quinn.

Tristan had once been given a special, majikally-spelled drink by a witch. A power highball, as Tristan described it, which had included the blood of immortal beings. He'd ended up with the ability for limited teleportation under the right conditions.

Teleporting here would be just as insane as shifting.

Tristan had no idea what area would be safe for landing.

Still, their dragon king had made Tristan his second in

command. Since then, Tristan had proven himself to be competent and loyal as hell. A real change from when Quinn had first met the young man, so he gave Tristan a go-ahead nod to show the team what he had in mind.

Tristan blinked out of view and all hell broke loose.

CHAPTER 2

Guttural voices roared and light shot from the middle of the room beyond where Quinn, Evalle and Devon remained.

What had happened to Tristan?

High-pitched screams sounded like kids, then deep shouts and bellows overpowered them.

Quinn rushed forward just as the glamour hiding all of that fell away.

Tristan appeared in the center of the space now, fighting two trolls. A third troll with black eyes and long, spiked teeth stood in front of a series of large cages containing two terrified teenagers and three adults. With a horn sprouting out of his thick head, hair everywhere, and standing seven feet tall, the guard troll held a short axe in each hand. He looked ready to bludgeon anyone who dared touch the cages.

Devon said, "He's mine."

Evalle rushed over to help Tristan.

Using kinetics, Quinn knocked one of Tristan's attackers backward so Evalle and Tristan could battle one at a time.

The eight-foot monster troll Quinn had knocked away rolled and came up on his huge feet. He had linebacker shoulders if someone wanted a giant on the football squad. A vicious tusk jutted down each side of his mouth where saliva drooled. When he charged Quinn, he opened a maw filled with needle-sharp fangs.

Shoving up a kinetic wall, Quinn prepared to drive the monster back.

But the troll opened his hand and tossed sparkling dust in the air that blasted Quinn's invisible wall apart.

Those sparkles stank of burned limes. Noirre majik?

Screw being careful.

Quinn shouted to his people telepathically, *They're using Noirre. Don't link and do whatever it takes to win.*

That countermanded his original order of bringing in the kidnappers, or at least one they could use for intel. Right now, he was more concerned about all of his team surviving.

Fighting a troll had inherent risks for anyone.

Fighting one that wielded Noirre majik turned the odds against even a Belador.

Devon struggled with the shorter, black-haired troll who had been guarding the cages. His telepathy didn't always work as well as the others so Quinn didn't know for sure that Devon caught the message authorizing him to use deadly force.

Evalle had thrown her power in with Tristan to battle his adversary. They had their troll on the ground. As soon as one of them could get free, Devon needed help.

Monster troll roared, yanking Quinn's attention back to staying alive. The troll swatted a beefy power hit at him, but the power blast connected with Evalle instead.

She went flying across the room backward and hit a wall, bouncing to the ground with a groan, but still upright.

Tristan's troll was back up and now had Tristan by the throat.

Quinn kept slamming kinetic hits at his big troll, hoping the miserable beast wasn't schooled in how to use Noirre majik effectively. If so, this troll would have already done a better job of wielding it as a weapon.

Growling, Evalle ran across the room, leaped into the air and flipped, landing on the back of the troll choking Tristan. She lifted her spelled blade and reached around, shoving it through the troll's forehead.

She shouted an order for the spelled blade to stay put.

Quinn got hit across the middle with an invisible bat. He blinked at the monster troll, who drooled through a snarl. "Die, Belador."

"Not yet," Quinn said, gasping for air and catching his balance.

Tristan fell back, holding his throat and sucking in air.

Quinn's troll pulled out another fist of sparkles.

Where was he hiding the bag of that crap?

Fuck this. Quinn would rather dive into sewage than enter the mind of a troll or a demon, but this one appeared to be running the show and had control of their Noirre supply.

When Tristan's troll fell backwards, Evalle leaped away then yanked out her blade. She turned on Quinn's troll, who cocked back his arm to throw the Noirre at her.

No time left.

Quinn shouted at Evalle, "No!" He pushed inside the troll's mind and shoved power hard into that thick skull. Dull pain slugged through Quinn's head. This shit would hurt later.

The massive troll slapped his head with the hand holding Noirre crystals. He smashed the sparkles into his eyes and howled, jerking his head back and forth.

Evalle swung around with a *what-are-you-doing?* look.

Quinn gritted out, "Help Devon!"

"I'm on it." She spun around and dove toward Devon, who was on the ground in a wrestling battle with the guard troll.

As long as Quinn had forced his way into his troll's head, he might as well find out what was going on. But the deeper he pushed, the more it was like digging face first through a clogged toilet. Flashes of faces and names came through, but nothing he could grab hold of except ... *get Belador children.*

The harder Quinn fought with his mind lock, the louder the troll roared and finally ran himself head first into a wall.

Quinn jerked out of his mind a second before the troll's head literally exploded. Murky-colored blood splattered everywhere, choking the air with a sewage odor.

Damn, that was too close. If Quinn had stayed in there, he might have suffered serious brain damage through the connection.

"Way to go, Evalle," Devon complimented.

Quinn looked over to see Evalle standing over her blade shoved into another forehead. At close to six feet tall, with dark brown hair and wearing black cargoes and a long-sleeved T-shirt instead of her usual BDU shirt and jeans, she was *the* role model for badass women.

She cut her eyes at Devon, gave him a half grin, and

shrugged.

Tristan walked up to Quinn, looking like a magazine model gone to war. He kept his tawny hair cropped in the messy look of today's young men, and filled out his black ensemble with cut muscle. Coughing, he pointed at the exploded head and said in a hoarse voice, "There goes our intel."

"Better to lose intel than any of you." Quinn gave Tristan a long look. "How did you know you could teleport inside their glamoured area?"

"I didn't, but it seemed like a good idea."

Bloody hell. Quinn had seen Tristan go from a loner who cared for no one except his foster sister, to someone who had tried to sacrifice himself for Evalle and their cause as he fought alongside her. Tristan had helped Evalle and their new leader, Daegan, escape the Medb stronghold. Now this young man was their dragon king's *Rí Dtús*. Daegan had come from an era where that title designated a right-hand man.

Taking Tristan's new responsibility into consideration only made his teleporting stunt that much worse.

"What would I tell Daegan if we'd lost you?" Quinn asked.

"Shit happens?" Tristan lifted his arms, then seemed to notice the odd quiet that had settled over the room. He frowned and turned around to face the cages.

Quinn peered at the enclosures, too.

All five humans were silent. Three were staring in wide-eyed shock.

He took in the red-haired pair of human teenagers who fit the description of the seventeen-year-old boy and fifteen-year-old girl missing from a Belador family. Those two were shaken up, but they wouldn't be overly surprised to witness Quinn and his team battling trolls. Belador families were aware of the preternatural world but kept its secrets.

The other three humans sat slack-jawed, no doubt trying to process the battle that had just taken place.

Tristan whispered, "We should ask the humans a few questions before calling in Sen."

Evalle walked up. "Why?"

Devon was right beside her. "Because, *cher*, they'll tell us anything right now. We're their saviors."

Quinn said, "Good idea, Tristan."

Tristan's smile jumped to cocky, so Quinn added, "Much better than the one where you teleported into a pile of trolls that could have killed you. I would rather not have to share *that* detail with Daegan."

That wiped the gloating off Tristan's face.

"Hey, what the hell are you people?" a man in the last cage called out.

Devon murmured, "There we go."

Quinn asked Evalle, "Would you go talk to the two children? Confirm they're our Belador family?"

"Sure."

There were ten cages. The first one held both teens, then there was a gap before the last three. Quinn would like to think keeping them together had been out of consideration for the kids, but it was probably simpler not to listen to those two complain and whine if they were left apart.

Evalle opened the cage and slipped inside, squatting down to speak softly with them.

No one could come out of the cages until the cavern was cleaned up. Noirre sparkles scattered around still had the potential to harm a human. This place stank like crazy.

Tristan had stopped at the cages with the other two adults and tried to talk to the men. Both were around thirty and looked snatched straight from the 'hood. They scooted back into the corners, as far away from him as they could. He shook it off and moved on to the guy who appeared anxious to engage.

As Quinn joined them, he was surprised at the candor of the human speaking.

This guy looked closer to forty, with thin brown hair that had been cut nicely but looked ratty right now. He'd been captured wearing a suit that was now dirty and sweaty.

Shoving a wary gaze to Quinn and Devon first, the man turned to Tristan and said, "What *are* you?"

"That's rude," Tristan said. "Most people ask names first."

Quinn barely managed not to roll his eyes at Tristan.

"Oh, uh, I'm Marty." He wiped his mouth with a shaky hand, but his eyes said he had a thousand questions. "What's your name?"

"Tristan." Pointing at Quinn, Tristan said, "This one is the boss. His name is Quinn, and that one is Devon. The woman with us is Evalle. How'd you end up here?"

"Those things ... uh, sorry, I don't know what to call them. I don't want to insult anyone, but, are you guys ... aliens?"

"No. We were all born here on earth. Those were trolls."

"No shit? Trolls really exist?" Marty's eyes bugged out when he stared at the closest troll. Evalle's blade remained buried in the troll's head. Marty sank onto the single broken chair against the wall in his cell. His attention returned to Tristan. "I'm a freelance reporter. A lot of my articles make the local news. I've been following wild stories about trolls, witches, warlocks and demons. I'll be honest, I thought it was all a hoax until one of those ... trolls caught me one night and knocked me out."

"He hit you and you survived?" Devon asked in disbelief.

"No. I mean he put some kind of mojo on me and I just passed out."

"Oh, yeah, that makes more sense."

Marty said, "I woke up in this cell."

"Did you hear anything they said?"

"I always heard them, but they didn't always speak English. Sometimes it sounded like maybe Swedish or Nordic or hell I don't know. Weird." He caught himself, quickly addressing everyone. "I'm not calling anyone weird. I don't judge."

Quinn noticed Tristan's eyes twinkling.

The Alterant was enjoying this. Quinn might have too if not for how bad this place smelled between the Noirre majik, troll BO and stinking blood.

Marty had quieted for a moment, concentrating on something.

If Quinn had to bet, he'd say the reporter was thinking about how much he should share. He probably thought he was going to get an exclusive on this.

Devon must have read the same thing. He scratched his jaw and his next words came out sounding like a Cajun from the back woods of Louisiana instead of the Ivy League graduate Quinn knew him to be. Devon was a warrior who would use any method at his disposal for withdrawing intel.

"I can understand a human bein' too terrified to get anything useful from a troll," Devon said.

Affronted, Marty sat up straight. "I'm an award-winning journalist. I've been in the middle of military operations that would turn your hair white and I've gotten exclusive interviews with world leaders. My network didn't expect me to come back alive from those campaigns."

Tristan said, "I'm impressed. We work for a top-secret arm of the government to protect humans. It's imperative that you share anything you heard so we can find the other missing humans."

Devon coughed to cover his choked laugh.

Quinn managed not to smile.

Tristan remained dead serious while he faced Marty.

"I understand. I want to help save others, too. The troll you fought was called Arto. The big troll that Quinn fought was called Gils," Marty said. He glanced at the third one, which had guarded the cells. "I don't know his name. He said very little and just did whatever Gils said. Right before you showed up, Arto was trying to convince Gils to grab their stash and run. He said they'd end up dead if they didn't."

Quinn looked at Arto. He'd been right.

Evalle joined them. She whispered, "Those are our kids and they're good."

Thankfully, Quinn could now face the warrior who hadn't expected to get any of his family back, and return his children safe and sound.

Marty said, "Gils argued they'd made a deal for, uh, something that sounded like no-war-ay."

Tristan nodded. "Noirre majik."

"Right." Marty frowned in thought then continued. "Gils contended they had to make good on their end of the bargain. If they backed out now there would be nowhere to hide from some goddess. He also called her a queen." He looked up at all three of them. "Do you have a queen?"

Tristan turned to Quinn, letting him answer.

"Yes, we do, but not the queen the trolls were talking about."

"Oh, man. Do these goddesses and queens have powers?"

"Yes."

Marty's face exploded with enthusiasm as if he'd just found the Holy Grail. "I thought I was going to die, so this sucked at first, but now it's gonna be amazing."

"Not if you don't have more to tell us, Marty," Tristan said in a mild warning tone.

That snapped the reporter back to the moment. "Got it. Arto argued that they didn't have everything the woman wanted and the longer they stuck around, the less time they had to hide from her. Arto would have made a much better leader," Marty mused.

"What else?" Quinn asked, trying to move this along. He was ready to call in Sen for cleanup, plus he had a child of his own to find and no decent leads. The only positive point about *his* child was that few knew of her existence and no one knew where she lived.

He hoped that was the case since *he* hadn't been able to find her even with his considerable resources.

"Gils flat-out said no," Marty continued. "He said he'd rather cut out his own heart with a dull knife than face what that woman would do if they ran without delivering on their end and she caught them. He said they had plenty of food and could finish this the right way." Marty's eyebrows dropped low over his eyes in a look of deep concentration. "You know what? I never saw them bring in any food."

Tristan snorted and covered his mouth to hide his reaction.

Poor Marty didn't realize he was sitting in the cupboard.

Evalle asked, "How did they catch the other people?"

Marty stood up and dusted off the minute he realized she had noticed him.

Smoothing his wild hair to now be neat, but grimy, Marty said, "Hi. You're really amazing."

Evidently he found spiking trolls in the forehead with her blade hot.

Evalle quirked an eyebrow at the obvious flirt. "Thank you. My mate would agree."

"Mate? What kind of mate?"

"He's a Skinwalker. He turns into a jaguar about this tall." Evalle held her hand level with her chest, which wasn't an exaggeration. "He killed a troll bigger than these because it hurt me."

Marty swallowed and toned down the charm.

Sounding pleasant, Evalle encouraged, "You were telling us how the trolls were getting humans."

"Oh, yeah. The two guys over there were following ads offering money for information on paranormals."

Tristan tensed. "What kind of ads?"

"That's the crazy thing. There are two ads. They look identical and I've seen the one from the guy in Atlanta who has been hunting paranormals for a long time, but I think the trolls copied it and put out their own."

Muttering a curse, Tristan told Quinn, "I know people at the company he's talking about. They're legit humans and only one woman there knows about us, but she keeps our secrets. Until we get this troll problem handled, I'll see about having their ads pulled. Then we can go after the phony ad."

"Good." Quinn recalled Evalle mentioning that Tristan had met a young woman with that group. The damned ads had apparently become a chum line for trolls.

Marty snapped his fingers. "Hey, I want to interview each of you and get pictures."

Evalle snickered. "That's not going to happen."

"Okay, forget the pictures. I can appreciate you want to remain anonymous like *Batman*, but this is huge."

"*Batman*?" Tristan scowled. "We're real."

"Of course you are," Marty said, rushing ahead. "Look I'm ready to get out of this cell."

"It's too dangerous for you to walk around the Noirre majik," Devon warned him. "You get that stuff on you and hoo-man, that'd be bad."

Marty's eyes widened when his gaze dropped to the floor, searching it as if man-eating scorpions would jump out of the cracks. "Okay, I understand."

Tristan sighed and suggested, "We might as well call in Sen. Time to wipe their minds."

"What?" Marty started looking back and forth, immediately agitated. "No. You can't do that ... can you?"

"Yes, and it's for your own good," Evalle pointed out. "You don't want to be involved in any of this. You're lucky you didn't get eaten."

"Eaten?"

She nodded. "The trolls were trading those two teens, but you three were rations."

Marty went from excited to frightened to disappointed all in ten seconds. "I'm glad I didn't get eaten." He shivered. "But this is the story of a lifetime."

"We'll make you a deal. If we ever go public, we'll let you do a story," Devon offered.

"Thanks. I appreciate that potential story, but do you really have to wipe my mind?"

"Yes."

"Well, shit. At least tell me this. Is there really a dragon?"

Everyone froze and looked at him. Quinn posed the question, "Why would you think that?"

"Arto said he'd do his part for that woman's event, but he was leaving the minute the dragon showed up because he didn't believe that she could keep them safe."

CHAPTER 3

The realm of TÅµr Medb

"Why is there a problem with using trolls?" Queen Maeve demanded of the warlock reporting in from her Scáth Force, an elite group of warriors. She'd designated a six-man team for a special mission.

"The older trolls are more cautious and won't get involved," her warlock said. "We're having to deal with young ones, who are often careless."

"If we lose a few of those trolls, so what?"

"You are correct, my queen, they are no real loss, but their mistakes have resulted in Beladors recovering some of the children before we were able to retrieve them."

"Do not allow that to happen," she warned in a voice that sent one of the warriors behind him stepping back. Either that or she'd lost some physical control and her face had altered shape.

Taking in the stunned expressions, it must have been the latter. She swirled away to buy a moment to compose herself, then eased the anger from her voice before turning to address them again.

"I'm pleased with the results so far." When their faces relaxed, she added, "But I do wish to capture more Belador children in the next few days. Allow no harm to come to the nasty little brats, and be sure to feed them, just in case my plans change."

"That's not a problem, my queen. We've been targeting twelve-to-seventeen year olds. They tend to be less trouble since they grew up in Belador households and are resilient, for humans."

"Very well, continue on and keep me informed if anything significant changes." Finished issuing orders, Queen Maeve dismissed the contingent of warlocks, teleporting them to the human world.

Power flushed across her skin just before Cathbad the Druid appeared in his usual dark suit, which allowed him to blend in better among human men. Or so he said.

She preferred the shoulder-length hair he'd worn when robes were in style rather than these shorter, brown locks that curled in small tufts around his face.

His beauty had destroyed hearts in his time, but not hers. She would never be so foolish as to give a man her heart.

Cathbad had adapted easily to life in the modern human world.

Lately, he reminded her of a well-dressed thundercloud. In fact, he was scowling yet again.

"What's your issue now, Cathbad? You've been in a far worse mood than I for weeks, yet I'm the one who's been slighted."

Giving her a stern expression, he demanded, "What are you up to with our people, Maeve? I see only a skeleton guard in the tower. We're goin' to lose what force we have in the human world if you keep settin' them up to be killed."

She floated toward him. "Those are *my* people who do my will whenever I choose."

When he said nothing to that, she added, "Unlike you, I have not sat idly during the weeks since my mistreatment at the hands of the Tribunal."

"Mistreatment?" His smile fit the sarcasm in his voice. "Oh yes, it was simply a lack of manners on their part. That's why you cost us an alliance with VIPER." A vein pulsed in his throat during his angry tirade. "I could have maneuvered past Daegan's challenges, but I didn't get the chance to save our position, because you couldn't control your temper *or* your form."

"None of this is my fault," she hissed, realizing he'd been brooding since they returned from that Tribunal meeting.

"It's not? What about growing into a giant at the Tribunal? You couldn't even maintain your normal body shape!"

"That was just a sign of my powers getting stronger." She wished. She had no idea what was going on with her body. One minute she'd feel fine, then the next she'd get sick to her stomach and the world around her warped out of shape.

Or she warped out of shape.

This had been happening ever since she reincarnated, but until right before that Tribunal meeting she'd been able to hide it from everyone. Even Cathbad.

It didn't matter.

She was not about to admit a weakness to a druid as powerful as Cathbad. She bluffed, "I am in full control of my body and powers."

He leaned closer. "I hope so, but we've lost the upper hand we had by being part of the coalition. I keep tellin' you to let me deal with Daegan, but all you do is argue with me. The minute you had to face him in the Tribunal, you let him win. That makes us look weak, so don't whine to me about being slighted."

"Don't push me, Cathbad," she warned, feeling her body twisting inside.

"Oh, I'm gonna push you. If you had kept your head together, we'd have gotten Kizira's body, too. All that maneuverin' only to leave empty-handed. We had a plan, a great plan, which would have allowed us to work our way deep into VIPER and eventually take over Treoir. What is wrong with you, Maeve?"

"Nothing!" Energy shot from her. Colors raced through her vision. Her body undulated and her stomach heaved.

When she blinked, she'd doubled in size and was staring down at Cathbad.

"So this is full control of your powers and body, eh?" Cathbad said in a stinging tone.

Energy boiled inside of her. She snarled and flipped a hand in his direction. Her air slap knocked him backwards. He hit the wall and landed flatfooted.

Straightening his suit, he walked back over. "Do not make that mistake again, Maeve. We've known each other a long time, but I am not one of your servants to suffer your abusive whims."

She felt her insides kink and tighten as she shrank back to her normal size. She was not about to apologize to anyone. Not when all others were below her, but she needed to bring Cathbad back in line with her plans.

Turning him into an enemy would be unwise and dangerous.

Offering her best imitation of a repentant expression, she said, "You're right."

His anger fell away, leaving shock in its place. "What did you say?"

She narrowed her eyes, because acting docile would be unbelievable to the druid who had known her so long. "Don't rub it in my face, Cathbad. I said you're right. I need your help. I'm suffering some kind of side effect lately. I'm not sure why. But fighting with you isn't helping."

Studying her, he nodded slowly. "I can accept that, but I am still concerned about what *your* witches and warlocks are doing in the human realm. I've heard of some takin' Noirre majik with them. What are they usin' it for?"

He would go ballistic if he knew why and just how much. In a haughty tone, she said, "We have plenty of Noirre that even those in the Scáth Force have never seen. I use it as I see necessary."

"What do you hope to gain by creatin' chaos in that world?"

She hadn't begun to cause the level of chaos she had in mind. "To get my dragon back, for one."

Cathbad looked like he was heading for a seizure this time. "That bloody dragon has caused enough trouble. You should have killed him here in TÅµr Medb when you could have. You had him at your mercy when he was cursed as a throne."

"I will not allow him an easy way out," she snapped. "No one tries to kill me and gets away with just dying. I want centuries of payback."

"That was two thousand years ago, Maeve. Get over it."

"No. I was not around for most of that time to see him suffer. He will serve me another two thousand years. Maybe then I'll put him through a slow, painful death."

Cathbad paced away, staring at nothing, then turned back. "I hope the loss of physical control is not a sign of you deterioratin'. I have cared many years for you, my love, but lately I find myself waitin' on the Maeve I know to return."

He could be incredibly sweet and charming when he wanted to be, which was how he'd slipped inside her emotional defenses so long ago.

But he could also be a vicious enemy when crossed.

She said, "I'm right here."

"I hope so, because I'm very concerned. I do not intend to spend the next millennium stuck in this tower. I didn't wait two thousand years to reincarnate into this body only to end up in a livin' prison. I want to know I still have a partner in all of this."

Just when he was winning his way back into her good graces, he pissed her off again. She would not tolerate anyone dictating to her.

"You want a happy partner, druid? Then get my dragon back."

Cathbad's power grew until it felt like the air couldn't hold it. "Even if we got Daegan back, we'd still be stuck here. Do. You. Not. Get. That?"

"Careful, Cathbad. I *am* gaining power," she lied, just to make him worry. "I will not allow anyone to insult me and live. You haven't considered that if we bring the dragon here I could compel him. That might return Treoir to us even more quickly and without having to fight a battle."

Chuckling in a dark way, Cathbad looked down and muttered something to himself, then swung his stern gaze at Maeve. "Did you not see what Daegan did in the Tribunal meetin'? He backed down every god and goddess there by pointin' out that none of us know the identity of his birth mother, who was clearly a goddess. I, for one, do not want to find out she was some favorite concubine of Zeus. It could have been a great bluff, but if his mother turns out to be as powerful as Daegan alluded, she could breach this realm."

Maeve would have explained more of her thinking if he hadn't pissed her off. She'd tell him enough to send him on his way. "If my plan goes as I intend, Daegan will never have a chance to call in his mother once he gets here."

Cathbad's gaze remained steady with a look that said he thought she was not entirely sane.

He'd find out soon enough, she was not only sane, but brilliant when it came to getting what she wanted.

Ready to change the topic, she asked, "Where is Ossian? He hasn't reported in recently."

"I was on my way to meet with you and bring him in when I

noticed warlocks leavin' for Atlanta."

Using only her eyes, she dared him to raise that subject again, but he didn't. She'd compelled one of the Scáth Force team to do her bidding without telling anyone her orders, including Cathbad. The only way he'd find out would be if he singled out that warrior, who was the lowest ranked.

Cathbad said, "Once I determine that Ossian is alone, I'll have him open the connection for me to bring him into the tower." He closed his eyes for a few seconds, then lifted his hands and gave a wave.

Ossian appeared, but not looking like his normal self. He lifted his hands to indicate his collared red shirt and black pants, which suited the olive skin and black hair of his current persona. "I apologize, my lord and queen. I was on my way to VIPER headquarters to check in. This is how I appear as Emilio, the Italian mage working for VIPER."

"You may remain in that form to conserve your energy," Cathbad said. "Please tell the queen how nothing new is happenin', because everyone at VIPER has a kill-on-sight order for our people."

Ossian's eyes showed his surprise for a second before he settled in to say, "Basically, that's true."

Maeve ignored Cathbad's negativity. "What else have you to report, Ossian?"

Brightening, he answered, "You asked for more on the witch known as Veronika. As she is held in the highest security beneath the mountain housing VIPER headquarters, it's difficult to access her. I did gain one opportunity when I physically impersonated a Belador guard, but the liaison, Sen, mixes up the list for guard duty to prevent anyone building a relationship with those in high-security lockdown. Most guards are given that duty once, maybe twice a year."

"I'm not hearing good news," Maeve commented dryly.

"I do have some. I've seen an opportunity to return to guard duty."

"Oh?" Maeve smiled, then caught Cathbad's sour look. What could be the problem now?

With her one-word encouragement, Ossian continued. "I also picked up part of a conversation about Veronika between two

Beladors. One had recently taken his turn at guard duty on her level. He has to check on the inmates once each shift. When he walked past her cell, which is warded and hidden behind a rock wall unless Sen clears access to view her, the guard heard her whisper, 'I know what your Maistir is hiding.' The Belador intended to tell his Maistir, but his friend warned that guards weren't supposed to interact with inmates. He pointed out that Veronika could just be trying to get Beladors in trouble, because she could then lie and say he'd engaged her in conversation. The one who heard the whisper concluded that it would be foolish to repeat. They both agreed to tell the Belador Maistir if they heard her say anything that would matter to him."

"Have you heard anything else to corroborate this?" Maeve asked.

"Not exactly, but I guarded her high-security level the day Belador Maistir Vladimir Quinn brought the Sterling witch to see Veronika. I couldn't hear the conversation since I had to remain at the entrance, but just before Quinn and the Sterling witch reached me on their way out, I heard Veronika screaming 'I know your secret,' which I reported to you and Cathbad."

"I recall that, but at the time we expected to have a solid resource on Quinn," Cathbad noted, referencing the plan for Maeve to use necromancy on Kizira's body, which they'd lost.

"Exactly, my lord. Quinn looked shaken as he left the secure area. At that time, I thought merely talking to Veronika had rattled him, but now I'm thinking she knows something very important that Quinn wants kept hidden."

Cathbad crossed his arms and lines formed at the bridge of his nose. A sign he was deep in thought. "This could be useful."

"Could be?" Maeve asked, wondering how he could take this so lightly. Addressing Ossian, the warlock whom Cathbad had poured majik into for days to make him a one-of-a-kind operative, she asked, "When can you go back to guard that level?"

Cathbad reacted quickly. "Careful, Maeve. I will not lose Ossian after all that I've put into creatin' a polymorph. He is the only one we have who can change his entire physical appearance at will. That was no easy task and every time he alters his appearance it drains him, which is why I told him to stay in his current state."

Sighing loudly, Maeve said, "When did you become so whiny, druid?"

His face darkened and his power expanded, pushing against her until Cathbad snapped his fingers and vanished.

She released a deep breath, enjoying the lighter air in her domain with him now gone. In fact, having him leave made her next decision that much simpler.

"Now, Ossian, back to what we were discussing. When can you see Veronika again?"

Ossian glanced at the empty spot where Cathbad had been, then shifted his gaze to Maeve. "Tonight."

Seeing his discomfort, Maeve turned on her own charm and smiled at the young man. "That would be excellent. By the way, you do know that ultimately, you work for me, since I rule this realm. Right?"

"Yes, your highness."

His quick answer was perfect. The man was not stupid.

She said, "Then you also realize that on occasion I will need you to perform an activity specifically for me and to hold what I tell you in confidence."

This time, though, he hesitated just a second. "Yes, your majesty, but Cathbad said I should run every mission past him so that he could advise me on any limitations I might have."

She waved off that comment. "Have you had any problems since becoming a polymorph?"

"No."

"Then you're fine. I would not send you to do something I felt you weren't capable of handling, and I was privy to all the work Cathbad did in recreating you."

Ossian's forehead smoothed as his stress lessened. "You make a valid point, my queen."

She poured a little power into her smile this time. While Ossian might be a polymorph, he was a man underneath all of that. She could sense his desire and spoke in a lusty voice, "I would reward you greatly for a successful mission."

"I understand, my queen," he said without a smidgeon of doubt in his words.

That was more to her liking.

"Tell me exactly how you'll get to Veronika so I can hear if everything sounds safe for you," she asked, just to make him believe she had his best interest at heart.

"I've been waiting for a Belador guard to be chosen who doesn't have a spouse or family locally. I had to kill the last one whose place I took. I used this Emilio persona to help hunt for his killer, which was never found due to my being given a way to hide my Medb scent."

"What if VIPER sends you out on a mission as Emilio before you can take the image of the Belador guard?"

"I've developed the Emilio identity as a not-so-powerful mage, which means I'm not in demand. Plus, I've also managed to annoy Sen to the point he doesn't call on me often. This allows me a lot of freedom to move around on my own schedule."

"Nicely done," she complimented. "Can you reach Veronika to actually speak to her?"

Ossian literally beamed at the sudden attention and became animated with the chance to show his wit. "Sen controls the rock covering her cell and a ward that contains her inside the room. I have an idea how I might access the witch. Even if that doesn't happen, I can still talk to her, since she clearly whispers through the rock." He pondered something, then added, "I doubt she'll share information unless she's going to receive something she considers of equal value in return."

Laughing lightly, Maeve said, "I would be disappointed if she made it that easy. I will give you something she can't afford to pass up."

Bowing, Ossian said, "I am ready to carry out your orders."

CHAPTER 4

Evalle and Storm's building in Atlanta, Georgia

Daegan walked through a dark part of the building that held those contraptions they used for traveling. Odd structures. He preferred teleporting. "What day is this?"

Evalle had been leading him through the building. She turned. "Tuesday. Barely. It's about two in the morning here."

When she continued on, he ducked his head to enter the space Evalle called a conference room. She had said the room would be suitable for a round-table meeting with five of his closest advisors joining him.

It would be if the table had been a round shape instead of rectangular and the room could expand to double in size.

He'd found people would speak more freely when they were comfortable.

Leaning against a wall on the far side of the room, Storm wore jeans and a black T-shirt, the only thing Daegan had ever seen him in.

Storm spoke. "Hi, Daegan. Welcome to our place."

"Good to see you back in Atlanta. Thank you for helping our warriors to the north and for providing a place to meet in the city." Getting a simple nod from the Skinwalker, Daegan eyed the table again, where Adrianna and Tristan sat far apart. Quinn had taken a seat at a corner near where Storm stood.

Evalle had paused on Daegan's left. She drew his attention when she cleared her throat and politely asked, "Is anything wrong, Daegan?"

To answer honestly would insult her and Storm. He said, "No. Why would you think so?"

After a brief glance in Storm's direction, she replied, "You're looking at that table like it might bite you. I know the reasons you prefer a round table, but that shape wouldn't offer an efficient setup for a business conference space."

"Your furnishings are exceptional. I did not intend to give you the impression otherwise, but perhaps we could meet in that first area I came through."

Storm observed it all without chiming in. He clearly wanted to allow Evalle to take the lead. Wise man.

Adrianna watched the byplay between Daegan and Evalle, allowing a smile to tease her lips.

Tristan frowned, probably at a loss for how to offer Daegan something better. That one worried too much.

"You want to meet in the garage?" Evalle asked, irritating him with her incredulous tone.

Daegan looked to Storm for help, but he remained silent.

Evalle's face took on a thoughtful expression. "Okay, you're always saying we should speak our minds, Daegan. I'm speaking mine. Something is bothering you. What is it?"

Now what could he say?

Tristan jumped in. "Do you want somewhere a little more ..."

"Open?" Storm filled in, finally offering some aid.

Daegan couldn't get a lie past Storm, which might be a problem at some point, but for now he simply gave in. "Yes."

Speaking to Evalle, Storm said, "Let's take them to the roof."

She snapped her fingers. "Great idea."

Tristan stood. "Good thing it's in the middle of night so you can enjoy it. Bet you don't get up there often, Evalle."

"Every day," she shot back. "In fact, I like sunset the best. Wait until you see what my mate created for me," she said with no small amount of pride.

Storm stepped away from the wall. "Let's go."

Daegan said, "Visualize the area and I'll teleport all of us."

"Works for me." Storm focused and said, "I've got it."

Drawing on his power, Daegan teleported them all to the roof and grinned as soon as he arrived. The room covered the entire top level of the building, with a large seating area on one end.

Thick sofas and chairs were covered in colorful material. Plants of all sizes were placed on small tables and in large pots. Small trees were scattered about. A comfortable table and chairs to serve ten had been arranged at the other end of the room. Thick rugs softened the slate flooring.

Daegan drew in a deep breath of air that smelled fresh and lively. He grinned, opening his arms wide. "Now *this* is fit for a king."

"Actually, it's fit for a queen," Storm said, kissed Evalle on the temple, then went to a cabinet built into the side. He opened a door to what these people called a refrigerator and pulled out bottles of water and beer.

The world had progressed in some very handy ways since Daegan's youth.

Adrianna and Evalle accepted water.

Daegan nodded his thanks at the beer offered to him, glad to see Tristan and Storm also drink a brew. It wasn't as if any of them could be intoxicated with a few beers.

Perched upon her chair and wearing a tidy outfit of jeans, small boots and a frilly red shirt, Adrianna's blond hair had been fussed into an attractive, but all-business, style on top of her head.

Daegan had learned that the human named Isak had treated Adrianna poorly, but this woman was no wilting flower to be wronged easily.

Evalle and Storm took the wide lounge seating, which stretched halfway across the end of the room. Once they did, Tristan sat on the next available chair, looking around and clearly impressed by what appeared to be his first visit as well.

Adrianna asked Storm, "Evalle told me about this room and how she can sit up here without the sun affecting her. How did you do that, Storm?"

"I brought in a shaman who spent a series of days blessing this area, plus I created a special ward," he said, not really giving specifics. "There's a little more to it than that and I'd appreciate it if you all kept this secret. From the outside, it looks like bricks along the exterior of this level."

When Tristan caught Evalle's eye, he leaned over and quietly said, "Nice crib, E. Glad you can finally have a place to call home."

"Thanks."

Settling into a chair, Daegan sighed in delight at the comfort. "Okay, time to get down to business. I've managed to visit most of the North American Belador divisions and quite a few of the European ones. I'll meet more of our forces as I have time. For now, word should be spreading about my taking over Macha's position and that I will protect my people." Allowing that to sink in, Daegan asked, "What is this Tristan tells me about Belador families being targeted, Maistir?"

Quinn filled everyone in on a troll nest raid that had been successful earlier that evening. He said, "We saved two teens, but we still have six more missing and three dead Belador spouses."

"Six? This has to stop," Daegan announced with heat. "Do we know who is behind it?"

"The trolls are being paid with Noirre majik to kidnap the children, so our guess is Queen Maeve."

Daegan agreed, "Sounds like her. She's tucked inside TÅµr Medb with Cathbad the Druid. Between the two of them and their coven, they could hold off a Belador army if we tried to invade that tower."

"That was our thought as well," Quinn said.

"We are not leaving here without a plan of attack, but I want to hear everything before we strategize." All of this reminded Daegan of another pressing issue with Queen Maeve. "Speaking of children, what progress have you made in locating your daughter, Quinn?"

"Sadly, very little. I spoke with Garwyli after you asked him to assist us. He's been searching on his own. He's checked on all female Beladors born under the PRIN star who would be the age of my daughter, but there is no guarantee that she was born under that star."

Adrianna spoke up. "If it's not asking confidential information, I've heard Garwyli mentioned, but could someone explain who he is and what you mean by someone being born under a star?"

The other four looked to Daegan who said, "Adrianna is part of my inner circle, and as such, she is trusted with all that goes on with the Beladors."

The petite Sterling witch gave him a deep nod. "Thank you. I will never betray that trust."

Evalle spoke up. "Now that you're cleared for any classified information, future Belador warriors are born under the PRIN star, but that doesn't mean all Belador children will be. The way I understand it, when it does happen, our druids locate them as children and whisper a Gaelic phrase into their ears. As they come of age at eighteen, the druid returns to tell them of their destiny. He gives them the opportunity to join the Beladors as warriors, or not."

"Hold it right there," Tristan said. "No one came to see me or my foster sister as kids or when either of us turned eighteen."

"You know, I think you mentioned that once but we don't talk about this much, so I forgot," Evalle admitted. "We should ask Garwyli about you two when we're in Treoir again. I'd say it's because we're Alterants, but a druid did come to see me at eighteen. That's how I got out of the basement where I was locked up. When he asked if I wanted to be a Belador warrior, I jumped to escape."

Storm curled his arm tighter around her shoulders and hugged her to him. "You're amazing."

She beamed at her mate. "Thanks."

Tristan made a curt noise.

Storm sent him a look that promised pain.

Daegan snorted at the two, then wondered aloud, "That is strange about Tristan and his sister not being contacted. We'll look into it at some point."

Tristan shrugged. "I don't care how I got here. I was just clearing it up that not all future Beladors are found as kids."

Adrianna had been listening with her head cocked to the side. "Good point. Now, what about Garwyli?"

Evalle continued, "He's an old Celtic druid."

Tristan said, "Ancient is more like it. He's older than dirt." Then Tristan caught himself and looked at Daegan and said, "Unlike our dragon king, who is robust with health."

Evalle laughed. "Nice save. While you drag your foot out of your mouth, I'll finish. Garwyli normally stays in Treoir. I don't really know his history, but from all I've seen he's powerful and wise." She smiled at Storm when she added, "He gave us a gift that we may never be able to repay."

By the look of thankfulness on Quinn's face, he must have known of the gift Storm and Evalle received.

Storm nodded then glanced at Daegan. "Seems to me Garwyli lived during your time. Did you know him?"

"I knew of him. We were aware that Garwyli was a powerful being, and he received high respect as a druid during my day, but I didn't know him personally back then."

At that, Quinn sat forward, leaning his elbows on his knees. "Now that everyone knows some of the Belador history, you'll understand why I had hoped Garwyli could shed some light on locating Phoedra, but that hasn't happened. I have no idea if she's inherited Belador powers from me or Medb powers from Kizira, something from both or nothing at all. The biggest problem is that I can't expose her presence to anyone outside of our group, which limits the resources I'm able to access."

"I've tried to tap Witchlock for locating your daughter," Adrianna admitted, raising eyebrows around the room. "It could be possible, but I'm nowhere close to being proficient with the power, I'm sad to say."

"How close are you?" Storm asked.

Adrianna folded her hands neatly in her lap. "As you have all trusted me with your world, I want to tell you the truth about where I am with controlling Witchlock. When I bring up the power, like this ..." She paused and extended her right arm, then opened her hand where a tennis-ball-size, white energy spun. "I can feel energy that would allow me to easily topple a building or kill a mage without question."

Murmurs fluttered around the room at that admission.

Daegan was glad to have Adrianna on his team and not as an adversary.

Adrianna said, "However, I keep the majority of that energy contained. Let me give you a reference point for what all of Witchlock energy feels like. First, visualize standing in front of the Hoover Dam, which has thousands of gallons of water pressing against it."

"I think I read forty-five thousand pounds of water per square foot," Evalle supplied.

Everyone looked at her.

"Hey, before Storm came along, I spent a lot of time alone with a computer and a miniature gargoyle whose vocabulary consisted of ten numbers."

Adrianna smiled then returned to her example. "Okay, now that you have visual of the pressure against that wall, think about a mouse standing there trying to figure out how to release a little water at a time, but knowing one wrong move could crack open the wall and all of that power would crush everything in its path. If I unleash Witchlock without being sure I can control it, I could kill myself and millions in the blink of an eye."

"Wow," Tristan uttered.

Daegan had never known anyone who admitted to possessing that level of power and yet being unsure how to use it. Tristan had filled him in on whatever he knew about each person on Daegan's team. Tristan had known Witchlock was formidable and put Adrianna into her own witch classification, but the amazed look on his right-hand man's face indicated the word *formidable* had been a severe understatement.

Quinn said, "Thank you for trying, Adrianna."

"You're welcome, Quinn, but I also want to share that I'm having visions when I sleep."

"Do they relate to Phoedra?"

"Not necessarily, but I can't rule that out. I always had visions growing up, but once Veronika took my twin and used her to generate power, I gained an unwanted connection to Veronika."

Daegan said, "Tristan filled me in on Veronika, but is she still an issue?"

"She shouldn't be. She's imprisoned beneath VIPER for an undetermined amount of time. She'll likely live out her days there because she threatened every being with any level of power."

"Even gods and goddesses?" Daegan clarified.

"Yes," echoed around the room.

That surprised Daegan. "Based on everything I've heard about the Tribunal, I would have expected them to put her to death. Why didn't they?"

Evalle said, "I think they're afraid of her. I would be very careful killing her after meeting her ancestors. Adrianna and I went to a realm where the spirits of Veronika's ancestors continued to thrive as the landscape, animals, insects, anything in that realm." She shuddered. "Creepy place with a buttload of power constantly being generated, and she has a strange connection to it."

"Why did you go to her ancestors' realm?" Daegan still had much to discover about this group.

"Evalle was trying to help me free my twin," Adrianna replied, giving Evalle a look of appreciation. "Veronika had put my sister there to drain her power and use it to boost her own abilities when it came time to take control of Witchlock."

Daegan shook his head. "I've never heard of such a thing."

Tristan said, "Glad Adrianna took Witchlock. Veronika's realm sounds like a place we need to make sure she never accesses again."

"Evalle is never going back there," Storm stated in a tone that dared anyone to contradict him.

Evalle rolled her eyes, but agreed, "I have no desire to go back."

"Anyhow," Adrianna said, pulling everyone back to the point. "I was getting at the fact that I've had dream visions, but I can't give you specifics. I just sense that Veronika may be trying to open a connection to me."

"What does she say or do?" Evalle asked.

"That's just it. I can't pinpoint what's going on. It feels like she's testing a potential link between us. I'm telling you this for one simple reason. My sister died helping me take possession of Witchlock before Veronika could call the power to herself. If Veronika ever does open a path between us and I lose my grip on Witchlock ... " Adrianna paused, meeting the gazes of every person in the room before finishing. "You all need to realize that you can't allow her to live, even if I go down with her."

Evalle broke the silence that dropped over the room. "That's not going to happen as long as we can kick her butt. You may get a few bruises, but you're not dying any time soon."

Adrianna gave Evalle her signature wry, half smile. "Just know that I told you so."

"Understood," Daegan said in tone intended to let everyone know he was ready to move ahead.

"I will continue searching every way possible for Phoedra," Quinn said, tilting his head at Adrianna in thanks. "But for now, we must focus on stopping trolls and Medb from getting to our people. That's why I asked Tristan to have you meet with us, Daegan. On the way here, we learned of some missing Belador families."

"More families being attacked?" Daegan boomed.

"Possibly. But it's also possible that some warriors may have packed up their families and taken them into hiding."

A heavy layer of quiet settled on the room until Daegan said, "We have not yet established my rule to the point the warriors are ready to trust me. First, we will make it safe for all of their families. At that point, those who have gone into hiding will be given a chance to return and see that from there on, we must stand together to protect all."

"I think that's generous," Quinn said. "Since yesterday morning, there have been five attacks on the human families of Belador warriors. We're investigating more reports every hour. I'm going to speculate that any *entire* missing families are Beladors who have pulled away, because it appears the trolls and Medb are after teenagers. I say we put our resources to finding those children first."

"I agree." Daegan rubbed his head and dropped his hand. "We need a castle."

"You have one," Evalle pointed out.

"I mean in this land. We need a place to keep our people safe."

"That's not realistic when their lives are spread out in different areas."

"I understand," Daegan allowed. "We will round up every troll and member of the Medb coven if that's what it takes to protect our people."

"It may take more than that," Tristan pointed out. "I have a troll I consider a friend, and I caught up with him on the way here. He told me he believes the trolls we're hunting are coming in from outside of Atlanta for the Noirre majik bounty. It's not local trolls, because he has heard nothing of the bounty and the locals know they're allowed to reside here as long as they don't touch humans. They don't like this trouble any more than we do."

Daegan asked, "Can we bribe them to give us information on the new trolls coming in?"

"No." Tristan held up his hand to stall any argument. "They would help us for free just to clear any dark cloud over their people, but one of the elder trolls brought this problem forward yesterday at a meeting. He was killed right after he left. The rest of their people have gone underground, literally, which means they aren't out and about to see what's going on. I was lucky to get a cell call to connect, and my friend won't say where he's got his family stashed."

"I do hate to add to our troubles," Quinn interjected. "But on top of all this, our people are running hard around the clock to deal with terroristic preternatural activity popping up in different places. Humans are reporting strange beings sighted around the city, which sounds like trolls and/or the Medb are actually *trying* to out us all to humans. Plus there's also been a rash of missing adults from the human community. Nothing about those crimes points to a human serial killer and from what we saw earlier, we think the trolls are taking them for a food source."

Frowning in thought, Daegan asked, "Do you think this trouble is related to me meeting with our Belador warriors?"

"I doubt it." Quinn looked around and everyone agreed with him. "You've been gone from two to three days at a time over the past six weeks, so I don't see an obvious correlation. We had an increase in demon and troll activity for a while, but we thought it was Queen Maeve's witches and warlocks retaliating for her getting booted from VIPER."

"And?"

Evalle lifted a hand, asking Quinn for a chance to speak. "During the raid tonight on the troll nest, we found three human men, which was where we got the idea adults were being held for food. But one of the men is a journalist who …"

"Journalist?" Daegan asked.

Evalle quickly explained the media and what reporters were. Daegan nodded. "Carry on."

She smirked and replied dryly, "Yes, your highness."

Storm coughed in the middle of drinking his beer, but failed to cover his smile.

Tristan and Quinn just gave her a look of no-you-didn't.

Daegan rolled his eyes. "Mouthy wench."

She laughed, then turned serious as she got back on track. "This journalist said people were following advertisements for information on paranormal sightings."

Evalle looked over at Tristan who said, "I know the group behind those ads."

"Can you not track this advertisement back to those who created it?"

Tristan said, "I can, but at the moment that group is harmless and not a threat to us. I have someone on the inside keeping me posted if that changes. Someone else is placing look-alike ads online to use as a trap for humans."

"Online what?" Daegan asked, starting to be annoyed at the things he didn't recognize.

Two thousand years had passed while he was out of touch.

"Online means they're using computers. It's difficult to trace illegal activity on the internet."

Quinn said, "I have people working on that, but their first feedback is that we're not going to find the source of these ads, as is usually the case with tracking hackers."

"We have to find out who is arranging the deals with trolls on behalf of the Medb. I doubt Queen Maeve will risk coming to the human world herself," Daegan said. "More than that, we need to figure out what the devil she has in mind for those children."

"That's just it," Evalle said, picking up the thread. "The journalist overheard the trolls arguing. One wanted to forget their deal and run, but the leader said once they accepted the Noirre majik they had no place to hide if they didn't do their part. The journalist said they spoke in another language at times so he only got pieces, but he picked up that the trolls were being paid in Noirre for something a queen wanted. This is how we put together the theory that the queen in question is Maeve, and that she is trading for teenage children of Beladors."

That bitch. Daegan would crush her for harming a child.

"As I mentioned earlier, we are woefully shorthanded and it's getting worse every day," Quinn added.

Daegan found that hard to accept. "We should not be shorthanded considering how many warriors we brought in recently from areas with low paranormal activity in central states."

"You would be correct in assuming so, but with the increase of troll and Medb problems, our people are all pretty much working double shifts, plus they're slipping away to guard their homes."

"Did you inform Sen of Belador families being targeted, Quinn?"

"I did so when I called him in to clean up the troll nest tonight. He said VIPER has its hands full trying to keep humans safe from the sporadic paranormal attacks. He contends the Beladors will have to take care of their own problems."

Daegan fisted his hand and energy rolled up his arm.

Evalle's eyes widened. "Uh, Daegan, your arm is glowing."

"It is only power surging."

"You're not going to spontaneously combust, are you?"

When Daegan didn't answer her confusing question, Tristan said, "She wants to know if you're going to explode into a fireball."

Wanting to grin at that thought, he shook his head. "If that were to happen, you wouldn't have a chance to ask me."

"Comforting," she muttered.

"Truth," Storm told her and she snorted.

Turning deadly serious, Daegan said, "I want patrols formed for all of our Belador families immediately."

"That will ... cut the resources allocated for VIPER in half. Maybe more," Quinn pointed out.

"I don't care what it does to VIPER," Daegan said, making it clear no one would naysay him, least of all VIPER. "Our children will not be left exposed to deadly threat. Their parents are to be protected, too."

"I'll meet with our people and set up a schedule," Quinn said. Staring down, he said, "I would not kill anyone without reason, but I will not stand by as the Medb harm our children either." He lifted his head and the sick worry poured from him. "We are going to be even more shorthanded, Daegan."

Quinn's haggard expression revealed responsibility he'd carried for weeks as the maistir, on top of not being allowed proper time and support to hunt for his own child.

That would change now.

Daegan had heard enough. "Quinn, as of this moment, your number one goal is to find Phoedra."

"But I—"

Daegan gave Quinn a look that brought silence before he continued. "Take today to speak with your next level of command so our people have a sense of order about the change. Then I will take over your responsibilities until you locate your child and bring her home."

"Wait a minute." Evalle waved her hands to interrupt. "We didn't get to tell you all of it, Daegan. The journalist asked if dragons were real. He said when the trolls argued, they agreed that once they delivered the kids they were getting far away before the dragon showed up. They don't believe the queen can protect them from you. The point we were trying to make is that kidnapping these teens appears to be about Queen Maeve trying to get to you and probably kill you."

"No, she doesn't want to kill me."

Everyone exchanged looks with each other, then Daegan explained, "She would never be satisfied with simply ending my life. She wants me back in her domain and probably as a throne again."

Quinn stood. "Either way, you can't be in this world."

"Point taken, but that is my decision to make." Taking in the room, he stated, "I am not leaving my people to face Maeve alone. I have things to do in Treoir, which includes meeting with Tzader, Brina and Garwyli. Before that, I will meet with Sen. Once I return later today, be ready to focus all of your energy on finding your child, Quinn."

This world at times confused him, but Daegan still knew the rules of war.

Never let your enemies see you bleed and never stop fighting until the light goes out in the eyes of your opponent.

If Queen Maeve wanted him, she'd have to come to the human world to capture a dragon.

First, Daegan intended to give Sen one chance to explain this nonsense about not supporting the Beladors.

CHAPTER 5

Evalle kept her eyes closed tight and her arms wrapped around her middle until she heard Daegan say, "You will live, Evalle."

She opened her eyes slowly and peered at the dragon king through her dark sunglasses. "It's not a sure thing for me when I teleport."

"It is when you travel with me."

"I'll admit that Air Daegan beats all the others who have transported me, hands down."

He made a snorting noise that sounded an awful lot like a dragon grunt.

She expected smoke to curl out of his nose.

The entrance to VIPER was oddly quiet. Normally there were plenty of agents coming and going at just before daylight. She should be glad for the empty reception area since her unauthorized arrival into headquarters via teleporting would have, at one time, sent her to lockdown.

Back then, she could sneeze and Sen would try to have her imprisoned for eternity.

From what Quinn said about Daegan putting Sen in his place during the last Tribunal, she wouldn't have to worry about that again. At the moment, though, she and Daegan were alone in the VIPER power base run by Sen, the egomaniac liaison who hated her for reasons she never had figured out.

She asked Daegan, "Are you ready to deal with Sen?"

"The question is whether Sen is ready for me." Her dragon king strode away with a confidence that Evalle wanted to have when she grew up.

She'd come a long way and had gotten far stronger thanks to Storm's, and now Daegan's, support.

Maybe it was a matter of having the right men in her life.

Still, no one was allowed to use majik inside VIPER headquarters except the surly liaison.

Why hadn't Sen appeared at the entrance to bust on them for teleporting in without permission?

And where was everyone?

Daegan stopped in the center of the room and crossed his arms, appearing content to stand there for as long as it took.

Evalle wouldn't leave him, but as soon as this was over she had somewhere else to go. Lanna Brasko had texted her right before Daegan teleported them to VIPER, asking Evalle to come visit. The young woman was Quinn's cousin, and she'd recently suffered a brutal physical, emotional and majikal attack.

A nurturing white witch, along with the witch's powerful Fae half sister, had been overseeing Lanna's healing. Both had refused visitors until they decided Lanna was ready, which had not gone over well with Quinn.

Evalle couldn't wait to see her young friend today.

"Something's off," she murmured to Daegan.

Daegan angled his head. "What do you mean?"

The stillness raised hair on Evalle's arms. "There's no activity. This area is normally busy throughout the day and night, especially with so much going on in the city and outlying areas. I mean, where is Jack? He's in charge of opening and closing the cave entrance."

"Who is this Jack?"

"A miserable troll who gets on my nerves during the best of days."

"He isn't afraid of you?" Daegan asked with a hint of surprise.

She gave him a half grin. "He might be after I threatened to rip off his balls and use them to make him a pair of earrings if he messed with me again."

Horror climbed into Daegan's gaze. "Hell. He would be well advised to never cross you."

"My point exactly."

Power rushed through the room.

Evalle turned around to stand at Daegan's shoulder when they faced Sen. She'd been chosen to accompany Daegan after shutting down a debate between Quinn and Tristan. Those two argued over who should go with Daegan to watch his back inside VIPER headquarters.

After assessing the options, Evalle told everyone she was the obvious choice for Daegan's backup.

Tristan's mouth had dropped open and Quinn grumbled something sharp. She pointed out that everyone had work to do and with dawn coming soon, she'd be limited.

The way she saw it, Daegan could teleport her to VIPER, which meant she'd be safe from the sun and of use to someone.

The dragon king agreed, but then she realized what she'd suggested and quickly advised Daegan to alert Sen first.

Daegan had scowled that he needed no one's permission to enter VIPER.

Storm had been more amused than concerned. He'd kissed her soundly and whispered, "Promise me you'll stick close to the dragon."

Evidently her mate was fine with her teleporting into VIPER without authority as long as she had a dragon close by.

Men were so funny some days.

Not Sen, though. He was never funny.

Sen gave her the usual stink eye and dismissed her presence, turning to Daegan. "You're new so you're not up on all of VIPER guidelines, but an important one to remember is that no one uses majik inside this mountain except me. That includes teleporting in unannounced."

Daegan stood with his massive arms crossed and a smile on his face.

He was the first person Evalle had met who found Sen amusing.

Her dragon king said, "What would be the point in my wasting time to tell you I'm coming to headquarters? It's not as though this will be a social visit, requiring time for you to prepare refreshments."

A muscle in Sen's jaw ticked. "The point is that we deal with hundreds of beings possessing all levels of power on any given day. Allowing even one to use those powers here opens the door for conflict. I won't allow it."

Daegan shrugged. "I'll take that into consideration, but you should keep in mind that I have no intention of being limited by anyone's guidelines."

Evalle had heard a full accounting of how Daegan had given Sen a smackdown in the Tribunal meeting. Their dragon king had made it clear the Beladors, Evalle, Tristan and the rest of Daegan's trusted circle were under his protection. Not that she'd doubted Quinn's rundown of what happened, but she just couldn't imagine anyone facing off with Sen who wasn't a deity.

This was worth teleporting any day.

Sen scratched his chin with a condescending expression. "I know you think you have the upper hand after that moment in the Tribunal meeting, but you have no idea what Loki and the other deities are doing at this moment."

That was not good news.

Daegan drew a deep breath and slowly let it out, everything about his posture saying he was not interested in Sen's nattering. The dragon king said, "I don't spend my time worrying what anyone else is doing. Unlike you, who must wait for direction, I rule the Beladors, which means I give the orders and take action rather than hovering around waiting for an order."

Oh, crap. He'd just reduced Sen to the status of a VIPER errand boy.

Sen's facial muscles hardened and his blue eyes turned almost black.

Evalle could feel his power generate and flow out around them.

Daegan said, "Save your posturing. I'm busy and will make this brief. We've been spreading Beladors out to other parts of this country in recent weeks to supplement weak spots in VIPER security. In spite of bringing in additional Belador resources from other continents, our people are being run ragged."

Maintaining an I-couldn't-give-less-of-a-shit expression, Sen said, "So? What's your point? We have a lot of troll and Medb activity going on."

"That's what I've heard. But let's be clear. The Medb activity is due to Queen Maeve and Cathbad the Druid being allowed to join VIPER to begin with, even though the coalition knew that the Medb and Beladors have warred for centuries."

Sounding cocky now, Sen said, "Guess the Beladors just didn't have the pull they thought they had. Besides, that was when Beladors were part of *Macha's* pantheon. Now, they have no goddess. Just you."

If Evalle gave points for this verbal match, she'd have to award a few to Sen for that nasty dig.

"I can see I'm wasting my time trying to have a productive conversation with you," Daegan said, sounding almost bored. "You asked what is my point? It is this. The Medb are now targeting Belador families. Children of those families, to be specific. What do you intend to do about that?"

Smirking, Sen said, "Sounds like an internal problem to me. I don't handle domestic issues."

Evalle clenched her fingers, wishing she could lock them around Sen's neck. Children were at risk.

The liaison's eyes cut over to her. Noting her fisted hands, Sen's lips twisted in a dark smile intended to taunt her. He'd gotten under her skin in the past and she'd paid the price.

Not now.

Her job was to cover Daegan's back and her dragon king didn't need anyone interfering while he was dealing with Sen.

"I see." Daegan nodded as if agreeing with Sen, which couldn't be the case, could it? Then he changed the subject. "As I understand it, you represent VIPER, correct?"

Sen's attention shot to Daegan. Had he heard a note of warning in Daegan's voice?

Evalle had.

"Yes, I represent VIPER."

"Very well, consider VIPER informed that we're cutting the Belador force assigned to the coalition in half, maybe more, to ensure our families are protected."

Sen's lips started to part and he caught himself. "You can't do that."

Totally unruffled, Daegan asked, "Why not?"

"Beladors have a commitment to VIPER."

"I would counter that VIPER has a commitment to Beladors."

Sen spoke through clenched teeth. "The Tribunal will not agree to a change this severe."

Daegan gave it a few seconds before he said, "You misunderstand me. I'm declaring the rule of Belador Cosaint. What this means is, since VIPER refuses to show us the same level of support our warriors have given to VIPER for so many years, we will take care of our own and we will use however many of our warriors are necessary to ensure the safety of Belador families. I suggest you go out and find more VIPER agents to fill the void you're about to experience."

Evalle glanced from Sen to Daegan, both steely gazes locked in silent combat.

Neither blinked.

Sen said, "If the Beladors do not fulfill their agreement with VIPER, consider yourself warned of potential repercussions from the Tribunal."

For the first time since teleporting in, Daegan's voice turned brutal and cold. "Consider yourself reminded, should VIPER choose to become an enemy of the Beladors, that we possess the greatest force in the preternatural world, which now includes a dragon. If VIPER wishes for a war, my people will be ready and I will lead them."

Game, set and match to Daegan.

But Evalle felt a chill race over her skin at the idea of going to battle against VIPER and the Tribunal deities. Would VIPER really start a war over this?

CHAPTER 6

Surprised at being called into VIPER headquarters at noon for a group agent meeting, Ossian entered the underground amphitheater in his Emilio persona.

Sen had no respect for Emilio as a mage, thanks to Ossian's bumbling on two missions. It was imperative for him to maintain a distant relationship with Sen, and being called in worked against his need to come and go at will.

Ossian had gained the attention of his queen and he would make her proud. His star was rising in the Medb. He intended to keep proving himself worthy to be the next person in line behind the queen and Cathbad.

His former Medb warrior team hated him. He could live with their jealousy. Anyone with a bit of ambition would jump to be in his place.

Queen Maeve had far less patience than Cathbad, but Ossian had to admit that he'd enjoyed receiving her entire focus on his last trip to the tower. He'd never considered who was specifically in charge once the queen and Cathbad reincarnated, but it was clear that his queen ran things. Ossian would make her happy and make Cathbad proud of him, but only if Sen did not screw up his mission.

What could have happened for Sen to call in so many agents for this meeting?

In fact, who were all of these people?

Ossian saw a couple of faces here and there he'd seen before, but none were Beladors. He didn't recognize many of the other agents. Not that all VIPER agents were clean-cut, upstanding types, but the majority seemed to be similar, cookie-cutter versions.

These strangers dressed in an assortment of rugged jeans, weathered leather, tactical vests and wifebeaters, with everything from shaggy beards to shaved heads and tattooed sleeves. They carried everything from hatchets to swords, and they smelled odd, like some tool pulled from a shed left abandoned for years.

The simplest description he could assign to this group was predatory.

Most of them clearly didn't like waiting, but Ossian could stand here for as long as was needed. The others rumbled in low conversations with the occasional curse or shout at each other.

"Listen up, people," Sen called out, his voice cutting through the rumble of chatter.

Ossian jerked around at the sound and lowered his gaze to the stage where Sen stood *way* down below rows and rows of tiered seating cut into the stone. "We've had a large number of vacancies open up for VIPER agents due to the Beladors bailing on their responsibilities."

Now *that* was interesting.

Sen didn't slow down. "Thanks to VIPER's relationship with Dakkar and his bounty service, we now have a large group of his bounty hunters willing to step in and help. Current VIPER agents are to offer any needed assistance to the new agents."

So these new people were bounty hunters.

Ossian couldn't wait to share that with the queen and Cathbad.

He mentally ran back over all he'd studied about VIPER, the Beladors and other groups he'd encountered as Emilio. Dakkar ran a large group of international bounty hunters and had an unusual deal in that he didn't have to align himself officially with VIPER. The coalition allowed him to operate throughout this region as long as he performed occasional tasks for them.

But this was more than a task. A sea of deadly operators filled the room.

Bounty hunters as VIPER agents.

Dakkar didn't have a reputation for taking on people burdened by principles.

His hunters were given free reign as long as they produced,

and all of them were nonhuman.

What kind of nonhumans?

Sen continued running down the list of priorities and how it would be refreshing to be able to send them out on their own without the need for partnering.

Now Ossian understood what was going on.

Generally, the agents worked in teams whenever possible and lately that had been a requirement due to all the paranormal incidents that had popped up around Atlanta.

Ossian had heard more than one rumor about Medb witches and warlocks being behind the trouble, but not so much lately. Once Cathbad separated him from the Medb Scáth Force unit, allowing Ossian more mobility, he had less solid street intel. The unit now answered directly to Cathbad, and to be honest, Ossian didn't mind the change at all.

The rest of the elite unit had made it clear they didn't care for Ossian as a leader.

They just didn't like that they were overlooked when Cathbad chose one warrior to become a polymorph.

"One more thing," Sen said, holding everyone's attention. "We do still have some Belador agents finishing up assignments, but they're on thin ice with VIPER. If, or maybe I should say when, VIPER decides the Beladors have broken their agreement with the coalition, I will alert you to a change in their status from ally to enemy. Should that happen, I'll issue a kill-on-sight notice. In the meantime, if you come across a Belador who appears to be on a VIPER project who is not doing his or her job, alert me. If you see Beladors breaking *any* of our laws, no matter how slight, you have the freedom to use any force you deem necessary to apprehend them and deliver them to me."

That sounded like open season on Beladors.

The queen and Cathbad would be thrilled to hear this.

Sen began handing out assignments to the motley group. The new agents took them and walked out without another word. There might be something to say for agents who wasted no time getting a job done.

As everyone dispersed, Ossian moved down the stairs and waited nearby for Sen to recognize him as the Italian mage, Emilio. When it happened, Sen seemed to pause, then muttered something to himself. He shoved an assignment at Emilio without so much as a hello, then continued on to pass out instructions to the rest of the bounty hunters.

Finding a place off to the side, Ossian leaned against a wall and lifted his document to appear as though he were reading his assignment details.

In truth, he powered up his hearing to catch what Sen was saying to each of the last hunters.

Each one was given an assignment in a different part of the city.

Come on, Sen, get to the one I need.

Finally, Sen turned to one scruffy looking guy with a thick beard who wore a long duster battered enough to suggest he had plenty of street cred to back up his deadly appearance.

"What's your name?" Sen asked.

"Bull."

"You take the next guard duty in our high-risk area. Shift starts in fifteen minutes."

"What? I'm a bounty hunter, not a babysitter. I don't do guard work."

Standing eight inches taller than the six-foot-tall bounty hunter, Sen snarled down at him, "I will deduct a premium from Dakkar's payment for any of his girls who whine."

"Fuck." Bull muttered something else, then said, "Fine. How long am I stuck down there and what do I have to do?"

"You've got a twelve-hour shift. We have three high-risk criminals." Sen told him where the three were located on that lower level. "Don't take your mobile phone down there. I just increased the security. The power will fry any electronics. Be sure to get the ID badge from the guard you relieve and keep it on except when you patrol. You patrol that area every hour. When you do, leave the badge on the chair each time. If you go missing, we'll know you didn't leave the building."

"What kind of security does it have?"

"I infused a special energy into the walls on that level. You'll see it when you get there. If something goes wrong, touch a wall and call out the problem. I'll hear you. Think you can handle that, Bull?"

"I'll be there in fifteen minutes." Bull turned to leave.

Sen called out, "Where are you going?"

"To my truck. Luckily I have a magazine that doesn't need a WIFI connection," he smarted back.

Shaking his head, Sen watched Bull for a moment, then vanished.

Ossian had his opening.

He left quickly, but not so fast he'd draw attention. When he reached the nearby wooded area where vehicles were parked, he waited as the agents left, except for Bull, who slammed his door, cursing to himself about arrogant pricks.

Standing still, Ossian listened for anyone else approaching, but it was just him and Bull. When the bounty hunter realized he wasn't alone, he looked Ossian up and down with a narrow gaze. "Who the fuck are you?"

"Emilio. I'm a mage with VIPER."

"Get out of my way, Emilio the mage, or I'm going to twist your head off just to brighten my day."

Drawing on the power Cathbad had given him, Ossian murmured a spell and pushed power into it.

Bull leaned in with his ear cocked, then pulled back. "You bastard." By the time he lifted his hands to unleash whatever preternatural weapon he possessed, Ossian had blinded and muted him.

Grabbing at his eyes as if that would turn them back to brown from the milky white they now were, Bull made odd noises behind his lips, which wouldn't open.

Ossian couldn't use more of his power. He had a limit and needed the majority of it for morphing into different physical appearances. But he did have enough to knock Bull onto his back and drag him to Ossian's nondescript white sedan and shove him into the trunk. Lifting a folded blanket, he smothered Bull until he was deathly still.

Once he changed into the image of Bull, Ossian pulled on the hunter's clothes. They stank, but to alter that might give him away. He made his way down to the high-security level beneath VIPER's mountain.

He recognized the man on duty right away.

His last name was Jordan, but his friends called him Casper for some reason. He had the easygoing attitude and boots that branded him a cowboy, but Ossian had little intel on this man. He'd like to find out just what power this cowboy wielded.

Casper was friendly with the Beladors, often working with Evalle and Quinn, which made him the enemy. Emilio had not been part of a team with Casper yet, but he'd noticed that the man seemed perpetually happy.

Ossian suffered a moment of jealousy over Casper's easygoing life and freedom.

Medb members were subject to a queen's rule from the moment they were born. Ossian's first chance of stepping above all Medb warlocks, even their Scáth Force, had come when Cathbad singled Ossian out to be a special operative.

He quickly brushed away any lingering envy of Casper. That would be the last thing he wanted Cathbad or the queen to find if either one entered Ossian's mind, which had happened twice already. Cathbad said the mental invasion was so that the druid could be sure Ossian's polymorph ability continued to be strong and precise. Failing to morph entirely into a new person would expose his gift to their enemies.

That sounded reasonable, but Ossian believed there was more to Cathbad's searching Ossian's mind than maintaining his abilities.

It didn't matter. One did not question those two beings.

The initial adjustment to becoming a polymorph had been painful, and the agony had persisted for weeks.

Still, he had no regrets.

Cathbad had also bestowed additional power on Ossian that was woven into his very being. He would never match the levels of power Cathbad or Queen Maeve controlled, but he wouldn't need to match them as long as he was the top man on their team.

"You're new," Casper said in a southern drawl, leaning against the wall next to an empty chair. He dropped a rolled-up magazine on the chair.

The action reminded Ossian that Bull had failed to get the reading material he'd gone to retrieve. Ossian cared nothing about casual reading, but he'd rather not leave a tiny detail for Sen to notice after Ossian completed his mission successfully. The perfect outcome depended upon blaming the escape on someone else. Casper had a magazine, but then most people would bring something to read during a boring assignment.

Time to switch mentally from Ossian to Bull, right down to the belligerent voice.

"I'm Bull. One of Dakkar's men."

Suspicion entered Casper's voice. "You an agent with VIPER?"

"I am now, dickwad. You got a problem with that? Take it up with Sen."

Casper eyed Bull up and down, but who would dare to come down here without Sen's permission? He must have concluded Bull was telling the truth, because Casper said, "No problem. It's all yours."

When Casper leaned down to pick up the magazine, Bull said, "Shit, left my magazine in the truck."

Giving an exaggerated sigh, Casper offered, "You can have this one ... dickwad."

Bull chuckled, because that seemed like a good way to defuse the tension. "You're okay, asshole."

Not acknowledging that comment, Casper gave Bull the usual end-of-duty debrief. "Everything has been fine. I just made a walk-through before you got here, which reminds me..." Casper lifted the lanyard over his head and handed Bull the ID badge. "A word to the wise. When you go on patrol, don't slow down near that Veronika. We've had some crazy bad stuff locked up down here in the past, but she's in a league all her own. Sings crazy shit on and off. A loony bird, that one. I swear I can feel her nasty shit touching me through that damn wall when I slow down."

Giving a shudder for effect, Bull said, "Thanks for the warning, cowboy. Think she can get out?"

"Not with the system Sen has in place."

Bull made a point of cutting his eyes at the energy flowing across the walls. He'd seen it the first time he'd changed from Ossian to a Belador named Lionel Macaffey. He'd killed the Belador and taken Macaffey's place as guard in this area.

The rock surface had some kind of shiny coating that moved like a wide stream of energy from floor to ceiling, and reflected light in a sparkling array of colors. It wasn't as if he had to touch the walls, which were twelve feet apart, but he had walked dead center to avoid the energy Sen had injected into the rock itself.

Dismissing it as unimportant, Bull said, "I'm glad that crazy bastard has decent security. I've heard rumors about Veronika. Someone said she crippled one guy. Might be true, might not, but either way I got things to do when this gig is done. I got no reason to risk bleeding over some bitch."

Casper just said, "With any luck, she'll never get out, or she'll mow down everyone with any power."

"Shit, she can try," Bull boasted, making it clear he wouldn't be run over. Ossian could get used to this beefy body and killer attitude.

A knowing smile ghosted Casper's lips. "I'm outta here." Walking past Bull, Casper said, "Not sure I can say you're okay, asshole."

"Good for you to realize that," Bull quipped.

Casper didn't even acknowledge his words.

Perfect.

Waiting ten minutes, Ossian placed his ID badge on the chair. Evidently in the past, some guards had disappeared, and VIPER wanted to be sure they disappeared *inside* the tunnels. Not that it would help the poor guard who hadn't made it out alive. Sen just wanted to know for sure that someone had entered the tunnels willingly.

Ossian had never heard of a prisoner escaping, which made what he had to do today seem impossible.

But he was not just anybody and he had a plan.

After passing the first two incarcerated beings, the second of which made his skin crawl even though it never made a sound, Ossian slowed his approach as he neared Veronika's cell.

He couldn't clear the rock covering without Sen's approval.

That created one obstacle he had to work around.

"Veronika?" he called softly as he approached the area of her cell. He knew the minute the witch realized she had company. The hair on his arms spiked and his skin felt too tight all of a sudden. Was she doing that?

She hadn't responded otherwise.

His skin tightened more.

How was she getting to him from inside a stone-covered and warded cell?

Taking a shallow breath, since he had trouble breathing at all, he said, "Veronika. I've come to help you."

Now he felt on fire.

What was she doing to him? Was this a test he had to pass before she would talk to him?

His eyes burned and floated in liquid. Moisture ran down his cheek. He sniffed at the coppery scent. He couldn't move his hand to check, but he felt sure his eyes were bleeding.

"I tell ... the truth, Veronika. I would never ... risk ... your wrath. Please allow me ..." He forced out the last words, "To help free you."

All the pressure and heat on his skin vanished.

He grabbed his throat and breathed in and out, just to be sure he could still do it.

Her words floated out on a tune. *"Tell me, tell me, who dares enter my domain. Tell me, tell me, why I should trust that you are sane?"*

Licking his dry lips, he said, "I come to present an opportunity offered by my queen."

Seconds ticked off as he waited for her reply, but she did not sing this time. *"You are here because you need me."*

What should he say to that?

He'd expected her to jump at the chance to escape. Cathbad had trained him to be an emissary, an assassin and a negotiator. Drawing on all that he'd been taught, Ossian said, "Every good agreement is based on two parties who have something of value to trade. I am authorized to offer you assistance to escape in return for your sharing information my queen believes you possess."

"Do you really believe I will share anything while I am still in here?"

What had Queen Maeve said? That she would be disappointed if Veronika made it easy? She'd been right about that.

He said, "My queen realizes you would not do so, which is why I will help you escape, but you must give me your word to work with her in gaining what she's after."

Another long pause, then Veronika said, *"Why should I believe that you can help me?"*

"Because I am a very special operative created just for this mission. This is the second time I've been a guard for the high-security level in the past six weeks." He gave her a moment for that to sink in. "I'm sure you've figured out that VIPER does not allow anyone to repeat guard duty more than once in six months and seldom twice in a year. If we come to an agreement, I will launch my plan to get you out of here."

"What plan? How can you do this?"

Her answer was quick.

He'd clearly gotten her attention.

Smiling now, he said, "I have told you enough. If I do not free you, then you will have lost nothing in giving your word and allowing me to try. I have one question I must have answered first."

"What would that be?"

"You often sing that you know the Belador Maistir's secret. Are you singing about Vladimir Quinn, and is his secret one that Kizira also knew?"

Again, Ossian waited patiently, but for almost ten minutes this time, for her to answer.

"You are still here. You are determined," she said.

"Yes. I am loyal to my queen and will face any threat to complete my mission." Something odd just dawned on him. "You haven't asked me my name or that of my queen."

"I know who you are and that you have been here recently. You were pretending to be a Belador warrior the day Quinn and the Sterling witch visited."

She'd realized he'd been impersonating a guard? Even without seeing him?

This time, the hair on his arms stood up sharply out of an emotional reaction to her words. He didn't want to call it fear, but serious respect.

She said, *"You can tell Queen Maeve the answer to both of her questions is yes. I sing about the Belador Maistir, Quinn, and the secret he shared with Kizira. If you free me, I give you my word to tell your queen that secret."*

Queen Maeve would be so proud of him, but did his queen realize he was dealing with someone truly insane?

He shook his head at himself. *Who am I to question someone as powerful as Queen Maeve? She knows what she's doing.*

Right now, he had to keep his excitement under control. The mission was not yet complete.

He told Veronika, "The moment we leave, I'll take you to Queen Maeve and allow you to share the secret with her. You can join forces with her and she will be able to protect you when VIPER sends an army to hunt you."

Veronika said, "*What are you waiting for?*"

What a churlish attitude. This witch had no manners. She should show her appreciation for all that he was about to do.

She'd agreed to share her secret, which was step one.

Once Queen Maeve had Veronika in TÅµr Medb, this witch would soften her attitude if she hoped to survive.

Ossian said, "Here's the plan."

CHAPTER 7

Still impersonating Bull, Ossian ran to the closest wall and slapped his hand against the stone, shouting in a panicked voice, "*Veronika is gone! I repeat, Veronika is gone!*"

He wiped damp palms on his pants.

Sen appeared, eyes blazing mad. "How did that happen?"

Ossian had expected Sen's immediate and angry response, but not the primal fear that arose in him from the surge of Sen's power. He was in up to his neck. No going back now.

He either pulled this off or Sen would unleash a vicious fury on Bull. Ossian wasn't sure he could maintain his Bull façade if Sen tortured him.

Wrong thing to think about.

"What the fuck is going on, Bull?" Sen ordered.

"Hey, you said this place was secure. You didn't say nothin' about that crazy bitch bein' able to open her cell."

Sen looked past Bull to where Veronika's cell was hidden behind a stone wall. "It's still rock."

Giving a sarcastic snarl, Bull said, "Of course it is. She opened it and reset the wall, then freakin' vanished."

"Why didn't you stop her?"

"I go after trolls and an occasional demon that skips out on a deal. Fighting crazy witches is over my pay grade, bud."

Sen's face looked like a monster hid inside, waiting to be released. He strode over to the wall and cleared it with a flip of his hand.

When the rock disappeared, red smoke filled the space that should be her cell.

"Veronika!" Sen shouted. "If you're screwing with me using some illusion tactic, you will not like the way you spend the next hundred years."

Not a sound came from the cell.

"Told you," Ossian said in Bull's deep voice.

"Shut up," Sen warned. Then he bit out a string of words and opened the ward sealing her in.

Red smoke boiled out of the room.

Bull coughed and choked, but he followed Sen in and almost ran into the liaison, who turned around and shouted, "Get the fuck out of here so I can tell if anyone else is in this room."

"Ah, hell. You tell Dakkar I quit. I don't need your shit."

Sen pointed at Bull and flipped his hand.

Still appearing as Bull, Ossian ended up outside the mountain, standing in the wooded parking area. *Shit, shit, shit.*

Where was Veronika?

Ossian changed to his Emilio image, which drained his energy, but he needed to dump Bull immediately with Sen on the warpath.

He walked over to his car, mumbling, "What am I going to do now?"

"Anything I ask."

Ossian spun around to find Veronika standing ten feet away in a red robe that flowed to the ground. The woman was a knockout with thick, black hair streaked with white, and blue eyes full of fire.

He started laughing. "We did it."

"Yes, but I am the one who left Sen locked in that cell." She smiled and he felt his body reacting to her. "He will escape, but I will be hidden by then."

She'd been a bitch back in her cell, but who wouldn't be in a bad mood in there? He let out a quick breath of relief. "All I have to do is contact Queen Maeve and—"

The air around him blurred and heated at the same time.

He heard Veronika's voice at a distance, but none of the words made sense. The harder he tried to see her, the more his eyes burned. His world tilted out of shape. Then his body twisted back and forth, changing from one shape to another as if his majik had corrupted.

"Do you understand me, Ossian?"

He shook off the dizziness and said, "What?"

"I asked if you're ready to do your duty."

He lifted his hands and touched his face. Yes, he was Ossian, instead of Emilio. Duty. He did have a duty and it wasn't to this witch. He stepped back. "What are you trying to do? I am Cathbad's best operative. Don't make the mistake of trying to mess with me or my majik."

"Forget about Cathbad and Queen Maeve. You now work for me."

Shaking his head, he said, "Never happen." Opening his mind to call Cathbad, he tried to reach out and hit a wall of pain that dropped him to his knees.

Veronika spoke in a language that sounded almost Russian, but that shouldn't be right. He'd studied her history. She was part of the ancient KievRus dynasty of witches, which originated in Ukraine.

When he could breathe again, he looked up to find dark spirits hovering just above the ground in a circle that started and ended with Veronika. They had him in the middle.

She said, "These are my ancestors. I do not disturb them often. You will do as I say, or I will hand you over to them."

Standing again, he said, "You don't want to do this, Veronika. Queen Maeve will come for me."

"I do hope so. She's on my list of people to teach a lesson for trying to enslave me."

His heart sank, but he bluffed, "That's not true. She and Cathbad want to form an alliance with you."

Veronika laughed out loud and the spirits mimicked her laugh, silencing when she did. "No one is my equal."

Ossian suffered true panic. He searched for a way to get through to her. "Don't you want Witchlock back? Queen Maeve and Cathbad will help return it to you."

Veronika looked at him with disdain. "You really expect me to believe that your queen will lend a hand in returning Witchlock to me when it will make me more powerful than the deities ruling your miserable Tribunals? Queen Maeve is not that stupid and I'm insulted that you think I am so easily manipulated. Now, it's time to bring you into the fold."

"No. You gave your word!"

"And I intend to keep it. I did not say *when* I would tell her Quinn's secret. If she lives long enough to meet me, then I'll tell her."

Ossian started sweating, big-time. Desperate now, he shouted, "Cathbad, call me home now!"

Nothing happened.

Nothing except giving Veronika more pleasure. "I do love to watch one like you squirm. You can stand still or not. The power of my ancestors will prevent anyone from seeing us or entering this spot until I'm finished."

"You can't compel me. Cathbad built in preventive measures in case I was captured."

Ignoring him, Veronika continued explaining, "Relax and ... well, it won't make this any easier for you. In fact, it's going to hurt. A lot." She pointed both hands at Ossian.

He stood strong, trying to convince himself that she could not break Cathbad's majik.

She could not compel him.

She could not ...

Pressure expanded in his head. Words shot around his mind like poison darts, stabbing him with excruciating pain.

He screamed and screamed. His body twisted in and out of shape again. His eyes bled. Foam poured from his mouth. He started choking.

Veronika said, "Do not die!"

His eyes bulged. *My duty is to die.*

CHAPTER 8

Evalle parked along the curb in front of Mother Mattie's house in the Emory area of Atlanta, waiting for the sun to drop out of sight. Until then, she couldn't leave the safety of Storm's Land Cruiser, which was warded against the sun.

Mother Mattie, the elderly white witch who lived here, was taking care of Lanna, as well as Mattie's granddaughter, Sissy. Both girls had suffered brutal attacks by Grendal, a powerful dark wizard who was now dead.

Adrianna unlatched her seat belt and peered out the passenger-side window. "It's close. Another few minutes and you won't turn into a toasted marshmallow."

"You're a laugh a minute."

"I could cloak you from the sun's rays."

"Thanks, but it's almost sunset, so no point in doing that when it's not necessary." For someone Evalle hadn't wanted to work with in the beginning, Adrianna had turned out to be a good friend. Which was why people should never assume they knew a person because of a name. Adrianna was practically royalty in the Sterling witch coven, one of the deadliest dark witch groups known, but she was not like them.

The Sterlings had mistreated Adrianna and her twin sister.

Adrianna had never forgiven them. In fact, she avoided dark majik.

"We now have a large group of beings with similar abilities to reach beyond our realm," Adrianna said, breaking the silence. She counted off on her fingers. "Me, Storm, Lanna and Mother Mattie, just to name a few who could help Quinn search for his daughter."

A Sterling witch normally did not partner with a white witch like Mother Mattie, but Adrianna had played a role in saving Mother Mattie's life. In turn, the elderly witch had shared with Adrianna how to break Daegan's curse, and Mother Mattie had asked her Fae half sister, Caron, to help them save Lanna.

Evalle asked, "What are you saying? We should have a séance?"

Rolling her head to the side to stare at Evalle, she said, "Sure. If that doesn't work, we'll grab a Ouija board."

"You can be one sarcastic bitch sometimes."

Adrianna laughed. "It's so easy to get your goat sometimes."

"Hardy har har."

Shaking her head, Adrianna said, "Hardy har har? You watch too many old television shows."

"Feenix likes them." Evalle and her sweet gargoyle had spent many hours alone watching television and surfing the net in the past. She looked around. "Sun's down. Let's go."

Evalle had shut her car door and met Adrianna at the back of the truck when the witch's smile fell away.

Adrianna put a hand on her chest, grimacing.

Evalle snarked, "I told you being a bitch would give you indigestion."

Looking around first, the witch opened her hand and the white ball of energy appeared, but it was spinning back and forth erratically.

Oh, crap. Evalle also checked to see that no human stood nearby or at a window. "What's wrong?"

"No idea. Something is affecting Witchlock." Adrianna sounded angry more than worried. "I wish there was some place to research this power without drawing the attention of someone from Veronika's family. The best place would be in her ancestors' realm."

"I'm with Storm. We should never go back there."

"Agreed." Adrianna struggled to stand upright, as if something kept forcing her body to contort. "I feel like I've been given a Ferrari with a monster engine, but no idea how it will handle, and dropped into the driver's seat at a hundred miles an hour in the mountains. One wrong move, I hit a wall and explode."

Evalle lifted both eyebrows. She took a step back, but in a teasing way.

Adrianna muttered, "Coward."

About to open her mouth and point out that a coward would survive this, Evalle's joking faltered when energy surged up Adrianna's arm. Veins glowed and shot around her arm like lightning strikes under her skin.

Breathing fast, Adrianna said, "On second thought, you may want to run."

"I'm not leaving. Tell me what's going on right now."

Forcing the words out, Adrianna said, "I've been pushing the energy a little more at times when I'm alone somewhere, like on a mountain top. Right now, it feels like the energy is trying to power up, but without me calling it. Or, wait, maybe it's ... reacting." Adrianna stared off into the distance, focused on something no one else could probably see.

As quickly as it came upon her, the sizzling energy disappeared and Witchlock spun happily in the normal direction, back to the shape of a tennis ball above the palm of her hand.

The witch released a long breath. "Finally."

"Finally what?" Evalle asked, staring at tendrils of white drifting away from the ball of energy.

"Everything is back to normal, or at least what I call normal." Using her free hand to brush long, blond hair over her shoulder, Adrianna explained, "Now that I can think more clearly, it felt as if the power was stretching out of shape or in one direction."

Evalle considered possibilities and still came up with only one. "Do you think it was Veronika?"

"If I hadn't recently seen her in the cell beneath VIPER with all of Sen's badass security, I might think that. She would have jumped on the chance to get to me when I stood that close. She couldn't. I have no idea what just happened. It could be nothing more than a reaction to my testing the power recently. Maybe the bulk of the Witchlock energy is trying to pull what I carry with me back to the source."

"That's not good."

"No, but I don't even know if that's the reason." Adrianna's frustration coated every word. Closing her right hand, then reopening it to an empty palm, she stretched her fingers and said, "Let's go see Lanna."

Letting the moment pass without further examination, Evalle led the way to the front door and knocked, expecting to see Mother Mattie when the door opened.

Instead of the elderly witch, her half sister, Caron, stood there. The Fae who'd killed Grendal. "What?"

"Lanna asked me to visit," Evalle said, getting to the point for Miss Personality.

Without turning around, Caron called out, "Lanna? Did you contact this Belador and ..." Her gaze swung to Adrianna, whom she asked, "Just what kind of witch are you?"

"To answer that I'll need a reference point," Adrianna answered smoothly. "What kind of Fae are you?"

Caron didn't smile.

Lanna showed up before that conversation could go any further and rushed Evalle, who opened her arms to the young woman.

To see Lanna happy warmed Evalle's heart. Quinn needed to see his cousin and let go of the guilt he carried for not keeping her safe.

Releasing Evalle from the hug, Lanna turned to face everyone. "Caron, this is my good friend, Evalle, and my other friend, Adrianna."

Evalle started to point out that Caron had met her and Adrianna, but that would mean bringing up bad memories for everyone.

Still not impressed, Caron said, "You can come in, but if anyone makes a threatening move toward Mattie, Lanna or Sissy, I'll have to turn you to dust." With that, Caron left.

"Please do not be bothered by Caron," Lanna said, her eyes showing how much she wanted everyone to get along. "Come. We have tea."

Adrianna smiled and gave Lanna a hug. "I'm glad you're better."

"I am fine. I need to see Cousin soon."

Evalle saw shadows in Lanna's eyes. The young woman was not as fine as she claimed, but Evalle knew from experience that sometimes you had to keep telling yourself you would survive just so that you could.

When they entered the kitchen, Mother Mattie had placed four mugs with steeping tea bags on the small table in her kitchen.

Evalle said, "My apologies, Mother Mattie. I should have called to tell you Adrianna was coming with me."

Lanna laughed. "She knew. That's why she has four teas. Caron will not join us."

Once they were settled, Lanna took a sip of her hot drink, then placed it carefully on the table. Evalle noted Lanna's deliberate mannerisms, which were so ... *managed* compared to the bubbly and vivacious young woman who had come to Atlanta only months ago.

"Thank you for coming," Lanna started. "I must help my cousin. He needs me."

Evalle lifted her hand. "I know he appreciates how much you want to help, but Quinn can't handle you getting hurt again. He has asked me constantly about when he could come to visit. I told him you would call when you were ready. He misses you and loves you very much."

"I know he does, but Cousin must learn that he is not responsible for everyone else." Lanna turned bright blue eyes on Evalle that were far more mature than they should be at eighteen. "I have not broken Cousin's confidence, but Mother Mattie knows about his search."

Hmm, Quinn would not be happy.

Evalle asked, "How did you find out, Mother Mattie?"

"While using my natural healing on Lanna, I saw things that troubled her. I had to ease her worries to push her beyond the grief she'd experienced."

Grief, yes, but in Lanna's case it was probably loss of innocence as well as loss of confidence in herself.

Evalle reached over and squeezed Lanna's hand. "You have no idea how proud of you I am. Quinn will be thrilled when he sees you again. I'm sure he's going to be fine with Mother Mattie knowing." She hoped. Poor Quinn was running a daily race to find Phoedra without an enemy discovering that she was his and putting a target on her back.

"Thank you." A little of the happy Lanna peeked through before her eyes darkened again. "But Cousin may not be so glad when I tell him what he must do."

Adrianna had listened intently and now asked, "What, Lanna?"

"I know you have visions. I have heard," she told Adrianna. "I too have them, but maybe not the same. I also have had dream meetings."

That announcement didn't faze Mother Mattie. No doubt, the witch had seen and heard a lot during Lanna's recovery.

Everyone waited for Lanna to finish speaking.

"My visions have been confusing and my dreams have been ... difficult."

Evalle's heart clenched at the nightmares Lanna had to be suffering.

"But I now think I know how to find my cousin's daughter," Lanna finished. She gave Adrianna a weighted look. "It will take all of us to find her."

"I've told Quinn I'll help in any way, Lanna, but I haven't had any dream visions that clearly relate to this," Adrianna admitted. "At least, as far as I know they don't."

Glancing over at Mother Mattie, who gave the young woman a solemn nod, Lanna said, "I have finally realized that I could do more than touch the bracelet given to Cousin." At Adrianna's frown, Lanna explained, "Kizira gave Cousin small bit of his own hair braided with Phoedra's. The bracelet burned my hand, but there is another way to find a connection to his child. It's inside him. We must bring together our power in one circle while I hold his hand. We can find this girl."

Evalle couldn't breathe for a moment. She turned to Adrianna and Mother Mattie. "Can we do this?"

Adrianna gave her a thoughtful look. "I don't know, but I also don't know that we can't."

Mother Mattie smiled. "It is possible. Lanna came up with that all on her own."

Lanna looked around, leaning forward and peering toward the hallway, then shook her head. "I would like much more power, but we will try it with me, Adrianna and Mother Mattie."

Had Lanna been looking for Caron?

"What about Storm?" Evalle asked.

"His majik is different," Mother Mattie clarified. "We are all some form of witch majik." She pointed at herself, then Lanna, then Adrianna as she said, "White majik, white majik, neutral majik."

Adrianna suppressed a smile, but Evalle could tell she was touched that Mother Mattie had not called her dark.

But if Storm's majik was different, then surely Caron's was, too.

Ready to find Quinn's daughter and give her friend some badly needed peace, Evalle asked, "When do you want to do this and what do you need?"

Mother Mattie held silent, watching Lanna who said, "Tonight. I would like to do this in your building, Evalle, if Storm agrees."

"You know he will. He'd do anything for you and Quinn." Evalle remembered something. "The twins miss you, too."

Lanna's cheeks pinked. "I have missed them."

Evalle would bet Lanna's flush had to do with one of the twins in particular, but she would not put Lanna on the spot by bringing it up.

Bullfrog grunting broken up with cricket chirping approached from down the hall.

"I know that adorable sound," Evalle said. The last time she'd seen Oskar, Mother Mattie's familiar, he'd backed away from Lanna because she'd been tainted with Grendal's majik at the time. Oskar had recognized the scent of majik as the same one from Grendal, who had also captured Mother Mattie, but the little familiar had had no way to relay that to anyone when Evalle found him.

Evalle recalled her one encounter with Grendal at a beast fight and shuddered at the memory.

Oskar came trotting up on all fours, looking something like a shaggy bichon frisé with a salt-and-pepper coat. He smoothly stood up on his hind legs when he got to Lanna and turned his huge, yellow, owl eyes on her.

She cooed all over him, careful to avoid getting poked by the unicorn horn protruding from his head.

"You two made friends," Evalle commented.

"Not at first, but all good now," Lanna replied. "Oskar was not happy when he smelled scent of Grendal's bad majik on me, but Mother Mattie and Caron fixed that."

One look at Mother Mattie's concerned face told Evalle that neutralizing Grendal's influence on Lanna hadn't been an easy task.

Evalle remembered Mother Mattie's granddaughter and asked, "How is Sissy?"

The light in Mother Mattie's eyes dimmed. "She'll come back to us. It's just going to take a bit longer for her."

"I will spend time with Sissy once she is awake again," Lanna said, still leaned over and petting Oskar.

Evalle hurt for Sissy. Caron had gone after Grendal to save Lanna. She'd returned with Lanna in her arms and shared nothing about what happened, but from the look in the Fae woman's eyes, she'd made him pay with a painful death.

Sitting up quickly, Lanna announced, "We should bring Oskar to see Feenix."

"I can do that, but it depends on what Evalle and Storm say," Mother Mattie told her.

Evalle would share all that had happened today with Storm, including Lanna's idea for finding Phoedra. Once she did, she was certain he'd be okay with Oskar visiting. She'd promised Storm she would not bring unknowns into their home without talking to him first. He knew all these people and had met Oskar. If she had any doubt he would agree this time, she wouldn't offer.

"That's a great idea, Lanna," Evalle said, giving Lanna's arm another squeeze. "Everyone will be glad to see you tonight. In fact, you can move back in whenever you're ready. We all miss you, Feenix especially."

"I can?" Lanna's eyes lit with hope.

She was killing Evalle. "Of course you can, Lanna."

"I will bring suitcase."

"Awesome. Feenix is driving us crazy asking about you."

Lanna's eyes glistened. "I miss him, too."

Not used to so much emotional overload, Evalle said, "Ready, Adrianna?"

Rising to join her, Adrianna thanked Mother Mattie for her hospitality. The elderly woman shushed them away when they offered to help clean up.

Outside the front door, Lanna stopped Adrianna, who'd been smiling until Lanna said, "You must not let her have your power."

"What are you talking about?"

"Veronika. My visions come in pieces like mixed up puzzle, but right before you arrive I see Veronika clearly in my mind. She will come for you. You must not let her win."

Chills ran up Evalle's arms. "We won't, Lanna, but promise me you'll tell us about any visions and not try to fix something on your own."

"I promise."

Lanna's quick and sincere answer hurt to hear. Evalle never wanted the girl to go looking for trouble again, but the Lanna she'd known would have bristled and argued that she had powers others couldn't imagine.

And Evalle believed she did.

Would Lanna ever regain her vibrant confidence?

In Storm's truck, Evalle gave Adrianna a smug look and said, "I was right. Sounds like we're having a *séance* tonight."

"I'm never going to hear the end of this, am I?"

"Nope." Evalle drove out of Mother Mattie's neighborhood of quaint homes and had just reached the main thoroughfare when Adrianna made a pained sound.

She said, "Pull over. Now."

Evalle yanked the truck into a closed gas station.

The witch jumped out and backed away.

Evalle ran around to her side. "What's wrong?"

The muscles in Adrianna's normally smooth neck bulged when she strained. "Get away from me."

"Not happening." With a quick glance, Evalle said, "Too many humans."

Sweat poured down Adrianna's face. She croaked out a few words and all the traffic sounds dulled. Even with whatever was going on, Adrianna had managed to toss an invisible cloak over them so humans couldn't see what went on.

Hopefully none had been staring at Evalle and Adrianna when they basically disappeared.

Not the biggest worry right now.

Evalle shouted, "Stop worrying about hurting me and tell me

what I can do."

Adrianna's petite body looked like someone had sucked out the softness and turned every muscle taut. She opened her hand and Witchlock was the size of a basketball, but no longer round. It twisted in different directions, bulging out of shape.

Oh, hell.

Frantic to offer any aid, Evalle called out, "What can I do to help you calm it down?"

"Nothing ... but that's ... good idea." Adrianna reached out with her empty hand and stroked over the ball of power while speaking in one of her ancient languages. The energy seemed to slow down for a moment, but then it spun faster again.

Her words came out in harsh breaths, sounding as if each one was being squeezed out of her.

Fury and strain contorted Adrianna's face into a scary mask. She was clearly trying to force her will on the power.

Witchlock was fighting back.

Adrianna's body arched, toes barely touching the ground. Her eyes rolled up until only white orbs glowed in the sockets.

A lightning strobe of energy shot across her arms and hands, then up her neck and through her face. It had to be blazing through her whole body.

Evalle hated not being able to step in and fight with Adrianna.

Muttering and shaking her head, Adrianna's eyes were still white, but she started shouting.

Was she ... arguing with Witchlock?

The energy built up until the noise turned into a roar that meshed with Adrianna's unintelligible words.

Popping flashes like out-of-control fireworks shot around everywhere. Evalle dove to the ground and covered her head.

Power exploded.

Heat ripped across her back.

Soft murmurs filled the space.

Evalle sniffed. Was that the smell of singed hair? She checked her head. Not bald.

She slowly uncovered her head and looked up to find Adrianna standing on the ground again with her eyes shut, but pale and shaking. She'd been through one hell of a power storm.

Gaining her feet, Evalle asked, "Adrianna? You still in

there?"

Nodding slowly, Adrianna opened her eyes and looked first at the small ball of energy spinning happily in her trembling palm. She released a burst of air, sounding relieved.

Evalle had seen this woman in more than one battle. Adrianna had ice water in her veins. To see her rattled was not good news.

Swallowing, Evalle asked, "You ready to tell me what the hell happened?"

"I would if I knew. The best that I can tell you is I was fighting to hold onto Witchlock. But while I did that, it seemed as if the power was struggling to figure out what was going on. I have a sense that it will remain with me as long as it believes I am powerful enough to host the energy."

"I know I'm not going to like the answer, but do you know who was trying to take Witchlock?"

"Veronika."

"That shouldn't be possible, should it?"

Raising seriously concerned eyes to Evalle, Adrianna pointed out, "You say that as if this power came with a troubleshooting manual."

"Good point. Are you ready to drop the cloaking?"

"Sure." Adrianna closed her right hand, concealing Witchlock, then lifted her other hand and swished the cloaking away.

Sounds from around them sharpened and grew louder.

Holding up her hand, Evalle said, "Let me double check that Veronika is still locked up."

"Good idea."

With Quinn busy getting their forces ready for Daegan to take over, Evalle called out telepathically to Trey since he was the central contact for Beladors in their area. *Trey, this is Evalle.*

I'm here, Trey called back. *What's up?*

Have you heard anything about Veronika today? Like her escaping?

No.

Any chance that could have happened?

Doubtful, but I'll contact Sen and see what he says. Stand by. After a sixty-second pause, Trey said, *Man, Sen's got his tighty-whities in a wad today. He said if we wanted a report, to send*

Beladors back in to work.

What does that mean? Is he avoiding the question?

Trey said, *I have no idea, but I'd think if Veronika had gotten out that Sen would be pushing a Tribunal to demand we come back in force. I'd also expect an apocalyptic display of Veronika's power just to show us the bitch was back.*

Good point. Let me know if you hear differently, okay?

Will do. Then Trey was gone.

Adrianna waited with an anxious look in her eyes.

Evalle said, "Trey just asked Sen, who blew him off because of Daegan yanking most of the Beladors out of VIPER."

"So nothing new on Veronika?"

"Doesn't sound like it, but I'll go hit up my Nightstalker when we get done tonight." Back in the truck, Evalle said, "I need to get ahold of Quinn so we can hold this séance tonight."

"Stop calling it that. It's not a séance."

"Is too."

"Is not." Adrianna lifted her hand. "You need to find Quinn, then please drop me at my house."

"Sore loser," Evalle remarked, smirking. She considered the gravity of what Adrianna had experienced and decided it was worth reaching out telepathically for something brief. *Quinn, can you talk?*

Quinn's deep voice answered in her head. *Quickly. I'm in the middle of something. What's going on?*

Just like she'd thought. He wasn't where he could deal with Sen. With traffic getting thick, she hurried to tell him, *I have to jump, too, so I can drive, but we need you to meet at my place at seven tonight. Good news. Lanna has an idea on Phoedra.*

No, Lanna is staying out of this.

Evalle debated for a moment what to say and decided on, *Just be on time.*

Evalle, did you hear me? I do not want Lanna using her powers in any way. Is that understood?

I hear you loud and clear. Gotta go so I don't wreck Storm's truck. Later.

Evalle ended the telepathy.

They had to find Phoedra. Lanna believed she could do it and Quinn had found no one else who could help.

What was the worst that could happen if she held the séance tonight and included Lanna?

Evalle's gaze tripped over to Adrianna, who looked seriously disturbed over that last power battle.

A lot could go wrong tonight.

CHAPTER 9

Treoir Castle in the Treoir realm

Daegan teleported into Treoir Castle with plans of tracking down Garwyli. He'd barely seen the old druid since taking over this realm. At the last minute, Daegan changed his direction and terminated his teleporting in the sunroom.

He expected to find his niece, Brina, which he did.

She and Tzader, her fiancé, were wrapped up in each other's arms.

"Have you two been locked from your bedchamber?" Daegan asked dryly.

Brina stepped back from Tzader, smiling like a young woman in love who deserved to be happy, but Daegan was in a hurry.

She said, "No, Daegan. We simply have not seen each other much today and slipped in here for a moment of privacy." She gave him a censuring look, then gave up. "What ails you, Uncle?"

"I'm huntin' Garwyli."

She asked Tzader, "Have you seen him?"

"No." Tzader suggested, "I can ask the guards to find him."

"That won't be necessary. I will find him sooner than they can." While Daegan was there, he reminded these two, "You were to be married by now. What's the delay?"

Brina lifted her hands in exasperation. "I'm waitin' for you to tell me our people are no longer under threat. Until then, I doubt we can have our friends stop what they're doin' for a weddin'." She frowned hard this time.

Daegan couldn't help laughing.

Tzader murmured, "Oh, hell."

"And what's so blasted funny, Daegan?" she scowled.

"You, niece."

Tzader put a hand over his eyes. "Not making it better, dragon."

Scratching his chin, Daegan said, "I'm only imaginin' the fierce warrior you two will have soon."

Dropping his hand, Tzader smiled. "Nice save, but it might be a girl."

Brina had been smiling at what Daegan said, but now whirled on Tzader. "What makes ya think she won't be a warrior if she's a lass?"

"That's not what I meant, *muirnin*."

"Don't try to wiggle out by callin' me *muirnin*."

"I thought you liked that."

Brina opened her mouth and closed it.

"Carry on," Daegan called out and got a terse look from Tzader right before teleporting out.

After zipping from spot to spot, Daegan lost patience and stood with his hands on his hips in the middle of an arched hallway.

He bellowed, "*Garwyli!*"

The old guy turned a corner up ahead and meandered down the wide passage toward Daegan. With white hair falling past his shoulders and a matching beard that reached his waist, the druid wore a simple robe and carried books as he puttered along.

When Garwyli got closer, he said, "Don't be hurryin' me, dragon. I'm an old man."

"You're a powerful old druid who can teleport within these walls," Daegan chided him. "Maybe even beyond, but I have yet to determine what all you can do."

Garwyli waved that off with a wrinkled hand. "I find it takes more out of me to teleport these days."

The sincerity in the druid's voice bothered Daegan. He liked the old guy and anticipated having him around for a long time. There was no replacing the knowledge of centuries and all the wisdom that ran through Garwyli's veins. Plus, Brina and Tzader had spoken highly of the druid's confronting Macha when she'd ruled this realm, even though the goddess held the strong hand of power.

Evalle idolized the druid as well and now Daegan knew why. He'd asked Evalle about it before leaving her at home after their trip to VIPER. She went all starry-eyed when she explained about how Garwyli had returned Storm's soul. It didn't take much to realize that many of his closest round-table advisors considered Garwyli an ally. He did, too.

"I'm here now, *dragon*. What do you want?"

"Are you so senile you've forgotten my name, *druid*?" Daegan countered, wanting to poke at him a bit.

Garwyli's snow-white beard hid most of his smile, but his eyes twinkled enough to give life to his humor. "Perhaps. Of course, if that is the case then you're wastin' your time lookin' for answers from me."

Well done, druid. Daegan chuckled then turned serious. "I need your advice. We're losin' human children belongin' to Belador warrior families. We've retrieved some, but for every one we find, we lose two. I think Queen Maeve has her coven members in the human world workin' with trolls to steal the children, and I'm pretty sure she wants to use them to get to me."

"That would fit from what I know of her and the Medb."

"I'm concerned that she's usin' this to pull me away from Treoir so she can attack the island. I've had our guard beefin' up our security and I've repaired the areas breached when she sent the gryphons in to attack."

"Then we should be fine here."

"I hope so," Daegan said. "But I also worry about some Belador warriors who have packed up their families and moved in the middle of the night. That means they don't believe I can protect my people. I'm not sure what I should do about them."

Giving Daegan a long look, Garwyli asked, "Are you intendin' to sanction them?"

"No. I would do the same to protect my family, but ... you've been here far longer than I. Do you feel that once I stop the Medb from harmin' our children, the families who left will return?"

"I think they'll wait to see if it is indeed safe, then, yes. Why would they stay alone when they would be safer with Beladors they know?"

"That's what I think, but we have no castle in their world for protectin' them."

"You want another castle?"

"To tell you the truth, yes, but it's not so easy to do these days. I have not had enough time to prove myself to them or they wouldn't leave. I know I can build a formidable force if we can show the Belador families that we stopped the Medb attacks."

Garwyli said, "Then that is the answer to your question. A warrior will follow the leader he or she respects. Prove yourself by stoppin' this attack and I think you'll be fine."

Daegan hoped so. He found it frustrating to rule from Treoir when the bulk of his forces were in the human realm. "There is one more thing. I must protect Brina. I haven't told anyone except Tristan that I've been hunting the gravesite of my sister. It has to be on this island."

Garwyli stroked his beard. His wrinkled eyes almost closed when he narrowed them. "Are you sure her body is buried here?"

"It has to be for Macha to have retained power. She and Maeve made pacts with my father that involved my two sisters. Macha's pact was to protect the sister who came to live here, which she did a poor job of, and to take over protectin' future generations when my sister passed. My father made it clear that my sister had to be buried on Treoir for Macha to hold that power."

Cocking his head to the side, Garwyli said, "Why do you need your sister's body?"

"I need a ring my sister wore that increased her power as long as she was on the island. I want to give it to Brina." He held in his pain at talking about that sister. She had been his favorite, because the other one ... well, that one had been a disappointment. Even so, if Maeve had delivered the body of the sister given into her care, Daegan could have removed *that* ring.

He loved his father, but those had been terrible agreements. His father had even said so, which was why Daegan had been conceived with the plan for a Treoir dragon who could protect the land and his family.

Daegan had failed everyone when he allowed Queen Maeve to capture and curse him.

"You misunderstand me, Daegan. I'm askin' if you know for

sure your sister is buried here, as in ... are you sure she's dead?"

Daegan took a step back. "I heard of her death when I was trapped in TÅμr Medb, cursed as the queen's dragon throne. Where would my sister be if she had not died?"

"Perhaps that is the question you should be askin'."

This was no help at all. "Thank you, Garwyli."

"I was not here when all of that took place, Daegan. I came later at Macha's request."

Impatient to get back to his other problems, Daegan said, "I understand. You can't help me find her body."

Sighing long and loud, the druid said, "I'm not a crystal ball to spout answers at will, but I do see more with my eyes open than others do with their minds made up."

Daegan knew when he was being reprimanded for dismissing the old druid's question. "I'm not ignorin' what you say, Garwyli, but how could she still be alive?"

"'Tis a good question. I would ask how is it that you are still alive?"

"I'm a dragon."

"She inherited your father's dragon blood as well."

"You think she's still here? Somewhere on the island?"

"I have no idea where she is, but accordin' to what you've told me I think we should consider all possibilities, though I also don't want to get your hopes up only to have you be hurt again later."

Poor old Garwyli was doing his best to give Daegan reason to hope. If he told the druid what someone had said recently, would Garwyli be just as encouraging or finally tell him to stop chasing dreams?

Instead, Daegan joked, "While we're at it, maybe we'll find another dragon or two."

"Why would you think you are the only one to survive this long? You are immortal."

You don't even know about the others, murmured through Daegan's mind.

Those words had haunted him for over a month. Just talking to the druid raised a powerful longing for there to still be dragons.

Then reality set in.

The dragons were all killed because Daegan had not been there to fight alongside them.

Garwyli had a gift of bringing cheer into everyone's life and was trying to do that for Daegan, but some things had to be accepted.

"Weren't you around durin' the great dragon slaughters?" Daegan asked, bitter every time he thought of how he could have saved his father and their allies if he had not walked into Maeve's trap and ended up a throne.

"Yes, I was around. It was a dark time for all of us." Garwyli sighed with great sadness. "That was one reason I went away for a while, to find peace. But here I am today, talkin' to you when we both should not be. It is a puzzle of sorts to work out. But you can't solve a puzzle unless you believe an answer can be found."

Those words eating at Daegan pushed him to ask this so he could convince himself to let it go and get back to caring for his people. "One more thing, Garwyli. Did you hear of the battle we fought in the human world six weeks ago to keep Kizira's body from the Medb?"

"Tristan did inform me. He was quite proud to shift into his gryphon form to fight at your side."

"I was proud of him as well. He's turnin' out to be an excellent *Rí Dtús*. I couldn't ask for a better second in command. When we slew our enemies, we discovered the warriors had Belador abilities. They were Laochra Fola."

That surprised Garwyli. "Weren't those the warriors Belatucadros kept for himself after endowin' Beladors with powers?"

"Yes, but when we found them in Atlanta, they were being led by Lorwerth, a bastard brother to my father. He was condemned to live in the Anwynn underworld for eternity, but someone freed him. I did not find out who negotiated his freedom, but as Lorwerth died he said somethin' about 'you don't even know about the others.' I pressed him for more, but he only said *blood kin* and *she*." Daegan felt ridiculous for clinging to the words of a man like Lorwerth, but he wanted a straight answer. "A moment ago you challenged me to think beyond myself when I dismissed the possibility of my sisters or any other dragon being alive. Please, no puzzles or cryptic words. Do you think there could truly be more ... dragons?"

Pondering a moment, Garwyli said, "You must always realize that in our world of nonhumans, anythin' is possible. Before you returned, no one believed dragons still existed. The best answer I can give you is that it's possible."

Daegan was a fool to wish for this, but he couldn't stop wondering. The only way he could mate would be with one who possessed dragon blood.

CHAPTER 10

Realm of Tuatha Dé Danann

Dakkar felt like whistling, but Macha had been in a foul mood for more than a month and hearing anyone happy around her set the goddess off.

He hoped what he had to report would change her mood, though nothing short of handing her the head of that dragon was going to please her. Her frame of mind had gone so far downhill, he'd failed to tease her out of it with hours of making love. She was an insatiable wench, but without passion these days.

A weaker man would take that to heart and feel a failure, but he knew his ability with a naked woman.

It mattered not. He would keep Macha satisfied and partnering with him so that when he handed her the dragon and Treoir, she would in turn give him what he needed to reach his goal. One she need not know of yet.

"How's the most underappreciated goddess feeling today?" he asked as he strolled in.

Macha sat neck-deep in a marble tub, which required two steps up to reach the platform holding it. She soaked in a bath filled with ... he sniffed. Champagne and lilac. Interesting mixture and he had no doubt it was the finest champagne to be had.

She adjusted her cloud of hair the color of a deep-red sunset, placing the thick mass against a plush, silk pillow that hummed a melodic tune. He loved it when her green eyes turned dark as he made love to her. She had a face that challenged the word perfection and lips fit for a goddess, but he was the man who owned her in the sack.

Eyeing him with a pout, she said, "I am bored beyond belief. I want my island back."

"I know, love." He heard the same refrain every single day, which was why he spent most of his time out in the human world, digging for ways to give her that bloody island and dragon.

He waited for her full attention to say, "I come to you with news."

She arched a perfect eyebrow. "You always have something to tell me, just not what I want to hear."

Undeterred, he stepped to the end of her marble tub and dropped to his knees on a lower step, then reached into the water to lift out a foot, which he began to massage.

She closed her eyes.

He kneaded the muscles and received a sexy sound of pain, but nothing like what he could pull from her with a night of role-playing. When she lifted another foot for him, he continued working on her as he spoke.

"I have been making interesting progress." No overt reaction, so he went on. "I have good news and not-so-good news."

Muscles in her foot tensed.

"There is no benefit to having a meltdown, Macha."

She opened her eyes to glare at him. "I will do as I please here."

"We all know that, but your staff is weary from your constantly putting them in a panic."

Without any acknowledgment of his point, she said, "What is your news?"

"The Beladors have withdrawn a large percentage of their force from VIPER, leaving the coalition in a lurch."

She lifted her head and the pillow whined. Macha said, "Shh!" silencing the pillow. She asked Dakkar, "Why did the Beladors do that?"

"Daegan claimed some of the Belador families were losing children to the Medb. Evidently Sen didn't see that as his problem. He threatened the Beladors with repercussions, but the good news in all this is that VIPER needs agents who can handle deadly preternatural situations. For some reason, trolls are coming into Atlanta and helping the Medb steal children."

Sitting quietly as sparkling bubbles floated around her glorious breasts, Macha said, "What is Maeve after?"

"My best guess is she's come up with some new plan for capturing the dragon."

"No. I want his head!"

Water sizzled and sparked. Steam rose from her churning energy.

Dakkar did not want to be burned, which would happen if that water surged and hit him. He could heal, but he'd just as soon pass on being a boiled mage.

"Macha, please."

She looked around, just noticing the temperature of her bath and stared at it until the happy champagne returned. She leaned back on the pillow, which sighed and began humming again.

Dakkar dried his hands and stood. "Due to the Beladors pulling out of VIPER, Sen asked if I could help. I was authorized to bring in as many bounty hunters as necessary to cover the assignments. I said I'd do it if my people could stay once I brought them in. He agreed. This gives me an inside line on everything that comes up and an edge as we move forward."

Macha allowed a contented smile. "That is good news."

"Quite a bit of good news, right?"

"Yes."

"It will balance out the not-so-good news that Veronika has escaped."

Macha shouted, "No! How could they let that happen?"

"My words exactly. I have no idea how she got out, because Sen forbade us talking about it. He said he hopes she goes after the Beladors and the Sterling witch first. If they don't stop her, then he'll come up with an attack plan."

"He's a moron."

"Possibly, but I like the way he's thinking. I'm all for letting someone else deal with her. In the meantime, you need to stay as far from the human world as you can."

"This is terrible."

He didn't see the downside. "Why?"

"Are you sure Maeve and Cathbad are behind terrorizing the

Beladors?"

"That's the logical conclusion since the trolls are being lured in with the offer of Noirre majik. "

Macha fisted the hand draped on the edge of her tub. "If that bitch Maeve captures Daegan, I will lose my chance to kill him and take all that he has stolen from me."

"I don't know about that, Macha. Veronika may get to Daegan before anyone else."

"She probably doesn't know a dragon exists. He's a threat to deities. That means he's a threat to her as well."

"My people have been sending me any intel they can scrounge from VIPER. Word is that Veronika knows a secret the Beladors have been hiding, which has to do with their Maistir."

"Quinn? That fool? He had a fling with Kizira. I don't care if it did happen when they were both young. He allowed an enemy to manipulate him with sex."

Who was Dakkar to criticize someone who used his own tactics? "True, but after placing some of my people strategically to make Sen's life easier, I have learned even more."

Macha grimaced. "Why make that buffoon's life easy?"

"Because Sen is the one person in position to do us the most good. When I had possession of the tomb with Kizira's body—"

"—which you lost."

Dakkar tamped down on his irritation. "That body was merely a means to an end."

"The end being to trap that dragon and kill him."

He deserved an award for patience. "You're getting off topic. If Veronika does not kill Daegan, I will hand you the dragon. All in good time. But when Quinn was searching for Kizira's body, evidently he took the Sterling witch in to see Veronika in her cell."

Macha perked up. "Oh?"

Without changing his expression, Dakkar smiled to himself. "Yes, and when they left, Veronika went into a screaming fit. Since then, she's been singing that she knows his secret. I don't think it's that he had a relationship with Kizira, because everyone from the Tribunal to you to the Medb found out about that, so what else could he be hiding?"

Sounding stumped, Macha muttered, "I have no idea."

"I will know for sure very soon, but I'm going to make an educated guess and say that this secret will put Veronika at odds with Daegan. I've heard Daegan is taking over as Maistir so that Quinn can be gone to handle something personal. That makes me think Veronika is after something Quinn doesn't want her to get her hands on." Dakkar could tell Macha, but he wanted her to reach the same conclusion he had. He asked, "What could Quinn and Kizira have been hiding?"

The goddess sat up quickly.

Champagne rushed over Macha's creamy white skin and damn, what a pair of tits. He almost didn't hear her say, "You think they had a child?"

Dragging his gaze from her incredible body, he said, "If they did, everyone will be after a child with Belador and Medb blood. Think of the potential to manipulate *that* kind of power from the beginning."

"Daegan would never allow that to happen."

"Exactly, which is why Daegan will be busy hunting for Veronika while Maeve is stalking his ass."

"I hate to admit this, but in a one-on-one battle, he *might* kill Veronika."

"Yes, with *might* being the key word if the Medb stay involved."

"What are you going to do?"

"Sen is hiding Veronika's escape from his superiors as long as he can. He called me in to strike a deal for the return of Veronika, which we did. She took down one of my hunters. We found his body in a trunk. I intend to find her, make sure she kills the dragon first, then I'll set my bounty hunters on her."

She lifted a perfectly sculpted eyebrow. "What did you ask for?"

"Sen to support me when I tell the Tribunal you deserve the return of Treoir. Those deities will jump at the chance to have you back where you were."

Finally, he earned a smile and the promise of more to come.

CHAPTER 11

Atlanta, GA – Storm and Evalle's building

When the doorbell to their building dinged, Evalle left the conference room to open the garage entrance for Lanna and Mother Mattie. Storm had offered to pick them up, but Lanna declined politely, which bothered Evalle only because she knew Lanna was comfortable with Storm.

Why have someone Mother Mattie's age driving through Atlanta traffic when it wasn't necessary?

With a quick check of the monitor inside the garage, which was connected to a camera trained on the entrance, Evalle hit the button to lift the door.

A modest, ten-year-old, blue sedan pulled in.

Mother Mattie climbed out of the passenger side. "I like your building, Evalle."

"Thanks."

Evalle was glad Quinn hadn't been present to see Lanna pop out from the driver's side. "When did you get a driver's license, Lanna?"

Mother Mattie replied instead. "Four days ago. I figured she's eighteen and far more prepared for the world than most of the kids her age. She nailed the test and didn't use her powers to pass, either."

"Really? That's wonderful," Evalle said, sending Lanna a smile. It dawned on her that she had no idea of Lanna's birthday, which reminded Evalle the twin boys had recently turned eighteen. She should ask if they had a birthday celebration when they stayed with Isak's mother.

Evalle had never had a birthday party of her own, but she was sure with a little help she could put together something for Lanna or the boys next time.

Now if only Quinn didn't freak out about Lanna driving.

Lanna smiled. It was still not one of her vibrant, high-wattage smiles of the past, but a sincere one. "I know you worry about Cousin stressing. I will tell him about my driving after tonight. I want calm first."

"About that," Evalle said, trying to figure out how to avoid hurting Lanna's feelings. "Quinn told me in no uncertain terms that we could not involve you in hunting for Phoedra." She prepared for the blast of anger and argument, but it never came.

Lanna looked to Mother Mattie. The elderly witch said, "We'll talk to him."

"Cousin is hardheaded. He will not hear us."

"Then raise your voice, Lanna," a strong female voice ordered.

"*Caron!*" Lanna's face lit up as she spun toward the street. "You are here."

Everyone turned to where the beautiful Fae woman stood on the sidewalk outside the still-open garage door. Evidently, Lanna had wanted Caron to join them but hadn't expected Mother Mattie's sister to show up.

"Hi, Caron," Evalle called over.

Caron gave Evalle a double take. "Are those eyes real?"

Evalle lifted her fingers then dropped them, realizing she'd taken off her dark sunglasses. "Yep. The shade is Alterant green."

"Nice."

Coming from Caron, that was a huge compliment. Evalle grinned. She stopped short of saying thank you. "Come on in."

Lanna took two steps in Caron's direction. "Yes. You are welcome here. We need your help."

"No, but I appreciate the invitation," Caron said to Evalle then crooked a finger at the suddenly disappointed Lanna. When Lanna reached the sidewalk, Caron said, "What have I been telling you? You are more powerful than pretty much any witch I know, including Mattie and she's tough to top. You're either a mage or sorceress, but it really doesn't matter what you are other than powerful. I've taught you enough to protect yourself, but it's time to start trusting your abilities again."

"Grendal's majik is—"

"No longer a significant concern. Yes, you may have some issues, but even Oskar does not sense Grendal's majik in you anymore, and he's pretty sensitive."

Speaking of Oskar, a grunting-frog-interspersed-with-cricket sound erupted from the back seat of Mattie's car. Evalle glanced over to see Oskar standing on his hind legs, which she knew from experience he could do as long as he chose.

She waved at him.

More excited grunting came from the little guy, then he gently tapped his horn on the window.

Mother Mattie said, "I'll get you, Oskar."

"I understand," Lanna said to Caron in an obedient tone.

"Oh, I know you understand, sweet pea, but I need you to *believe*," Caron told her. "This is the time to start learning more about your powers. First be sure someone is watching your back ..." Caron's gaze slipped away from Lanna and touched on Evalle, who gave her a hard nod, acknowledging Lanna would be well protected.

Caron continued telling Lanna, "As long as you're around those you can trust, then push the boundaries and accept that you're going to hit limitations. Don't fight it and don't force it, but don't back away if you feel strong enough to go forward. This is one of those times you don't need me or Mother Mattie."

"Hey, speak for yourself," Mattie warned. "She needs as many witches as we can pull together, me especially."

Caron gave her a don't-screw-with-me-right-now look. "I'm talking about using *her* powers, Mattie, not needing additional power for the hunt tonight." Returning to Lanna, Caron said, "Just don't go off on your own for a bit. You'll know when you're ready. Don't come up with some half-baked reason for taking a risk. I trust you to be smarter than that. As for tonight, I'm not a witch. My majik would probably interfere. I have located people by calling on the elements, but the elements have to believe I have a vested interest. I have nothing against your cousin, but I also have no vested interest."

Evalle hadn't realized how deeply Caron had tapped her paranormal resources to find Grendal when she saved Lanna. Evalle appreciated all the Fae woman had done for Lanna, but especially Caron's obvious efforts to begin rebuilding the young woman's confidence and self-worth. Those had taken a beating from Grendal's abusive actions when he tried to drain power from Lanna.

Lanna straightened her back and filled her lungs with a deep breath. When she exhaled, she said, "I am strong. I can do this."

Caron gave her a look full of praise. "Attagirl. If Quinn gives you too much trouble, tell him he doesn't want me to come chat with everyone."

Mother Mattie said, "Don't threaten my friends, Caron."

"You know better, Mattie."

Lanna turned to the older witch with a knowing smile. "Caron does not threaten. She makes promise."

"Exactly. Okay, sweet pea. You staying here?" Caron asked.

"Yes." Lanna's voice was getting stronger with each word. "I am at home here. Storm, Evalle and Feenix are family."

Damn. That girl needed to shut up soon before Evalle's eyes started leaking. "We're glad you're back, Lanna." Evalle told Caron, "I know Quinn will want to personally express his gratitude to you and Mother Mattie."

Shaking her head, Caron groused, "You people have got to learn not to ask a Fae for anything and not to thank one."

Mother Mattie made a *pfft* sound at Caron. "I'll talk to Quinn and pass along his appreciation to the stick-in-the-mud."

"Mattie." That was Caron's warning tone.

The old woman waved her off. "I left you meatloaf and a baked potato in the warmer."

Caron practically glowed with happiness. "What about cake? Did you make a chocolate cake, too?"

"Yes, there's cake and milk. Now get out of here."

With a snap of sparkly energy, Caron vanished.

Evalle cringed. "Was anyone watching her, Lanna?"

"No. Caron hides her majik from humans." Lanna sighed. "I would like to eat everything and have beautiful body, too."

"You are beautiful," Evalle told her.

"Yes, but even Brasko women must work to good body."

There was a hint of the confident Lanna that Evalle had missed.

Mother Mattie opened the rear door to her car, where Oskar promptly hopped out and walked over to Evalle on his hind legs. The witch pulled out a large canvas tote bag, hooking the straps over her shoulder.

Evalle scooped up Oskar. "Hi there. Want to see if Feenix is up for company?"

Oskar danced his head side to side, upping the sound of his chirping and grunts. She took that as Oskar talk meaning he knew exactly where he was headed.

When everyone acknowledged they were ready, Evalle took the lead through the lower entrance area, then up to the second landing. She paused to say, "Your apartment's unlocked, Lanna. Go ahead and get settled. Everyone is supposed to be here in the next fifteen or twenty minutes. We'll take Oskar up to Feenix's level."

Lanna dragged her suitcase down the hall and disappeared into her space.

Evalle waited to see if the twins would stick their heads out from across the hall, but they didn't. Probably playing a video game.

At the next landing, she smiled at Oskar's enthusiastic grunting as she reached for the door to Feenix's space. Her sweet gargoyle had been upstairs with her earlier in the evening, where she'd kept a sharp eye on him so he wouldn't eat anything in her stainless steel kitchen.

But she did let him torch a pizza in the oven where his flames wouldn't harm anything. It took so little to make him happy.

Opening the door, Evalle lowered Oskar to the floor. "Mother Mattie, meet Feenix."

Her two-foot-tall gargoyle had been building some structure with brightly colored plastic blocks Storm had brought him. Feenix turned around, bright orange eyes glowing with excitement.

"*Evalle!*" Feenix flapped his little bat-like wings, taking to the air. He flew the length of the room and landed in her arms, chortling happily. She'd never get tired of the sound of joy he made every time he saw her, as if she'd been gone for months instead of hours.

She hugged her baby, then turned him to the witch. "This is my friend, Mother Mattie."

"Mattie?" Feenix asked.

"Yes, I am. Nice to meet you, Feenix." Mother Mattie was grinning and held her hand out, palm up.

Feenix studied it a moment, then placed his thick hand on hers. He closed his eyes and made a humming sound.

Evalle didn't interfere, which said how much she trusted the witch.

When Feenix opened his eyes, he started nodding. "Mattie friend."

Mother Mattie's eyes held the kind of warmth seen when someone coos to a child. The witch said, "You're something, Feenix. I have never met anyone like you." Her eyes slashed at Evalle in a way that said Mattie would like to know more about the little gargoyle.

Feenix twisted around and looked down. "*Othkar!* You play?"

Oskar lifted up on his hind legs and turned as he made bullfrog-grunting noises. He tapped back and forth from one foot to the other, clearly ready to play.

Evalle looked at Mattie. "Think we're good?"

"Yes. Oskar either likes you or he doesn't. No halfway with him. Feenix isn't going to hurt him and Oskar will not harm your baby, especially now that he knows Feenix is my friend, too."

"Now that you mention it, Feenix is pretty much the same as Oskar when it comes to liking or not liking someone." Evalle lowered Feenix to the floor. "Why don't you show Oskar around?" When she stood up, she told Mattie how Storm had kept Oskar contained in one corner last time for his safety.

Feenix had yet to move. He'd stuck one of his claws into his mouth as if debating on what to do.

Had he not understood what she was saying?

Or was he unsure about Oskar being loose in his area? Feenix had never shared his space freely with anyone except Lanna or the boys.

"Othkar," Feenix announced and walked past the little critter.

Mother Mattie's familiar spun as smoothly as a dancer and tiptoed after Feenix.

When they reached the other side of the room, Feenix dragged two of his beanbag chairs to the middle of the room, facing the wall where a huge flat-screen television had been mounted.

Storm had created a special panel with different-colored buttons the size of muffins, which he'd wired for controlling anything in the room that required electronic operation. Some buttons had designs and images painted on the surface.

Feenix said something to Oskar, who made a loud chirping noise.

In reply, Feenix laughed as he walked over to hit a big black-and-white checkered button.

Roaring engines of the latest Daytona 500 NASCAR race poured from surround-sound speakers mounted along the walls.

Oskar jumped up and down on his bag.

Feenix chortled and clapped as he waddled back to his stuffed bag.

It looked like they wouldn't kill each other.

Evalle had an app on her phone that allowed her to monitor Feenix via cameras when she wasn't with him.

"They'll be fine," Mother Mattie declared and stepped out, closing the door behind Evalle, who headed to the roof.

"Lovely place," the witch commented as they walked into the open space upstairs. Mattie placed her tote bag next to one of the cozy chairs, and took in the view of the city at night. "Are you only able to come up after dark?"

"Oh, no. I'm up here during the day, too." Evalle explained how the roof worked to protect her from the deadly sunrays.

Mother Mattie said, "That's some man you have, Evalle."

"I know." She beamed with pride. "He's the best."

"That's what I want to hear after a long day," Storm announced, walking up to Evalle from behind and kissing her soundly. One touch of his lips and her body started planning a party with his.

When he released her, Evalle whispered to him, "We have company, but save that thought."

"Oh, I won't forget," he assured her. "Sorry I'm late."

"No problem. I let Quinn know we're starting at eight instead and he was good with it. He needed the extra time."

Storm paused to greet Mother Mattie with a handshake. "It's

nice to have you visit us."

"I told Evalle that you have a wonderful building, but that was before I actually toured it. Very nice."

"Thank you." Storm kissed Evalle again.

Mother Mattie moved back to the plush chair she'd chosen and settled with a sigh. "To be that young again."

Quinn arrived next and Storm asked how long it would be until Daegan showed up.

"Daegan won't be joining us," Quinn replied. "He's working personally with our people in the Atlanta area to ensure all Belador families are secure. Once everyone is covered to his satisfaction, he's going to take any additional Belador warriors he's withdrawn from VIPER to areas in the country with heavy Belador populations and leave teams in place to replicate the plan in those spots."

Storm asked, "What about VIPER?"

Evalle interjected, "I haven't had a chance to tell you or Quinn, but we're on the outs with VIPER. Sen basically blew off Daegan's concern for Belador families being targeted, so Daegan invoked something called Belador Cosaint." She shared a quick rundown of what had happened with Sen.

Quinn mused, "He said it was a protocol created long ago. I'd like to hear more about Daegan's life prior to being captured and cursed."

"We all would," Evalle agreed. "I think he'll tell us in his own time."

Storm carried a tray of different beverages toward the coffee table as he commented, "I wonder how Sen took getting pushed back again. If Daegan keeps doing that, Sen's going to come after him."

Evalle said, "Sen didn't like it. In fact, Trey tried to ask Sen a question earlier today and Sen blew him off."

"After witnessing the way Daegan knocked Sen down a notch during the last Tribunal meeting, then issued a not-too-subtle warning to the Tribunal deities if they tried to take him on, I'll put my money on the dragon," Quinn said.

Evalle interrupted, "Hold on guys, before you start talking shop. Quinn, I thought you'd want to know that Mother Mattie is here." She gestured toward the seating area.

Quinn leaned to look past Evalle. "I apologize for not speaking sooner, Mother Mattie. Very nice to see you. I have so much to thank you for, and appreciate all you and Caron have done."

"It's good to be here and you're welcome. We were happy to have Lanna with us." Mother Mattie gave a definitive nod, confirming she'd been happy to have Lanna at her home.

Having started toward her, Quinn paused. "Wait, if you're here, does that mean—"

Lanna entered the room. "Hello, Cousin."

Quinn turned around and caught Lanna, who dashed into his arms. When he hugged her, his face relaxed a little for the first time in a long while.

Evalle was glad to see the pair reunited.

Quinn told Lanna, "I've been worried about you."

"I know, but I am fine."

Evalle didn't believe that for a moment and seriously doubted that Quinn did either, but she hoped he'd accept it for now. When he loosened his hold, Lanna stepped back and lifted her cocky little chin at him.

"I believe I can help you, Cousin."

His voice was gentle, but stern. "As long as you sit on the sofa and tell me your idea, I will very much appreciate any help you can offer. But if you try to find her by using your powers, then I will be quite displeased."

Offering him an unconcerned expression, Lanna said, "You will be very displeased then, because I will do much more than call up my powers."

"Lanna, listen to me—"

Evalle cringed and said, "About that, Quinn..."

Quinn shifted around. "You knew she planned to do something tonight?"

"Well, sort of, see—"

"I told you she was *not* getting involved again."

"I know that, but—"

"Please. Be. Quiet!" Lanna requested without raising her voice, but power rushed through the room and everyone fell into a deep silence.

Storm murmured, "Whoa, that's ... major mojo."

Evalle had always suspected Lanna had a lot hidden inside her, and Caron's words downstairs had backed up that instinct. Still, that surge she'd just experienced was insane.

Quinn looked shocked. "How did—"

Lifting her finger to her lips, Lanna shushed him.

Behind Quinn, Mother Mattie chuckled.

Holding her short frame as erect as she could, Lanna informed Quinn, "It is time for you to see me as adult, Cousin. I was careless with my abilities when I first came here." Her solemn blue eyes forced everyone to take her seriously. "I have learned much. Some things I wish I had not, but that is how life goes. I have healed and trained with Caron. You remember her?"

"The Fae woman."

Quinn didn't sound too happy about a Fae powerhouse training Lanna, but to argue that point after what Caron and Mother Mattie had done for Lanna would be digging a deeper hole than the one he already had going.

Nodding, Lanna said, "Yes. Caron and Mother Mattie have worked very hard. You should wait to see the results before assuming you know what is best for me. Caron does not know if I am mage or sorceress or ... something else. Caron says I am like witch with much power since they are all from same family of beings."

Quinn's gaze went to Evalle, who gave him a be-patient look and angled her head toward Lanna, subtlety suggesting that Quinn should listen to the girl.

Lanna continued. "Caron says I am very powerful. I knew this, but I did not realize how dangerous it was for me to use these powers without more knowledge. I am taking time to develop all that she has shown me about myself and I need people I can trust when I draw on this power. I *am* going to join with Mother Mattie and Adrianna to find your daughter. You must do your part when I ask and *not* interfere with me."

Well, damn. Evalle exchanged a look with Storm, whose expression said this was a far more mature Lanna than he'd last seen, too.

She'd put Quinn in his place, but she was fooling herself if she thought Quinn couldn't see the shadows in her eyes that Evalle had observed.

Adrianna walked in, saving Quinn from having to figure out how to respond to Lanna's set down. The Sterling witch called out, "Do we just have three witches for this?"

"Make that five," Kardos said in a deep voice as the first of two male witches entered. "Evalle told us you were having a séance."

Adrianna made a derogatory noise.

On the heels of Kardos, Kellman walked in. All similarity between the tall, fair-haired twins stopped at physical appearance. Both were attractive young men, but Kellman had a quiet reserve about him, unlike his boisterous sibling.

"Hello, Kardos and Kellman," Lanna said.

As Lanna spoke, Kellman lifted his head and stared at her with an unabashed adoration that had Quinn frowning.

Evalle knew that overprotective look. She sent a message to Quinn telepathically. *Stop giving Kellman the you'll-die-if-you-touch-her stink eye.*

Quinn glanced around at Evalle.

She crooked an eyebrow in challenge.

Quinn answered in the same silent communication, *I was not giving anyone a stink eye.*

Oh, yes you were. Kellman and Lanna like each other. We can all see it and Kellman would lay down his life for her, so she's not at any risk staying here with the boys. If anything, I think it will help her come out of her quiet shell.

She waited for him to argue, but he couldn't.

Quinn knew, just as Evalle did, that Kellman had proven himself to be the sane and upstanding one of the twins.

Worry scrawled across Kellman's face when he took in Lanna. Quinn might want to lock her away somewhere safe, but that wouldn't help as much as Lanna being around peers she trusted.

One more thing, Quinn, Evalle added just for him. *I believe Lanna is ready to begin moving past what happened to her with Grendal and tonight will actually help her. I wouldn't have gone along with this if I didn't believe it. We're all ready to watch out for her, but are you okay with the boys knowing about Phoedra? Lanna told me she'd like as much witch power as possible.*

He just nodded, ending their private chat.

"Thanks for joining us, guys," Evalle said out loud. "If you'll all grab a seat, Lanna can tell us what she has in mind."

"One thing first," Adrianna said as they all found places on sofas and chairs. Storm sank onto the soft cushions beside Evalle.

"Sure. What's up?"

"Did you tell anyone about what happened when you and I left Mattie's house?"

Storm came to attention. "What happened?"

Oh, boy. Evalle said, "Nope. I wasn't sure if you wanted me to share it so I didn't." She whispered out the side of her mouth. "I was going to tell you later."

Storm squeezed her leg. All was good.

"Thanks for that," Adrianna said with appreciation in her voice. "But I think Quinn and I may need to go back to see Veronika."

Quinn jerked at that. "Why?"

Adrianna proceeded to describe what had happened while she was out with Evalle visiting Lanna. The Sterling witch still sounded shaken by that second incident when she'd fought to control Witchlock.

She had been talking to the room, but as she finished, Adrianna asked Quinn, "What do you think?"

"I think I'll check with Trey and have him find out if any of the guards working VIPER's high security area have reported something going on with Veronika. I heard yesterday that she's singing crazy songs." Quinn's face had gone from serious to concerned in a blink.

"Good luck with that," Evalle grumbled.

"Why would you say that?"

She told Quinn about asking Trey to check earlier to see if anything had happened with Veronika and how Sen dismissed any request from a Belador.

"That bloody liaison. I'll give him an option to give me a report or give it to Daegan in person. This is too important to be screwing around."

"Nice to finally have a hammer to hold over Sen," Evalle said as she inched toward the edge of her seat, waiting on Quinn to contact Trey telepathically.

She studied his face, which normally showed little, but his hands curled into fists before he drew a deep breath and unfurled his fingers as he exhaled anger.

Before Quinn could say a word, Evalle and Adrianna both asked, "Did Veronika escape?"

"Yes."

Mother Mattie lifted her phone and started typing. "We have to alert all the witches."

"Wait a minute. Sen can find anyone who runs so he can find her, right?" Evalle asked.

Quinn's Adam's apple bobbed with a hard swallow. "Evidently not this time." He told Mattie, "As to alerting the witches, that will be wise, especially Rowan, but I believe we probably have some time. Veronika will most likely target Adrianna first, but Veronika knows Adrianna has the Beladors as allies so she will need time to organize a support team and to come up with a plan for gaining Witchlock without Adrianna destroying her."

"Understood," Mattie said.

Showing the kind of backbone that kept Witchlock from Veronika's claws, Adrianna said, "I'll go with Mother Mattie after we finish here so we can meet with Rowan in person and explain what we're up against."

"That's what I told Rowan in my text," Mother Mattie said, putting her phone away.

Shaking his head, Quinn stood and said, "I'm sorry, Lanna, but we're not doing this tonight."

Lanna started to speak, but Adrianna stood and told Quinn, "Veronika knows about Phoedra. She said as much when we saw her in VIPER. With that witch at large, I may be of no help to any of you after tonight. If Lanna doesn't locate Phoedra, then you, the Beladors and that dragon will have to find Veronika, Quinn, because I believe she *will* find your daughter. If you don't get to Phoedra first, you may not have a second chance if Veronika realizes what she can do with Phoedra's potential power. Every second counts right now."

CHAPTER 12

Quinn wanted to choke Sen.

How was it that Sen could find anyone, but not Veronika? Worse than that, Sen had sat on vital information when he should have been broadcasting that she was loose.

Based on what Trey related, Sen would say only that her escape was unusual circumstances. Quinn would have to find out more on that later.

Right now, he had to bring himself to allow Lanna to put herself at risk again. No matter what everyone said, this was not a normal search for a missing person.

Not when his daughter carried his genes plus that of a Medb priestess.

Everything about this search would be extremely dangerous.

"Cousin, please sit so I can explain what we need to do," Lanna called out.

Resigned to at least give Lanna a chance to try, Quinn ignored the headache that still nagged him since diving into that troll's head last night, and took a seat.

Lanna sat across the room from him with Kellman and Kardos on each side of her.

Sitting a little too stiffly to look at ease, Lanna said, "Cousin, am I correct to think it is okay to talk freely about what we're doing and who we are looking for?" At his nod, she said, "I will tell you that Mother Mattie knows, but I did not tell her intentionally. It came out during our ... healing sessions."

Guilt hammered him over not keeping Lanna safe from Grendal. "I understand and trust Mother Mattie to hold a confidence."

The elderly witch tilted her head at him.

He added, "I am in your debt for anything you need in the future and I'd offer the same to Caron, but I understand she does not wish to be thanked."

"You're correct. I'll pass along your appreciation to Caron." The elder witch sent a look to Lanna, giving her the floor again.

With her hands tucked in her lap, Lanna continued. "I have always been able to find those in our family. Is that not right, Cousin?"

"That is correct. You showed an uncanny ability to do that early on."

She awarded him with the hint of a smile. "I find it easier to draw on that ability when I hold something connected to the missing person." She no doubt caught the worry Quinn failed to hide from his face and rushed on to say, "I am not touching the bracelet, Cousin. But your daughter Phoedra is now my family, too."

Leaning forward, he studied on where she was going with this line of thought. "That's true."

"I believe if I hold your hand while I call upon my powers, that I can find Phoedra, because she is connected to you."

That sounded so logical, but majik was rarely logical.

He asked, "I accept that it is your decision to do this, but I want the truth. Is there a risk to you?" He glanced at Storm, but the Skinwalker appeared determined to stay out of this exchange, so Quinn was on his own.

"There is always a risk with majik, Cousin. I will be safe, especially with four witches to share their power with me."

Quinn thought she might be overestimating what the two boys brought to the witch table, but he could live with an unsuccessful outcome as long as Mother Mattie and Adrianna kept Lanna safe.

He cursed himself for the hope racing through his heart when his job was to protect Lanna from harm. There was nothing he could do, though, about the fast beating of the savaged organ after weeks of hitting dead ends everywhere he'd gone.

Even Garwyli had come up empty, though the druid continued to try.

Quinn couldn't deny his anticipation at even a tiny lead.

Lanna stood up, sounding in control of the event. "I will tell you where to sit on the rug when we are ready to start. When I do, please make yourself as comfortable as you can. I have not tried this for many years. I apologize now if it takes much time."

Mother Mattie said, "This is not something to be rushed. Work at your own pace." She rose and handed the heavy tote bag to Lanna.

"Thank you." Lanna withdrew a large object wrapped in black felt. She placed it in the middle of the rug and opened the circle of soft cloth to reveal a polished black bowl almost two feet across, but shallow. The black cloth extended another six inches all the way around and had silver designs drawn on it. Next she pulled out three sturdy candles, one indigo, one purple, and one white. Once she had them arranged in the center of the bowl, she withdrew a velvet bag of crystals.

She placed the crystals in specific locations in the bowl before filling the dish with water from a small jug.

Did that tote hold anything else?

Nope. Lanna carefully folded the bag and placed it on her chair.

As Quinn watched Lanna, he realized he'd never seen her pay attention to detail the way she did now. Was there a reason the dark blue candle stood taller than the other two?

She began pointing out places on the rug for everyone. "Kellman there, then Mother Mattie, Kardos, Adrianna, Cousin, and I will be here."

Like the others, Quinn slipped off his shoes and found his spot, where he sat cross-legged.

Adrianna took her spot, looking like a perfect blonde package of class and confidence. Quinn was thankful to have her as an ally to Beladors, as well as a friend.

He knew about Isak Nyght, a human black ops soldier, who had been getting deeply involved with her until the chump acted like an idiot, in Evalle's words.

Lanna drew Quinn's attention back to the moment when she asked Evalle to lower all the artificial lights, then explained, "This will not be a scrying exactly. My majik works in its own way. When we join hands, please open your power to me. I have learned how when we bring our power together, we form a stronger connection to the universe. I will open myself to what I can learn about Phoedra, but I will need all of you to remember whatever I say. I may recall what happens, but I may not."

Taking her place next to Quinn, Lanna extended her hand, which he grasped, noting how small her fingers were against his huge hand. Lanna would rush into a burning building for those she cared about, but in spite of her inner strength, which humbled him, she was still a vulnerable young woman who had been through hell.

"Everyone please hold hands." Lanna grasped Kellman's hand, then squeezed Quinn's and said, "Relax, Cousin. It will be fine."

Lanna closed her eyes, silent for a moment, then she began speaking in an earnest tone. "We call to you, guardians of the innocent, to ask for your wisdom and your vision. We open our hearts to your counsel and our minds to your advice. We seek one of our blood who needs our prayers and our strength. We wish to wrap Phoedra, child of Quinn and Kizira, in our love and protection."

The only sound Quinn heard next was soft breathing as Lanna sat perfectly still.

He forced himself not to fidget.

If she could put herself out to do this then he could do as she asked and open up to her power, but it was difficult to do so, knowing Veronika had escaped.

Lanna lifted her chin, eyes still shut, and moved her lips but no sound came out.

The flames of the candles began to grow, with the indigo one climbing the tallest, to eye level with him.

Opening her eyes, Lanna leaned forward slightly and stared down at the bowl.

Quinn couldn't help leaning a little forward himself and gaped at the reflection of her eyes. He looked over to see if it was a trick of the lights on the water, but no.

Her blue eyes had turned bright as two diamonds with pinpoint pupils.

Looking up above the circle of bodies joined by hands, he saw a halo of white hovering over them.

When he checked Evalle and Storm, they both looked at the

halo, then Evalle sent Quinn a reassuring smile.

Lanna moved her head as if studying something intently in the water. Then her face eased and she whispered, "Phoedra."

Did that mean she saw something?

He didn't dare say a word.

Adrianna had closed her eyes and her lips were moving with silent words, too. Was she sending Lanna power?

How the hell did this work?

Mother Mattie also sat with her eyes shut, but the boys were following Quinn's actions by watching every move.

Actually, Kellman only had eyes for Lanna.

"Where are you going?" Lanna asked in a confidential tone. "Show me your world."

Quinn held his breath.

Was Lanna actually *seeing* his daughter? He had no idea what Phoedra even looked like. His pulse climbed, but he maintained his calm. The last thing he wanted to do was distract her.

Lanna pulled back with an odd expression on her face then leaned forward again. "Who is that woman?"

What woman?

Damn, Quinn had to bite his tongue to keep from shouting out a question. Wouldn't Lanna call out an alert if she saw Veronika? Could Veronika find his child this quickly when Quinn had been searching constantly for weeks?

Adrianna murmured, "Who is the woman?"

Without looking at Adrianna, Lanna said, "Pretty face. Brown or maybe reddish brown hair. Curls."

"Macha?" Adrianna asked softly.

"Not Macha. Not a goddess."

And neither did the description sound like Veronika. Quinn released a breath of relief for that much, but he still didn't know who was with Phoedra.

Mother Mattie opened her eyes and focused on the murmured exchange between Adrianna and Lanna.

Should that worry him?

The elderly woman glanced at Quinn who gave her what he hoped conveyed a look of confusion.

She shook her head slightly, indicating he should not interfere, but she remained with her eyes open, watching closely.

"Where is Phoedra?" Adrianna asked in a quiet voice, sounding as if she were in a trance.

"Is near water. Maybe ocean."

That didn't narrow the location down much for Quinn, but it was a start.

Adrianna turned her head to the side, flinching as if in pain, then the moment was gone and her facial muscles relaxed. Still in a monotone, the Sterling witch asked, "What about ... the woman?"

Lanna frowned at the water. A ripple chased across the surface. "She has dark energy. Not human."

Quinn's heart dropped. Who was with his child?

"What ... town or street?" Adrianna breathed out.

Lanna studied whatever she saw in the bowl for a long couple of minutes and finally said, "Very warm. They are walking. Candles. Another woman." She leaned forward sharply. "No ... no."

"What?" Quinn uttered and Mother Mattie sent him a visual threat he interpreted as shut up or expect to be hurt.

"Watch out, Phoedra!"

CHAPTER 13

San Diego, California

Reese O'Rinn strolled down a quiet section of the La Mesa suburb at a loss for how to cheer up her twelve-year-old neighbor and dog sitter, Phoedra.

Wait, not twelve. That would really set off Phoedra. She was now a teenager at thirteen.

Until now, Reese had a go-to list for bringing a smile out of the adorable teen, but not today.

Everything she'd suggested had been met with indifference.

What else could she do at five in the afternoon that would be fun?

Normally, Phoedra would be bubbling with excitement over the smallest thing and full of opinions, which never failed to show her mature side. It usually took so little to make her happy. She'd turn her face up to the sun, which was currently on its way to setting, and smile, then prance around to show off whatever she'd worn in her favorite colors.

Nope. Today she kept her chin tipped down and wore a slouchy, long-sleeved, gray T-shirt and jeans with her worn sneakers.

A far too subdued look for her.

Just like her silence.

Reese knew zero about raising a child since hers had died without ever having a chance at life. That had been ten years ago. Not a day went by that she didn't feel the loss.

But Phoedra was such a special girl in so many ways that

being around her had patched over some of the holes in Reese's heart. Everything about this child was unique except for her last name. Smith didn't really fit.

Phoedra's bright gaze had an exotic appeal, and for a thirteen-year-old, she was wise beyond her years.

Who knew? There might be other kids her age who were just as wise, but Reese felt justified in her subjective opinion since she'd been around to watch this one change. From a lanky braniac who had always been an adorable kid, Phoedra was budding into what would be a stunning young woman. She took in the world through inquisitive blue eyes and wore her black hair chin-length ... with a dash of pink.

She'd sported an entirely pink head of hair until last week.

Phoedra had major endearing qualities like loving Reese's shaggy mutt, Gibbons, and looking at Reese on occasion as if she were some kind of superhero.

That right there qualified Phoedra for saint status, because while Reese did a smash-up job of pretending to be human, she would never be a superhero.

She would also never expose Phoedra to the fact that Reese was not human, or to the nasty demons hunting the energy inside Reese, which was why she had to keep the girl inside this demon-free zone east of downtown San Diego. Reese had stopped hunting demons so that the pain-in-her-butt person who gifted her this safe zone would not take it away.

Phoedra had been acting strangely lately, for ten days actually, and Reese was running out of geographic area to keep a thirteen-year-old entertained and safe.

Was Phoedra close to starting her period? How young did girls start nowadays?

I suck at knowing what to do for a teenager.

The movie Phoedra had wanted to see was sold out. Now what?

"What's going on in that head of yours, Phoedra?" When at a loss, go rushing forward with a stupid question.

The girl lifted her slim shoulders.

Reese squelched a growl of irritation.

Where had the perpetually sweet young lady gone? Was this the infamous evil hormonal stage coming upon Phoedra?

At Phoedra's age, Reese had been a real pain in her mother's backside, but that had been more about Reese possessing demon blood than anything else.

Maybe all thirteen-year-old girls had demon blood. Heh.

"Got something you want to do?" Reese asked, feeling desperate.

Phoedra shrugged again.

"Come on, Phoedra. Talk to me."

"You didn't have to come with me."

Technically, Phoedra *was* talking, but that was not what Reese had wanted to hear. "I'm actually a little hurt that you headed out for a movie without me."

"I forgot."

Reese was no lie detector like that demon Skinwalker named Storm whom she'd met in Atlanta six weeks back, but she called the bullshit flag on Phoedra forgetting.

She'd seen Phoedra leave her apartment after the girl's foster mother, Donella, had departed for work.

Reese had told Donella a long time ago that she'd keep an eye out for Phoedra any time Donella couldn't be there, and in return, Phoedra and her foster mother took care of Gibbons.

Reese was pretty sure this wily teen had slipped out without telling her foster mother, but she would not betray Phoedra's trust when she was generally such a good kid. Something was clearly bugging her, but what?

Phoedra asked, "Do you ever get premonitions, Reese?"

"Uhm, I, uh..." How to answer that? Reese saw visions sometimes, but not the way humans had premonitions from what she understood of them. *Think, Reese.* Phoedra had opened a door. She needed to keep her talking. "Sort of. Why?" Always redirect the question when in a tight spot.

"I asked Donella, but she doesn't have them," Phoedra said, instead of answering why she was asking.

Reese bit her lip, keeping quiet, hoping the tactic would push Phoedra to talk. It worked on adults.

Swiping a handful of black hair and pink highlight behind her ear, Phoedra admitted, "Sometimes I have a feeling something will happen. You know?"

That sounded right for a premonition.

What was a safe answer?

"I know what you're saying." Then it hit Reese that maybe this was part of Phoedra's female cycle coming on. "I think it's a female trait. I've heard some women say when they have their period, their intuition increases." Total bullshit, but damn that sounded good.

Phoedra slammed to a stop and spun on her. "What? I'm not having PMS!"

Oh, crud. Backpedaling, Reese raised her hands in supplication. "Hey, I wasn't suggesting that. I was just saying what I've heard from other women." Not that she socialized with any besides Phoedra and Donella.

Time for a subject change. Reese went for Phoedra's favorite topic. "How's Joey doing?"

Phoedra's eyes teared up. "He's a jerk."

Oy. Was there no safe direction?

But Reese did have experience with the opposite sex and shared her best advice. "Boys, and *all* men, are idiots most of the time. They don't usually deserve the women they get."

"But I really like this one," Phoedra said in a watery voice.

Reese could commiserate.

With the exception of a casual encounter when loneliness got the best of her as a younger woman, she'd spent years avoiding intimacy with men. Who could blame her after the man she'd fallen for at nineteen had gotten her pregnant, then abandoned her.

Then she discovered he'd been married.

Then she lost the baby.

Then ... life didn't matter a whole lot for a long time.

But in fairness to men in general, she'd met Quinn, who was unlike any other she'd ever encountered. So much that Quinn was the cause of her suffering weeks of stupid fantasies since she'd come back from Atlanta.

She couldn't get him out of her mind.

He was in a hot and incredibly wonderful category of males all his own. He'd fought to protect the body of a dead priestess from potential necromancy. Not just any priestess. Kizira had been a Medb, an enemy of the Beladors, and Quinn was the North American Belador Maistir.

Who did something like that these days?

Sleeping with the enemy didn't get much closer than a Belador bedding down with a Medb.

Reese didn't know for sure Quinn and Kizira had done the horizontal tango, but she felt certain something serious had gone on between those two.

She couldn't shake the disappointment that had latched onto her and still followed her around since she'd figured out that connection.

It wasn't as if she had an attachment to Quinn.

Sure, he had stood between her and a horde of demons, and he'd played fair with her even though she never came clean with him about why she'd been sent to retrieve Kizira's body. She'd like to think Quinn would have understood if she'd told him she'd been offered the return of her powers for delivering Kizira's body and keeping it out of the Medb queen's hands.

In the end, she couldn't bring herself to take the body from Quinn, who was clearly grieving the loss and willing to protect Kizira's body from everyone. She might be cursed with being a demon magnet because of her blood, and she would do practically anything to have her powers returned, but not at someone else's expense.

Phoedra said, "I told him about my premonitions yesterday and he said I was special."

Reese started to ask what she was talking about, but recovered in time when she realized they were still discussing Joey-the-jerk who had made this girl cry.

"You *are* special, Phoedra. You're beautiful, intelligent and gifted." Gifted should cover premonition territory. "Never settle for anyone who doesn't treat you right." Reese mentally ran back over what Phoedra had said and asked, "So, if he said you were special, what's the problem?"

"He didn't want to meet me at the movies today and I know he's not working."

Aha! Reese felt much better knowing Phoedra had not been dumping her so much as meeting a boy on the sly.

Wait a minute.

That didn't sound right at all.

Who was this guy Joey? Reese carefully said, "I wish he had

joined us. I would have liked to meet him. What does he look like?"

Phoedra warmed to that topic, sounding breathless. "He's got a great body. Maybe eight inches taller than me and has a green Mohawk. He's a, uhm ... "

Reese supplied, "Bad boy?"

Pink embarrassment flushed Phoedra's cheeks. "I guess. He's not like anyone else I've ever noticed." She released a sad sigh. "I mentioned inviting you and that's when he backed out. I told him how you're a good friend, but I think he didn't like that you were older."

Twenty-nine was not old. Reese would like a chance to explain that to Joey-the-jerk. She was starting to think he might be someone older who was lying about his age to be around Phoedra. If that was the case, Reese would find him later and let out her inner evil bitch to make him think twice about ever coming around this girl again. She'd also send in an anonymous pedophile report. She would not tolerate some creep getting near Phoedra.

Still sounding hurt, Phoedra said, "I thought Joey might show up anyhow when I told him I changed my mind and I would go alone. But I didn't see him at the theater."

Reese would bet Joey had seen her with Phoedra. This guy was sounding more and more like some manipulating slimeball trying to get Phoedra alone to get frisky with her.

Phoedra's eyes lit up. "Look!"

Reese spun around, ready for an attack.

Cars cruised by slowly. People strolled down the street. The sky was blue and full of fluffy clouds.

She looked at Phoedra. "What?"

"A psychic," Phoedra whispered conspiratorially. "I've been wanting to go to one."

Reese had yet to meet an honest psychic, but that didn't mean some didn't exist. She considered calling Donella first to clear it, but the minute she suggested that, she'd destroy the moment with Phoedra, who was actually smiling now.

Besides, what could be the harm of some woman staring into a crystal ball?

Reese would be right there with her. "Good idea."

Phoedra started nodding. "I know, right?" She took off and Reese kept up with her as the girl cut across the street to the front door for Madame Salina.

Phoedra waited as Reese opened the door. Evidently this looked a little intimidating up close. Reese blinked her eyes to adjust to the dark interior lit only by candles and a small lamp with a yellowed shade that had tassels along the top edge. Incense burning in the corner failed to cover the old smell in the air.

A woman with dark-brown hair streaked with gray, decent makeup and black-outlined eyes walked into the room. Her red-and-black dress fell in filmy layers over her plump shape. She might be fifty, but her face wore it well.

"I am Madame Salina. May I help you?" she asked with the welcoming smile of someone happy to make money.

Phoedra looked at Reese with pleading.

What could Reese do but say, "My friend would like a reading. Do you have an opening?" Maybe the woman would be booked for the day.

"Actually, I saw my last appointment a few minutes ago and was going to leave—"

That's the ticket. Reese gave a good apologetic look. "No problem. Sorry we didn't call for an appointment."

Phoedra looked crushed.

Crap.

"Oh, no, I was about to say I had a regular client call just now. She'll be here in about an hour, so I have time."

"Wonderful," Reese said, but a weird feeling crept over her. Was she making a huge mistake? If Donella got upset, she might not let Reese around Phoedra again.

The change in Phoedra was instantaneous. "Thank you so much, Reese."

The pressure of friendship.

Reese had two friends and did not want to lose either one. "What luck, huh?" she said to Phoedra, then asked the psychic, "How much?"

Madame Salina said, "I sometimes offer first-time visits for free. This will be my gift to her today."

Phoedra's eyes lit up. "Really? You're the best."

Reese felt unseated by a stranger, but she let it go. The woman probably sucked a person in with a free reading, knowing they'd come back for more.

Seeing Phoedra truly excited over something for the first time in a week and a half was worth it.

Waving her hand toward the opening behind her, Madame Salina said to Phoedra, "Please come in."

Reese started to follow, but the psychic asked, "Do you want a reading as well?"

What if this woman was for real and somehow exposed Reese's true nature? She shrugged. "Not really."

"Then please wait out here." Madame Salina walked through the opening and pulled two sliding wooden doors together.

Reese paced quietly for a minute before misgivings got to her. She'd always respected the privacy of others but what if that woman told Phoedra something crazy about her premonitions?

Or what if she told Phoedra something about Joey that caused the girl to get into trouble?

Or ... heck, Reese didn't know. She wasn't a parent.

She wasn't even human.

Stepping close to the sliding doors, she eased them apart a tiny fraction at a time until she could see into the room.

Fifteen feet away, Phoedra sat in a chair upholstered in gold brocade and positioned to the left of a round mahogany table. The psychic settled opposite her in an identical chair. They were in a cozy spot framed with draped curtains pulled back at the sides and a small sofa against the far wall. Candles gave everything an intimate glow.

The furnishings in this place belonged in an antiques display for the late eighteen hundreds.

Thankfully, the room where Reese waited had a similar amount of candlelight, which wouldn't give away her snooping. She suffered a moment of guilt, but dismissed it.

Phoedra's safety came first and Reese would never share anything she heard.

Conscience put at ease, she stilled her breathing as Madame Salina finished her initial small talk and got down to doing her psychic thing. She uncovered a crystal ball in the center of the table.

Huh. Reese hadn't thought there'd really be one.

Phoedra asked, "I'm not sure what to do about a boy I like."

Madame Salina held her hands just above a ball and studied it. "Your relationship is going through a difficult time."

Reese almost laughed. What young girl wasn't in a rocky relationship? Phoedra was no pushover. Any minute now, she'd put Madame Salina to the test.

Phoedra asked about premonitions, which Reese had expected.

Madame Salina said, "You are quite gifted."

I already told her that, Reese thought with a grumble.

"You must trust your instincts," the psychic went on. "You are strong and you have wonderful things coming your way."

Phoedra squinted at the psychic.

Uh oh. Reese knew that suspicious look in the girl's eye.

Here it comes ...

"Can you tell me who my mother and father are?" Phoedra asked.

Reese's heart hurt from the longing in Phoedra's voice.

Madame Salina said, "I ... I don't like to say some things to one your age."

"What do you mean?"

"It sounds as if you don't know if your parents are alive or not."

"I don't," Phoedra admitted sadly. "I want you to tell me."

The psychic looked up with concern in her face. "I would not like to be the one to tell you that sort of thing if they are not alive."

"Is it because you don't know?"

Staring into the ball again, the psychic said, "I know about one of them."

Phoedra gasped and sat forward. "What? Which one."

Hell, Reese was leaned in, too, waiting on that answer.

"I feel a spirit close by."

Reese's heart thumped wildly. She should grab Phoedra and get her out of here. That woman couldn't know if her mother or father was dead, could she?

"You think one of them is ... dead?" Phoedra asked.

When Madame Salina nodded, Phoedra swallowed hard and

said, "I want to talk to whoever it is."

Reese shut her eyes. *What have I done?* Donella would kill her.

Madame Salina opened her hands and raised her chin, eyes closed. She said, "If you are this child's parent, please let us know."

Reese heard Phoedra sniffle and dropped her head against the door. She couldn't take listening to Phoedra in pain. This had gone on long enough. Reese lifted her head and looked through the crack, preparing to go in and drag Phoedra out of there even if that meant the girl didn't speak to Reese for a while.

A smoky figure in a hooded robe took shape behind Phoedra.

Reese checked the psychic, who still had her eyes closed and seemed oblivious. Heh.

Now what am I supposed to do? Reese chewed on her lip. What if that really was one of Phoedra's parents?

The psychic said in a low tone, "I feel someone who cares about you close to us."

Phoedra blurted out, "Ask why they left me."

The ghost's hand stretched out from the sleeve. Narrow fingers with sharp nails looked to be feminine. The ghost balled her hand into a fist. The floor trembled.

Oh, no, no. Reese's palms dampened. She gripped the doors.

The psychic's face gave away her surprise.

Hold everything. Reese lowered her hands. Did the psychic know someone was there or not?

Madame Salina now stared at the crystal ball, licking her lips and showing no sign of acknowledging the ghost standing behind Phoedra, who made no move to touch the girl.

Damn. What if that was Phoedra's mother? If Donella knew who it was, wouldn't she have told this girl? This couldn't be the first time Phoedra had wondered about her parents.

This might the girl's only chance to find out.

The ghost wasn't a demon. Seeing how the ghost now held a hand above Phoedra as if protecting her, Reese took a breath and gave the psychic another minute.

Madame Salina said, "O spirit, if you are this child's parent, move the candle flame."

The ghost unfurled her other hand from the deep sleeve.

Reese watched the candle closely for any tiny change, which ended up not being necessary. The flame flickered once then grew and twisted unlike any flame Reese had ever seen.

Riveted in place, Phoedra's gaze locked on that braided flame as if it was a direct cyber connection to the afterlife. She whispered, "Which parent is it?"

Madame Salina had lost some of the pink in her cheeks, but she said, "O spirit, if you are her mother, give us a sign."

The candle bent to one side.

Yes, it tilted toward Phoedra and wax drizzled from the candle. Reese couldn't see what the wax looked like.

Phoedra got excited. "It's an M. It must be my mother!"

The psychic looked less thrilled by the minute. Could she feel the power vibrating in the room that Reese felt even from behind the door?

Who was that ghost?

Madame Salina must have felt something. Her skin turned pasty. She lifted her disturbed gaze to Phoedra.

Reese expected the psychic to finally comment on the ghost standing in her line of sight, but Madame Salina didn't say a word. She seriously couldn't see it?

Practically bouncing now, Phoedra asked, "Who is she? What's her name? Did she ever care about me?"

The table began to vibrate, making the candle dance around.

Madame Salina slapped her hands on the table and shouted, "O spirit, please show your love and cross over. Be at peace."

"*No!*" Phoedra shouted. "*Don't send her away!*"

The melting candle lifted up, the flame blinked out, then the candle flew against one of the door panels where Reese hid. She jumped back, then lunged forward and shoved the doors apart, determined to get Phoedra out of there now.

A loud crack sounded as the table ripped in two with each half falling to Phoedra's right and left side.

The psychic made panicked animal sounds.

Madame Salina's chair spun around and shot her out of it onto the floor. She jumped up and ran to a door at the back of the room, screaming.

Reese had made it two steps inside when everything calmed except for Phoedra crying.

The spirit floated toward Reese, stopping between Reese and Phoedra.

In a furious move, the ghost pointed a finger at Reese then shoved the same digit in Phoedra's direction in a silent order. Then she vanished.

But not before Reese recognized the face she'd seen all too often on the darknet.

That face belonged to a dead Medb priestess in Atlanta.

The same body Reese had left with Quinn.

Holy crap.

Was Kizira of the Medb coven Phoedra's mother?

That made no sense. No Medb priestess would leave her daughter to be raised by someone else, and definitely not a human.

Had Kizira's spirit shown up because Reese was present at the reading?

That seemed more logical, but why?

Was Kizira trying to get Reese to help Phoedra find her mother and father?

Again, why?

This was like a twilight zone episode of that old show with Timmy and Lassie, but with Kizira's spirit playing Lassie's role of pointing out trouble.

None of that made sense either.

Reese gave up for the moment. She got a shaky Phoedra up and held the girl as she cried herself out.

When she caught her breath, Phoedra said, "I know you had to have heard some of that. Do you think it was my mother?"

So Phoedra wasn't wigged out over a spirit wrecking the room, only that it might have been her mother?

Reese wanted so much to tell her yes just to give Phoedra something to hold onto, but she wouldn't lie to her.

"I'll be honest. I know it was someone's spirit, but I have no idea if it was definitely connected to you. If I thought it was, I'd tell you." Wiping Phoedra's tears, Reese said, "I'm not making any promises for success, but I will help you try to figure out where you came from and the identity of your parents. Okay?"

"Thank you," Phoedra blubbered, hugging Reese.

Poor girl. Reese meant her words.

She wasn't sure what she could do, but she'd give it her best effort. Hopefully Donella would support her research and share what she could. Reese had spent recent years building a following as a celebrity photographer, selling her pictures under a pseudonym to media for the gossip columns. She had a way to shield her demon energy, which allowed her to leave this area to work, and now she would use her resources to track down Phoedra's parents.

Patting Phoedra's back as she nudged her toward the door, Reese said, "You ready to blow this popsicle stand?"

"What?" Phoedra wiped her face.

"Hey, don't tell me you don't remember Skipper saying that in *Madagascar Penguins*. We watched that last year."

"Oh, you're right." Phoedra smiled a little. "I'm not thinking straight."

"I know, hon. Speaking of dessert, I'm hungry for a banana split."

Glancing back at the psychic's building after walking outside, Phoedra said, "I'm in, but I still want to talk about what happened in there."

Reese expected that but had no answers. "Let's get you somewhere you can freshen up and we'll talk. Deal?"

"Okay."

Avoidance plan working fine.

Reese caught a break in the sparse traffic and crossed the street, then turned south to hunt up an ice cream shop she'd taken Phoedra to before.

They were walking past glass windows covered in brown paper on the inside. Still trying to cheer up Phoedra, Reese said, "Maybe this is a new clothes shop."

Phoedra walked over to look into the glass pane on the door with her hands cupped on each side of her eyes. "I can't even see ..."

The door opened and Phoedra fell in.

"Hey!" Reese rushed over behind her and dove inside.

Someone shoved her hard enough to take her to her knees, but she'd seen no one. Nonhumans? Her eyes adjusted quickly. The only reason she hadn't fallen on Phoedra was because the girl was being dragged away kicking and screaming.

I might not have my powers, but I still have some preternatural moves. Reese rolled to her left and flipped up to her feet, then raced after Phoedra, knocking over silver clothing racks set up between bulging boxes of clothes.

Someone swiped her legs out from under her without even touching her.

Reese was ready this time and rolled up to land on her feet again then turned, hands up for the attack.

Finally, an actual body to fight. A wide one at that. He came at her, silhouetted from behind by the bright light coming through the open door to the sidewalk.

A woman walked by without looking in.

Somebody had shielded this attack from view.

The guy lunged for her. When his big hands touched her, she latched onto arms twice the size of hers, rolled back using his momentum, and shoved her feet into his gut to flip him over.

He crashed against a stone fireplace that was under construction, and crumpled. Blood rushed down his face from where his head had taken a beating on the rocks. If he had any serious powers, he should have thrown a spell at her or used his ability to pin her better.

Maybe he underestimated her and saved his majik.

Everything about his rough look made her think merc.

Or bounty hunter.

But that would mean Phoedra was the target, because they didn't seem interested in grabbing Reese.

She didn't hang around to find out how much that headache was going to piss off the guy behind her. Racing through the back storage area, she jumped over piled boxes marked with designer names and landed in an open space.

Why couldn't she still hear Phoedra screaming?

At the back door, she burst through to the rear loading area in time to see Phoedra slumped over the shoulder of a big guy with a full tattoo sleeve and green hair. He tossed the girl into a van, jumped in after her, and it peeled off.

Reese leaped off the steps and raced after the van, using every ounce of extra demon juice she had, but the van blurred, then disappeared.

Had someone cloaked it? She didn't think so since cloaking

should be more immediate. Either you're cloaked or you're not.

Same with teleporting.

Had the van driven into a bolthole?

Reese stopped and stared at the empty space where the van had been. She mentally reviewed everything she'd seen so she didn't forget any details.

One major detail hit her between the eyes.

Phoedra's kidnapper had a green Mohawk.

Joey-the-jerk was not human.

CHAPTER 14

Atlanta, GA – Storm and Evalle's building

Energy strummed through Quinn, threatening to break free if he had to sit silently for one more minute of this séance. At what point was it over, and how would he know if Lanna was in real trouble?

She'd stopped shouting about Phoedra, and although she still breathed rapidly, she'd begun to calm.

Quinn took in Mother Mattie, who had yet to say anything but kept her attention bouncing from Lanna to Adrianna and back.

No help there.

Looking over at Evalle, he found her sitting forward, with her elbows on her knees and one knee bouncing. Storm put his hand on her thigh, calming the busy leg.

Quinn spoke to Evalle telepathically. *How can we know Lanna is safe?*

Evalle's bright green gaze shot to his. She replied in the same silent way. *You have to trust Lanna. Caron stopped by for just a moment when Lanna and Mattie arrived. Caron told Lanna that this was the next step she had to take. From what Caron was saying, Lanna is a powerhouse who can handle this. She just needs her confidence back as a person. Lanna doesn't appear distressed physically. She's only reacting to what she's seeing. Just sit tight for a little longer and maybe we'll have a way to find Phoedra.*

I will wait a little while, he conceded.

Lanna lifted her head and opened her eyes, which were a

normal blue color again.

Quinn's patience was shot to hell. "Are you okay, Lanna? Do you need to stop?"

Mother Mattie hissed, "Silence."

"Not if I think she's in danger."

"I am fine, Cousin. Please give me a minute." Lanna squeezed his hand again and sounded strong. She asked Mother Mattie, "Are you hearing everything?"

"Yes. It sounds like Phoedra is in danger. Do you remember any of it?"

"Not much, but I do remember a man stalking her."

Quinn asked, "Could you tell if the woman with Phoedra was a friend or helping the man?"

"I do not know. I may need questions when I am seeing into the water."

Mother Mattie said, " Adrianna has been prodding you, which seems to help."

"Good." Lanna's gaze went to Adrianna, whose head was bent forward.

The Sterling witch must still be in her trance state.

Closing her eyes again, Lanna whispered words more to herself than anyone else. In less than a minute, she opened her eyes, which were bright crystals once again, and leaned forward.

Adrianna's head lifted. Her eyes were also shut. "What man follows Phoedra?"

Lanna studied the water with her blind-looking eyes. "Three men. Not human. Maybe ... trolls or warlocks. They have powers. Very foggy. Hard to see faces."

What are they doing, Quinn wanted to shout.

Lanna tensed and rocked forward then back. "Can not see her."

Maybe his daughter had escaped the stalker.

Lanna was showing the first real signs of stress, even if Quinn was the only one who could recognize it. He'd seen this young woman grow up and she was cracking around the edges.

Kellman shifted his grip on Lanna's hand and said, "I'm here. You're safe."

She visibly relaxed.

Well, damn. Quinn would have to allow that the young man

could be important to Lanna's recovery, just as Evalle had suggested.

He could feel Evalle's eyes on him, so Quinn glanced over.

Evalle had a warning eyebrow lifted. She feared he'd overreact again.

Quinn sighed, resigned to accepting that Lanna was no longer a child. Any remnants of childhood clinging to her had vanished during Grendal's vicious attack.

"Where did you go?" Lanna asked the water.

Adrianna turned her head in a way that said she was focusing hard on something. "Where is she?"

Clearly Lanna and Adrianna had their own conversation going on. Would Adrianna recall any details once she came out of her trance?

"Men have ... van at brick building first. No more. They are ..."

Jerking upright and blinking her eyes until they returned to their normal color once more, Lanna said, "I know where Phoedra is, Cousin. She is in this country, but very far away. You must go fast to find her."

His heart tried out for the drummer position with the Guns N' Roses band. He said, "Just tell me where and I'll head to the airport immediately."

"Where is she?" Adrianna called out louder and in a sharp tone.

Everyone turned to the Sterling witch.

Evalle walked over and put her hands on Adrianna's shoulders. "Hey, Lanna is done."

Adrianna lifted her face and snarled in a different voice than hers, "Where is the girl? Tell me now!"

Mother Mattie reached into a pouch at her waist that Quinn hadn't noticed. She pulled out a pinch of something and shouted a blistering string of words when she threw the sparkling dust at Adrianna.

The sparkles swept up as if on an invisible wind and dusted the top of Adrianna's head.

The Sterling witch's face twisted. Breaking away from the hands of each twin, Adrianna grasped her head, jerking back and forth. Sweat glistened on her face.

Kellman stood up and helped Lanna to her feet.

When Adrianna finally stopped struggling, she dropped her hands. Evidently Mother Mattie's dust had broken her out of the trance.

Sounding panicked, Adrianna asked, "What did I say?"

Evalle told her the gist of what happened.

"Why didn't anyone stop me or ask what I was doing?"

Confused, Mother Mattie said, "I thought you were prompting Lanna."

"No." Adrianna shook her head, looking not a bit happy. "I could hear some of what was being said, but it turned into a mash of voices in my head."

"But you were asking Lanna questions," Evalle argued.

"Not me. Veronika. She was listening in through me. You have to keep me as far from Phoedra and Lanna as possible."

Quinn hadn't thought this could get any worse.

What a foolish thought. He said, "I'll leave Evalle and Storm to figure this out, but I want Lanna safe."

Storm had stepped over next to Evalle. "She will be. Lanna is staying with us."

Adrianna stood, a bit wobbly, then pulled herself together with that core of steel that made up her backbone. "I'm not sure what I'm going to do until Veronika is caught, but no one should trust me with any information."

Evalle said, "Don't go hiding from me. It's going to take all of us to stop Veronika."

If that were even possible, but Quinn would not give voice to the negative thought.

"Right now, I'm going home where I can think."

"You shouldn't be alone," Evalle argued.

"I have Witchlock," Adrianna said as if that were her nuclear defense. "If I have to unleash it on her, I will, but right now I need some time to think. I'll run a blood ward around my house using Witchlock. If Veronika gets through that, then nothing you or anyone else can do will stop her."

"I'll walk you out." Evalle left with Adrianna.

After a moment, Storm said to the room, "She's out of hearing range now."

Quinn pulled Lanna into a hug. "Lanna, you are amazing.

Thank you for doing this. Give me the location. I'll have my driver here by the time I get downstairs and he'll take me straight to the airport."

She swung a sad gaze to him. "No, Cousin. You do not understand. That is not fast enough. You must go there *now*."

"You mean ... teleport?"

"Yes. The men are using a bolthole. One is looking to make deal with someone. I did not see where they went. I heard one say they would not stay long. A lot of voices." She clutched her forehead with her eyes clamped shut. "They are in building with boards on windows and sign that says NO TRESPASSING. Bricks are faded yellow. Not painted in much time. It is near a ... uh." She looked to Kellman. "What is place American football played here?"

"The dome."

"Yes!" Lanna snapped her fingers. "Phoedra is near dome with ... letters on it." She closed her eyes, concentrating hard. "B ... O ... and I think maybe K."

Quinn asked, "Bok or is it Book?"

At the same time, Kellman and Kardos said, "The BOK Center."

Kellman added, "It's an indoor sports arena in Tulsa, Oklahoma."

Lanna beamed at them. "Thank you for being here."

The boys grinned like idiots.

"I am sorry, Cousin. I wish I could teleport you, but I am not good for that distance."

He grabbed Lanna. "You have done astonishingly well. Thank you for that. I don't want you doing anything else. Just stay safe for me while I'm gone."

"I will."

Bloody hell. Quinn wasn't even sure he had the right place. Was that location correct or some distortion of what Lanna had seen? She said Phoedra was near this dome structure and in a building with signs warning against trespassing.

Probably hundreds of those in any major city.

That building could be in any direction from the dome.

It mattered not. Quinn had to find Phoedra before those men opened another bolthole.

CHAPTER 15

San Diego, California

Reese stomped around a moment, cursing the reason she had no powers. She could have saved Phoedra, but no.

How was she going to get that child back?

She finally started walking across the back parking area of the shops as she sorted through her limited options.

She snapped her fingers. Quinn had said if she ever needed any help, just ask. She'd get her car and head to Atlanta. The only problem was the time she'd lose getting there and finding him.

That was assuming he'd know someone who could find Phoedra after the girl had traveled through a bolthole.

How many beings could open one of those?

A flock of crows descended on her, creating a swirling cloud of black.

"You can't be serious," she groaned. Reese was in no mood for this crap right now.

The swirling black band of feathers widened.

A giant raven glided down and turned into a man clothed in a dark sport coat, slacks and black pullover. *Yáahl* had left the top of his mountain peak in Haida Gwaii Islands west of Canada. There stood the raven god of the Pacific Northwest Haida tribe. Her mother's tribe, which had booted Reese a long time ago.

White glowed around the black centers of his eyes. He was upset about something.

Tough shit. Reese wasn't having such a good day either.

He was also the person who had taken Reese's powers after she lost her baby.

No time like the present to piss him off.

She started in, "You're in a bad mood and I'm in a hurry. I'll make this easy. Either give me my powers right now or get out of my way, Yáahl."

"*You lost her!*"

"Who?" He can't mean—

"Phoedra. Who else? How could you let them take her?"

That just shot her pissed-off level into the stratosphere. "Because I couldn't stop preternaturals. In case you forgot, some asshat stole my powers. Why do you even care?" Her mind flashed with images of Kizira. "Wait a minute. Is this your fault?"

Looking stern, he admitted, "Yes."

Shaking her head, Reese muttered, "I should have never gotten out of bed this morning, because reality isn't supposed to be weirder than a dream. Okay, start from the top. How do you know Phoedra?"

"We do not have time to waste. You need to—"

"No, dammit." Reese charged up to him. "I've had it. For years you withhold my powers and put me through bullshit games. You send me after Kizira's body and now you know about Phoedra? I want to know what you know and I want it now. Everything about this freakin' stinks."

"Some things are not for you to know. You have to find Phoedra." This time he said it more as a plea than a demand.

"I fully intend to, but I'm not leaving here blind on some crazy errand for you again. Time to come clean."

He gave her his best intimidating look.

She crossed her arms and waited.

"You are impossible."

She gave him a pithy look. "Thank you. It's nice to know my best qualities are recognized. Come on. How do you know Phoedra?"

"Her mother gave her into my safekeeping as an infant, and asked that she grow up like a normal child until the time came for her to accept her heritage."

Oh, crap. "Let me guess. Her mother is Kizira."

"When did you find that out?"

"Just a little earlier when Phoedra went to see a psychic who tried to call up her parents."

"What? Where was that?"

"Oh, that's right. Your pack of flying minions couldn't see inside a building. Back across the street."

"Taking Phoedra to a psychic was a stupid thing to do."

"Me? No, no, no. You not telling me *who she was* tops anything I've ever done. The bloody Medb might have her now."

"I don't think so."

"Why not? It makes perfect sense."

"Did you see warlocks?"

She was not arguing with him when Phoedra was still at risk. "I don't think so. Looked like bounty hunters to me."

"Why would they target her?"

"Phoedra liked this guy Joey, but he was with the group who grabbed her. She told me she was having premonitions, but I didn't know she was a child of the Medb so I didn't take it seriously. Hey, don't give me that look. You're the all-knowing one here."

"Continue."

"Phoedra told Joey about her premonitions, which I'm thinking might be actual visions. He must have detected some sort of power around her." That's when Reese reminded Yáahl, "If I had my powers, I might have known, too."

"Precisely."

What he wasn't saying hit her between the eyes. "You withheld my powers because I was around Phoedra?"

"No. I bound your powers because you were reckless. Allowing you access to your powers would have ended with you dying many years ago. I have kept you alive."

"I'm trying to dredge up some appreciation, but not feeling it."

Yáahl stared down at her as if pondering something. He said, "The Medb and trolls are stirring up a storm of trouble in the southeast. It appears they're trying to bring the preternatural world out to humans."

"Are you kidding me?"

"I do not joke about such things."

"What's that got to do with finding Phoedra?"

"Due to all the trouble, VIPER is shorthanded. They brought bounty hunters in to cover the shortage, and they're sending them out nationwide."

"I thought VIPER banned bounty hunters for the most part and approved their use only on occasion."

"That is correct, but it appears something significant has changed in VIPER. Due to that, there's no telling what else the bounty hunters are doing now that they have run of the country. Phoedra may have been taken by one of them."

"Wouldn't your crows know?"

"I task my minions with keeping me informed of general situations I'm interested in. I did not send them for specifics. That issue is significant only if it relates to Phoedra. They reported she was with you when she was kidnapped."

What a bunch of snitches. Reese realized something else. "Does Donella know about all this?"

"Yes. She is one of my guards for the girl."

That could mean Donella was some type of nonhuman.

"Why did Donella work a job?"

"Because I was tasked with giving Phoedra as normal a life as possible."

Reese could argue that Phoedra had a safe life, but not a normal one, because Donella didn't want the girl out of her sight when she was home. She made sure Phoedra excelled in school, but limited the people she could spend time with, pretty much to just Reese.

That's why Reese had tried to give Phoedra some freedom and allow her to just be a kid. Reese had mixed feelings on all of this crap with Yáahl, but not about knowing Phoedra.

She'd never regret having gotten to know the young girl and would hurt anyone who stopped Reese from finding her.

Yáahl asked, "How did Phoedra vanish?"

"I'm thinking a bolthole based on the way the van was slowly swallowed into invisibility."

"If that's the case, I feel Queen Maeve and Cathbad do not have Phoedra. They would have teleported away. It could be someone working for Macha since she would never dirty her hands, or ..."

"It could be a third party like a bounty hunter just filling a ticket for any of them, or another player we don't know anything about." Ready to get rolling, Reese said, "I'm going after Phoedra immediately, but first I need all that you have on her."

"You're not in a position to make that demand."

Reese cursed vividly and asked, "Can you send your minions to find her?"

"No, whoever took her has gone somewhere they can't follow."

"You suck, Yáahl."

"Careful with that tone."

"*No!*" she snapped. "You were supposed to watch out for her. Well, she's gone and you need my help, because I *will* find her and get her back. Are we clear?"

He gave her dark look. "Very well. I hear a bargain coming."

"Not this time."

That shocked him silent.

Score one for the low woman on the totem pole. Reese explained, "I'm not bargaining with Phoedra's life."

His face went blank. "One shock after another from you today."

"Be careful. That almost sounded like a compliment, but don't get carried away. We're not done." She hated to ask for anything, but this was for Phoedra. "Could you help me for once?"

Yáahl angled his head in a very bird-like manner as if trying to process what she was saying. He nodded once. "Of course I will help. What do you need?"

"I have no idea who I'm going up against, but they're clearly nonhuman. Would giving me back my powers be too much?"

Lifting a hand, he waited as a small raven came barreling down at them, then opened its wings and slowed to drop a medallion on a leather cord in Yáahl's hand.

She knew that medallion well. He'd given it to her once before, which allowed her use of some of her powers while she wore it. He offered it on an open palm. "I'll grant you the ability to tap your powers and ..."

"Sounds good. Thank you." She snatched up the medallion and turned to leave.

He snapped his fingers and Reese froze in place. She couldn't even feel her heart beating. Really?

"As I was saying," Yáahl continued, "I will also allow you to teleport twice."

That was more than she'd expected from the tightwad who had kept her on a short leash for years. This way, she could teleport to wherever Phoedra had been taken, if she could determine where that was, and back when she had the girl in hand.

Yáahl inquired, "Can you locate her?"

Reese grunted at him with eyes shooting out a WTF message.

He released her body.

She shook off the awful feeling of being paralyzed. "I'll know as soon as I sit in the location where I last saw the van." If that didn't work, she would burn one teleportation to reach Quinn.

He was her only backup plan.

With her mind bouncing around with all sort of thoughts, she slowed at one in particular about Quinn and Kizira.

Could Phoedra be *Quinn's* child?

Then she got her senses back. No chance.

She could understand Kizira hiding her daughter with Yáahl to keep Phoedra away from the Medb, but Quinn? He had an entire Belador army at his disposal to protect Phoedra.

Quinn was not a man who would abandon his child.

"What are you waiting for, Reese?" Yáahl asked.

"Follow me." She returned to the spot where she'd last seen the van and sat in the middle of it to access her distant viewing ability.

Waving at Yáahl, she said, "Wish I could hang out to give you the audience you so desire for your bore-me-to-tears monologues, but I have things to do. Oh, wait. There's a guy in that building." She pointed at the rear door. "He was bleeding badly. Can you do something about him?"

"There is no one in that building now."

She didn't even want to wonder how he'd vanished. "See ya."

"Do not fail, Reese."

"What? Or you'll take away my powers? Been there, done that, got screwed. I'm going to get Phoedra. All I ask of you is don't get in my way."

"Do not return without her."

"I know. Don't return or you'll take away what little I still have in this world," she quipped, but deep down she was terrified he'd do just that and she'd never see Gibbons again.

"We have spent many years as adversaries. You have a chance to return as a peer in my following."

She had no idea what the hell he was trying to tell her. "What are you saying, Yáahl? Plain words, please. No riddles."

Leaning down, he said, "Return Phoedra to me safe and sound, and I vow I will unbind all of your powers. You'll have them forever. No discussion. No questions. You won't need the medallion anymore and you'll be able to go anywhere you choose. Don't let your emotions rule your actions."

Her mouth slipped open. She'd already told him she'd bring Phoedra home, but he was right. She'd given up Kizira's body last time to Quinn, knowing she could have regained her powers just by showing up with a cold body.

She said, "Understood." No smart comeback when she'd just been assured of the one thing she'd waited ten years to have returned.

"I want no misunderstanding, Reese. If you fail to rescue Phoedra and return with her, do not return under any circumstance."

That was the Yáahl she'd come to fear and hate at times over the past ten years. When in doubt, he added a threat level meant to get what he wanted.

The good news for him was that they wanted the same thing.

She'd bring Phoedra home or die trying.

Yáahl straightened and gave her a solemn look that meant he'd said all he was going to say.

The swirling black cloud of minions that had surrounded them, which had clearly been a cloaking device, burst apart with black feathers floating down.

In the next second, crows flew high. When they disappeared, she looked back down to the ground.

Yáahl was gone and she was on her own.

Fine. She'd spent most of her life that way.

Once she had Phoedra in hand, she intended to press Yáahl to find out everything about her. Phoedra deserved to know who her parents were.

Reese looped the medallion over her head. Power flooded her body. Whoa. The last time she had this medallion, it had given her a limited amount of power, but this time it was far stronger.

That said how much Yáahl wanted Phoedra back.

It wasn't as if Kizira could harm him from the afterworld. Evidently Yáahl took his vows seriously, and right now he was breaking the one he'd given Phoedra's mother.

Reese searched back and forth across the rear delivery area. "Please don't let some truck run me over while I'm doing this."

Opening her senses as she gripped the medallion, colors flashed at her then a dark hole opened up, widening more and more. It took a minute, but once the hole opened up, she started to see a large dome, then streets running away from it. Huh? Her gaze blurred, then cleared. She turned her head to the side for a different view and spotted the van pull up to a rusty overhead door.

Leaning in toward it, she searched behind the van for a street name or landmark, but the edges blurred again.

If they traveled there through a bolthole, could she teleport to the same place? What happened to a body if it stopped in the middle of teleporting?

Would she just land someplace unexpected or would her body get caught in limbo ... or would she just disintegrate?

Yáahl could have given her a crash lesson on it.

A hand clamped down on Reese's shoulder. Pain and energy shot through her. Nonhuman. *Oh, shit, oh, shit.*

Whoever it was yelled, "Got one here."

No time left for pondering what-ifs or fighting this guy, because she'd lose her viewing location.

She called on the medallion to teleport her to the one thing she could recognize. That dome.

Power raced over her skin.

The world blurred ... was anything happening?

Big hands clenched her shoulders and pulled her backward.

All at once, her body jerked and stretched. She'd forgotten to question one more possibility.

What would happen if she got pulled between her destination and someone using majik to hold her in place?

CHAPTER 16

Tulsa, Oklahoma

Quinn went on alert as the teleporting ended.

Groomed grass and solid ground beneath his feet. Check.

Giant indoor event facility at his back, which appeared to be the BOK Center. Check.

No one saw him appear out of thin air thanks to arriving in Tulsa at around nine in the evening, if his calculations on central time were correct. He'd departed just after ten from Atlanta.

Almost perfect.

If Daegan had teleported him twenty feet to Quinn's left, he'd have been able to walk through an open area between trees fronting Frisco Avenue without having to jump a wrought iron fence.

Still, Quinn had no complaints.

He hadn't realized that Daegan had been in Treoir Castle in another realm—the dragon king's second trip that day—which meant Daegan had to drop what he was doing to teleport back to Atlanta to help Quinn and then send Quinn on his way.

That wouldn't have happened when Macha had control of the Beladors. The last time Quinn had seen her at the end of a Tribunal meeting, she'd told him, "I am done with you."

As a two-thousand-year-old dragon shifter, Daegan packed a ton of power, but he'd clearly been stretching himself thin to zip all across states, countries and realms throughout the day to protect his people.

He'd taken over Quinn's role of Maistir and had now

teleported Quinn at a moment's notice.

No questions asked.

Paying that man back would require ... he couldn't fathom how to do it and had told Daegan as much, to which Daegan replied, "Bring your daughter home. That will be payment enough."

Daegan was earning loyalty from all of his followers. The Beladors had a true leader.

Quinn hoped this was the place Lanna had seen. Now he just had to locate a faded yellow building with NO TRESPASSING signs. *If* everything Lanna had observed was accurate, that could be in any of four directions.

He dismissed any doubts. With more of a lead than ever before, now was the time for action.

He waited as people walked along Frisco Avenue in both directions. Thankfully, no event appeared to be scheduled at the dome for tonight. As soon as humans were out of the way, he used kinetics to leap across the wrought iron fence wrapping the back half of the sports complex.

Due to dealing with troll raids and the like in Atlanta, Quinn had been wearing dark-green cargo pants and a black T-shirt when he'd come to the meeting with Lanna. Storm had loaned him a hooded gray jacket, which allowed Quinn the ability to hide his Triquetra blades for easy access.

He could only hope that between those razor-sharp, triangular throwing blades and his Belador powers, he was prepared for whatever he went up against.

Didn't matter. He was getting his child away from her kidnappers.

He struck out in an easterly direction toward downtown Tulsa, covered a mile, then crossed over to a parallel street and headed back to the BOK Center. This was a tedious, but pragmatic approach to covering a mile out in all directions from the center.

It would be simpler and faster if he could use his Belador powers, which allowed him superhuman speed, but he had to do his part to protect the preternatural world from humans.

Not that he had much control of that at the moment. If Queen Maeve and her followers kept up their antics, they would all be exposed to humans.

He kept moving out and back on the parallel streets, using a counter-clockwise direction around the BOK Center.

On his third trip out, he had taken the cut-across to the next street heading back to the center again when his senses picked up energy moving somewhere ahead of him.

Two young men were walking toward him on the opposite side of the street, but they kept going without slowing down. Humans.

That strange energy could be any type of being these days, with trolls and the Medb coven on the move plus Dakkar's bounty hunters added to the mix, but when Quinn keyed in on the power, it dissipated.

Was the being moving away from Quinn?

Or had he been made and the being now hid its power signature?

He continued, walking quickly along the empty stretch. Not much foot traffic. During a game or event at the sports center, all the parking lots he passed would undoubtedly be full.

The odd energy stroked past his senses again.

He paused, turning slowly to see if he could pinpoint where it came from.

A vibration of energy pulsed hard, as if the being started powering up for something. Quinn picked up his pace and started to cross North Denver Avenue when a movement off to his right caught his eye.

Buildings and embankment walls bordered each side of the avenue, which ran beneath a railway bridge five hundred feet away.

Quinn had stopped at the corner and now eased into a dark area, then stood very still. He saw nothing at first.

Seconds later, there it was.

A dark figure emerged from the shadows and prowled along the narrow walkway that ran along the avenue, protected from the highway by a two-foot-tall concrete divider.

Any question he had about energy coming from that person disappeared when the being paused beneath the railway track bridge and leaped straight up at least ten feet.

He had nothing but instinct to go on at this point. Finding a preternatural being in this area raised his suspicions enough to take a closer look.

Quinn followed, found an opportunity to use his kinetics to leap the ten-foot height, then closed the distance between them. He allowed for a reasonable space to prevent being spotted. As he approached, the deep shadows spit out another figure, much larger.

The new player moved like a troll. At that size, a troll would have claws as long as Quinn's fingers.

In two long strides, the troll lifted its arms, preparing to attack the smaller person Quinn had been following.

Quinn raced forward.

The potential victim spun and lashed out with a whip of power that sliced horizontally across the troll's chest.

The troll made a nasty groaning sound, then toppled over.

But Quinn had lost the advantage of being clandestine since his footsteps gave him away.

The victor of the battle took off, running down the tracks.

Now, with no humans around, it was time to use his Belador speed.

Advantage Quinn. He rushed ahead in a blur. His prey was quick, but not quick enough. Quinn saw his opportunity. Someone working on the tracks had stacked a short pile of railroad ties on the side.

When he got within a hundred feet, he used kinetics to spin a wooden tie across the tracks into the path of his prey, sending the lithe figure flying through the air and landing in a tumble.

He barreled up and stopped just short of running over the now-prone body that was heaving air in and out.

Hair that could be red or brown spilled out as her cap fell off. Good goddess.

He stared down at a face he'd never expected to see again. "What are you doing here, Reese?"

Shock washed over her face for a split second before she shut it down to that blank expression he remembered so well.

"I've got business here."

He offered her a hand.

Instead of accepting his help, she jumped to her feet and backed away. "What are *you* doing here?"

She'd been in Atlanta, hunting Kizira's stolen tomb and never said why she wanted it. Now she was not only in Tulsa, but in the area where Phoedra should be?

A coincidence by definition was an extraordinary concurrence of events or circumstances without an obvious causal connection.

He had yet to believe in coincidence, especially when on a mission.

"What business do you have here, Reese?"

"I didn't tell you?" she said innocently, then snapped her fingers. "It's because I figured out a long time ago not to explain things to people. Otherwise they start thinking they're entitled to know everything I do."

That smart mouth verified he had the real Reese.

But what *was* she doing here?

"Tell you what, Quinn. If you tell me why you're here, I'll tell you why I am. But if you try to bullshit me, I'm gone."

"I believe we've established that I can outrun you."

"You think that's all I can do?"

The minute she referenced her powers, he scanned her neck for the leather thong holding the medallion she'd worn last time. There it was. For some reason, she could access her powers with that medallion, which meant whoever had taken away her use of them had not given them back fully.

"Who has you dangling at the end of puppet strings, Reese?"

Her cocky smile fell away at that. "I'm busy and I'm on a tight time frame so either meet me halfway or leave me alone."

"I have a third idea."

"What's that, sport?"

"I could use that baling wire over there to tie you up until I finish what I came to do, then take you back to Atlanta with me where you could finally answer my questions."

"You can't teleport."

"No, but I have someone on speed dial who can. Remember the dragon?"

She took a step back.

Shit. He hadn't planned on her calling his bluff.

CHAPTER 17

Using her peripheral vision, Reese took in her surroundings while keeping Quinn in front of her. He looked the same and yet different. Quinn had a way of being imposing no matter if he wore a suit or jeans. The hoodie might downplay him to a regular guy on the street, but only from a distance.

Anyone who got close to him would sense a level of power. Even a human would.

One look at this man, and a *woman* would start calculating ways to get him in the sack. Not that she was, because she'd already calculated about a thousand different scenarios.

Not one of them looked anything like this minute.

She could not use *her* remaining teleportation just to get away from him, but that left her few options. She'd seen enough during her trip to Atlanta to know he could back up his threat to contain and teleport her.

He probably had that blasted dragon on telepathic speed dial.

This wasn't how she'd envisioned facing Quinn again. Not that she'd planned to actually see him in person, but in her fantasies he was so happy to see her, he declared his undying love.

Okay, not really, but there was lots of great sex.

She'd definitely envisioned that part.

Threatening to tie her up would sound a lot better in a bedroom with silk scarves, not rusty wire.

Not the time to fantasize, Reese. Why was Quinn here anyway?

Did it have to do with Phoedra?

If Quinn *wasn't* here because of Phoedra, this was pretty damn coincidental.

He couldn't be involved in her kidnapping. The idea of that made Reese sick for the split second it took her to dismiss it. The alternative was ... that Quinn came here hunting Phoedra for someone else.

That would be even more disturbing if not for one simple fact. Reese had left Kizira's body in Quinn's care because this man epitomized honor. He wouldn't be hunting the girl for any bad reason.

The niggling, ugly, green-eyed monster poked at Reese now, reminding her about Quinn and Kizira's involvement, and how much he'd obviously cared for the Medb witch.

At least she was sure of one thing. Phoedra couldn't be his child, because Reese had spent enough time around Quinn to believe he would not have left Phoedra without a father.

Reese knew, firsthand, the kind of man who abandoned his own flesh and blood.

Maybe Kizira had somehow left Quinn a message asking him to protect her daughter.

Reese brightened at that thought. Her gut latched onto that explanation for now.

Still, her cynical side wouldn't shut up. She had to determine whether Quinn really was hunting Phoedra, and if so, why.

Not that any reason would overrule Reese's commitment to Yáahl, but she'd sleep better confirming Quinn was still one of the good guys.

She'd been the bigger person about Kizira's body and walked away empty-handed last time, but not this go-round.

Quinn watched her with an expression that said he was unwilling to let her leave until he had what he wanted. "Reese, please don't push me to do something I'd rather not."

"Let's put our cards on the table," she suggested.

"I'm in no mood for games."

"Makes two of us." She gave him a serious look to sell her point. She'd knocked aside the damn nonhuman bounty hunter who'd tried to grab her, then teleported away. Then she'd had to fight a freaking troll when she arrived in Tulsa. As much as seeing Quinn made her heart pitter-pat, time was a wastin' and she needed to get moving. "Tell you what. You start first because I was here first."

Sometimes an illogical argument was the best way to go.

He crossed his arms and eyed her with confusion.

Time kept ticking away.

She finally said, "Fine. I'll start first, but I'm trusting you to do the right thing and tell me the truth about why you're here."

He made no sound of agreement.

She banked on the fact that this man who had fought beside her against an army of demons, and stood in front of her when it looked like they were going to die, still had a core of honor a mile wide.

Brushing off her jeans from the tumble and shoving her hair off her face, she stood with her feet shoulder-width apart and hands on hips. "I'm looking for someone."

His lips parted then closed into a firm line. "Who?"

"See? You're not playing fair. You're supposed to tell me what you're doing now."

"Fine. I'm here for the same reason. Now, who are you looking for?"

"A young girl who got kidnapped."

"Why are you after her?"

Reese picked up some seriously suspicious tones from him. "If you'd just tell me—"

"You're looking for Phoedra," Quinn accused, clearly done with twenty questions.

Damn.

"Yes, but that must mean you're hunting her, too. Why?" Reese shot back at him.

"I have my reasons."

She hated this endless circle jerk. "How well do you know her?"

"That has no bearing on what I'm doing."

Her heart sank at his cold reply that sounded like business as usual. Evidently, she didn't know Quinn as well as she'd thought. If he'd at least indicated he was doing it for a friend, she could have lived with that, but nothing about his demeanor said this was personal.

Well, it was to her.

He'd just ruined the best fantasy lover she'd had in years.

Too many years.

Slamming her fist into her hand, she said, "Unbelievable. I help you get Kizira's body back and leave it with you when I had a lot on the line for delivering that body to someone who wanted to protect it. But I thought I was doing the right thing. My radar for men is so far off I can't even fathom it."

Quinn's eyebrows shot upward, but she wanted answers, dammit. On a roll, she demanded, "Who's paying you to hunt down this girl? Must be big money considering they sent the Belador Maistir. I will not let anyone mess with Phoedra so just back off and go home."

"You think I'm here to kidnap her?"

Reese offered her *duh* look.

Quinn snapped, "I'm not here to harm her."

"Oh, really? Then give me one reason to trust why you're here right after she's been kidnapped?"

His face lost its stern countenance. "Phoedra is my daughter."

Ah, hell.

Just ... well ... hell.

Reese's mind had been connecting dots between Kizira's ghost and Quinn being so possessive of Kizira's body, trying to show her this had been more than a quick tryst. It wasn't as though she hadn't *suspected* something intimate between Quinn and Kizira, but to be honest she hadn't wanted to accept that a powerful Belador had been actually having an affair with a powerful Medb. An affair based on real, deep, one-of-a-kind love.

She'd seen the evidence of his love for Kizira by the way he'd put his life in jeopardy to protect the witch's cold body.

But ... he'd had a *child* with her?

And he had clearly not been in Phoedra's life.

How many times am I going to allow a man to make me feel like an idiot?

Quinn crossed his arms. His eyebrows dropped low over his eyes and his voice had a chilling sound when he asked, "Did you know Phoedra was Kizira's daughter the whole time you were in Atlanta?"

"No." What happened? A minute ago she'd had the upper

hand, but now Quinn was on offense, questioning her. If Phoedra really was his daughter, and she doubted he would say that if it weren't true, he might tune up his mind lock trick and dynamite Reese's head.

"Who are you working for, Reese?"

"No one."

"You show up again, with that medallion you use to access your powers, and want to convince me you answer to no one?"

"I'm here on my own. The situation with my powers is my personal business."

"You showed up in Atlanta with some kind of blood that draws demons. Phoedra's safety is more important to me than anything in this world. How am I supposed to trust what you are when all I know is that you apparently have demon blood?"

That made her sound like a preternatural skank. "I can't help what kind of blood I have, but I'm not a freaking demon, if that's what you're implying."

Her short tone must have gotten through to him. Quinn said, "I have no issue with you as long as you don't get between my child and me. Stand aside. I'm going after Phoedra."

She would not let him see how he'd hurt her. "Oh, you're going all fatherly *now* when you haven't been around for the past thirteen years?"

His eyes flared at that hit.

Too bad. He had no reason to treat her like some demon that would kill Phoedra when he hadn't been around at all. "You do what you want, but I'm heading out, too."

A thought crossed his face. "Do you know where Phoedra is?"

"Oh, *now* you want information? Really?"

He cupped his chin as if processing something. "Do you know anything about her kidnappers?"

"Why, yes, Mr. Belador Maistir. I was the one who fought them to get her back. I can identify two of her kidnappers and the van they were in when they went through what looked like a bolthole."

"It *was* a bolthole." He said that as a statement, not a question.

Reese recalled how Quinn had needed her help in Atlanta to find Kizira's stolen tomb. How did he know it was a bolthole, and furthermore, how had he known Tulsa was the place to find

Phoedra without Reese's remote viewing help?

She glared at him and rattled off, "Yes, that's exactly how they escaped and I was there to observe it, but I'm just some lowly grunt with demon blood, so you might not want to take my word for it."

He muttered something that sounded like a curse in Russian. "If you truly care about Phoedra's safety, let's put our differences aside and share information."

She started to point out that there had been no differences until he'd treated her like a second-class citizen.

Reese scrubbed her hands over her face, trying to wash away her anger, because he had a point, damn him. "I've been here almost an hour."

"How'd you get here so quickly?"

"I have friends in low places," she shot back at him. "Anyhow, I've been covering the area around BOK Center to find the van, because I saw it go past the center."

"You used your remote viewing ability like you did in the cemetery in Atlanta?"

"Yes, but it wouldn't work as clearly because of these guys using the bolthole. It messed with my ability to see." She considered his extensive resources. "What kind of being can open one of those for escape?"

"Depends. A powerful mage or druid might be able to, but more often than not it's a gift passed through a family. Does that fit the kidnappers?"

"Not really. They seemed below that level. If it was a family connection, why have them land here and go to a decrepit building? I would have thought they'd go right to their superior and deliver Phoedra."

Quinn said, "I agree. In that case, they might have bought or traded for a majik-infused object that would open the bolthole. If we don't find Phoedra here, I'll put someone on tracking down a trade of that kind."

Reese's heart stuttered when he said *we*.

Then her brain bitch-slapped the unreliable organ so she could stay on track.

"Got it," she replied. "Here's what I've covered." She told him of the half-mile long streets fanning away from the center and he gave her his progress.

He hadn't covered nearly as much area as she had, but then he'd been going out a mile.

She acknowledged, "Based on where we've both been and the fact that you went further than I did, we only have two more streets to check. If she's not there, we'll have to fan out farther."

"Agreed."

She led the way back to Denver Avenue and watched for traffic to clear out before she dropped the twenty feet to street level.

She hated to jump this far. If she broke something, healing would cost time and medallion energy she didn't want to spend. But the medallion had helped her jump up here, so maybe she wasn't as limited—

An arm hooked around her waist just as she started to leap.

She went airborne, landing softly, and stood there a moment, enjoying the feel of Quinn's body against hers.

He removed his arm before her hormones got out of hand. With a touch of his hand lightly against her back, she got moving.

As she walked, she tried to convince herself not to be nice and thank him.

Damn. She wanted to stay pissed at him, but guilt weighed too much to tote around. She quipped, "Thanks for saving my knees."

"You're welcome. I wasn't sure if you had kinetics since you didn't seem to last time."

"No, but I have more of my powers this time." She kept searching the area as she walked. The possibility that the kidnappers had parked the van inside remained a constant worry since she'd arrived.

"What are your powers?"

Should she tell him? Why not? "I have this raw energy inside me that I can wield. You probably saw when I used it on the troll back there. It's what I used to crack that energy canopy over the gorge when we were in Atlanta. I have a remote viewing ability, which you also know about, but it's not a perfect science. If I'm not distracted by something like fighting to stay alive, I can hide the pull of my blood from demons, but it takes effort to do that.

Sometimes my powers work great and sometimes they just confuse me, because I never had training or enough time to become confident in wielding them. Other than when I saw you in Atlanta, I haven't used any of them in a long time."

She expected Quinn to ask again who had locked away her powers, but he surprised her by returning to Phoedra.

"About not seeing Phoedra before now, I didn't know she existed until Kizira told me as she bled out in my arms. Kizira died before she could tell me where she'd hidden our daughter. She said only that I must find her and protect her, and now some very dangerous people are hunting my child."

Reese tried to swallow the giant lump of guilt that formed instantly in her throat. She'd chastised him for being an absentee father. "Is the Medb queen hunting Phoedra?"

"Possibly, but we've had a powerful witch escape from VIPER lockdown who is looking for her as well. I have to find Phoedra first. I can't live if I let her down, too."

The pain in his voice hurt to hear.

Did Yáahl know about Quinn? Of course, he did. Why hadn't Yáahl helped Quinn find Phoedra after Kizira died?

Reese wanted to pluck a few feathers right now. She turned at the next left she could take and Quinn stepped up beside her.

She had to deal with her guilt before it ate a hole in her chest. "I'm sorry about busting on you, but I've known Phoedra for over two years and I never saw Kizira or anyone else nonhuman around her until now. I didn't know Kizira was her mother until today."

He gave her an odd look. "Who told you?"

"Someone who helped me get here." When Yáahl had offered Reese sanctuary when she was pregnant, he had required her agreement to never share anything about his existence without his permission. Holding up a hand, she said, "There are some things I can't tell you, Quinn, but this person is not a threat to Phoedra."

"Is it the same person who sent you for Kizira's body?"

"Yes, but he only wanted me to bring Kizira's body back to keep it from the Medb." Before he could prod further, she added, "I made a choice to leave Kizira's body with you and explained to him that you were the Belador Maistir and had a personal interest in protecting it from the Medb."

At the next corner, which was quick to reach since they were cutting from one long street to the next, Reese turned left again and grumbled, "If they parked the van inside the building, we may have to backtrack and look through all the windows."

"Actually, we won't."

"Why not?"

"My cousin has a different type of viewing ability. She located Phoedra and the kidnappers near BOK Center. She said to look for a two-story, pale-yellow building with boarded-up windows on the ground floor and NO TRESPASSING signs. Look up ahead on the right."

Reese paused and realized she would never have found that building without Quinn.

She understood Quinn's investment in this, but she'd made a promise to Yáahl to bring Phoedra back to him. She'd speak up for Quinn to see his daughter, but she could not let him leave with Phoedra, who didn't even know Quinn.

Thankfully, Reese had one teleportation left, which meant all she had to do was get a hand on Phoedra and she could vanish.

Quinn would hate her, but Reese could not let her growing— and unrealistic—attachment to him get in the way like last time.

Yáahl hadn't been joking when he said to return with Phoedra or don't come back. Until someone convinced her that doing anything else was in Phoedra's best interest, Reese was sticking to her plan.

CHAPTER 18

Easing up to the corner of the faded yellow building, Quinn turned to Reese and whispered, "If I get eyes on one of them, I'm going to slip into his mind to search for their end game."

"Sure you want to do that?"

He always suffered a moment of mental flagellation when he entered a mind, but these beings had kidnapped a child.

His child.

They were monsters as far as he was concerned.

Reese had been present when Quinn voiced reservations about entering someone's mind without permission. Over the years, he'd struggled with the moral dilemma of practicing the equivalent of mind rape by jumping into someone's head without warning.

But he had a personal code of honor. He would take that step *only* when someone's life was on the line or the person whose mind he entered had been committing a serious crime.

Touching his child soared to the top of both lists.

He said very clearly, "I will crack their heads open to see what pours out if I think it will get Phoedra back safely."

She rolled her eyes. "I wasn't questioning your reason for using your mind lock. I only wanted to point out that we don't know what these three beings are or who controls opening a bolthole. What if you jump into a mind and it starts some kind of chain reaction that puts Phoedra at risk?"

He had to give Reese credit. He'd entered the mind of a Laochra Fola during a mission in Atlanta six weeks ago. Someone had planted a self-destruct spell that killed the man when his mind was breached. That mental foray had almost taken Quinn with the Laochra Fola, whose head imploded.

"Good point," Quinn said.

"See, I'm not evil after all," she quipped.

Had he treated her so badly earlier that she thought he held such low opinion of her? "I don't think you're evil, Reese."

"You also don't believe that I'm friends with Phoedra or that I'm here just to save her."

"I haven't said that, either."

"You know what, Quinn? Sometimes you say a lot with your silence." She cocked her chin to stall his next words. "Save it. We can't afford this conversation right now. If you're willing to show me some trust, then you continue down this front side of the building and I'll go around back to see what I can find out. We can meet around the corners at the other end."

He was torn between allowing her to continue on her own where something might happen to her and showing that he was capable of giving her some trust. She'd tracked Phoedra to this city and nothing Reese had done in Atlanta caused him to think she'd harm his daughter.

But it was hard to get past the fact that someone else pulled her strings. Whoever it was had sent her to Atlanta more than a month ago to get her hands on Kizira's body and now this person knew Phoedra.

That left a few holes in her story about who she was and why she had this connection to his daughter.

Quinn had no idea who the mystery man was other than being a common thread between Kizira, Reese and Phoedra.

He didn't believe for a minute that Reese had accidentally met Phoedra, which raised serious concerns about how long she'd known his child.

Tired of the battle raging in his mind and heart, he gave up when his protective side won. "I agree with the plan, but you go along this front side and I'll go to the back."

"What-*ever*, your lordship."

His lips twitched with a smile. He'd love to kiss that mouth into silence.

I'm officially out of my mind to be thinking about anything except getting inside this building right now.

Reese stepped away before anything else could be said. He should thank her.

Quinn moved toward the back, trying to shake off the feelings Reese dragged to the surface.

What was it about her that had kept her on his mind? She'd clearly burrowed under his skin too far to ignore.

He and Kizira had burned fast and hot for two weeks when they were both very young. He'd cared for her deeply at the time.

Who was he kidding? He'd loved her to the point of madness at first, but then she disappeared and he never saw her again for years.

When he finally did see her again, every time they crossed paths since then they'd been adversaries, and Kizira had been compelled to commit crimes against the Beladors. Wounds and the subsequent scars had built up over time, turning the passion they'd once shared into something bittersweet.

It had taken meeting Reese for him to realize a truth he'd avoided admitting to himself. Because of having no idea of his history with Kizira when Reese met him, she'd forced him to take stock of his life and stop feeding into the ugly cycle of survivor's guilt.

He'd finally accepted that Kizira's death was not his fault.

During the months since she'd died, Quinn had done some hard soul-searching. He now realized that if the war between Beladors and Medb had somehow miraculously ceased, he and Kizira could never have had what they'd once shared when they were young. They would never have managed a stable life with mutual trust and affection at its center.

Too much heartache under the bridge.

The hardest thing he'd been forced to accept was that Kizira had never fully trusted him with the knowledge of their daughter or she'd have told him sooner, before the point of her death. She allowed Phoedra to live for thirteen years with no father. *No parent at all* it seemed, if what Reese insinuated was true—that Kizira had not been part of Phoedra's life either.

Quinn struggled to process that last part.

He wouldn't hold it against her.

As a child of the Medb, Kizira had been taught to never trust anyone. The fact that she'd successfully hidden Phoedra from the powerful coven spoke of Kizira's true nature and her love for their child.

If he could find his daughter now, he'd have the chance to explain all of that to Phoedra and then work to gain her trust.

As he made it to the rear of the building, he stepped onto a dirt-and-gravel parking area ravaged with weeds. He suddenly realized that if the kidnappers were actually here, he'd finally see Phoedra for the first time.

And she'd see him.

Hell of a way to be introduced to your child.

His heart jumped into hyperdrive the closer he moved toward the walk-in door next to a tall garage door. The harsh cut of tire tracks showed someone had been in a rush and turned hard on their way into the building. He was no tracker like Storm, but those tracks appeared to be fairly new compared to softer-edged ones nearby.

Pausing at the walk-in door, he leaned his ear close, listening for voices.

He heard nothing at first and tested the rusted doorknob. Locked.

Using his kinetics, he slowly turned the tumblers until a tiny click sounded. He opened the door and stepped inside the pitch-black space.

When his eyes adjusted, he made out the walls of a hallway with a door on each side. Offices, most likely. Slowing to listen at each door and hearing silence, he continued moving to the one at the end, which he hoped allowed him to peek into the garage without drawing attention yet.

He listened and caught a conversation.

Someone with a deep baritone voice was saying, "... and that's not okay. You said we could turn this bounty quick. What are we doing here? I need my money."

A younger, less gruff male voice replied, "I did not say it would happen in a day. Didn't I pick the perfect spot to grab her and get us out of there? No one is following us through that bolthole, but I can't just jump to the next spot without sending word first."

"That's bullshit, man. Where are we going next and when are we getting paid?"

"You're on a need-to-know basis, Charlie."

"Well I fuckin' need to know *now*, Turbo. I can't stay around that ... that, hell whatever she is. She hurts my head."

Was Phoedra using a power? Were her abilities already evident? What were her gifts?

Or had being under duress caused her gifts to surface?

Who knew, since she was the product of a powerful Belador and Medb priestess?

Turbo said, "Her hands are contained. Stay away from her and you'll be fine. Touch her and you'll hurt a lot worse when I'm through with you."

"I'm not going near that thing. She's your problem."

They were afraid of Phoedra.

Those words were music to Quinn's ears right now, but that didn't dismiss whoever was paying Turbo to kidnap her.

Quinn had his hand on the doorknob to open it when Charlie said, "What's that noise outside?"

Quinn dropped his head against the door. Was Reese trying to get in?

"Shit, man, someone's fighting out there."

"Take Buzz and go check it out."

Quinn jerked upright. Had a demon attacked Reese? He turned to rush out, then hesitated. What about Phoedra?

He had to keep them both safe.

He had seconds to make a decision.

If he could take down two of the kidnappers outside where Phoedra wouldn't be caught in an energy crossfire, that would up his odds of getting to Phoedra before the third guy could use her as a hostage or turn her into a human shield.

Plus, he couldn't leave Reese to fight off a demon even if she had her powers. She'd admitted that she hadn't practiced with them much.

Quinn raced outside where light flashed from the far end of the building.

When he made the corner, ashes were floating in the air.

Reese had disposed of what had probably been a demon, but two guys with nonhuman energy—had to be the kidnappers—had her by her arms, which meant she couldn't get her fingers on her medallion.

She dropped to her knees.

That pulled the one on her right off balance.

She jerked her left hand free and nailed him in the groin. He doubled over, cursing, and reached for a fist of her hair, yanking her onto her back.

The man on her left lifted a hand and swirled it into a fireball, preparing to strike Reese with it.

Quinn dove into his mind and drove energy into it, then withdrew just as quickly.

Fireball guy's eyes rolled up in his head. He fell to the ground, slapping his body with the fiery hand, which caught his clothes on fire, but he was stone-cold dead in the next second.

With that one down, Quinn ran to Reese, who was still pinned to the ground by the one she fought. Quinn didn't want to kill that one yet if it wasn't necessary.

She grabbed her medallion and hammered a wild chop of power across the back of the guy who still cupped his groin with one hand.

His hand fell away from her hair as he dropped face-forward, and she sat up, shoving hair out of her face by the time Quinn reached her.

Lifting her so she could stand, he asked, "Are you okay?"

She looked at what was left of the body smoldering on the ground. "What'd you do to him?"

"I stopped him from hitting you with a fist of fire. The rest was self-inflicted."

Reese twisted around toward the front of the building. "They came out of the street-side door. But there's one more in there."

"I know. I was inside when the third one sent them out here because they heard you fighting what I assume was a demon."

She whipped her head back to him. "You were inside? Is Phoedra in there?"

"Sounds like it. Now we have two against one. Let's do this. When we get inside, I'll take on the last guy and you protect Phoedra."

Amazingly, Reese didn't argue. "I'm in. Let's go."

Quinn led the way, sneaking up to the rear entrance of the building again. He'd made it inside and down the hallway with Reese right behind him, when he heard a grinding noise that caused his heart to miss a beat.

The garage door motor had been engaged and the van engine cranked.

Shoving the door open, Quinn ran into the garage, but fifty-gallon barrels blocked his way.

He couldn't blast them out of his way without risking harm to Phoedra. He did an about-face and rushed back the way he'd come.

Reese had already raced out the door ahead of him.

The van blasted through the half-open garage door. Metal squealed and twisted.

Reese launched herself at the van, grabbing a door handle and getting dragged.

Using his kinetic power, Quinn lifted the rear wheels to take away the van's traction. He tried to lift the entire van into the air, but the front end was blurring out of shape as if something had a grip on it.

What else could he do without endangering Phoedra or Reese?

In a blink, the van vanished from the front to the back as if someone had passed a majik hoop over it. That had to be the bolthole opening up and swallowing it.

Quinn lunged and grabbed the back doors of the van, yanking with his kinetics engaged to rip them off. Energy wrapped the van, burning his hands, but he wouldn't let go.

Phoedra was shouting, "*Help!*"

In a massive flash of power, the van lurched forward, out of Quinn's hands, and disappeared.

"*Fuuuuck!*"

Wait a minute. What happened to Reese?

Yelling came at Quinn from a distance and, out of nowhere, Reese barreled toward him in midair.

He caught her against his chest, falling back as momentum sent them skidding through the dirt.

She slapped the ground next to him. "*Damn! Damn! Damn!*"

Catching his breath, he pushed them to a sitting position that ended with her on his lap. Her face, arms and hands were scratched and bleeding in some places, but she paid no attention to her injuries.

"I'm sorry, Quinn. I almost had the door open, but I couldn't let go to touch my medallion. I could see Phoedra. She looked okay. He was shouting at her to stop messing with his head, so I think she's got some type of defense."

"I know. I heard one of the men we took down say he was afraid of her. That she hurt his head every time he got close. The only positive is that Turbo, the name of the guy who still has her, warned his associate not to touch her or he'd suffer worse. I think she's at least safe until she ends up wherever he's taking her. Based on what little I heard, he hadn't intended to leave for another day or two. We still have time to find her."

"But she was *right* here," Reese said in a pitiful voice. "We should have had her."

He put his head against hers. "I know and I appreciate what you did, but I don't want you harmed either."

"I'm in this until she's safe." She lifted her head and put her hands on his cheeks. "I'm tough and I'll heal. We can't hold back no matter what if ... I mean *when* we get another shot."

"First we have to find where he went."

Reese's disappointment washed away. "That's right. Give me a minute." She jumped up and looked around, then she took five steps. "This should be about where the van disappeared."

Quinn followed her and took up a guard position to watch for demons. He knew from experience that she was vulnerable when she attempted remote viewing.

Reese clutched her medallion in one hand and closed her eyes, sitting perfectly still with her legs crossed. She leaned forward, squeezing her eyes tight. "Don't do that."

"What?"

She paid him no mind and kept muttering. "Stop it. Just one more ..." Opening her eyes, she looked up at the sky, raised her fist and shouted, "Do not summon my inner bitch, Universe. She doesn't play nice."

Quinn's heart hit his feet. She couldn't find Phoedra. "It's okay, Reese. Thank you for trying."

"What?" She pushed to her feet and dusted at the layer of dirt covering her. "I know where she went."

"You do?" That booted his heart back up close to his throat.

She held up a hand. "Let me be clear. I know the *city* he took her to, but I only got a glimpse before he sealed the bolthole behind him so I'm not sure where they are in that city or if he is only driving through."

"Doesn't matter. I'll arrange to get you home then I'll leave immediately to go after her as soon as you tell me where she is."

"No."

Shock robbed him of words at first. "Why not?"

"First, you needed me to find her just now, which means you might need my remote viewing again. Second, she doesn't know you."

He took that one straight to his heart and it must have shown.

"Oh, hold it, Quinn," Reese said in a rush. She put her hand on his arm. "Let me rephrase that. Phoedra doesn't know you *yet* and might think you're another person trying to grab her. She's known me for two years and trusts me. I need to be there for her, for both of you."

He couldn't argue with that logic. He had yet to even see his daughter's face. Contrite over his thoughtless decision, he said, "You have a valid point. I didn't mean to sound unappreciative, as I am anything but."

Giving him a wary look, she said, "Does that mean you're taking me with you?"

"Yes, of course. You're working just as hard as I am to get her back and I welcome the aid you offer." He admitted the truth. "I had not intended to put you at further risk, but I would be a fool not to acknowledge that we are better as a team." When she gifted him with a smile, he felt forgiven and moved ahead. "Now, where are we going?"

"New Orleans. I got to Tulsa on a one-way teleport, so how do we get to New Orleans?"

"Give me a minute." Quinn called to Trey telepathically. *This is Quinn. Is Daegan somewhere you can reach him?*

I could, Quinn, but Daegan is leading a team that's on the trail of a missing Belador teen and we're a little shorthanded.

With the Beladors spread thin, Quinn was not about to bring his dragon king here to help retrieve Phoedra at the cost of putting another person's child at risk. *Don't bother Daegan. I can handle this.*

When he closed the telepathic link, Quinn explained to Reese,

"We'll have to do this the old-fashioned way."

She frowned. "We'll need a credit card to rent a car. Did you bring any with you?"

"Yes, but we're not driving to New Orleans."

Taking a look down at herself then glancing at him, she said, "I doubt they'll let us through airport security looking like this and with no luggage. That just screams suspicious in this day and age. Also, I have no ID with me. I only carried cash when I left my apartment today."

Quinn had started punching numbers into his phone and paused long enough to ask Reese, "How did you plan to get home with Phoedra if you had no way to rent a car or fly?"

"I had a plan."

When she said nothing more he said, "But you aren't sharing that plan?"

She clammed up tight.

Using her words from earlier, he said, "You know what, Reese? Sometimes you say a lot with your silence."

CHAPTER 19

Reese finished washing up in the small lavatory on the airplane Quinn had arranged. She had avoided the mirror, but finally stared at the face looking back at her. "What was I supposed to do? Tell Quinn I had one more teleporting ticket home once I found Phoedra?"

Her reflection, aka Miss Guilty, offered no help.

"I'm so not in the mood to argue right now," Reese muttered, looking away and brushing her hair to help it air-dry. With no way to pull it back, she had to leave the curls to do as they pleased.

Even after she'd admitted to Quinn that she had no credit cards or travel ID for leasing a rental car or purchasing an airline ticket, he'd surprised her by not pressing her for more. Like not asking for her secret plan of escape had she found Phoedra on her own.

Even worse, he'd hired a private jet, which had been ready to lift off with only two passengers in a half hour.

A. Half. Hour.

Who did things like that?

Quinn had taken it all in stride, acting as though he chartered a Learjet from Tulsa to New Orleans at the snap of his fingers every day.

Did he?

In the weeks after she'd come home from Atlanta, she'd searched the internet for information on Quinn just to figure out more about him.

She'd found nothing.

And yes, if she were telling the truth, she'd been stalking the guy. It was a new experience for her and she wasn't sure she'd give it up any time soon. Not now that Quinn had popped back into her life.

Who was this man and what kind of stupid money had he paid to make this airplane happen?

What would he do when they found Phoedra?

She caught Miss Guilty's eye again and snarled, "I know. It's not what will he do, but what will *I* do? I don't have any choice. I have to return Phoedra. Hassling me is not helping."

Finished with her cleanup, she dressed in a pair of jeans with a long-sleeved, dark-blue, button-down shirt, which she left untucked and with the sleeves rolled up on her forearms. He'd had the set of clothes waiting at the plane by the time they arrived.

He'd made one freaking phone call, spoken so quietly she hadn't even heard the actual words, and clothes had been delivered.

She'd never heard of Josef Seibel Caspian sneakers, but the shirt had a Burberry tag. She didn't want to know how much this pair of casual gray shoes had cost.

She should tell him not to buy anything expensive like this again. These would end up like her cheap running shoes by the end of this trip—dirty and worn hard.

Being tough on clothes and shoes was just the nature of her life.

Who had anything delivered that quickly to an airport in a strange city, with a no-hassle phone call?

The same man who had a Learjet waiting at a moment's notice.

A man with unlimited resources.

Reese didn't begrudge him wealth. In fact, it meant he could give Phoedra a better-than-average life, but that wouldn't happen immediately.

From every appearance, Quinn was accustomed to a world where only the perpetually loaded could reside. On the other hand, he didn't hesitate to get dirty, and he wasn't put off by her mouthiness or any of her usual tricks. He made for an interesting puzzle stuffed into one seriously sexy body.

She jerked herself back to reality. It would be nice to have a button that could send her hormones back to hibernation.

But the more she was around Quinn, the more she had to face that what she felt ran deeper than hormones. If she lowered her guard and admitted it even to herself, danger waited in that direction. She could not be the woman in his life. Not when she would forever put him at risk as a demon magnet.

Still, deep inside she was just a woman who wanted that one chance to dream. That one chance to believe she wouldn't have to spend her life alone.

Just one chance to know the feeling of being cherished.

All of that was nothing more than fantasies. She mentally jerked herself back to the mission.

Stick to finding Phoedra.

What would it be like when they found the kidnappers?

Quinn had clearly never met his daughter.

Did it bother him that Kizira had kept him in the dark all these years about their child? *His* child?

At one time, Reese would have cheered Kizira for protecting Phoedra. Now that she knew the kind of man Quinn was, Reese admitted that such a judgment would have done Quinn a horrible disservice.

Just look at what he was doing now. Not only did he want his child, but he was fighting with everything he had to get her back from kidnappers.

Everything Reese knew about Quinn said he would never have offered money for an abortion, as her baby daddy had done.

Of course, abortion wouldn't have been needed in Kizira's case, since she could have ended the life of a child with her majik alone, but still.

She wouldn't compare the two men.

Quinn would never consider aborting his baby. She knew that deep in her gut.

Whatever Kizira's reason had been for hiding her newborn, Reese did not believe it was because of fear over how Quinn would react. He might not have been planning on a family, but he was a fierce protector who would have cared for any child he created.

Reese envied Kizira that.

She would never have a protector like Quinn as her own, but neither should she project one man's faults onto another man.

Phoedra's father was honorable and wanted his daughter.

What would Phoedra think when she met Quinn?

Reese hoped the enthusiasm she'd seen the girl exhibit at the psychic's office meant she'd be thrilled about Quinn.

Okay, maybe *thrilled* wouldn't be a reality at first, given that Phoedra would need some time to understand that Quinn hadn't been around because he hadn't known about his daughter.

If Reese did nothing else in this life, she would be sure to bring Phoedra and Quinn together once she showed Yáahl how important Quinn was for Phoedra.

That shouldn't be difficult. The girl deserved a parent who loved her. Phoedra had been so ready to find out anything on her mother, and then the psychic had tried to send Kizira's spirit away.

That had clearly upset Kizira and Phoedra, but where had Kizira gone?

Had Kizira's spirit actually crossed over?

Something told Reese that Kizira would not rest until her child was safe. That one moment when Reese had faced the angry ghost of the dead Medb priestess would give her nightmares.

Reese still hadn't decided if Kizira had been telling her to watch over Phoedra or to stay away.

For that matter, where had Kizira been back in Tulsa when they were trying to free Phoedra from the kidnappers? Reese and Quinn could have used a little motherly fury to slap *those* guys around.

Every time Reese answered one question, she gained three more.

Whack-a-mole investigation technique.

Story of my life.

She packed her bloody, torn clothes into a plastic garbage bag and stepped out of the lavatory. She was at the back of the plane, but the view between her and the cockpit amazed her. Lush furnishings with comfortable seating, deep carpet and blinds on the windows looked more like a living room than an aircraft cabin.

Quinn stood halfway between her and the cockpit, studying something on his phone. He paused and turned her way as soon as she shut the door behind her.

Shoving the phone in the pocket of his hoodie, he covered the distance between them quickly, slowing to touch her face. "You still have scratches. I thought you could heal with the medallion."

She winced even though his touch was soft. "These scratches are from being shot out of the bolthole. I don't know why they aren't healing quickly, but they just haven't gone away."

He seemed stuck in the moment, unsure what to say or do. What was going on in that amazing mind of his?

Unable to take the tension that wound her up whenever he was this close to her, she said, "Back off, Jack. You're nasty and I'm clean."

"Yes, you are. You clean up exceptionally well."

She fought back a smile. After expending so much energy going halfway into a bolthole that spit her out, she was physically spent, which put her mental state at low-discipline level. With a little encouragement, like that compliment, she'd go over the edge and do something insane like wrap her arms around him, because she could live with a little grime when it was on him.

She really wanted to hold him.

Instead, she cocked her head toward the bathroom end of the plane and gave him a clear signal to go on.

He didn't move.

In fact, he looked like he wanted to kiss her, which had to be a malfunction in her brain or her out-of-control imagination in charge. She was damned glad he would not enter her mind uninvited or she'd embarrass herself with the random I-want-you thoughts circling her brain.

This was his fault, all of it. There could be no other explanation for why she'd become a hormonal idiot now after managing to keep her icy distance from other men for years.

She could probably get into the *Guinness Book of World Records* for women her age with the least amount of booty time.

If Quinn didn't move soon, she would lose any chance at that record. Her body was sending loud blasts to her brain with the signal that jumping him on a Learjet sofa would heal all her aches.

Her mind had run roughshod over her body for years, disregarding her own physical needs, but no more, evidently. Every female part she possessed wanted to feel Quinn against her, skin to skin.

Clearing his throat, he said, "I'll be just a moment cleaning up."

Breathe. "Right, uh, take your time."

He stepped to the side to allow her to pass, but as she did he reached for the plastic bag. "I've got this."

That was another silly thing that turned her on.

Quinn could go from fierce warrior, bleeding out everything in his path, to total gentleman in a nanosecond. In fact, he was more of a gentleman in dirty clothes than the rest of the male population all decked out in tuxes.

Before Reese could find a seat, the male flight attendant, whose name she'd missed in all the bustle of getting onboard and airborne, stepped out from the galley and asked if she'd like something to drink.

He was as efficient as he was silent, bringing her a bottle of water by the time her butt hit the beautiful cream-colored sofa. She took a sip and watched clouds float past, finally allowing herself a chance to process a few things.

Such as the fact that evidently neither Phoedra nor Donella was human and that Yáahl had been pulling their strings, too. There were a lot of things that didn't fit together at the moment.

The raven god had a lot to answer for.

He'd known Reese for ten years.

He'd known Phoedra longer than that.

Reese had gone to Yáahl when the man she thought she loved had gotten her pregnant and walked away. She'd been a willing participant, so it wasn't as though she blamed the guy for more than fifty percent of what happened.

But she did blame the rat-bastard for tricking her, then leaving.

With the cursed blood she carried, she'd been told she couldn't give birth to children. She'd gone to Yáahl, the one person who could protect her from demons while she and her child were vulnerable.

Reese had been a shaky young woman back then. She'd asked for protection.

And that's exactly what Yáahl had given her. No more.

He hadn't lifted a finger to save her child, who'd died before he ever drew a breath.

Yáahl claimed he did not have the right to choose a person's destiny.

To this day, she did not accept that excuse.

She barely remembered those months after the birth when she'd thrashed around, blaming the raven god and everyone else she could think of for losing her baby.

Finally she had to grow up and accept that the fault was all hers.

Her mother had warned Reese about her demonic paternal genetics.

At nineteen, Reese had been foolish, in love and with stars in her eyes.

Until she wasn't, when the man she loved had offered to pay to *deal with it*. As though the person growing inside her was not his child, but an *it*.

She'd never met her own father.

Correction—the man whose blood she carried, since that's all he was to her. But that blood acted as a magnet for demons and cursed her children to die upon birth.

Those two men had taught her all she needed to know about love. It didn't exist. Since then, she'd decided to live in the moment. To take what she could from life.

Shutting her eyes, she gave in to the grief tightening her chest. Fighting it never helped. The pain would hit her at the most unexpected times. When it did, she opened her heart to allow it space, because the memory of her baby lived there.

The agony washed over her until slowly, it eased until she could think again.

Blinking, she wiped the hint of dampness off her cheeks, took a deep breath and forced her mind back to unanswered questions.

How long had Yáahl been toying with her?

It sounded as if Kizira had gone to him with *her* child once Phoedra was born, unlike Reese who had shown up pregnant and asking for sanctuary.

Why would someone as powerful as Kizira need anyone's help when she'd been next in line behind the Medb queen?

At least, that had been the case according to the darknet.

Reese snorted with a sarcastic chuckle, because everyone knew if something was on the internet it had to be true, right?

If only the internet had all the answers, like why Kizira had hidden her child.

Had she feared the Medb would figure out her child was part Belador?

That made the most sense.

Yáahl had to have known where Phoedra was during her entire life, which meant he also knew that Reese had moved in next door to Phoedra and Donella.

He'd probably orchestrated that.

What about Donella? Who was she in all of this or ... *what* type of being was she?

"Have you solved the problems of the universe yet?" Quinn asked, causing her to jump. "My apologies. Did I startle you? Or is that reaction the sign of a guilty mind?"

"It's the sign you're annoying me when I'm deep in thought," she snapped, but there was no heat to her words.

She leaned back and dropped a blank mask over her face to hide just how close Quinn had come with his question.

When she took him in from bottom to top, she forgave him for catching her off guard.

Her gaze climbed up his snug jeans and deep green pullover, pausing to appreciate the muscles shaping all that. Water drops clung to a few tips of his still-damp blond hair. He couldn't have done more than rinse the dirt out in the sink, but he managed to look refreshed and clean.

She drew in a breath and teased her senses with a scent her body apparently remembered from six weeks ago. She'd been chest-to-back against him in a tree with demons coming at them from all sides.

She silently shook her head at how easily he distracted her. That scent was starting to cook her brain now. Add that to the muscles playing beneath his pullover every time he moved and she lost a few more chips of gray matter. She crossed her arms in case her nipples decided to give away just how much she enjoyed the scenery.

Her body showed little regard for her sanity any time Quinn was close. She'd have to be on top of her game to stay out of trouble around him, because he would be the kind of trouble that could get her in over her head.

Quinn swung around, providing an optimum view of his backside before he sat down. Of course, that butt ranked ridiculously high on her sexy-man derriere scale.

When he dropped down beside her, he swung an arm along the top of the sofa behind her head.

Every cell in her body took notice.

The nerves along the side of her body closest to him paid even more attention due to the heat rolling off of him.

"Reese?"

"Hmm?"

"Stop looking at me that way unless you want to end up horizontal on this couch."

Her eyes flew wide open. She looked up to see that, yes, she'd been busted for ogling.

If there was a penalty, she hoped it involved getting naked.

Too far, imagination, way too far.

Shifting around to sit more upright, she realized what he'd said and backed up mentally.

Did that mean Quinn *wanted* to get horizontal with her?

And how was this helping her rein in her overactive sex drive, which had clawed its way back to life after meeting him in Atlanta?

His gaze hadn't moved from hers.

She searched for something to say. "What time is it?"

He gave her a look that said he knew where her mind had been and it had nothing to do with time. But he said, "Around midnight. We'll arrive at two in the morning local time. I've been thinking about New Orleans."

She thanked the stars that he had something to talk about that would shake her mind loose from visuals of naked Quinn with naked Reese.

She tried not to sound breathless when she said, "What about New Orleans?"

"I did some research while you were cleaning up. One of my resources confirmed the name of the person to help us there."

"Really?" She sat up, looking him straight in the eyes. "You know him? Who?"

"I know *of* him. He's called the Keith. He's a major kingpin in the preternatural world in NOLA. His family was among the first French to settle in Louisiana, but their ancestors go back to the fourteenth century in Europe. It's the family of Inchkeith wizards."

"Never heard of them."

"They're not all wizards, but the majority of the males carry that power and are trained to wield it."

"What kind of name is Inchkeith?"

"It's not their actual name. It has to do with the Island of Inchkeith, which is in a firth in Scotland."

"What's a firth?"

"A narrow sea inlet. There's an interesting history involved. Back during the Scottish Wars of Independence it was used as a strategic military location as well as a place to quarantine those with disease. King James IV was known for his strange experimentations and for working with an alchemist, and his men either revered or feared him."

Reese shook her head. "How is that related?"

"*Listen* and you'll find out."

Her glare affected him not one bit. He went on. "One of the king's most loyal generals had a son whose mother did not survive childbirth. This son caught syphilis while in the military and was sent to the island to be put under quarantine until he healed."

Reese snorted. "How'd that work out for him?"

Quinn gave her a droll glance.

She pantomimed zipping her mouth shut and throwing away the key.

"As if," he muttered, then shifted, moving closer to her side.

Moving away would interrupt his story again.

That would be rude.

She didn't want to be rude, right? Made sense to her.

He said, "Anyhow, this next part is known only among our kind. The general knew his son would not survive, because doctors then had no way to cure that disease. Being one of the king's more open-minded followers, this general was willing to try less-traditional methods. He searched everywhere for a witch who could help him, and found one in France where rumors indicated that she was part Fae and part witch. He offered her anything to save his only child."

"Bad move." Reese slapped a hand over her mouth, but Quinn's smile quirked, then he shook his head and continued.

"The witch said she'd try, and if she succeeded that she wanted a child by the general."

"See?" Reese said. "That's why you don't make a deal with a witch."

"Hush. The general had no intention of impregnating the witch, but he agreed and took her to the island. He put her and his son in a private space. She spent ten days working her majik, which the general later said was horrifying. At the end of it, she declared his son healed and stronger than his father would ever be. When the general took his son and the witch back to the mainland, he told her he'd pay any amount she wished, but he did not want to have more children."

Reese lifted her eyebrows to say *what else?*

Quinn finally smiled at her, full-on, and the world became a happy place. He said, "The son left the military without notice, tarnishing the general's reputation, but that wasn't the worst of it. The general soon discovered the witch had transferred syphilis from his son to him. It had to be the witch, and she'd used majik to do it, according to his diary, because he hadn't been with a woman in almost a year. As the story goes, the witch had drawn power from the island, which she used to save the son—"

"*That's* the reason for the Inchkeith name," Reese interrupted. He rolled his eyes and she said, "Oh, sorry, Mr. Grimm, please finish your fairy tale."

"Anyway, then she charmed the general's son into following her home to France where he gave her many gifted children."

"Can I talk now?"

"Would it matter if I said no?"

"Not a bit." She laughed. "So this NOLA wizard has Fae blood?"

"Possibly. If he does, he won't admit it to us."

"But he *will* help us, right?"

For the first time since driving to the Tulsa airport and lifting off, Quinn's confidence seemed to slip. "That will depend upon whether I can convince him to agree to see us. It's a little complicated getting in to meet with the Keith."

CHAPTER 20

Bloody hell. Quinn frowned as he peered out the cabin window as the Learjet parked after landing at New Orleans Lakefront Airport. This put them closer to downtown than if they'd flown into the major international hub.

Rain pounded the exterior from a nonstop downpour. A weather front was moving across New Orleans, which could take only so much water at any given time since the city was actually below sea level.

Quinn lifted a rain poncho he'd retrieved from the flight attendant and offered Reese a hand to stand. "Go time."

"I'm ready." She popped up from the sofa, eyes alert. Everything about her said she was on edge, but obviously, nothing would hold her back.

"We'll likely be drenched even with umbrellas." Lifting the clear poncho above her head, he straightened it until the plastic covered enough to satisfy him. This was a change.

He'd spent most of the flight thinking about pulling clothes off of Reese. If she knew that, she'd probably unleash her demon energy on him.

She stepped away. "Thank you. You'll make Phoedra a great dad."

Considering how he'd failed her so far, he shouldn't welcome that vote of confidence, but he did. "I owe it to Kizira to do my best."

Reese's face fell for a second, then she gave him an empty smile. "Yes, you do." Then she got busy gathering up the magazine she'd been reading and returning it to the end table.

What had he said to draw that odd reaction?

He'd spent too much time watching Reese, and not enough of that time looking closely. But the woman could sigh and pull his attention away from everything except her bright blue eyes and sweet mouth.

She'd entered the bathroom a roughed-up ragamuffin and stepped out looking too perfect for what she'd been through. Every time she turned her head, the light would catch on red highlights in her brown hair as it flared in soft waves around her face. It was damn distracting.

Now his gaze traced over the perfect shape of her mouth. He itched to run his fingers along those soft cheeks and that lovely figure, clearly evident even in a blouse and jeans that were a bit too large.

Quinn pinched the bridge of his nose. If he kept taking stock of her natural assets, and there were plenty, his own jeans wouldn't fit.

As it was, he'd have to stand here a minute or he'd give away the direction of his thoughts the second her gaze landed on his straining zipper.

Reese had intrigued him from their first meeting, but once she left, he'd never expected to see her again. Quinn rarely found himself caught unprepared, but this intense attraction had thrown him off his game.

The fact remained, he'd been caught up in his own issues, and failed to really listen to her or to look beyond the surface.

Unacceptable.

"What's wrong, Quinn?"

"Nothing." Lie. *Nothing other than me standing here lusting after you like a sailor on his first shore leave.*

He had no business thinking of Reese that way.

If he were being honest, he'd tell Reese how much he'd missed her once she vanished in Atlanta, but he still didn't even know who she really was. He'd been angry when she'd looked at him with disappointment and pointed out that Phoedra had never met him, but what else was she to think at that moment?

Reese could have brushed him off and still blamed him for being a deadbeat dog, getting Kizira pregnant, then failing to accept his part in Phoedra's birth, but Reese had accepted his explanation. She'd believed what he said.

That trust meant something to him.

And she thought he should be with Phoedra even though Kizira had hidden his child from him.

That kind of support made him feel like he could be the father Phoedra deserved.

And someone Reese would not run from again.

Still, now that he'd started paying more attention, he'd caught disappointment hovering in Reese's face.

He would get to the bottom of that soon.

Rain that had been battering the fuselage settled down to a steady shower by the time they were close to deplaning. Quinn had requested a car to be waiting with their packed luggage in the trunk. He spotted a black limo on the tarmac with lights on and wipers flipping back and forth. Nice to see something would go right.

When he looked around for Reese, she had moved to an open spot in the cabin. He watched as she did a couple of quick stretches, punches and calf kicks. Was she practicing a form of personal defense?

He'd like to stand here for hours enjoying that view of her backside, but they needed to head out. "What are you doing?"

Jumping around and landing in a stance with her hands up, she replied, "Making sure I can move in this outfit."

"You're not fighting anyone."

"You don't know that."

"I do at this moment. We're only going to a hotel."

She stood all the way up. "What happened to seeing the ..." She looked past him at the cockpit area and finished, "The you-know-who person we're here to see."

"I told you I have to arrange a meeting first and I can't do that until I'm in his hotel."

"Can't you just tell him what's at stake and get in to see him right away?"

"If I could, I would be taking a helicopter instead of ground transportation." With a casual glance at the flight attendant, he suggested, "Let's continue this conversation in the car."

She nodded and let it go until their flight attendant had produced a huge umbrella and walked them over to the limo.

Once inside and with the privacy window raised, Reese started in. "I don't understand. Why do we have to waste time checking in?"

Quinn would have thrown everything under the sun at the wizard if he believed it would shave even ten minutes of waiting, but he knew better. "He lives here in New Orleans, but on a different realm. He deals with no one unless they are in his hotel first."

"It's a portal to his realm?"

"Yes." Quinn left it at that because explaining more would take too much time. It was a complicated affair, working with the Keith. "If I enter sounding desperate, the Keith might make me wait days instead of hours to meet him. It all depends upon what he feels will place him in the most favorable negotiating position once we meet."

She pushed her hands into her hair, muttering, "The Keith, the Keith." Glancing at Quinn she asked, "Is that his only name? The Keith?"

"Yes."

"Why? That sounds ridiculous."

"It's a sign of respect and something that has been passed down from the old clans in Scotland. For example, the laird of the MacDonald clan would be called the Macdonald. See?"

"Good grief. How does New Orleans contain his ego?" Reese must not have wanted a reply, because she then asked, "Why would he be a jerk about just helping you find Phoedra?"

"Because this isn't his problem and he owes me no favors. If anything, I'll end up owing him a favor no matter what I pay, and it won't be one that can be resolved with cash. But first he has to determine if I'm worthy of his aid. I've had business dealings in Europe with some of his family, but I've never met the Keith in person and I've heard stories about how he runs the Louisiana preternatural community."

"Is he a member of VIPER?"

"No. When the VIPER coalition formed, they spread far and wide, but they had to make allowances for those who were already in place and considered grandfathered in. As long as no conflict arises, VIPER and these isolated independent groups keep the equivalent of a gentleman's agreement. Basically they don't bother each other."

She shoved her elbow on the door support and leaned her head against her hand. "Does anyone have all this hierarchy and political division crap written down somewhere?"

"Not that I know of and I doubt anyone would want it in print. In the preternatural world, your currency is in *who* you know more than what you know." Quinn didn't know the Keith that well, but he did know the Inchkeith family and hoped that would benefit him when it came time to negotiate. "Beyond that, it's all about how well you know who you're dealing with, and writing down how each person operates would constitute rules. All the players from deities to wizards to trolls abhor rules."

"Good grief. I'm glad I don't have to live with all these politics."

"You would if VIPER knew about you, but you've managed to remain off their radar. How is that, Reese?"

She pointed at her chest. "Demon blood, remember? I'm the complete opposite of whatever royal line you hail from."

"Royal line? Why would you think that's my background?"

Her shoulders went up in a careless move. "You're the North American Belador Maistir. Kizira was a Medb priestess, daughter to the queen. Shoot, now that I think about it, that has to make Phoedra some kind of princess." Reese smiled. "Phoedra will love that."

He was as far from royalty as the old guy they'd just passed who was pulling an empty aluminum can from a sidewalk trashcan, oblivious to the rain.

"Where are we going?" Reese asked before Quinn could return to their conversation.

"Maison du Keith."

She interpreted, "Home of the Keith? Just in case someone doesn't realize it's his hotel?"

"Yes."

"Oh, yeah, no major ego there. Why do I get the feeling this isn't going to be a normal hotel stay?"

"Because it won't be."

They pulled up in front of the Inchkeith wizard's elegant hotel in the French Quarter. Quinn had gained invitation to Maison du Keith on the way here. That had required creativity on his part.

Visitors suffered no crime within a block of this place, in any direction.

Human criminals unaware of the wizard's property became ill as soon as they entered the space and turned worse with each step, which forced them to do an about-face and leave.

That took a hell of a load of majik to maintain.

Reese's gaze jumped everywhere. "Can anyone stay here?"

"No. You must be invited and, by all means, please be on your best behavior. The Keith's word and rule is without question once we step inside." He put his hand on her arm, drawing her eyes back to him. "I can send you back to the airport in this car and have that same Lear take you home, plus have a car waiting at the other end. All you have to do is say so and tell me where you need to go."

"No. Like you said, we're a team. I'm not bailing on you."

She'd humbled him again.

His heart did a happy dance that she was staying, but his conscience had to accept a new load of guilt. This was not a safe place for Reese, but Quinn knew the quickest way to get answers on anything preternatural that came through this city was through the Keith.

The driver opened the door on Reese's side.

About to exit, she hesitated and turned back. "How exactly did we get invited?"

"I sent a message to pique the Keith's curiosity enough to open his doors. His people sent word of a hotel reservation, so we've gotten past the first step."

"Way to go, Quinn." She stepped out and was immediately shielded by two black umbrellas with the hotel name on them.

He hoped pricking the Keith's curiosity turned out in their favor. If the wizard didn't care for Quinn's message, he had no idea what awaited him and Reese. Rumors floated about a mage who had visited last year, supposedly looking for aid in a land battle in Europe, and no one had seen him since.

That's why Quinn would have preferred to meet the wizard without Reese, but the invitation came back for Quinn plus one. He had not mentioned anyone traveling with him.

The Keith had impressive intelligence resources.

No point in arguing with Reese. Once she made up her mind,

Quinn would have to tie her up and leave her, which he couldn't bring himself to do.

Outside the limo, her mood visibly perked up from being fawned over by Maison du Keith's staff.

Quinn slid out and put his hand at her back, leading Reese to the covered entrance where he paused to remove her poncho and hand it off.

"Shouldn't we keep that?" she asked.

He leaned close to her ear. "We have officially entered an interim area. You won't need a shield from weather. If you did, it would vanish if our host did not want you dry."

She nodded solemnly, then whispered, "Not in Kansas anymore. Got it."

His gut turned into a pretzel, warning him about bringing Reese here. Quinn couldn't use telepathy, kinetics or any other power inside the hotel. No contact with Beladors.

Not even access by phone.

Quinn had agreed to those terms just to be allowed to enter.

If the Keith deemed him worthy of an audience and it didn't go well, Quinn would offer to secure Reese's freedom at the loss of his.

Now to find out just what went on inside this place.

CHAPTER 21

The realm of TÅμr Medb

"Where is Ossian?" Queen Maeve shouted for the third time, rattling the walls of TÅμr Medb. *"Ossian!"*

Energy pulsed through the room and Cathbad appeared just as smoothly attired and groomed as the last time he'd visited her. No hair out of place. Beard nicely trimmed. He was the image of a flawless male with the exception of his morose attitude lately.

Her patience waned every time he complained that she no longer followed their original plan.

Plans changed. He should know that.

Especially when their initial strategizing had been two thousand years ago. Life changed. The key was to adapt.

She waited out his silence and finally gave up. "Why are you in a snit, druid?"

Still he stared her down.

"I have been handling everything on my own," she pointed out and considered how few times she'd seen him recently. "Where have you been?"

"Away."

"Doing what?"

"Remainin' calm when I want to destroy everythin' in my path."

That's when it hit her that this was no snit. Cathbad was extremely angry.

She'd never admit it to him, but having Cathbad this irate did give her some pause. Was this due to what had happened in the

Tribunal?

When would he let that go?

Taking a compromising tone, she offered, "I admit that leaving the coalition was not as we'd intended, but that relationship would not have lasted long anyhow. You can't trust a bunch of deities."

"Oh, I agree that trust is not somethin' to be gained easily and should not be misused once ya have it."

"If you're tossing that dagger at me, take care, Cathbad. I will allow you room to be angry, but I will not tolerate a lack of respect from anyone, including you."

He stepped across the room, taking his usual stroll as he thought. When he turned back to her, he said, "Did we not have an agreement that we would return in this time and rule together?"

"Basically, yes."

"No, Maeve, there was nothing basic about our deal. We spent weeks hammerin' out an agreement we could both live with and puttin' that in a blood bond. I stuck to my part of our arrangement from the moment we reincarnated. You, on the other hand, have continually ignored the partnership and put us all at risk. You're creatin' chaos in the human world like a child scatterin' toys when you're unhappy."

She floated over to him, remaining a foot off the floor to force him to look up to her. "Do not reduce my strategic planning to a tantrum. I am still committed to our arrangement, but I am flexible enough to adapt and change with the times in which we find ourselves. You think what is happening in that realm is chaos? If I lose my control, you would see true pandemonium."

"Then tell me, what is the point of your attacks on the Beladors, because from where I'm standin' I see no purpose that serves the Medb."

"We will spend decades or longer trying to flush out Daegan. Pushing *all* of the preternaturals out in the open means there will be no reason for Daegan and others to remain hidden. In fact, he'll be even more exposed as he tries to protect the Beladors and Treoir at the same time. Once our kind is out in the open for humans, it will become easy to move around, because VIPER will be too busy dealing with humans acting irrationally and attacking preternaturals."

"None of that sounds like a good idea, Maeve."

"Of course it does." She swirled around in a blast of sparks. Flames in candles at multiple levels around the room grew stronger, powering up a glow that washed over her as she moved and talked. "Even now, there is word of Daegan leading teams to hunt down missing Belador children and arranging guards for the families. He's putting himself at risk every time he's in the human world." She spun around again and floated back to Cathbad, her voice revealing the excitement she felt throughout her body. "I am close to finishing my plan. I hear the dragon is rabid over the kidnapped Belador teens. He will do anything to get them back to their families. That will force him to be the most vulnerable and he will then kneel at my feet."

Cathbad's jaw flexed with muscles tightening and loosening. When he spoke, his deep burr poured out with hot anger. "You're doin' *all* of this just to bring that bloody dragon back to TÅµr Medb and make him a throne again? *All* this just for your childish vengeance?"

Muscles clenched in her throat, but she didn't yell at him. She had to stay calm to show him how she was the one in power who would rule today and forever.

But there was no reason to hide her irritation with him. "You miss the entire picture, Cathbad. I'm disappointed. At one time you would not have been so narrow in thought."

"By all means, educate me on this brilliant plan," he said, his voice dripping with sarcasm.

Her energy boiled, searching for an outlet, but if she lost her control now she'd never convince him to stand by her through reclaiming Daegan.

Struggling internally for a moment, she remained still until she felt calm flood her mind and body. She said, "I no longer intend to allow Daegan to simply live out eternity as a throne."

Cathbad blinked with surprise, but quickly hid his reaction. "Daegan should be thrilled to hear your change in plans for him."

Ignoring Cathbad's snide tone, she said, "Once I capture that dragon, I plan to compel him to do whatever I want. He will become a major weapon for us."

"That's your idea?" He cupped his forehead, cursing quietly.

"Please, by all means, tell me what I've missed, oh mastermind," she countered with her own snippy tone.

Lowering his hand, Cathbad stared at her in a way that made her think he didn't recognize her. "Have you forgotten the curse you placed on him before we went into our deep sleep, Maeve?"

"No, but clearly you have." She smiled, taunting him so that his anger would steal his control.

Cathbad fisted his hands then forced them to flex open. He spoke slowly as if addressing an imbecile. "My dear Maeve, when you cursed Daegan to be a throne for eternity and to remain in this room, you also included that no one could compel him. You did that so no one else could gain an advantage with him while we were out-of-pocket, but that is also the reason you can't force him to answer your questions now."

She started laughing and floated away. It felt good to win with Cathbad.

He called out, "Have you truly lost your mind? I've wondered if the reincarnation damaged you."

Zipping around the room just to feel her long hair flying behind her, she kept laughing until she whipped in front of Cathbad with the speed of a snake on attack.

She lowered her face until she was inches from him to enjoy the impact of her words up close. "Let me educate you, druid, as you seem to have forgotten one very important point. I did include that part in the curse about not allowing anyone to compel Daegan, but he destroyed all the elements of the curse when he broke it to free himself from being a throne and returned to dragon form. I. Can. Compel. Him. Now."

Finally, she got to enjoy the surprise that blossomed in Cathbad's face when that clicked in his mind.

Crossing her arms, she said, "Well?"

"I stand corrected, Maeve," he said, humility seeping through his words. "You are unmatched as a queen at this moment and I am not worthy to stand in your presence."

She should punish him for all the aggravation he'd caused her, but she did have a tender place for this druid. Floating down to the floor, she hooked her arms around his neck. "Apology accepted."

He kissed her with enough heat to melt their clothes.

She bit his ear and raked her nails through his hair.

Cathbad snapped his fingers and her gown burst into tiny pieces that disintegrated. "This is how I remember my Maeve." His hands were pure majik when he reached for her breasts and brushed her nipples.

"Are you going to leave me naked all by myself," she teased, and his clothes disappeared just as quickly, leaving him in all his glory. The gods would envy his body.

She dropped her gaze. Oh, yes, this man was gloriously naked and ready to take her. He liked sex rough and rowdy. She would give him everything he could imagine and then a few of her own ideas. When she finished with him, he'd be too weak to leave her bed. Maybe hours of invigorating sex games would put an end to the annoying man he'd turned into recently.

Cathbad slowed his kisses to ask, "I heard you call for Ossian. Where is he?"

If Cathbad didn't know, she wasn't going to admit she'd expected Ossian to deliver Veronika long before now. The druid would go ballistic if anything happened to his precious polymorph. She trusted Ossian to do her bidding and would allow him the time he needed.

She nipped Cathbad's lip. "I was actually looking for you." Reaching down, she closed her hand around her favorite part of Cathbad and he groaned with pleasure.

That was nothing compared to what she would do to him in order to keep his mind off the polymorph until she could determine whether Ossian had been successful.

She'd learned a long time ago how to lead men to do her bidding and this druid was no different.

He asked, "Ya still have not told me where Ossian is, love."

"Off doing a task for me. He should be along soon."

Cathbad gripped her wrist, pulling it away from pleasuring him. He released her and backed up, clothing himself as he moved away.

The momentary heat turned into a chill at the abrupt change in the druid.

His eyes burned hot, but not with desire.

Cathbad was just as angry as when he'd entered.

She'd seen the face he showed now, long ago when someone

had crossed him and killed his mistress. He'd gone insane for a bit and nothing Maeve had said would calm him down.

He announced in an icy tone, "I should be able to reach Ossian at any time, but he has yet to respond. I will find him. I hope for your benefit that he is on a task I've assigned and you have not put him at risk. I've told you more than once that I put a lot of myself into turnin' him into a polymorph. I consider him far more valuable than your entire army of witches and warlocks, includin' your Scáth Force warriors."

Saying anything right now would ignite the rage simmering behind his eyes.

Lifting a hand and waving it across the front of her, Maeve clothed herself, holding his gaze the entire time. "You have become dull, Cathbad. Find your servant and while you're at it look for your humility. It would serve you better than this pugnacious attitude when you return."

"You assume I will return," he retorted.

Her lips parted in true shock at his statement.

Cathbad was not one to bluff, but ... he had no castle or realm. In the next instant, he was gone.

"He'll be back," she muttered to the empty room. "He needs me and TÅμr Medb."

CHAPTER 22

Reese had her back to Quinn as she took in the opulent room. From the black, king-size bedframe with delicate settings of trees and animals carved and gilded into the finish, to the lavish gold faucets in the bathroom and the collection of exotic body oils next to the bed, it treaded that fine line between gorgeous and gaudy.

This room belonged in a palace.

Or a Manhattan prostitute's suite.

Running her fingertips over the smooth, silk comforter, she muttered, "So how does this work?"

"What exactly are you referencing, Reese? The bed or meeting the Keith?"

She turned to find Quinn still standing just inside the now-closed door where she'd left him when they'd entered the room. "You know what I'm talking about, Mr. Comedian."

"We literally have to wait to hear from him. If we show any sign of being impatient, he'll delay the meeting."

Her gaze landed on the Louis Vuitton carry-on bag Quinn had ordered someone to purchase and fill with clothes that would supposedly fit her, plus toiletries and shoes. He'd explained all of this on the way to the hotel after having made another one of his brief, quiet calls.

She couldn't imagine that level of financial power. More than that, she had this deep feeling that Quinn had not always lived this way. Something about the way he was just as at home in the middle of a battle as in a luxury hotel said there were layers she had yet to peel back.

She'd like to know if he had, indeed, come from more humble beginnings, but he had yet to share much about his early years.

Or himself at all, really.

Next to her designer luggage sat a black duffel bag with no obvious brand ID on it. The bag had also been packed with whatever he required for clothes and incidentals.

What made him think she needed the snazzy suitcase?

She'd lived her whole life in the world of the extraordinary, but being with Quinn forced her to reassess the meaning of peculiar.

She didn't care what she had to use for a travel bag or even what she had to wear as long as the Keith obtained the information they needed on Phoedra. Quickly.

The sooner they left this place, the better she'd like it, but it was nice not to be on the constant lookout for demons here.

Falling backward on the bed, she grumbled, "Why can't we go out and look for the kidnapper's van while we wait on the Keith? Don't you have human intelligence contacts?"

Quinn walked across the room, looking out the window. "I do, but we already know that the kidnappers are not human, so that substantially limits human investigation. As for the nonhumans, I'm trying to keep Phoedra's existence hidden for as long as possible. Even more troublesome, if one of the kidnappers is related to the Keith, which I think he is, humans will not be able to track him here at all."

She pushed herself up on her elbows. "Why would you think any of those guys would be related to the Keith?"

He turned and leaned back with his arms crossed. "Because only a family member would be so bold as to enter New Orleans through a bolthole. The Keith would have security watching the city for anything odd and entering via bolthole would stand out."

She hadn't considered that, but then she hadn't even known the Inchkeith wizard existed. This situation gave her a whole new appreciation for Quinn as an ally. She asked, "Have you negotiated a lot of weird stuff like this?"

Nodding, he said, "It was part of my job description prior to becoming the Maistir. I have a team which oversees Belador investments, another of my responsibilities, but one I've always enjoyed since it helps our warriors everywhere. When something significant required expertise at negotiation, I have been the go-to person the majority of the time."

How had he gone from business guru and negotiator to Belador Maistir? That seemed like a position for a warrior. Not that Quinn wasn't an absolute tough guy all the way, but he was a refined tough guy.

He wore jeans and a pullover with sizzle, but she bet he'd rock a pair of snug jeans with *no* shirt and swinging a sword.

She closed her eyes. That might be her new favorite Quinn fantasy.

It needed to remain a fantasy only.

When she opened her eyes again, the lights were softer in the room. When had that happened?

Quinn walked to her side of the bed and reached for the hem of his pullover.

Wait. A. Minute. How had this happened?

He lifted it over his head.

Cut abs and a dust of golden hair stole the saliva from her mouth.

She immediately forgot keeping him only as a fantasy.

Why had she made that stupid rule anyway? She stood up and started unbuttoning her blouse. When the shirt fell open, leaving her lacy bra exposed, she couldn't move, captured by the dark look in his eyes.

He stepped toward her, unzipping his pants slowly.

Her breath was coming in choppy gasps. Her nipples hurt from wanting him to touch them. She reached up to relieve them herself.

The world faded away until there was nothing left but her and Quinn in this moment.

She licked her lips. "I want you to ... "

"What, sweetheart?" Heat smoked through his eyes. There had to be a fire somewhere.

"Want you to touch me."

He paused, his face shifting through emotions rapid-fire. "I ... "

"Please, Quinn. I haven't been touched in forever."

He emitted a groan and lifted his hands, unclasping her bra and capturing a full breast in each hand. "You're so beautiful."

She wanted to believe him.

His fingers moved and she grabbed his biceps to hold herself up. "Yes. That. More."

He lowered his head and kissed her. She knew this mouth, missed it and him.

Blue and silver colors swirled around the room. She wanted to float along with them. His hands were moving down her body. "Yes, keep going."

"Reese."

Why did he sound so far away?

She slid her hand inside his pants and ...

"*Reese!*"

The world sucked back into focus.

Quinn now stood over by the door.

He still had all his clothes on.

Grimacing, he seemed apologetic. "This is the Keith's world and I was told that, uh, some guests might feel the hotel's influence. I should have warned you, but to be honest I wasn't entirely sure in what way the influence worked."

His eyes dropped to her chest.

She looked down to find her shirt open. Oh, crap. At least her lacy bra was still in place, but she had her fingers holding her breasts with her thumbs in the perfect position for brushing her nipples.

She yanked her hands away then jammed her shirt together and tried to button it with trembling fingers. How was she going to face him after she'd had an out-of-body sexual experience with him in a starring role?

"Don't."

She looked up to find him standing in front of her. "Don't what?"

"Don't feel embarrassed."

Sending him a death glare, she said, "I'm not. I'm an exhibitionist at heart."

He called her on the lie with the look in his eyes, but when he didn't press her further she dropped it. Once she had herself pulled back together, she had a little talk with her inner wild woman.

This trip was about finding Phoedra, and the hotel must have some serious mojo to have distracted her from that goal.

This little jaunt was not about having a fling with Quinn.

Besides, Quinn still had feelings for Kizira, which was understandable since she was the mother of his child.

Hands off. Period.

"What's wrong, Reese?"

Plastering a fake smile on her face, she said, "Nothing besides being stuck in this dump with nada to do."

His lips curled up at her dissing a room most saw only in magazines for the rich and crazy. He said, "We can do nothing until the Keith sends for me. There's no telling when that will be or how long we'll be on our feet once he does call for us. In the meantime, you might want to get some rest."

Did that mean he thought she was getting cranky?

Or more like crazy after that strip act. Ugh.

Probably. In truth, she *was* drained from being up for a long night taking photos and coming home just in time to follow Phoedra, then fighting preternaturals in San Diego, teleporting to Tulsa for another round and ending up here.

But ... she cut her eyes around to the ginormous bed. If it only slept half as good as it looked, that would be awesome.

Now that she had shown him hers, she couldn't be coy. It wasn't her style. The sooner she got past the humiliation of a moment ago, the easier it would be to work with him.

She had one more concern. "Will this place influence me when I'm asleep?"

"I was told that it does so only during waking hours."

"Joy for joy. Okay, what's our sleeping arrangement, Quinn? Just to be clear, I'm not sleeping on the floor and I'll be disappointed if you pull some kind of noble crap about sleeping on the floor. That bed's big enough for both of us as long as you keep to your side."

He chuckled under his breath. "I shall control myself so we can both rest while we have a chance."

Maybe he should be worried about her controlling herself.

Shoot. After what she'd just done, maybe he *was*. Heh.

She kicked off her shoes and climbed onto the massive bed, which swallowed her.

This had to be what sleeping on a cloud felt like.

Quinn stretched out next to her and he seemed pretty relaxed, which lightened her heart. She'd have been disappointed if he'd acted uncomfortable to be on a bed with her after that slutty display.

She couldn't recall the last time she'd lain in a bed and looked at a man.

He turned to her, bending his elbow to prop his head. "Why did you leave without a word in Atlanta?"

"I had a commitment to someone and a deadline," she lied, but that was simpler than explaining Yáahl.

"Is that someone the mysterious person who controls your powers?"

She reached for the medallion, checking to be sure it was still with her. "Yes."

"I worried about what had happened to you."

Stop being so wonderful, Quinn, her mind cried out. "Thanks, but I can take care of myself."

"I know you can, but ..."

Curiosity just had to make her ask, "But what?"

"But I wouldn't want anything bad to happen to you." He leaned over and kissed her.

His lips felt incredible and could this man kiss. He'd caught her so off guard that she had no time to prepare a defense and caved immediately. She cupped his neck and held him close, kissing him back.

When he stopped and pulled back just enough to look her in the eyes, she asked, "Was that the room's influence?"

"No."

"Why'd you do that?"

"I didn't want you to think you were alone in your thoughts."

Was he saying he had fantasies about her?

He kissed her again. "Sleep now."

Oh, sure. No problem. All she had to do was to stop thinking about him, that kiss and a bed in the same sentence.

Quinn lowered his head to the pillow and turned onto his back, then dropped his arm over his eyes.

Sleep would be a trick to pull off.

Closing her eyes, she went to her fallback for getting to sleep, where she pretended to live like any other woman her age. She had Gibbons and a nice house in the country ... apple pies. Kids were playing in the yard ... no, not kids. More dogs and maybe a cat. Her mind wandered until she was out.

Why is it so hot in this place?

She blinked awake sometime later, feeling suffocated by the warm air. Reese preferred sleeping with the air cold enough to hang meat. She might as well get up and find the stupid temperature control.

She opened her eyes to darkness.

It wasn't daylight yet? She felt like she'd slept for hours.

She distinctly remembered the light on the corner table being on when she'd climbed into bed, and the first hint of daylight coming through the blinds on the windows.

Had Quinn turned off the lamp?

How long had they slept?

Rolling to her right, she dropped her feet down to the cold, stone floor.

That couldn't be right. This room had thick carpet.

With a shake of her head to clear away the fog from going under so deeply, she padded in the general direction of where she recalled the table with the lamp. Holding her hands out in front of her for protection, she touched a surface. Then she felt around until she recognized the shape of a candle. With a little more effort, she located a box of matches.

Had the power gone out?

Could that even happen in a wizard's hotel?

After two tries, she lit the candle, which *really* illuminated the room and ... the slate floor. Something was off. She would have remembered that detail.

Taking a slow turn, she tried to bring to mind what she'd seen before going to sleep.

Not a thing in this room looked familiar, from the stone walls and slate floor to the two high-back chairs constructed of heavy dark wood and upholstered in lush red velvet trimmed in gold. The bed frame now appeared rough-hewn from the same dark wood as the chairs and was decorated with erotic scenes of men and women carved into the headboard.

A dark-red, satin bed cover trimmed in gold draped across the super-thick mattress.

She searched the room for her things, but the chic rolling suitcase and Quinn's duffel were nowhere in sight.

Neither was he.

Don't panic. He'd said this place was strange.

Her gaze wandered to the wall where the window had looked out on the French Quarter in New Orleans. When she'd first entered the room, it had been a tall, multi-paned window, framed with long curtains on a wall covered in textured wallpaper.

Not anymore.

The space now had a small arched window that had been cut a foot deep into thick stone. Walking over there, she pulled open the beveled-glass pane that swung to the inside on a crude hinge.

The moon gazed down, lighting the blackest night.

Instead of buildings defining the modern day tourist area of New Orleans during early morning, the scene below was of men in medieval clothing, which appeared to be soldiers carrying torches at night as they walked along the top of a monstrous wall.

Uh, nope. Not men exactly.

The bodies were human shaped, but their heads looked like gargoyles with horns sticking out the tops of their skulls. Below her, more soldiers marched in procession on the hard ground, each armed with a sword and shield.

Now. *Now,* it was time to panic.

She put a hand over her racing heart, a weak effort to keep the terrified organ in her chest.

Reese closed the window and swung around with her back against the cold stone.

What had they done with Quinn?

If he'd only gone to a meeting with the Keith, he would have left her a note.

Quinn's words rambled in her head ... *first the Keith has to determine if I'm worthy of his aid.* What if the Keith called Quinn to visit him and decided he was unworthy?

Preternaturals had to be the most screwed up people on this planet. She'd fought demons over the years.

Demons made sense most of the time.

They attacked with the intention of bleeding her power dry then watching her die slowly. Simple. No confusion. They just hunted their prey and took the power.

Once that was done, they moved on.

What was the Keith up to and what did he expect *her* to do? If he'd planned on her staying in the room, he would have locked the door, right?

She stepped over and tried the door.

It pulled inside a half inch.

That was enough for her to deduce that she could leave the room. In fact, maybe that was the point.

How was she supposed to know without a playbook?

Quinn had said they were entering a different realm.

She started using logic to work her way through this puzzle.

The Keith had to invite a guest. Said guest had to wait for an audience and had to prove their worthiness. Now Quinn was gone, the room had changed and the door was open.

What did all that say?

The Keith enjoyed toying with people.

Fine. She'd play because sitting here wondering what happened to Quinn would drive her crazy.

When battling any opponent, the best strategy was to first determine their goal, then figure out what prize they hoped to win. Once their motivation was clear, you could ferret out your opponent's weakness.

Everyone had a weakness.

What did the Keith want?

She wouldn't be able to answer that until she left this room.

What was his weakness?

She had no clue.

So much for figuring out a strategy. She moved on to survival. What could she use as a weapon? Tearing up furniture or destroying any part of the room might land her in a dungeon.

A real dungeon.

On a hunch, she opened the tall armoire that now stood against the wall opposite the bed and was also covered with artwork depicting carnal pleasure.

She was starting to see a theme in the Keith's thinking.

She found a man's armor and a robe that would likely fit Quinn, but it would drag on the floor if she wore it. Sliding the robe forward, she exposed a set of cubbyholes with lacy underwear, a thin sleeping gown and five sheer scarves as long as her leg. Each scarf was in a different iridescent color.

She bent to a low cubbyhole and withdrew two of them, a butter-yellow one and the other a glowing, pearl white. Running her hand across the sleek material, she closed her eyes thinking about how this would feel if Quinn dragged the scarves across her naked skin.

Standing up quickly, she grumbled, "What the hell, Reese?"

She faced the mother of all insane situations and her mind went to sex?

Maybe she shouldn't take the scarves.

They can be used as garrotes for strangling someone or tying them up, she reasoned and shoved them into her vest pocket.

Then froze.

Vest? For that matter, when had her button-down blouse turned into a billowy shirt?

Walking over to a standing mirror in the corner, she took in the cream shirt with extra-full sleeves, cinched at her wrists. The vest had a stiff collar that stood around her neck and flared open at each lapel. Intricate designs she didn't recognize had been embroidered in gold over the black leather. Her long black pants of thin material had a similar fullness, but the pant legs were tucked inside boots that laced up to mid-calf.

Yep, definitely time to panic.

The Keith might just be having some fun in his own twisted way, but this was starting to be too much.

She slashed out with her feet in a series of kickboxing moves.

Good flexibility for fighting.

What if she had to run?

She looked around in the armoire and under the bed. No more shoe choices.

Where was the bathroom? Only one door and she was fairly certain it opened into a hallway. Or it had at one time.

Considering the era of this castle, she didn't want to know what they'd offer for a bathroom and just said a quick thanks she didn't need one.

Releasing a rush of air, she prepared to leave.

At the door, she drew it open just enough to stick her head out. The hall extended left and right with torch sconces lighting both directions. Both ends of the hall were identical. On each end, a set of two steps led to a narrow landing where a guard stood next to an arched wood door painted red.

The Keith had a thing for red.

She hoped it wasn't an omen about getting bloody.

Regardless of which way she went, she had to get past a guard.

This called for diplomacy.

Quinn had told her to be on her best behavior. She would not insult the guard no matter how much he argued with her.

Closing the door behind her, she walked to the right.

In the first few seconds, the hallway seemed longer than it had upon first glance. Looking back, the door to her bedroom and the door at the opposite end with the second guard were fading out of sight.

She'd only gone fifteen feet. Why did it look more like seventy?

Facing forward, she made the decision to keep her eyes on whatever was in front of her. Up ahead, the guard wore an armored chest piece, leather pants and boots. He had that weird head with the horn and had to weigh over three hundred pounds with no flab.

He held a shield in one hand and a wicked looking sword in the other.

When she finally got within twenty feet of the guard she had to pass, she said, "I'm looking for the kitchen. Can you—"

He bent his knees and leaped down with a bellow. He covered half the distance between them when he landed and swung his sword in a high arc.

"Oh, shit." Reese flipped to the side to avoid being slashed in half. She yelled, "What the hell? I'm a guest."

Clearly, he hadn't been informed, because he whipped the sword up high to swing it again.

Screw manners.

She was in save-my-ass mode right now and lunged around behind the guy.

He looked like a body builder left in the gym too long and all those muscles had pulled his body tight so he had no flexibility. He couldn't continue twisting as quickly as she ran circles around him. She kept up the defensive measure until he finally stopped, looking confused.

Bad move, buddy.

She slammed her boot heel into the back of his knee. His leg folded and he hit the ground face-first with a howl of pain.

"Ha!" She shoved a fist in the air.

The guard burst into tiny sparks then disappeared, leaving his shield and sword that had fallen to the floor.

She did a quick look around.

No other guard was anywhere nearby because the opposite end of the hall had blurred out of existence.

The Keith was one seriously mental guy.

Snatching up the shield, she lifted the sword that had been a heavy broad sword, but was now a finer piece of craftsmanship. It fit her hand nicely and had perfect balance.

Had she chosen the correct direction to take from the room?

Only one way to find out.

Covering the last twenty feet to the door at the end, she climbed two steps to the landing where the guard had been on duty.

"Now what?"

The door opened on its own.

CHAPTER 23

Reese used the tip of her sword to push the door open wider, surprised when it easily swung all the way into the next area.

That was the end of the good news.

On the other side of the threshold, it looked like a bunch of mirrors were reflecting an arched hallway so the image repeated over and over. It was all brightly lit from above.

She poked her sword across the threshold.

The part of the blade that crossed through vanished.

Cursing softly, she lifted her chin and stepped through the doorway.

The minute she crossed over, the multiple mirror look was gone, replaced by a beautiful enclosed courtyard with four white, marble statues that made her think of Michelangelo's masterpieces. Each of them was a foot taller than Quinn and they'd been placed on a raised platform in the middle of a fountain.

The fountain was in the center of a circular patio made of smooth stones.

Large-leafed palms, lush shrubs and tall stalks of plants with bright yellow flowers filled parts of the lush tropical backdrop for a cozy sitting area of low marble benches.

If she knew her art history better, she could probably identify the statues, all men without a fig leaf in sight, and they stood facing out. Intermittent water spewed up from different spots in the fountain, sometimes splashing the two-foot-tall retaining wall built of sparkling stones.

If those streams of water started dancing in sync, she wouldn't blink an eye at this point.

If those statues became animated and attacked her, she would do her best to kill them.

The patio area had to be seventy feet across, bordered all the way around by a two-level structure the same white as the statues. Vines twisted around the columns and sprouted purple flowers the size of her hand. Walkways with railings went all the way around the second level of the circular enclosure, mimicking the lower level where a walkway also ran the perimeter of the area. Intermittent columns supported the upper balcony walkway.

Arched doors had been placed every ten feet along both the upper and lower walls. All black, except for one gold door on the lower level, directly across from where she stood.

Was that her next passage to access?

Could it be as simple as walking over and opening it?

Not a chance.

She moved forward slowly, keeping her eyes on the vegetation, the structure, anything that could be a threat.

"You have one opportunity to reach the gold door," the closest statue facing her said in a smooth voice.

Reese lifted her gaze until she had to bend her neck to see him. "Do I have to fight you?"

"No."

"Do you know where my friend Quinn is?"

"Yes."

"Are you going to tell me?"

"No."

Like that surprised her? "What can you tell me? We're trying to save a young girl's life and we're losing time."

"Time is not relevant here. If you depart this realm it will be the same moment in time as when you entered."

That sounded great.

Wait, he'd said *if.*

She felt a sense of relief that they weren't losing ground on finding Phoedra while here. That was encouraging, but she still needed to figure out what the hell the Keith wanted from her and if Quinn was with him or out here somewhere.

Standing in the center of the patio, she counted a total of ten doors on the top level and ten on the bottom.

She had a bad feeling about those black ones. "Sir?"

The statue's bored expression never changed. "You have been informed. What more do you require?"

Informed?

Don't snap at the statue that can help.

Offering a smile, which seemed stupid when talking to a chunk of rock or marble or whatever he was made of, she said, "If I go through that gold door, will I find the Keith?"

"You will not receive an audience unless you earn it."

She sighed. "So I've heard. How do I earn an audience?"

"By surviving all attempts on your life."

Doors flew open on the top level and demons of all types stepped out, took a look around, then down.

At her.

The energy in her blood churned, sending out the equivalent of demon pheromones.

Quinn had said not to use her powers in the hotel, but what about here?

She should have asked Stoneface.

Screaming, the demons leaped over the edge, landing hard on the ground. One broke his leg. That was promising.

She jumped to the outer ledge of the fountain and ran around the pool with her back to the statues, hoping he hadn't lied about not fighting her.

"Here goes nothing." She reached for her medallion.

It wasn't there.

Oh, hell.

When she reached halfway around the fountain, she dove at the first demon, slamming her shield at his head. It cracked faster than an egg. Spinning into a living dervish, she kicked and slashed her way through the first seven. Every one of them burst into a cluster of sparks before disappearing.

This felt like a ... video game.

One of the demons raked a claw across her back. Shit, that hurt.

Okay, not a video game at all. The Keith was not kidding around.

She slashed the demon's arm, cutting it off clean. When he stopped to look at the stump, she sliced the sword across his neck. There went his head.

All her hours of training to fight with anything she could get her hands on were paying off. But that had been for defeating the unexpected demon.

Not to become a video game avatar.

Two demons left.

One crawled toward her with a broken leg.

She ignored him for the one that had been stalking her from behind. Demonic energy rushed through her body, carried on a tidal wave of furiously pumping blood.

Her back burned from the claw wound.

Nothing she could do for it right now.

She took two steps toward the crawling demon and heard the swoosh sound of the stalker making a leap.

Spinning around, she dropped to her knees and shoved the sword blade up, hitting him under the breastbone and destroying his heart.

Nasty smelling blood should be raining down on her, but the same crazy splash of little fragmented sparks erupted and he was gone.

Breathing hard as she stood up, Reese started to leave when a claw cupped her ankle. She'd forgotten him.

Twisting hard, she sliced off the demon's head.

"Eleven for me. The Keith, zip," she whispered, trying to build up her confidence to open that golden door.

Casting a quick look at Stoneface, she could swear he smirked at her.

Evidently men were jerks as statues, too.

When she got close to the door, it clicked and began to slowly open.

This might feel like a game, but the bleeding wound on her back was burning even worse now. She couldn't even recall what kind of demon had clawed her, so she had no idea if she would die soon or heal.

What are you thinking? Without the medallion, you have zero chance of healing.

"Well that's encouraging," she muttered. "Good thing I didn't become a doctor with that fatalistic bedside manner."

This time she didn't even look into the open space on the

other side of the door. Might as well avoid whatever mindfuck the Keith had put in place. Instead, she stepped through to find herself in a grassy area with three paths.

"Oh, come on." Sweat dripped into her eyes.

The paths were all smooth, stone walkways that turned into long suspension bridges.

Moving forward carefully, she found a boulder taller than she was and climbed up to take a better look.

One bridge stretched over a burning volcanic pit. While she studied the structure of linked metal sections, flames shot up all around it and even through the slats she'd have to walk over.

The next crossing hovered above a glacial valley of ice-capped sharp mountains. Thousands of icy tips spiked up everywhere. As she watched, one of the spikes jutted up with no warning and broke off, crashing across the swinging walkway and knocking it sideways.

Lovely.

The last bridge appeared to be a swinging footbridge made of ropes, with wood slats for the walkway. It stretched over a beautiful canyon where a river ran peacefully a thousand feet beneath it.

Clearly, that's a trap.

But she doubted any of them would be a cakewalk.

Had Quinn gone through this same gauntlet?

Would he have had his powers? No. Even if he did, he wouldn't use them in the Keith's realm. Had he survived? Was he lying somewhere bleeding to death?

Focus! She'd think about Quinn later if she survived. *One* of them had to make it through to help Phoedra. She didn't want to die, but if it came down to one of them, she hoped it was Quinn who survived, so Phoedra had a father.

Stalling would not make this easier and the wound on her back continued to ache. At some point, she might not be as mobile.

Whipping the sword back and forth, she warmed up her wrist.

"Okay, paradise, what have you got?" Reese started walking forward at a steady pace, alert to everything that moved.

When she reached the bridge, she took a tentative step.

The bridge didn't try to eat her.

There you go. Think positive.

The bridge had originally looked about a hundred feet long, but a quarter of the way across, something shifted. Now it stretched as long as a football field ... or two. She picked up her pace.

The sky changed from beautiful blue overhead to dark storm clouds gathering.

Was that a sign for her to hurry-the-hell up?

She needed Phoedra, who played way more video games than she did, but Reese would never want the girl to be in this place.

She started running, but lightning and rain immediately bombarded her. Then came the ice. She lifted the shield to protect her head from frozen water bullets the size of golf balls.

Her shield cracked.

She ran three more steps and the shield split completely in half, each part falling into the gorge. She tossed the handle in after it.

Below her, the peaceful river now rolled into a raging blast of flash flooding. Waves ripped trees loose and dragged them along in the river.

She slipped and slid down to her knees on the water-drenched wooden slats, then fought her way back up, clinging to the sword.

Without that one weapon, she seriously doubted her chances of reaching the next doorway.

Lightning struck the bridge behind her, setting it on fire.

Reese ran with all she had, taking the brunt of the ice balls battering her body. She tucked her head to protect her face as the hail hammered her scalp and popped her arms. She was almost to the other side when the bridge gave way from behind and slipped out from under her.

Nothing but air.

She lunged for the rope railing, snagging a link with one hand and clinging with all she had when her full body weight yanked her down. She flew toward the mountain, clinging to the ropes with one hand and trying to grab on with the hand holding the sword.

For a second, she almost let the weapon go out of fear of falling, but gripped it tighter and instead looped her arm around a wad of ropes. Muscles burned and the shoulder bearing most of her weight felt as if it might pull out of the socket.

Wind whipped her outward, then slammed her back against the rock wall, rattling her teeth. Her fingers slipped. She kicked wildly for a foothold.

"Here, give me your hand," called from above.

Leaning back, she looked into the downpour, blinking to see.

The face of a young man with short brown hair and odd, bright-gold eyes looked down at her. He was dressed in nothing but a loincloth attached to a rope belt. Tarzan?

Rain and ice struck her face.

None of it seemed to bother him.

He offered a hand. "Give me your sword. I will pull you up."

Not a chance she was handing over her only weapon.

His face twisted and changed from the stranger with creepy eyes to Quinn's face, then back to the stranger.

Was he doing that or was her mind wishing so hard for Quinn that she was doing it?

She shoved her feet around frantically for purchase and one landed on a loop of rope.

"Hurry, miss, before you fall."

"No." Pushing up, she found another foothold and leaned in to slide her hand up for a higher grip.

Maybe he was a mirage that would disappear if she made it to the top. That sounded like a good game suggestion.

Rain and thunder held a war party.

As she got closer to the stranger, his body began altering from human to ... beast.

Clearly, the Keith wasn't going with the mirage idea.

The beast warped into something with jaws wider than her head, black eyes that still looked human but with red outlines. Tusks shot out from each side of his jaw and curved down.

Claws tipped his hands, which changed right in front of her to paws more suited to the four-legged body he shifted into. He snarled louder than a lion's roar and slashed a massive paw at her.

She clung to the rope with one hand and sliced off the leg he stuck down at her.

No explosion of sparkles this time.

Crap.

His body contorted again, keeping the hideous head, but changing into a twenty-foot-long orange serpent that slithered down the bridge.

She whacked at the body, but her blade bounced off the glistening orange scales. Clinging now with both legs twisted into the ropes, she was still a good eight feet below the ledge she needed to reach. The downpour of rain gushed over her.

Jerking around, she leaned over to see what her slimy friend was doing.

The monster serpent kept growing longer and longer until his body had woven itself in and around the dangling bridge she clung to, giving his hideous head a perfect support as he curled back up.

He bit her boot, yanking her foot back and forth.

She clutched the rope, fighting panic, and jammed her other boot hard at his nose, assuming he had one.

Keeping a stranglehold on the ropes and the sword, she saw no way out of this. The longer she struggled to hold on, the more fatigued she became and the less mobility she had for fighting.

The beast-serpent growled, sinking its fangs deeper and yanking the boot free, exposing her foot. She pulled her bare foot up closer and kept kicking at him with the other boot, trying to break his fangs.

Two snapped off.

He had a mouthful left.

He ripped the other boot off and spit it out. The boot fell forever, lost in the oblivion of fifteen-foot waves crashing everywhere.

The serpent lunged up and wrapped around her body. He circled her waist then lifted his head slowly to eye level.

She couldn't breathe. He coiled tighter.

Scales had now run up onto his head. She wouldn't be able to lop that off.

He reared back, jaws open.

With the serpent holding her in place, she was free to use both hands. She flipped the sword with the point sticking out.

His massive open maw dove at her.

She drove the blade deep into his throat.

He tried to bite down, but she twisted the blade back and forth, using all the strength she had in both arms.

She heard a loud pop.

Bright lightning shards shot from what had been a serpent monster.

She smiled.

And fell.

Nothing held her.

She flailed around to grab the tangle of ropes. Her heart jumped in her throat as she slid downward. Lunging, she caught the rope with both hands and yanked her body to a stop.

The sword went tumbling end over end out of sight.

Rain splattered her face.

She hung there, unable to do anything except breathe. Slowly, the rain subsided. The sun came out and the river below calmed.

But her sword was gone.

Clinging to the ropes, her heart raced. She didn't want to accept losing and she'd keep going, but logically the challenges would become more difficult.

She'd barely survived this one, even with a sword.

Leaning back, she looked up fifteen feet and realized she hadn't survived this yet.

Her arms burned and her body ached.

She wouldn't win another fight, maybe not even if she had the sword. She would never see Quinn again.

"Don't think that way," she barked at herself.

Quinn might be out here, fighting just as hard. Besides, one of them had to live to find Phoedra.

Struggling with every move and wheezing for air, she started making her way up, hand over hand. It felt like forever before she finally got to the cliff and hauled herself along the rope until she could fall down on the thick vegetation.

That seemed like a cushy place to die.

Her back continued to burn from demon poison, but she didn't care.

All she wanted to do right now was wait for the end.

When it didn't come right away, she cursed herself for being a wimp and stopping. Pushing to her feet, she weaved a bit, but she was standing.

Looking over her shoulder, she took in the beautiful vista of mountains in the distance with splashes of green as it fell away to the quiet stream below.

Not a bridge in sight.

Can't go back that way.

Shoving wet hair off her face, she wiped water from her arms, but the heavy humidity continued to give her a steam bath. One button held her shirt together and her pants weren't in much better shape.

The vest was gone.

Her last weapon—the scarves—had vanished with the vest.

She hoped there were no poison stickers ahead since she had no shoes, either.

Moving forward, she climbed over fallen trees. This place felt like a rain forest. Her hair and clothes were wet, but the temperature was at least tolerable.

She discovered something positive about all this humidity. Before long, she felt fairly clean.

But the demon juice was working on her, because she was losing energy with every step. Her muscles felt leaden.

How long before this ended?

Keep thinking about Quinn.

Got it. She'd learned to trick her mind to get past pain by taking it to a place that felt good. She imagined being with Quinn in a pretty place where they could stroll through the woods. Flowers were blooming and birds chirped. They came to a lovely clearing where they sat down, then Quinn started kissing her. He took her clothes off and started making love to her.

"Really?" She shook her head. "I wonder if I'll still have fantasies about him when I'm dead."

She tried to make light of it, but she regretted not telling Quinn that she'd missed him over the past six weeks. That he was special to her. If she truly bared her soul, she'd admit that she wanted to find out what it would be like to make love for real with a man that fantasies couldn't match.

Her miserable conscience piped up. *That's not all you want to find out with Quinn. You want a relationship.*

"No," she argued with herself. "I'm not so selfish as to want something more with Quinn when I would be a liability to him because of this demon blood."

That shut her conscience down.

She scanned the jungle constantly for some path or sign that she was moving in the right direction, but nothing stood out as obvious so she kept her heading.

It didn't take long before she came upon an arched door.

No building, just the door.

Right.

Leaning to the left, she looked past the door to find more of the same jungle.

"No weapon. What am I supposed to do now?" She waited for a tree to start talking, but nothing answered her. "Screw it." She reached for the wrought iron handle and pushed, then pulled, but the door would not open. "Really?"

"Open Sesame."

Nothing happened.

Heh. It had worked for Ali Baba.

Scratching her head, she considered everything she'd seen until now and finally came up with only one idea.

Lifting her fist, she knocked three times.

The door whipped opened and she was yanked inside.

CHAPTER 24

"I've been sick with worry." Quinn hugged Reese, so damned glad to see her. He'd tried to tell himself it was because he felt responsible for Reese's safety, but that only contributed to his being a crazed lunatic waiting for her to arrive.

He had begun to believe he'd lost her.

The possibility of her dying here threatened to bring him to his knees, and that had rattled him.

He never wanted to go through the longest hour of hell again.

Her hair and clothes were drenched. She dug her fingers in, holding on to him. "I was worried about you, too." When she pulled back, her wild gaze raced over him with urgency, clearly taking in his ripped, dirty clothing and the gashes, now healing, on his lower arms. She started to say something, then shook it off.

"What, sweetheart? Just say it." More than anything else, he wanted to kiss her at this moment.

Not true. After the battle he'd fought to reach this point, his body throbbed with the desire to drag her underneath him and feel her as he shoved deep inside her.

But Reese needed comfort, not to be ravaged by a wild man.

She'd fought just as hard to be here. She'd battled her way through unimaginable obstacles, though hopefully not as bad as the ones he'd faced. That had been the deal he'd cut with the Keith when Quinn discovered he had to run a deadly gauntlet and that he couldn't prevent Reese from running an obstacle course, alone, too. Quinn had been offered the chance to lighten her challenge, but that meant his course would be even more difficult.

Reese cursed lightly under her breath, then muttered, "I earned this." She lifted up and kissed him.

Well, hell. Who was he to say no to that?

When Reese kissed, she gave it her all.

No holding back.

She did everything with her whole being and kissed him now as if she wanted to imprint her mouth in as many spots as she could. It was more like imprinting her very soul on him and binding their bodies in this one moment.

More, sweetheart.

Quinn swept his tongue past her lips to entangle hers. She tasted of life and hope. Her warm body molded to his, letting him know she wanted him just as much.

That was so damn hot.

He felt everything about Reese. Her presence demanded his attention and he gave it willingly.

In many ways, this was a new sensation for him, to feel what he did for Reese.

He'd been a machine for too long, doing what was required of him and allowing no room for impulsive actions.

No chance to feel true emotion.

He wanted more than what he'd had with Kizira when they'd first met as young adults.

Talk about unhealthy relationships. That one deserved its own category.

It was in this moment with Reese that he realized the difference between what he'd experienced in the past and what he felt now. The sad truth was that Quinn's own burden of guilt and shame over his secret relationship had kept him from moving on emotionally. His heart had wandered around lost while he'd clung to his grief and focused on duty. He'd denied himself any semblance of a normal life, justifying his actions as being necessary to perform his duty.

He'd betrayed his people even though he hadn't known who Kizira was that first time.

For that, he'd truly believed he deserved no one.

But then Reese had burst into his world, planted her feet with force and refused to tiptoe around his pain or ignore the subject of Quinn's own self-delusion. Reese had refused to be ignored, period.

He had no words to describe the fear he'd experienced in the past hour of waiting with no idea if she'd survive the Keith's maniacal game. Quinn had paced constantly, listening for any small sound alerting him she'd survived.

Reese had her hands in his hair and on his face now.

Heat whipped across his skin at her touch.

By the goddess, he wanted this woman. Here. Now.

Nipping his lip, Reese said, "Stop thinking about anything but me."

Damn, he loved that demanding side of her. No one compared to Reese when she wanted something. No one.

Quinn growled, "Yes, ma'am," then reached for her ragged shirt and ripped it open, leaving her bare except for a frilly bra.

She gasped and looked at him with wide eyes.

That caused him to look around and realize where they stood. In the Keith's realm.

She latched onto the collar of his shirt and yanked him down to eye level with her. "What's wrong?"

"This could be happening because of the Keith's realm influence, like back in our guest room."

"Do you really think that?" she challenged, breathless.

"Honestly? No."

"Me either." She lunged up, smacking his lips with hers, hard enough to make him laugh. She grumbled about having to do everything herself.

Not on his watch.

He wanted her to feel as much as he did right now. He'd known beauties that a king would go to war for who could never reach inside Quinn and grip his heart the way Reese had.

One minute she massaged his heart with tenderness and in the next she crushed the brittle parts so they couldn't re-form into the hard shell it had been for so long.

Reese had blown into his life like a breath of fresh air with a sharp bite. She'd pushed and prodded, forcing him to acknowledge feelings he'd long denied.

Reese was a force that called to him on every level as a man.

A woman he wanted in his world.

For more than just this mission.

Fighting through the Keith's live-or-die game and wondering whether Reese would survive her challenges, had shown him that.

She might not trust him entirely yet, but he was willing to trust her and take the first step in keeping her close.

Quinn clasped her face in his hands, taking over and kissing her with fierce abandon.

But his conscience wouldn't stand down. It reminded him that Reese deserved to know what he felt for her before he continued pawing her.

His body argued for talking later.

She pleaded, "Touch me, please, touch me. I want to feel your hands, Quinn."

Evidently, their bodies were in agreement.

Her heated words snapped the thin resistance tugging on his fevered mind and locked his conscience out of the picture.

His hands were just as happy to join in as his mouth. He popped her front-clasp bra, appreciating the easy access, then filled his hands with her breasts.

"Oh, yes," she moaned between kisses.

Her hands joined the party, pulling his tattered shirt apart. He slowed his attention to her breasts just long enough to shrug out of it.

She grabbed his hands and brought them back to her glorious breasts, demanding, "Me, me, me."

He grinned in spite of the heat building between them. He lowered his head to take a nipple into his mouth and tease the tip with his tongue until it stood erect and happy.

The throaty sigh she released did him in.

Now he was glad the room he'd been stuck in while waiting for her had a bed and a bathroom and food on a table. There were candles. Quinn had lit one in the bathroom and had been on the way to light more out here when he'd heard three knocks.

He had no idea how she'd known to knock, but that had been the key to opening the door.

The Keith had left Quinn a message in his battlefield indicating that *if* Reese made it to the final point with Quinn, the Keith would send for them between three and one hundred hours after she arrived.

That wizard had a twisted sense of humor.

The only relief he'd given Quinn was to inform him that time stood still while Quinn was in the Keith's realm. If he and Reese survived and left with Phoedra in hand, or at least information on how to find her, the time and day would be the same when they left as when they'd arrived.

Quinn hadn't missed the Keith's specific point of *if* he allowed them to leave.

Reese hooked her arms around his neck.

Quinn lifted her by her hips and she wrapped her legs around him. She moved her hips against his surging erection in a rhythmic motion that no man could resist. He could feel her steamy body and smell how much she wanted him.

She reached for his snap. "Off. Now!"

Smiling at her, he shucked his pants then nipped her ear. She bit his shoulder. Using one hand, he tore off her thin, shredded pants.

The instant realization that no underwear shielded her heat untethered him completely.

Now they were bare to each other.

Time to get serious.

He wanted to see her face when he brought her to orgasm.

Hooking his hands under her, he lifted her sweet body until he could take a breast in his mouth and suck hard on her nipple.

She trembled and clenched her legs around his ribs. The sound that came out of her was so erotic it shot heat through his groin.

He lifted her further, forcing her to unwind her legs.

She grumbled and grabbed a fistful of his hair.

Staring intently at her, he backed her against the wall and ordered, "Put your legs on my shoulders."

With a little twisting, which was no problem for a woman as athletic as Reese, she slid a leg over each shoulder.

That brought her most delicious spot up to mouth level.

He dove into her heat, using his tongue to torment the sensitive layers. She gripped his hair and cried out. Her legs hooked tighter around his shoulders and locked him to her as she arched backward.

Lost in pleasuring her, he kept teasing her near the edge and pulling back, then pushing her closer again and again. He could do this for hours.

She fisted her hands in his hair. "I can't handle any more."

Her legs shook with strain.

He wasn't stopping to argue.

"Quinn! Please do it," she pleaded and ordered at the same time.

Damn, this woman would drive him crazy and he'd go happily. With one last lick, he toyed with her sweet spot once more then gave her what she wanted.

She bucked and yelled, straining as she hit that pinnacle, but still holding on. Her tremors shook through her as he caught her around the waist and lowered her slowly until her legs flopped loose. She couldn't stand yet.

Her fingers released his hair then caught his shoulders. Her eyes turned dark as night and met his. She whispered, "I want you, all of you. No stopping. Ever."

His heart rolled around in his chest, wanting to take her literally, but accepting her at her word he picked her up then lowered her onto the tip of his erection.

He froze.

"What?" she asked with an unsteady breath.

"Condom."

Her face shifted with hesitation, then she nodded. "Glad you remembered. Find one." Her gaze slashed over to the bed.

Angling to look in the same direction, he saw an array of condoms where there had been none before. *Screw the bloody power rules.* Quinn freed a hand to kinetically lift a package and pull it to him, catching the package with the same hand. Nothing negative happened.

He ripped the foil with his teeth.

She snatched the condom and tossed the foil away. She ordered, "Lower me down."

Leaning over, he put her in position to slide the condom in place and now *he* shook. Damn, that was ... just damn.

Lifting her again, he slid home inside her. Feeling her this way shot stars across his gaze.

He dropped his head to hers, his hard-on throbbing in her

heat. "You're so incredible."

"More," she whispered the word in a soft plea.

Pushing deeper inside her, he lifted her slowly then pushed her down.

He'd never forget her face in this moment, with her eyes fluttered shut and her lips whispering words his mind couldn't translate.

Not while he was buried deep inside her warmth.

She opened her eyes and a vixen stared back at him. She held his gaze and aggressively moved with him in that ancient dance males and females had been perfecting since the start of time. Quinn had no problem doing his part to get it right.

Gripping his shoulders, she rode the wave up and down.

Perspiration beaded on his face. "I love to watch you as you come."

She gritted out, "Don't blink. I'm—"

He reached between them, using a finger to push her over the edge.

Her words meshed into a high-pitched cry. She dug her nails in and her entire body tightened.

Trying to control himself while watching her reach that pinnacle was an impossible goal. He followed her into the vortex and roared through his orgasm.

They both shuddered as he slowed his motions.

Falling against him, she held onto his shoulders with limp arms. "Thank you for a truly fucking wonderful moment."

What man wouldn't grin at that compliment?

She had a mouth on her and he loved it.

When she let her legs fall loose, he held on until she could stand. "Ready for a shower?"

"This place has one? I figured you'd have to catch rain water and channel it to me with palm leaves."

Turning toward the bathroom, he put his arm around her.

"Ow, ow, ow." She leaned away from his hand.

He took one look at her back and lost it. "Why the hell didn't you tell me you were hurt?"

"Because you would have gotten all cranky and then getting naked wouldn't have happened."

Truth. He'd lost his mind when she kissed him. He wanted to

get out of here and be sure he hadn't allowed the Keith's realm to manipulate the two of them.

"Reese, about that—"

She jumped down his throat. "Listen to me, Mr. Too-proper-for-his-own-good. You can say you've wanted to do that since the first time you met me. You can say you were overcome with lust. You can say you were worried you'd never have this chance again."

All three statements were true, but he held back from speaking until she unwound.

"Just pick one, Quinn, but if you start with saying this was a mistake, I will make you regret it as soon as I have my medallion."

In the face of her words, he could only admit the truth. "I regret nothing as long as you aren't upset with me."

"Me? I just had the best sex of my life and you think I'm going to complain?"

He should be cheering her cavalier attitude about what had just happened, but he couldn't shake the disappointment tumbling through his chest.

Setting all that aside, he said, "We have a few supplies. One is a cream to heal wounds."

"Oh, really. So nice of his lordship the Keith to give us that."

He herded her into the bathroom, which had a strange mix of rustic walls and floor, but upscale facilities.

Opening a jar that had been left on the counter, he said, "Turn around."

She crossed her arms and her breasts bulged. "That gooey stuff could be something that turns us into houseplants."

Quinn shut his eyes. "I've used the cream. It's fine. Please give me your back, Reese."

"Okay."

He opened his eyes and she was still standing there with her glorious boobs facing him.

She laughed. "Made you look. Twice." Then she turned.

Heathen. He put a healthy layer of cream on a long slash across her back. "What did this to you?"

"A demon. I'm going to be pissed if they gave me the harder gauntlet to run without my powers. This was some kind of screwed up game. What happened to you?"

"When I woke up and realized I was not in the room with you, I was informed I had one chance to prove myself. I would have to play the Keith's version of a live video game."

"I knew it had to be something like that."

Quinn took his time smoothing the cream and enjoying the delectable back, which was just as nice as her front and beginning to heal already. "He offered me a choice of which gauntlet to run, but seeing your back infuriates me."

"Why?"

"He said the only way I would see you again was if we both survived our challenges. We could both face level two, or one of us could take level three and the other would get level one."

She stepped away from him and shifted around. "You took level three, didn't you?"

"Yes." He hoped some of those creatures would not return as nightmares.

"You're too good, you know that, Quinn?"

No, he was not good at all.

He wanted this woman and she might trust him with her body, but his gut was squawking that she hid secrets that controlled her life. He planned to tap every resource he could when he returned to find out who she answered to, because no one deserved to control Reese.

Looking over her shoulder, she said, "Huh. Feels like it's healing. Think it will continue working while I shower?"

"Probably. If not, we'll reapply the cream."

Once she'd entered a steamy shower, he turned to pull off the condom and discard it in the receptacle provided. Before it hit the bottom of the empty trash can, the condom paused and twinkled into tiny sparks then blinked out of existence.

Had the can caused that or had the condom only been an illusion?

He had to stop questioning everything or he'd go mad here.

The condom had felt real. Enough said.

CHAPTER 25

Reese kept listening for someone to call them to the Keith. She didn't care that time stood still while they were in this place. She wanted to get moving and find Phoedra.

Dressed in a clean pair of jeans, a soft pink shirt that she left loose and a pair of ballet-style, slip-on shoes, Reese brushed her hair, which had turned into a hot mess of wild waves.

Quinn seemed to like it. He couldn't keep his hands off her hair.

She smiled.

He stepped into view behind her and kissed said hair.

See?

"You have a fetish about crazy hair?" she asked.

"Possibly."

"How much longer do we have to wait?"

Quinn said, "The Keith indicated he would send for us between three and one hundred hours."

"Lunatic wizard." She put the brush down, still shaking her head at all the things her host had arranged for them.

The kind of host who tried to kill you first.

If you survived, he then decided whether you were worth wasting oxygen on. She and Quinn had showered, changed, made love again, and finally eaten the fruit and cheese left for them with a carafe of red wine.

Decadent and unnerving at the same time.

Putting the sink and mirror to her back, she looked up. "This wizard had better come through."

Quinn twisted a lock of her hair around his finger. "The

Inchkeiths are a family who live by their word. We made it through the Keith's gauntlet and proved worthy of his aid. He'll at least listen to us. If he believes in our quest, he'll do his part."

She considered what had happened earlier when they'd made love. They'd used a condom, but they'd also kissed every inch of each other. She wasn't concerned about either of them being clean as she couldn't hold a disease in her body and Quinn had the ability to heal anything in his.

Plus, she hadn't been with anyone in so long, she'd been mostly just worried about remembering how it all worked. No problem there. Quinn proved to be a master at making love.

He had even remembered to use protection.

He'd never know how much she appreciated his attention to that detail.

From what Quinn had told her, the Keith's realm controlled all consequences of actions that happened within it. She took that to mean that if the Keith allowed them to live, they would be absolved of any crime against his people or creatures during the live-action games.

Seemed like that rule of the Keith's personal universe would also cover consequences from making love, but in addition to using condoms she was between her cycles.

No problem, right?

Quinn asked, "What's worrying you?"

No big deal. I'm just terrified of getting pregnant again and putting another baby at risk. Instead, she said, "I can't find my medallion. I haven't seen it since I woke up in the room without it."

"The Keith probably has your medallion. Nothing goes missing unless he deems it to be."

"Exactly. What if he decides he likes it and wants to keep it?"

"I'll address that when I speak to him."

"You mean when *we* speak to him, right?"

"Yes, of course."

Why didn't she believe Quinn? She hated playing mind games. "Yes, of course, but ... what, Quinn? What are you not saying?"

"It's impossible to get anything by you."

"Glad you realize it, now give." She curled her fingers in a give-me motion.

"I don't want you here."

"Wow, not feeling the love after all I just went through and what we just did."

He muttered, "At one time, I knew how to say the right things to a woman, but I've clearly lost my touch." He ran a hand through his hair, which was nicely messed up.

She liked when he lost that perfect look, the one that fit with the chartered jets and limos.

A life she didn't fit into.

Explaining further, he said, "I love having you here right now, but I hate having you neck-deep in danger. I'll be honest that if the Keith gives me any opportunity to let you out of this place, I'm taking it."

How could Quinn be so incredibly different from the first man she'd met, who had stomped on her fragile love? When faced with both of them taking an equal route to this room, Quinn had opted for the more difficult, and definitely more dangerous, path. He'd left her an easier course.

She had a hard time imagining just what he'd faced after what she'd gone through.

Now he was willing, yet again, to throw himself on the blade for her safety. She said, "We are a team. I want you to repeat that."

"Reese, please."

"No, you can't make my decisions. I entered this realm of my own free will. I've been banging around on my own for a long time. I'm perfectly capable of taking responsibility for anything I decide. So, say it."

He gave her a fierce stare.

She laughed. "It's not possible to make me shake in my boots. I lost them."

His face broke out of the dark glare and he said, "You're impossible. We are a team."

She enjoyed her win, because with control-freak Quinn, that statement was *definitely* a victory.

"If we are a team," he began, each word pronounced with precision, "then when this is over, promise me you won't vanish into the ether."

Oh, crap.

She pushed past him and scrubbed her hands over her face. "This is temporary, Quinn." Turning back to face him, she said, "You're special. I won't deny what I feel, but you don't know me. I'm not someone you want in your life."

"Why?"

"There are things I can't tell you." Actually, she'd like to share some of it, but Quinn was a protector and fixer. He'd immediately dive into fixing her life.

Then he'd find out it wasn't possible and he wouldn't walk away.

She would not drag him into the hell of living with a demon magnet.

"I only asked that you wouldn't vanish like last time, Reese."

What could she tell him? *I have a one-way teleportation ticket and have to return with Phoedra?* The minute she showed up empty-handed, Yáahl would lose his shit.

Coming into this realm and being with Quinn had shifted her thinking. She'd been trying to convince herself that she was taking Phoedra back no matter what, but she wasn't sure she could do it.

Her heart made a sound of longing every time she looked at this man.

What if they didn't make it out of the Keith's realm alive?

She had to give Quinn something in return.

Let him know that if she had it within her power to change her life she would stay. "I don't always have control of my world or my decisions, but I'll promise to try my best not to disappear. Okay?"

"I can accept that." Crossing the room to her, he said, "I assume the medallion is part of those things you can't share with me, but wearing it around your neck is not a good plan. You should have a ring you can curl your hand around and access your powers."

"I said the same thing but got overruled." She needed to distract him, which was ridiculously easy. She went up on her tiptoes and kissed him.

He was trying to hold back, but he cursed and kissed her all the way down until she stood flatfooted. Her breasts ached, wanting their share of attention from those amazing hands of his.

Just as his fingers moved up to touch her, two hard knocks on the door startled her.

Reese jumped back, then felt like an idiot. She could kiss anyone she wanted.

Quinn kissed her again quickly and said, "It's time."

CHAPTER 26

Quinn kept his hand on Reese's healed back as they walked through the Keith's palace, where guards lined the walkway. The Keith's healing cream had even repaired the scratches from when she'd been shot out of the bolthole. Yes, Quinn felt protective, but mostly he just couldn't stop touching her.

The arched ceiling rose twenty feet, covered with paintings that showed the style and ability of a master artist. Recessed areas in the walls were filled with red marble sculptures of men and women in golden clothing, when they had any.

Reese smirked.

Quinn whispered, "What?"

"He has a thing about red and gold."

"You noticed that?"

She nodded. She'd changed into dark-blue silk pants with a matching full-sleeved top and a filmy wrap around her shoulders, which had been delivered to their room with the request that she wear them.

Her clothes shimmered and caught the light of hundreds of candles floating through the palace on crystal butterfly wings larger than his hands.

Reese lifted her gaze to him.

He was taken by how beautiful she was, with her soft hair flowing over the gauzy wrap. She licked her lips and he clamped his mouth shut to stifle a sound of need.

Her eyes narrowed. "Mind on business," she hissed.

Just like that, she snapped him out of his lusty haze and lightened his heart. "I'm ready, if you are."

She swallowed, the only hint of her nervousness. "I am. I would be irritated at dressing up for this meeting if you didn't look so good in a tux." She lifted an eyebrow and whispered, "And out of one."

Laughing right now would send the wrong message to anyone watching, but holding back was an effort.

They paused outside a pair of doors that belonged in the Emerald City of Oz. The tall doors swung inward with no sign of physical aid.

Reese stared in awe. "Who lives like this?"

An immortal wizard who enjoys life on his terms.

One of the wizard's guards, who had accompanied them to this point, announced, "May I present your victors, my liege?"

The Keith's large blue eyes and almost feminine mouth resembled the rest of the men in his family, whom Quinn had met years back while brokering a major business deal. This man could thank his French ancestors for the long, dark-brown hair he wore loose, as well as thick, black lashes.

His white tunic and matching loose pants suited a man surrounded by a half-dozen women wearing casual gowns and similar loose clothing, but all in bright colors.

He lounged on piles of furs with his women positioned just as comfortably all around him. One female massaged his head while others flipped through magazines and chuckled with each other. Some even had electronic tablets in hand.

How did any electronic work here?

"Welcome, Quinn and Reese," the Keith said, not bothering to rise. He waved a hand and all the guards left.

That made it very clear he could handle any threat on his own.

Quinn touched Reese's back, guiding her forward until they were within a few feet of the steps to the Keith's raised dais.

Sending a chalice he'd been sipping floating across to one of his women, the Keith watched as she refilled it with a dark liquid and waited for her to send it back.

He sipped and said, "You have proven yourselves worthy to reach this point. I must admit, I considered bringing you here for immediate execution when I receive your message, Quinn, especially when you did not share your identity beyond a first name."

Reese frowned, but remained still.

Quinn had asked Reese to leave the talking to him.

He said, "I hoped you'd find my message interesting and I had no doubt that you could determine my identity," Quinn pointed out, to give credit to the Keith in front of his harem. There was no other word for this group of women hanging on his every word.

Give me a smart-mouthed pistol with fire in her eyes any day over a roomful of cookie-cutter women.

"True," the Keith agreed. "I did find your message intriguing. You said 'An honorable man would never allow a debt to go unpaid.'"

Reese turned to Quinn with her eyebrows climbing as high as they'd go.

Yes, he'd questioned the Keith's integrity and honor.

Quinn patted her back, reminding her to keep all attention on the Keith, as he was sure the wizard had more to say.

"Now you can explain your message, Quinn," the Keith said, stretching to allow one of the women to massage his feet.

"I met your Uncle Jacques a few years ago in Marseille. I negotiated a trade with someone we'll call a financial opponent of his. I handed him the shipping lanes he needed to move his people and products without any human or preternatural issues."

The Keith sat up, dropping his feet to the fur-covered floor. "I remember him telling me about a Belador who saved him a lot of trouble. That was you?"

"Yes."

"Well done, but that is not my debt."

"No, it isn't," Quinn agreed. "I merely wanted to establish that I do have some history with the Inchkeith dynasty and, as the Belador Maistir, I have knowledge of your extensive family."

The Keith managed to hide his surprise at hearing Quinn was a Maistir. Quinn had withheld any information on his background to prevent the Keith from denying him a meeting outright.

Beladors outnumbered Inchkeiths, but the wizard's family possessed powers of magnitude that few could imagine. Still, in the wizard's position, Quinn would have denied this meeting and kept his hands clean.

Quinn nodded. "If meeting with you was not of such extreme importance, I would never have imposed upon you." Always good to let the Keith know Quinn respected the wizard's position. "I am searching for a thirteen-year-old girl who has been kidnapped by a member of your extended family."

The Keith jumped to his feet, cursing in French. His face erupted with fury. "*Mon dieu!* You dare to come here and claim such a thing? We are not pedophiles who touch children."

Quinn held his hands up for a moment. "You misunderstand me. He has not kidnapped the girl for that reason. We are dealing with preternatural chaos in Atlanta. There are bounties out for anyone who possesses power. I believe the man has taken the girl for a bounty, but he should not have chosen this particular one." Quinn shoved power into his last words unintentionally, but no one touched a member of his family, especially the females, without drawing his wrath.

"Why do you believe this kidnapper is of my family?"

"Because he opened a bolthole to enter New Orleans right before I sent my message to you. It is my understanding that no one would dare enter this city in that manner without permission ... unless they had Inchkeith blood."

"A bolthole?"

"Yes, and he calls himself Turbo."

French cursing torched the air then the Keith snapped out, "*Chasseurs!*"

Keeping her attention on the Keith, Reese whispered from the corner of her mouth, "What's going on?"

"He's bringing in hunters, or what we'd call trackers."

Edgy looking men and women flooded the room. They were in their mid-twenties to thirties and dressed in normal attire for locals walking around New Orleans. Probably to blend in.

There had to be seventy of them. Maybe closer to a hundred.

The Keith boomed out, "Find Turbo of the Inchkeiths. Bring him and any female with him to me. A fist of gold to the one who shows up first."

Spreading his arms wide, the Keith whipped one hand in a horizontal arc across the room while spewing a string of French words that tested Quinn's grasp of the language.

As the Keith's hand moved in reverse, every hunter blinked

out of sight. The wizard was using one hell of a spell to send his people outside the realm that quickly.

Hope shoved Quinn's heartbeat into overdrive.

After all he and Reese had been through, getting Phoedra in hand right now would go a long way in easing his guilt over bringing Reese to this place.

"How long?" Reese asked softly.

"My *chasseurs* are the best and most efficient when tracking anyone in my domain," the Keith said, directing his words at Reese. He studied her a bit too long.

Quinn wanted to shove her out of sight.

The Keith had an admiring glint in his gaze.

While Quinn agreed that Reese was a delight for the eyes, he'd rather not have to bloody the wizard who held ultimate power in this realm.

Quinn would end up a memory if he crossed the Keith, but no one was getting near Reese.

She didn't shy away. If anything, the Keith's full attention seemed to be a curiosity for her.

The wizard asked her, "What do you desire?"

Reese made him wait for her reply. "Are you a wizard or a genie?"

Several women snickered at that and the Keith smiled at them. Returning to Reese, he said, "I can make your greatest wish come true."

If only Quinn had telepathic ability with her right now.

Reese said, "That's quite an offer, but lacking in that I'm not sure you can deliver anything I want."

"You should test me."

Quinn felt perspiration at his neck. No, she shouldn't test him or the wizard would take it as some sort of agreement. With no way to relay that to Reese, Quinn waited to see what she said. If she stuck her foot in it, he'd jump in before the wizard could accept.

Reese tapped a finger on her lower lip, thinking. When she removed her finger, she said, "You like games, right?"

His eyes lit up with the promise of a challenge. "I love games. No one defeats me. Is this not true?"

The harem paused in whatever they were doing to nod and

give him a quick round of applause.

He preened.

"Very well," Reese said. "If you can solve this puzzle before Turbo is brought here, and not tell your people to slow their search, then I will take what you offer. You must first figure out what I most desire."

Quinn cursed himself a hundred times over for bringing her to this realm.

The Keith rubbed his hands together. "Yes, this is exactly how we should proceed. On my word, my chasseurs will return very soon, but what do you request if I fail? I will not, but I always like to know that everyone has skin in the game."

"If you lose, you give me back the medallion I was wearing when I entered your hotel."

"This?" He lifted her medallion from where it hung around his neck. "I am attached to the energy in it. I will agree, but if I win, you will stay and explain this medallion to me."

Swinging his gaze from Reese to the Keith and back to Reese, Quinn couldn't decide which idiot to throttle first.

Rubbing his hands together, the Keith said, "Give me the puzzle."

Smiling at the wizard, Reese said, "I do not want wealth. I do not want majik or power. I'm fine with the way I look. I do not want any person or any tangible item. What do I want?"

Quinn had been worried for Reese, but now his concern shifted to the wizard, who was no longer grinning.

How would the Keith react if she stumped him?

She might have to give him the medallion to get out of here.

The wizard paced back and forth.

His women stared at him and whispered to one another, no doubt trying to help their ruler.

Turning a serious expression on Reese, the Keith said, "You wish to be a bride?"

"Nope, that would imply that I wanted someone."

"True." Casting an odd look in Quinn's direction, the Keith shrugged and paced some more. He snapped his fingers. "You wish to be happy?"

"No, but you're getting warm."

That tiny encouragement brought back the wizard's infectious grin, which swept through his harem.

Power brushed Quinn.

The Keith roared, "*No!*"

One of the larger male hunters held a man with a green Mohawk high in the air with one meaty hand wrapped around his captive's throat. The hunter looked concerned. "Is this not Turbo, my liege?"

"Yes, yes. It is, but your return ended a most enticing game. Well done, Nino." The Keith descended the steps and walked to Quinn's left, where Turbo struggled against an iron hold.

With the noise covering her words, Reese whispered to Quinn, "That's Joey, the jerk who kidnapped Phoedra."

He nodded. Turbo, aka Joey, would pay dearly.

Turbo held out a hand, silently pleading for help.

The Keith told his hunter, "You will be rewarded once my guests leave, Nino. Release him."

"Thank you, my liege." Nino did as ordered, then bowed. "I will call back the others."

"Yes, please do so."

As Turbo's feet hit the floor, he clutched his neck, coughing. "Thanks, man, I—"

Nodding at the hunter who walked out of the room, the Keith grabbed Turbo in a chokehold and raised him a foot off the floor in spite of being far smaller than his hunter. He told Turbo, "I have allowed you to live only because I love my aunt, but even your mother would kill you over this insult. How dare you harm a child *and* bring her to my domain?"

Turbo's eyes bulged. His face turned red, then purple.

No one should interfere right now unless they wanted to die, but Quinn couldn't stand by as the Keith killed Turbo.

Quinn said, "Pardon me for the interruption, but where *is* the girl?"

The Keith turned a vicious look at Quinn. "Do not interfere."

Irritated after all he and Reese had been through, Quinn said, "If you wish to kill him, I'm all for it. In fact, I'll do it for you, but Reese and I only want the girl who is clearly not here."

Turning to Turbo, the Keith shook him and said, "See what you have done? No one causes me to mistreat guests."

Reese gave Quinn a look that questioned the wizard's

definition of hospitality.

Lowering Turbo to stand on his own feet again, the Keith released his throat. "Where is the child you kidnapped?"

Rubbing his bruised neck, Turbo sounded as if his windpipe was half crushed. "Sorry, but it's been ... tough week ..."

"Turbo!"

"Right. Had a bounty for her." When that didn't absolve him of any crime, Turbo said, "Some guy called Ossian contracted for her."

"Who is this Ossian?"

"I don't know much about him. He said he represents a powerful witch in Atlanta looking for a girl with powers and named Phoedra."

Sharp claws of apprehension climbed Quinn's spine. Who was this Ossian? Quinn would unleash every resource to find him and his benefactor. He could only pray that it was not Veronika.

Turbo continued to blather. "But this guy showed up who Ossian knew and took the girl from both of us."

"Who?" Quinn ordered, no longer willing to wade through more of Turbo's verbal garbage.

"Ossian seemed surprised. He called the guy a Scáth warrior, whatever that is."

Reese cursed softly.

Quinn fought to breathe. He needed to bloody something and Turbo was a prime target. He'd allowed the Medb to get their hands on Phoedra.

"You might have reduced your penalty if you had delivered the girl here," the Keith said.

"Oh, man, I'm sorry. Did you want her?"

A dark glow pulsed out from the Keith. "I do *not* touch children. You compound your crime by insulting me. I have told you more than once to never use an Inchkeith bolthole except to protect your life."

Turbo's face fell. "Who, uh, told you I opened a bolthole here?"

As Quinn had thought, Turbo had committed a greater crime by opening a bolthole in the Keith's domain than by committing the kidnapping. Screwed up priorities, but if it helped him find

Phoedra, Quinn was glad for the rule.

"Do you deny it?" the wizard asked in quiet voice that carried a scary threat. "If you lie to me, Turbo, the punishment is far worse."

"Okay, fine. I did use a bolthole, but I was desperate. I was being chased. I needed the money and couldn't get any from my mother and then I—"

"*Aarrghh!*" The Keith raised his fists, his power rocking the room. Dark waves of energy spun around his body.

Turbo fell to his knees crying.

The harem huddled into one group.

Lifting a hand over Turbo, the Keith spit out some incantation and a black smoke rose from the ground, twisting into wide bands that wrapped around Turbo. He watched with terrified eyes as the bands covered him from chest to knees, forcing him to stand and pinning his arms to his sides.

Turbo sobbed, "Please, don't... "

Lifting his hands, the wizard said, "You can never do these things again."

"I won't, I swear I won't ever—"

The Keith opened his fingers wide and shoved them forward.

Twenty miniature silver spears appeared in the air and flew at Turbo, driving through the black straitjacket in all directions.

Turbo screamed.

Blood streamed from the bottom edge of the smoky wrap. One spear had drilled low enough to strike his balls. He passed out standing upright.

Calling his guards, the Keith said, "Take him away and guard him until I have decided what his punishment will be."

Quinn had to admit he'd wanted to kill the bastard, but leaving him to the Keith would be a suitable sentence for his crime.

Once the Turbo mess had been removed, leaving the spot where he had stood perfectly clean, the wizard turned to Quinn. "I would have delivered the girl to you if that had been possible. Unfortunately, it is out of my jurisdiction."

"I understand. Thank you for a lead on locating her."

"As I told you before, when you leave my realm, time will resume from the point of when you entered, so you have lost no time here. You have entertained me greatly. For that, I will give you a parting gift."

Quinn was afraid to find out what the wizard considered a gift. All he wanted to do right now was get out of here alive with Reese and race to Atlanta to figure out how to get Phoedra from Cathbad and that bloody queen.

In a hurry, Quinn said, "Your hospitality has been gift enough."

Reese snorted and Quinn wondered if they would get out of here after all.

The wizard said, "I insist on the gift." Then he turned to Reese. "But first, what was the answer to the puzzle?"

"It's simple. I want to be a normal human and I doubt you can change what I am."

She'd clearly stumped the Keith who frowned with confusion. "What are you?"

"Something that would take too long to explain since we're in a hurry." She held her hand out. "By the way, pay up."

"You are a lovely and fierce warrior. I would make a special place for you here." Reluctantly, he pulled the thong necklace over his head and dropped the medallion into her hand.

Quinn was not leaving Reese even if she said yes.

Reese snapped her fingers shut and said, "That is an exceptional offer, but I politely decline. I have responsibilities at home and I have never been one to share."

She'd lifted Quinn's spirit with that, but when she slipped her hand in his in a possessive move, his heart did backflips. He held a new hope for his future if he could just get to Phoedra.

The Keith took note of their hands and sighed. "As I said, you were both entertaining. Come back some time when you want to test yourselves again."

Reese said, "Yeah, that would be—"

Quinn squeezed her hand. She was about to ruin a perfect exit.

Reese finished by saying, "—an invitation unmatched by any other."

The wizard's face had started to lose amusement until she recovered. He clapped his hands together. "Now for your gift."

Anxious to get on the move, Quinn said, "If you'll just point us to the front door, that would suffice."

"That would take far too long."

"You said time would remain the same no matter when we left," Reese pointed out.

"Hush, imp. That is true, but do not deny me a last moment of pleasure." Grinning with evil delight, the Keith lifted a hand and drew an invisible vertical circle that encompassed Quinn and Reese.

She looked down at herself then at Quinn. "I don't feel anything. Do you?"

"*Au revoir.*" Using his hands, the Keith made a pushing motion toward them.

The room blurred.

Noises blasted at Quinn from every direction.

He prepared to protect Reese, but from what threat?

CHAPTER 27

Ossian strode into the clearing where Veronika had indicated she would be upon his return. He trembled at having to return without Phoedra in hand.

This bitch witch was proving to be more insane by the minute.

Why else would she have stolen a throne and placed it in the middle of a clearing in Kennesaw National Battlefield Park northwest of downtown Atlanta? She must have stolen it, since he doubted she could conjure up one with such an intricately carved frame finished in gold, which also showed decades of natural wear.

Why hadn't she conjured a comfortable mansion to use while she was at it?

The throne couldn't be placed in a more ridiculous spot, sitting on the grass-and-twig-covered ground beneath a canopy of thirty-foot-tall oak trees.

No humans would wander into her spot. This witch would secure the area to prevent intrusion.

He'd be the first to acknowledge that Veronika was a power capable of threatening many nonhumans. She'd been gaining more strength through her ancestors and clearly had a plan for drawing power from Phoedra.

He had a high regard for her level of crazy after she'd taken him from the jaws of death three times and sent him back when she cooked his majik again and again.

She'd jacked up his majik so much that Ossian struggled to hold one physical shape for more than a few hours. She'd pushed him nonstop since she'd snapped the link between him and

Cathbad. Ossian desperately needed rest for any hope of regaining full control of his morphing ability.

He couldn't accept that he might not ever do so.

What were Queen Maeve and Cathbad thinking about him now? That he'd jumped from one side to another?

Pausing several steps from where Veronika perched on her throne with a sour expression, he bowed at the waist then righted himself.

Now he had to utter disgusting words. "My queen."

"You're empty-handed."

How nice to be enslaved to a queen who noticed the obvious.

"Please allow me to explain what has happened," he implored.

She nodded her assent.

"The bounty offers I put on the darknet were productive. As you said, there couldn't be many young girls named Phoedra who possessed powers." To say he'd been surprised when someone found a girl to match that description would be an understatement. He'd tried to tell Veronika the girl could be called by another name.

But that had not been the case.

He was likely not helping his case by explaining that Veronika had been correct, but she allowed him to continue.

"Phoedra was located on the other side of this country and transported to an unauthorized location. My instructions in the darknet ad specifically said that once a potential target was found to contact me, then I would bring her here."

Ossian paused to draw a deep breath, but he really wanted to give her a chance to say something so he could gauge the trouble he faced.

When she did not comment, he said, "The bounty hunter ran into some kind of trouble, so he instead went to New Orleans, a region protected by his kin. He would only hand her over there, stating he would not trust anywhere else when he had a safe place to meet. I understand how important it is for you to have this girl and her power, so I agreed. I was in the process of taking possession of Phoedra when a Medb Scáth Force warrior appeared as if teleported in. I don't believe they have that ability, so I'm guessing Cathbad or Queen Maeve sent him. He took the girl before I got my hands on her. It all happened very quickly."

Veronika listened intently then asked, "How did he know where to find her?"

Ossian lifted his shoulders and shook his head. He reminded her, "You have ensured that I can tell no one what I am doing for you, especially an enemy of yours, which is pretty much everyone."

Veronika leaned forward, her seething anger causing the air to shimmer with dark energy. "This makes no sense. I will repeat this only one time, Ossian. How could this Medb warrior have known how to locate Phoedra?"

Swallowing hard, Ossian said, "I'm guessing Cathbad has been looking for me, which I did warn you he would do. Logically, he would send one or more Scáth Force warriors to find me. Once Cathbad revealed where I normally reside in this world, the warriors would have found my computer." He'd been proud of using the accelerated learning ability Cathbad had bestowed on him to become proficient in all electronics. "If that happened and the Scáth Force discovered my user ID they would have had access to the darknet history and could have begun tracking my movements through the features in my phone. They would have been privy to messages I exchanged with those hunting Phoedra."

"User ID?"

"Sorry. I forget you're a Luddite."

Veronika tensed and Ossian felt power rush past him to her. She was loading herself, probably through her connection to her ancestors.

That could be very bad. "Have I said something you question, my queen?" he asked.

"Do you dare to curse me, Ossian?"

Ah! "Uh, no, I would never do such a thing. A Luddite is someone not familiar with technology. I can't help what I say. Cathbad's majik forces me to tell the truth to him. Evidently, that now extends to you as I am under your control."

She relaxed and leaned back, but in a pensive mood. "Do not use that term again. I don't like it."

"Absolutely, my queen." Ossian rushed ahead to say, "The Scáth Force warrior did relay a brief message for you that he was taking Phoedra, but that the Medb intend to return her as part of a deal with you."

Her lips parted in disbelief. "Now they expect me to trade in good faith? That druid and queen should suffer having their eyes dug from the sockets with a rusty spoon." She slapped the arm of her throne. "Is there no honor any more among preternaturals? I will forgive no one for stealing what is mine."

He wouldn't respond to that even if he stood behind an impenetrable wall.

She wanted respect from the rest of the nonhuman community?

Ossian had to move her away from dwelling on his loss of Phoedra and onto the potential for gaining what she wanted.

And if Cathbad could pull a miracle out of his bag of tricks he could save Ossian from this wacked-out witch.

Ossian began, "My queen, this may turn out quite well. I do believe the Medb want a partnership with you, which would explain their bold act." He added a little something to bring her around to his way of thinking. "In fact, grabbing Phoedra to use in trade clearly shows how you intimidate Cathbad and Queen Maeve."

Veronika cocked her head with interest. She no longer appeared ready to dispose of him. "Go on."

Ossian had struck a positive note by embellishing to stroke her ego. "The Medb warrior said that his superior wished to meet with you at midnight tonight." Ossian explained the location, which was south of the city and used for an annual Renaissance Festival.

"What about the humans? I want no more interference."

Ossian said, "I have no doubt that Cathbad will guarantee a protected area as neither he nor Queen Maeve wish to be found in the human realm at the moment. Queen Maeve insulted the deities at a Tribunal meeting and they have barred the Medb leaders from returning here. I do believe the Medb witches and warlocks would have been sent home if Sen had spoken up, but he enjoys irritating the Beladors. I believe I can say for sure that Cathbad will control the area where we meet."

"What do he and Maeve want in exchange for the girl?"

"I was not given that information. The Medb warrior literally rattled off the terms and departed immediately, probably teleported again by Cathbad or the queen. Even so, it would be unusual for the Medb queen to share any details. She would never trust a warrior with the terms of an important negotiation."

Veronika remained still while she processed everything. Slashing a suspicious look at Ossian, she said, "You are a product of Cathbad and Queen Maeve's machinations, so what do *you* think they want in trade?"

Ossian bristled at being considered one of the many faceless warriors for the Medb. "To be specific, I am an entirely unique creation by Cathbad. With that said, I can only tell you what I believe would be their aspirations. I'm thinking that prior to your wiping the planet clean of beings with power and turning their minions into your slaves, that the queen and Cathbad will wish to form a pact with you to protect them and their Medb warriors. Think about it. You would end up with Phoedra, from whom you could mine power, plus gain a powerful group as ally."

"Very well, we will meet, but not entirely on their terms."

Ossian's moment of excitement dampened. He had no idea what Veronika would do, but if he had to wager on her approach to the meeting, he'd say she was stacking a heavy defensive force in her favor.

Technically, he was wagering with his life as the ante.

CHAPTER 28

One moment Quinn stood next to Reese in front of the Keith, and in the next, he lost all sense of time and place.

Everything came back into focus suddenly.

Quinn realized he was on a roof in the dark. Thankfully, Reese had landed next to him. He asked, "Are you okay?"

Her hair flew around her face in the night wind. "I'll live, but I don't want to do *that* again."

"I believe the Keith sent us through a bolthole. I say that because it felt like an amusement ride that had jumped the tracks. We certainly didn't have any control over it."

"Got it. Where are we?" She tucked the filmy, dark-blue shawl around her shoulders against the cool air moving briskly around them.

"Give me a minute." He stepped past a heating and air structure mounted on the roof to take in the city. "It appears we're in downtown Atlanta."

"How are we going to find Phoedra from here?"

"This is actually a good place to end up. I have resources available with one telepathic call." Reaching for her hand, he asked, "Do you still have the medallion?"

"Yes." She opened her fist to show him.

Quinn took the necklace and hooked it around her neck. He wanted her capable of defending herself.

"What are we going to do, Quinn? How are we going to get Phoedra back from the Medb?"

"I have an idea, but it needs a little work."

She pulled him around to face her. "I hate that sound in your voice."

"What sound?"

"The sound of pulling back from me and everyone else to do something all by yourself. I'm here. The Beladors are here. You've got a freakin' dragon."

"And even with all of that muscle and power, I can't get to Phoedra in TÅµr Medb without incurring major casualties, even if we could insert while the queen and Cathbad are there. Both were away when our people broke into their tower to rescue Daegan. I feel certain Cathbad and Queen Maeve will have better security in place this time."

She tightened her grip on his arm. "Just don't leave me behind."

He didn't say a thing.

"Damn you, Quinn. I can't take being left in the dark on this. I want to know what you have in mind."

Would she be ready to meet him halfway? "Can you swear to me you won't vanish into thin air at some point?"

Guilt spread across her face. "I told you I'm going to do my best."

That sank a rock deep in his gut. He'd thought after they shared such intimacy that he'd get an absolute yes this time.

Who held power over Reese and why wouldn't she let him help her break that hold?

He wanted time with Reese. He cherished the gift she'd given by sharing her body with him in the Keith's realm, but he wanted more than sex from this woman.

He wanted her trust.

This connection he felt with Reese ... he couldn't explain it, only that it was new and special. Something that deserved nurturing. He needed time with this woman to show her that he was not like the person who had hurt her so deeply in the past.

He'd come to realize someone had damaged her emotionally, so badly that she feared getting attached.

She already cared for him. It was obvious.

She just needed to open her eyes and heart to see that he cared for her as well.

No, it was his job to show her he cared.

If his idea for rescuing Phoedra went sideways, he'd never

have a chance at more with Reese or his daughter.

But if he died gaining Phoedra's freedom, he knew she'd always have Reese watching over her as well as his Belador clan. All of that depended on Reese staying alive.

"We're at a draw," he said to ease the tense moment, but he was not about to give in all the way. "In answer to your question, I will do my best to keep you informed of my plans. Now, give me a minute to reach out to Evalle."

Reese tossed him an uncompromising glance and turned away.

Perhaps that was just as well.

He dreaded putting Reese in further danger. When she discovered his plans, she would not be happy with him. First he had to make sure Reese would be safe once he took a step he couldn't undo.

A step that might destroy his relationship with Daegan.

Regardless, Quinn intended to do his best to protect Daegan and the Beladors right along with those he loved.

He would prefer to include Daegan, but if the dragon king knew what Quinn intended to do he would not stand by and allow it.

That meant not informing Tzader or Evalle either.

Both of them would jump in with Quinn and lose all that they had gained.

No, this was his fight, and his sacrifice, if it ended badly. Phoedra was his responsibility and he was going to give her a chance at life.

Reese was his responsibility, too, even if she fought his attempts to help her at every turn.

After reaching out to Evalle telepathically and determining she could pick them up a short distance away at Woodruff Park, he walked Reese downstairs and onto the sidewalk.

After crossing two streets, they reached the park at an area known as Five Points, due to five roads coming together in one central downtown spot. The digital clock on the iconic Coca-Cola sign blinked with a temperature of sixty-three, and the time, just after two in the morning. Few people moved along the sidewalks this time of night, and exhaust from earlier traffic hung in the humid air.

If not for the dire situation, he could imagine strolling along the quiet sidewalk with Reese after a night on the town.

Normal people lived that way. He should try it sometime.

Reese said, "Gibbons would like this park."

"Who is that?"

"My mutt. He loves to play Frisbee."

"Then you should take him to Piedmont Park on a nice day. That's where everyone in the city goes."

"Uhm hmm." She walked along, silent now.

He hated when she shut down. His beautiful perpetual ball of energy was normally ready to take action and give her opinion, whether he asked for it or not.

He wouldn't want her any other way.

The fact that he might not see her again after this gnawed his insides. When he thought about how she'd helped him save Kizira's body from Queen Maeve weeks ago, then rushed to rescue Phoedra now, he struggled for the words he owed her.

In the end, he said, "Thank you, Reese, for everything. You have been amazing through all of this and you'll never know how much I appreciate your being Phoedra's friend."

She cursed and flashed him her signature you're-gonna-get-an-earful glare. "That sounds like a goodbye talk. Really, Quinn?"

He should have known better than to think he could keep this simple. "No, but things are going to get complicated quickly. With so many people around once Evalle picks us up, we won't have a chance to talk privately. I'm not saying goodbye, but I am making sure that if anything happens to me that you know how much I appreciate all you've done for Phoedra and for me. I also want you to know that you're important to me, but if something goes awry while gaining Phoedra's freedom, I hope you'll continue to watch over her so she isn't alone."

Quinn realized he'd walked two steps alone.

He turned to find out why Reese had stopped.

She was a vision, standing there with the dark, gauzy wrap poofed out around her and waves of coppery-brown hair flowing to her shoulders. Perfect full lips were set in an unhappy shape as she considered him, and fire filled those dazzling eyes that saw too much.

He should thank her for the breathtaking image burned into his mind. He would take it to his death.

"Don't make me hurt you, Quinn."

What a woman, full of piss and vinegar.

He should never have allowed himself the freedom to make love with her when he had no idea what tomorrow would bring, but he refused to regret one second of feeling her next to him and loving her for those hours.

Damn his soul, he wanted her again. He had a feeling that wouldn't change even if he had a lifetime to test it.

She paced forward and gripped his lapels, which was becoming her go-to action when he annoyed her. Probably her way of evening the difference in height between them when she wanted to get a point across.

She tugged him down until their noses almost touched, hesitating a half-beat before she kissed him.

His world flipped all over the place when they touched. He drove his hands into her hair, pulling her deeper into the kiss. Heat burned everywhere they touched and his body demanded he take her up on her offer.

When she released him, she warned, "If you go off on your own without me to back you up, I will make you sorry you were born."

No half measure with her. "That's a hard offer to resist."

"You are so infuriating."

"I know the feeling," he chided, smiling at her.

An old Land Cruiser pulled up with the passenger window down. "Hey, you two. Want to ride?" Evalle called out.

Reese jumped back, but Quinn caught her to him, warning, "Please do what I ask for any hope of us seeing each other again."

Her fire melted under that request. "Damn you, Quinn. You better not get yourself killed."

"I'll do my best to fulfill that directive."

"You're hot even when you sound like you have a stick up your backside."

"Dollar waiting on a dime, guys," Evalle called out, giving Quinn a narrowed look that promised an interrogation.

Kickass women might just be his downfall.

At Evalle and Storm's building, he, Reese, and Evalle met in the conference room.

Quinn waited for the ladies to take seats, then started the conversation. "First, I want you to know that we can speak freely around Reese. She's earned my trust and is the reason I even know where Phoedra is at the moment."

Evalle cut her gaze at Reese first then to Quinn and asked, "Where is she?"

"The Medb have her, but someone I believe is working with Veronika actually brokered the initial kidnapping."

Sitting back with a hand over her eyes, Evalle groaned. "We failed."

"Not necessarily," Quinn said. "I'll explain more on that in a moment. First, what's going on with the Beladors?"

"Daegan is running teams around the clock to track down families," Evalle said, placing her hands on the table in front of her. "I'm here only because I was on the way by our building to drop off my bike and pick up Storm's truck. Storm's tracking a troll who he thinks has kidnapped a human teen belonging to a Belador. Storm wanted a way to transport any victims because we sometimes find other humans and can't keep calling Daegan to teleport everyone. Tristan is blown out from teleporting warriors to different locations to save time."

Hearing how stretched Daegan and the Beladors were with looking for families that had been taken, Quinn silently acknowledged he was on his own with his plan. "I'm sorry I haven't been here to help, but—"

"No one expects you to be here, Quinn. Not until Phoedra is safe."

"Thank you. But I do think now that Reese and I are here, we can help."

Evalle gave him thumbs up. "Awesome."

Reese sent him a sharp look, but didn't start arguing. That was a refreshing change.

"Where does VIPER stand on all this right now?" Quinn asked.

Scoffing first, Evalle said, "After Sen blew off helping Beladors and Daegan declared the rule of cosaint, we've had very little contact with VIPER. Daegan got really pissed when he found out Veronika had escaped. By the way, she's still on the loose. As soon as warriors come off VIPER duty, Daegan puts them to either protecting their families or helping hunt down the missing teenagers. Due to that, VIPER brought in a load of bounty hunters, which hasn't turned out to be as simple as having Belador warriors."

"That's not surprising," Quinn commented.

Evalle nodded and continued. "I spoke to one of the warriors who just came off duty at VIPER and he said Sen may not admit it, but VIPER is in trouble. Trolls who are not involved with the kidnappings are filing complaints over attacks. Medb witches and warlocks are filing complaints of being persecuted. Everyone is a victim and everyone is a potential suspect. *Oh!* And we were almost exposed to humans twice in the last three hours, but Sen managed to fix it."

"That wanker Sen deserves the bloody headache he's suffering, but I am glad he did something right. Having our world exposed to humans would be an unimaginable crisis." Everything Quinn had heard so far reinforced his plan, which he hoped would also aid the Beladors. "Time is clearly of the essence. I don't wish to hold you up so I'll get to the point. I have an idea for how to get Phoedra back."

"Yes." Evalle fist pumped.

Reese didn't weigh in. Suspicion peeked out of her eyes.

"I am going to speak with the Tribunal to—"

"*No!*" echoed in the room from Evalle and Reese shouting.

"Hear me out," he snapped at his grumbling audience. "I believe from all you're telling me that the Tribunal would be open to negotiation. If they aid us in getting Phoedra back then we'll help them recapture Veronika."

"Huh. That would do it if the Tribunal could pull off their part," Evalle mused. "How are we going to capture Veronika, though? Daegan took Adrianna to Treoir to prevent Veronika being able to access her and so that Adrianna could work with Garwyli. That also helps protect Beladors and Phoedra from that wacko."

"I will offer only our *assistance* in trade, not guarantee that we will be the ones to capture Veronika," Quinn clarified. "She is too powerful for anyone to boast of a single-handed capture.

We stand to lose lives just by being involved with confronting her, though."

"True, but when Daegan finds out Veronika's role in Phoedra being captured and the Medb now having her, he'll definitely be all in. He's serious about keeping Phoedra away from both groups."

"I realize that, but I don't think we should interfere with what he's doing right now. I'll have more to tell him once I go to the Tribunal." Quinn hoped once he entered, he'd be able to leave again and with an agreement. This would test his negotiating skills. He explained, "We must assure two things no matter what, Evalle. One is that Phoedra is freed safely, and two is that we protect our dragon king at all costs. He is the future. Without him, it will be a *dark* future for the Beladors."

She stood. "Agreed. What else?"

"I would like to ask Reese to use her remote viewing gift to aid in locating the missing children."

Reese rose. "No. I want to go with you as backup."

"The Tribunal will not allow you to join me, and even if they would, VIPER doesn't know you exist. Show your face there and you'll be subject to their rule. I won't allow you to put yourself in that position."

Evalle added, "He's right, Reese. And if he trusts you, then I do. We need any help we can get. We've lost twelve children as of earlier tonight. It could be more by now. The Medb have managed to hit at the heart of the Beladors."

Clearly torn and disappointed, Reese nodded. "I'm going to need some clothes."

Giving Reese a long perusal, Evalle said, "I wondered about the party outfits."

Quinn said, "Trust me when I tell you that neither of us chose these clothes or wished to have been where they were foisted upon us, but that's how we found a lead on Phoedra."

"Ah! That sounds like a good story when we finally get a chance to breathe and catch up over wine." Evalle had recently tried wine for the first time, thanks to Storm, and only because she trusted him enough to let her guard down. She walked to the door, telling Reese, "Come up to the fourth level when you're ready. I'll find something you can wear even if we have to roll up sleeves and cuffs."

"I'll be there in a moment," Reese replied.

Once Evalle's footsteps thumped away up the steps, Reese walked over to Quinn. "Foisted? Where do you get these words?"

"Me? You never fail to surprise me with the things you say."

"We all have our gifts, Quinn. Mine is being annoying."

"Something I do love about you," he admitted.

Her eyes softened, pushing away the cockiness. She said, "This plan of yours is what you call doing your best not to leave me?"

"I said I'd do my best to keep you informed, which I have. I have only one move in all this and it must happen quickly. Please help the Beladors. They are a loyal lot who will not forget any aid. It would gain you ally status for as long as you never cross them."

"One of these days, you're going to have to stop taking care of everyone else, Quinn, and do something for you."

He had stolen a moment for himself back in the Keith's realm. "I'm doing it right now. I'm a selfish bastard who wants you and Phoedra to be safe, and I won't accept anything less." He leaned down and kissed her sweetly. "Remember what I asked you to do."

She tugged on his tux lapels, but gently this time. "Don't make me have to tell Phoedra that both of her parents are dead."

He could not make that promise, so he kissed her again and walked out. He was still the Belador Maistir of North America, which gave him the authority to contact Sen.

Once he was two blocks from Evalle's home, Quinn sent out a telepathic call to the liaison. He'd risk using telepathy to locate Sen immediately.

Power slapped the air when Sen arrived in person, snarling, "What the fuck do you want, Belador?"

"A Tribunal meeting."

"This is your lucky day. VIPER is pissed and the Tribunal is in a rare mood. I can't wait to drop your tuxedoed ass in there."

Quinn kept his eyes open, prepared to watch as Atlanta spun out of view for the last time.

CHAPTER 29

In Cathbad's private quarters of TÅµr Medb

Cathbad had never spent a lot of time around children, but he found Phoedra interesting. He could feel power seeping out of her, but he had no idea how much or what form it would take.

She might prove to be a more intriguing experiment than Ossian now that he'd shielded his mind from her random zaps of power.

She didn't even know she was affecting anyone.

Oh, yes, this one would be special.

He could compel her to answer his questions, but he'd rather leave that as his last option. He'd much rather hear her uninfluenced answers.

Phoedra sat across from him at a table covered with succulent meat, fresh fruit and enticing vegetables.

He'd warded this area of TÅµr Medb to prevent the queen from showing up whenever she chose. She might like all that traffic through her personal quarters, but he did not.

Phoedra cast a stony look his way. "What is this place?"

"It's a safe house of sorts." He'd gleaned that term from his visits to the human world and thought it might sound familiar to her. He admired the way she'd handled the strange things happening to this point, but his Scáth Force warrior had said she'd been in an enclosed vehicle, so she probably hadn't seen a lot of preternatural activity during her travels.

There was no reason to upset her, but he couldn't imagine possessing power and not realizing it on some level. Still, finding out she was not sitting in the human realm she'd lived in since birth would likely cause her distress.

Did she know yet that she was different from mere humans?

"How'd I get here?" she asked, face glum.

"My assistant brought you to me."

"Is he a cop?"

Cathbad found that amusing. "More of a special operative."

"Did he drug me? I don't remember how I got here."

"No. Do you feel drugged?"

"Not really." She continued to stew while her gaze flitted around the room fashioned for fine dining with furniture from the early eighteen hundreds of the human world. Candles gently lit the space from eight different spots. He could snap his fingers and replace it all with modern implements, but this was where he felt most at home.

Sounding defeated, she asked in a small voice, "Are you going to kill me?"

"Killing you would be a terrible way to start a friendship."

She rolled her eyes. "Well, no one is going to pay a lot of money to get me back."

Did she really not know her value?

Her stomach growled for the third time since she'd become lucid again, but she had yet to drink the water or touch the food he'd arranged to have ready for her.

Avoiding his face this time, she asked, "What *are* you going to do to me?"

She feared him.

He knew it without asking her, but she kept her fear hidden fairly well. Of course, he'd been doing everything he could to make her relax.

Smiling with a splash of majik to up his charm, he said, "I have nothing bad planned for you."

Phoedra looked surprised for a moment, then recovered. "Why should I believe you?"

"Why shouldn't you?"

Her face scrunched up with confusion. "Because I believed that jerk, Joey, who was some kind of *thing*. His weird friends helped him kidnap me. I don't know who to trust now." Her eyes filled with water, but she sniffed hard and fought against crying.

Cathbad would pay a king's war chest of gold if she managed not to turn on the waterworks.

He had caught her reference to Joey being a *thing*, which meant she at least suspected everyone was not entirely human.

He kept his voice in a soft, grandfatherly tone. "You are correct to question all of this, because it is unusual. That doesn't necessarily mean you're in a bad place. You're not. I will keep you safe. You're far better off with me than the person who sent Ossian to retrieve you."

"That freak? He ... he ... his face *changed*. That was crazy stuff. I don't think he could control it. He got upset when Turbo pointed out his head wasn't on tight. Ick. Made me sick to look at him."

Cathbad took offense at any criticism of Ossian, who had been a work of art before Veronika got her claws into him. Oh, yes, he had figured out what happened to Ossian. When Cathbad could not reach him telepathically, he put every Scáth Force warrior on tracking Ossian, which resulted in getting answers from his polymorph's computer.

The odd thing was that Ossian hadn't protected access to his computer. In fact, he'd left an interesting note about this child's mother.

Had he gone there after Veronika got her hands on him and left his electronic security weak so that someone would discover his activities? Quite possible since Ossian had to know Cathbad would come for him.

Cathbad regretted not developing Ossian further to the point of giving the polymorph teleportation ability. If he had, Ossian might have escaped the witch.

On the other hand, Veronika would have taken advantage of that power, which would have given her unlimited possibilities for moving around. She'd have escaped before anyone could have locked her up, and Cathbad would have missed the chance to nab Phoedra.

But she did have a way to shield Ossian from Cathbad when Ossian returned to Atlanta.

For now, only for now.

There would be time to deal with finding Ossian. At the

moment, Cathbad had a majikal prodigy to study and develop.

He explained to Phoedra, "If my man had not intervened when he did, you would have been handed over to an insane woman instead of sitting here, having a peaceful dinner." When Phoedra's stomach grumbled yet again, Cathbad said, "Please eat. You are hungry, right?"

She stared with heavy suspicion at the perfectly prepared steak.

Giving her a sigh worthy of any disgruntled father, he lifted a fork and knife. After slicing a piece of steak, he ate that bite, then stabbed a broccoli floret and consumed it, too.

After swallowing, he said, "I will test the rest of this if you're still concerned about being poisoned or drugged. It's very good. I have an excellent chef and I would not go to this much trouble if I wanted to harm you."

"Guess you have a point." Making a sound of frustration the young had perfected over centuries, she started eating. After the first bite, her face gave away how much she enjoyed it.

Finally, she might be more open to chatting. "Now, let's talk so we can get to know each other, Phoedra."

"I want to go home."

"I understand that and perhaps we can work something out."

That got her attention. "Really?"

Lying had always come easily to Cathbad. "Of course. I'm not an ogre."

"Who are you?"

"My name is Cathbad."

Another scrunched up look. "What kind of name is that?"

The young in this era had no manners. "The only one you need at the moment."

Putting her fork down and wiping her mouth on the cloth napkin, she said, "What I want to know is, why did you send someone for me? Who are you to me?"

"I will explain that, but not right this second. Just know that I am the only person who can protect you from some very dangerous and powerful people." He watched her face as that sank in.

"You mean those weird guys?"

That opened the door for him to test just how much she knew

about the preternaturals. "That is exactly who I'm talking about. By the way, have you experienced anything unusual recently?"

Phoedra had started eating a six-layer parfait. She paused with a bite halfway to her mouth. "What do you mean?"

"Like a supernatural ability or gift?"

She shrugged, and that action alone told him something. If she had not experienced powers, she would probably have said something tart or condescending.

Interesting. She truly didn't know?

Cathbad lifted a handful of nuts, munched on them, then took a drink of his wine. "Let's talk about something else first. Do you know anything about your mother or father?"

"No." The word had slipped out on a sullen note.

"Who raised you?"

"My foster mother, Donella. She said she doesn't know anything about my background other than I was handed to her as an infant. She was surprised when no one adopted me."

"I see." Cathbad kept casually snacking on nuts. Donella could not be human. Human babies were adopted quickly, especially a beautiful infant, and this child would have been one. No, this girl had been shielded from anyone with powers.

He hadn't believed Ossian's computer notation about Phoedra's mother being a Medb, but it all made sense now. Kizira was Phoedra's mother. His mind gathered pieces of the puzzle, adding to it the image of the Belador known as Quinn holding Kizira as she died.

The queen would kill to know what Cathbad had discovered. She should not have crossed him.

He allowed a pleasant silence to drift along until Phoedra felt the need to speak.

Staring at her food, she asked, "What would an ability feel like?"

There it was—that sound of curiosity rising up and forcing her to ask a question she had probably been keeping to herself. "Have you felt anything unusual that you can't explain, Phoedra?"

She didn't answer while she finished eating. Once she put her fork down, she murmured, "You'll think I'm a freak."

"No, child. On the contrary. I would never think that, because

I possess gifts and abilities. I've also known gifted people my entire life and feel certain you are one of a special breed."

For the first time, she looked at him as something other than a kidnapper. "Really? What kind of abilities? Show me."

He considered all the things he could show her and realized small would work best. Anything large might destroy this fragile moment of building trust.

Pointing at the fork in her hand, he said, "Allow me." Using his kinetic ability carefully, he moved the fork out of her hand and dished up a small piece of cake that he floated back up to her lips.

Her eyes got so large they threatened to pop out of the sockets. She whispered, "No way."

He waited for her to eat the dessert. "You may take the fork back. It won't bite you."

She tentatively reached for the utensil. When she grasped it, she lifted the utensil up and down a couple of times, then placed it on the plate.

Fearful at first, she sat there staring at the fork as if trying to decide what had happened. Then she started grinning. "I'm not a freak?"

What fool had told her that? "Of course, you're not. You belong to a very special group of beings."

"Beings?" Now she was back to sounding wary.

"Yes. Human beings," he corrected for her benefit.

"Oh. Got it. So it's normal for me to have premonitions?"

"Absolutely. How do you think I was able to find you? I was given a vision of you in that location." Not really, but she loved hearing that additional confirmation.

Cathbad's own ability with true foresight was unreliable, but until Veronika had messed with Ossian, Cathbad had been able to view through Ossian's eyes when he chose. Still, it took a great deal of power from him and the polymorph so he avoided it most of the time. He'd tried, though, after Ossian had dropped out of his reach. Cathbad had tried every way to locate him before turning to his backup plan and sending out the Scáth Force.

Phoedra was probably just gaining her ability to see into the future, which Kizira had been able to do according to what he'd heard about the deceased priestess. TÅμr Medb occupants who had known Kizira claimed her visions were never wrong.

Offering Phoedra a smile of camaraderie, Cathbad said, "Having visions or premonitions is more common in females."

"Ugh." She lifted both hands as if a rat had run across the table in front of her, which hadn't been the case at all. She had a dramatic way with her hands.

She said, "Please don't make this about being hormonal."

Cathbad chuckled out loud. He couldn't recall the last time someone had given him a true reason to laugh. This one would be a delight to train.

"No, I'm talking about genetics and lineage," he explained. "Clairvoyants tend to inherit that gift from their mothers."

"You think my mom could do this?"

"Yes." Cathbad snapped his fingers. Servants dressed in white tunics and pants trimmed in gold and black entered from a door at the end of the room and cleared the table, leaving their drinks.

Once that was out of the way, Cathbad suggested, "Tell me what you've seen and I'll help you figure out what it means."

She said, "I've had these, uh, weird images. In one, this big flying beast is attacking a woman."

That could be a vision of what happened to her mother, but Cathbad did not want to influence Phoedra so he just let her talk.

"I know that's too crazy to understand, so just forget about that one. The other dream or vision or whatever it is I keep having is about a red dragon fighting a bunch of people, but I can only see it with blurry edges. Some amped-up woman throws a laser or something bright at the dragon. They fight and he falls from the sky. Hits the ground like a ton of bricks."

Cathbad couldn't contain his excitement. "Does she kill the dragon?"

Phoedra turned glum. "I think so. I don't remember past that point when he was on the ground not moving. It makes me feel bad."

"Why?"

She looked at him as though he were a dunce. "He was this big, beautiful red dragon. I mean, dreams have meanings, right? So what could it mean if I see a dragon die in my vision?"

Cathbad sat back. It meant she'd seen the end of the Treoir

dragon king.

This child would bring Cathbad even more joy once he had groomed her to be a lethal weapon against all others.

CHAPTER 30

Tribunal meeting, Nether Realm

Quinn wasn't surprised when Loki appeared at this Tribunal. The unpredictable Norse god lived to meddle and toy with those beneath him, which Loki considered to be everyone with the exception of Odin.

If Loki were foolish enough to flaunt his arrogance to Odin, it would happen only once.

Loki could shift his entire physical self to appear as someone else, but all the deities observed a certain protocol within a Tribunal. That was only because they had instituted the protocol, though, and not out of deference to those who faced their judgment.

Quinn stood in the middle of a plane of ankle-deep grass, which wafted back and forth softly in a nonexistent wind. The area spread out in a large circle more than a hundred yards wide, with edges that vanished into darkness. Stars played overhead. This Nether realm might appear completely different next time, as it took whatever form the deities chose.

Straight ahead of Quinn, a raised dais floated above the ground, intended as a stage for a mix of three gods and/or goddesses.

At the moment, Loki reminded Quinn of a male runway model in a dark Armani suit, cream-colored shirt with the collar open and his hair in a contemporary cut. Quinn suspected Loki's formal clothing had happened instantaneously the minute the god of mischief arrived to find Quinn wearing a tux.

He doubted Loki did that for his benefit, but Quinn was actually glad to see someone else dressed for after-hours.

In the next blink, the Polynesian goddess Pele appeared on Loki's left. Midnight-black hair spilled across porcelain-white shoulders, left bare for this meeting. Her gown swept to ankle-length in a mash of silver and gold thread. Thin straps of her sandals wrapped her ankles and disappeared under the hem of the gown.

She wore her temper on display as blatantly as her beauty, with no apology.

To Loki's right, Justitia also took corporeal form. How apropos to have the goddess of justice for this Tribunal meeting, but that didn't mean the scales would weigh in Quinn's favor.

Where Pele's beauty boasted an exotic appeal, Justitia's attraction came from her moral strength as well as her physical attributes. Even in an ordinary gray gown that hid her feet, she would draw plenty of male attention in a room filled with beauties. Her golden blindfold fooled no one. She carried an ornate set of scales with her, reminding the world she would see justice done.

Quinn opened the meeting with a bold statement in hopes of gaining the attention—and support—of the Tribunal trio quickly.

"Veronika is free and gaining power. If she joins with the Medb, we may lose the human world to them. Once that is gone, your followings will disintegrate. There's a certain balance to a world where each of you has followers. If we allow that balance to be disrupted, first chaos reigns, then the power that gobbles it all up will continue until she finds a way to reach even deities hidden in their home realms."

None of those on the raised dais said a word, but each stiffened at the threat to existence. Evidently, Sen finally informed them.

Quinn added, "Daegan and the Beladors did not abandon VIPER."

Sen scoffed loudly and the three deities murmured words in disgusted tones, which Quinn could not hear.

He pressed on. "It's true. Daegan wants to support the coalition, but the coalition let him and the Beladors down when the Medb began stealing Belador children and VIPER refused to lend us aid. Innocent human children in all cases. We took a vow to protect humans. That means those related to our own people as well."

Loki walked across the dais with his hands clasped behind him, the picture of a being in deep thought. When he returned to center stage, he asked, "We have yet to see Beladors returning to the VIPER force. Why have you requested this meeting?"

The fact that Loki had not blasted Quinn out of the room said a great deal about their concern over Veronika and VIPER's lost resources.

"When VIPER refused to help us ... " Quinn paused to cast a hard look in Sen's direction before finishing. "We had no choice but to take care of our own first. While doing that, we discovered that the Medb have taken possession of not just a Belador child, but one whose powers are anticipated to be beyond estimation at this point." Quinn wasn't positive that was true about Phoedra, but it was a real concern and there was no evidence to the contrary, so his statement stood as truth.

If not, his body would have glowed red, the Tribunal's form of lie detection.

He continued, "This thirteen-year-old girl has no idea that she even possesses gifts or abilities, so you can imagine how she could be molded into something extremely powerful who could do great things or ... be an incredible destructive force. Veronika originally located the girl, but the Medb stole her away."

This time Loki glared at Sen, who maintained a stoic face.

Quinn wanted to move this along. He reminded the room, "I witnessed Queen Maeve's breakdown during my last visit here. I don't believe she can be reasoned with, which means our best hope is Cathbad. Considering how Cathbad and Queen Maeve's powers have not been truly tested since they reincarnated, we have no barometer for their joint abilities. Add to that a dynamic Belador prodigy plus a wrecking ball known as Veronika and ... that should paint a clear picture for our total annihilation if they join forces."

Grim silence fell across the realm.

Even Sen held his usually biting tongue. Daegan had exposed Sen as a demigod, which meant it would have taken a god to force Sen into the position of VIPER liaison, which he despised, but which pantheon had placed him here?

If Veronika gained control and Sen had no realm to hide in, she would mow him down as well ... or make him an offer to join her.

Pele asked, "What of the Sterling witch who now possesses Witchlock?"

Quinn explained, "Adrianna may one day become our greatest defensive unit, but she has not had time to fully explore that power. After Veronika escaped, Adrianna experienced episodes of power issues she attributed to Veronika's attempts to access the Witchlock power, so we placed Adrianna in a secure location."

"Where?"

He was not about to tell them the dragon took her to Treoir. "I'm not at liberty to divulge that to anyone."

Had he not caught their attention with a viable threat to their existence, they would likely have tortured the answer out of him. Refusing them had been a calculated risk, but an educated one.

They needed allies.

Loki turned first to Pele and next to Justitia, whispering with each goddess. When he faced Quinn again, he said, "You clearly came here with a plan of some sort. We are open to hearing what you have in mind."

That was the first step toward cooperation Quinn needed. Quinn said, "What I have in mind will require inviting Cathbad to this Tribunal, but he may hesitate to return after having walked away from VIPER under threat of reprisal due to Queen Maeve's loss of control during her last meeting here."

After another heavy silence, Loki nodded. "I'll call in Cathbad now and give him assurance that he is safe from any repercussion regarding his last visit."

That immediate agreement was an indisputable sign of the deities' trepidation over Veronika and the Medb joining forces, even if these deities would never admit as much.

A moment later, Cathbad's body shimmered into solid form. He took in everyone, pausing the longest on Quinn, then asked Loki, "Why have you asked me here?"

Loki said, "The Belador Maistir has told us what he believes is underway between the Medb and Veronika. We wish to hear both sides."

Look at Loki, being Mr. Diplomatic.

Quinn told Cathbad, "I know you have Phoedra. Is she unharmed?"

Cathbad didn't appear surprised by the accusation or the question when he admitted, "At the moment, yes."

"You must realize that Queen Maeve is not entirely sane and should be kept away from Phoedra."

Cathbad gave nothing away in his bland expression. "What I do with her is my concern."

"No, it is *mine*," Quinn made very clear. "If Phoedra is harmed, there is nowhere in this universe you can hide."

"Save your threats, Belador. The child is in my care only and perfectly content at the moment, though a bit confused by all this majik and teleporting. You should not have left your child so naïve, Quinn."

All eyes turned to Quinn in accusation.

Yes, he'd withheld that Phoedra was his child, but he had not lied. If the deities wanted to know, they should have asked.

"What do you want?" Cathbad asked conversationally.

Before Quinn got to his request, he wanted to state some things here so that everyone was up to speed. "As I understand it, the Medb are kidnapping other Belador children who are human."

Cathbad hesitated, then his forehead creased in a confused expression. "What? I know nothing about kidnappings."

The druid didn't glow red.

Well, hell. Quinn wanted this very clear. "So you don't know about Queen Maeve's witches and warlocks using trolls to capture children of Belador families in exchange for Noirre majik?"

Taking his time to answer, Cathbad said, "I knew she was stirring up trouble in the human realm, but I am not a party to *her* kidnappings."

As if that exonerated him because he'd stolen only one child?

Loki asked Quinn, "Why does this matter?"

"Because in order to stop Veronika from turning every being into a slave and wiping out anyone with power who she cannot enslave, you all need the dragon king to bring Belador forces to this fight." Directing his comment at Cathbad, Quinn said, "Daegan is furious that children have been taken. He will hunt the kidnappers to the ends of earth and beyond to return the children and make the guilty pay. If those children are returned unharmed, I believe he could be convinced to partner with a coalition force to defeat Veronika."

When Cathbad made no comment about Veronika, Quinn went for the jugular, but this time he took a different tactic since it appeared the queen was operating autonomously. "Is it true that Queen Maeve sent someone called Ossian to broker a deal between the Medb and Veronika?"

Finally, Quinn had surprised Cathbad, but that would not work in his favor if Cathbad didn't know about the deal with Veronika.

Loki turned to Cathbad. "You have been given amnesty from your queen's antagonistic action here last time, but you are now answering for yourself."

"I understand," Cathbad said, regaining his stern composure. "Yes, the queen did send an emissary to Veronika with the express intent of creating an alliance."

Quinn missed something. Cathbad hadn't been surprised about Veronika, so what part of his accusation had Cathbad not expected?

Loki unleashed his anger on Cathbad. "What are you thinking, druid, to partner with a witch who has made it perfectly clear she wants to destroy all of us? Do you really believe we'll allow you and the queen to form that type of union without sending the best we have after you?"

Holding up a hand, Cathbad calmly pointed out, "I did not say *I* was trying to do that, only that I know Queen Maeve desires such an agreement."

There was the opportunity Quinn had been waiting for and could not allow to pass. "Cathbad, I am here to ask that the Medb cease hunting Belador families, that those kidnapped, including Phoedra, are returned and any potential partnership with Veronika terminated."

"I have no part in any of that with the exception of taking Phoedra on to raise."

Don't attack the druid. Don't attack the druid. Quinn

struggled to keep from lashing out with mind lock. This man dared to claim his daughter? He had better turn her over or they were looking at a dead druid.

Quinn said, "You are a part of the Medb and therefore guilty by association."

When no one on the dais contradicted Quinn's statement, Cathbad scratched his chin. "If I were to agree, what could you possibly give me in return to satisfy my loss?"

Your loss, you son of a bitch? Quinn would not be baited. Not when so many lives were on the line, especially a child who did not deserve to be in the middle of any of this.

Quinn said, "In return, I will voluntarily go with you, for you and the queen to do with as you choose."

That surprised even Loki, who appeared overly concerned about the offer. He asked Quinn, "That means Queen Maeve could compel you to do her bidding, even against the Beladors, once she had you in TÅµr Medb. Does Daegan know you just offered to join the Medb?"

"No. Do you think he would have agreed to my coming here if he had?"

"I don't believe you," Cathbad said.

"You have no choice, Cathbad." Quinn held his arms apart. "I am not glowing red. That is precisely why I wanted this meeting at the Tribunal. All cards on the table. No lying by either side. So, will you accept me in trade for Phoedra and the other children?" Quinn would go with Cathbad once the children were safe, but the minute he entered TÅµr Medb, he would dive into Queen Maeve's mind and she would obliterate him on the spot.

"No."

Cathbad had spoken so softly that Quinn didn't believe his ears. "What did you say?"

"No, I do not accept that agreement."

Quinn ran a hand through his hair. Hell, what was he going to do now? He cut his gaze to the dais where the trio seemed just as perplexed.

Was that druid really willing to go up against the Beladors and this Tribunal to retain Phoedra?

Quinn's palms dampened.

The Beladors and all of VIPER would go to war with the

Medb after Quinn had called out the Medb for cutting a deal with Veronika.

"Call in the dragon," Cathbad said to Loki. "I have one offer to make. If he refuses, then you will all have to make your own deals with Veronika."

CHAPTER 31

Veronika stood on tamped-down ground near wooden bleachers where she'd cloaked herself and Ossian while they waited for Cathbad to show up. She had always enjoyed being out in the night, but could do without the smell of horse dung.

She took in the painted buildings, which appeared to be an empty stage setting for an outdoor theater. "You said a Renaissance Festival is held here, Ossian? What is that?"

Ossian said, "The humans enjoy reenacting medieval life. I spent some time here this afternoon to get the lay of the land. Those who participate, and the audience, are quite authentic in dress and manner. It's very entertaining."

"I suppose." She had not enjoyed traveling through Atlanta to reach this location by dark, but soon she would rule everything. The first thing she would do is rid this city of the obnoxious traffic.

Peasants should walk.

Ossian added, "This is the middle of the week and the festival doesn't actually start for another nine days. No humans should be here after midnight. I'm sure when Cathbad arrives he'll have a protection in place."

"Did you really think I would leave that to him?"

When Ossian looked lost for an answer, she said, "I placed a spell around this arena to shield us and deter humans from coming close." She gave a lift of her shoulder. "If someone interferes, it requires little power for me to kill a human."

Where was the druid?

From everything Veronika had dragged out of Ossian about

Cathbad the Druid and Queen Maeve, she felt confident she could maintain the upper hand in this meeting.

She knew better than to trust that druid.

But she'd take this slight risk to gain Phoedra. The world would bow to her once she drained the power of a child born of a powerful Belador and a Medb priestess. Veronika had been considering the different ways to handle this discussion tonight.

Perhaps she and Cathbad could test working together at some point. She would enjoy having a man around again and from what Ossian had shared, the Medb queen was having serious issues with control over her body and powers.

Maybe this Cathbad would be looking for a change of partnership.

Were Cathbad and Queen Maeve stronger after having reincarnated, or were they the same power level as before, or weaker? If Queen Maeve was having problems physically, what had being asleep for two thousand years done to her?

Ossian said, "He approaches."

Cathbad stood alone at the opposite end of the field Ossian had told her was part of a mock jousting arena. Humans today were strange creatures.

The druid was not so strange, though, except for the cape. Dramatic, but eye-catching. She'd pictured an older man, not this attractive one somewhere around mid-to-late thirties. She would definitely entertain the idea of spending time with him.

Cathbad called out, "I know you're close by, Veronika. Show yourself. The faster we make this deal, the sooner we will both be less exposed."

She uncloaked herself and Ossian, then led the way toward the center of the open area, stopping before she reached it.

That left Cathbad forty yards away.

Ossian took his place at her right side. Her loyal servant had experienced a few malfunctions after surviving her ministrations, but overall he was turning out to be a true benefit.

Veronika said, "I am here, Cathbad, but I do not see Phoedra."

"If we strike an agreement, I will produce her."

"Very well, what do you want in exchange?"

"I want Ossian."

She looked over at Ossian, who stood rigid, showing no sign

of having heard Cathbad's demand. Just as well. He was going nowhere. "No. Ossian is mine, and to be honest, he's of no use to you or anyone other than me at this point."

Cathbad did not seem surprised by that announcement. He shrugged and said, "Then you have nothing to offer me."

Was he giving up so quickly?

The druid wouldn't last long if that was the limit of his ability to negotiate. "I have something to offer that you would be wise to consider, Cathbad."

"What is that?"

"Your life. I am willing to accept Phoedra in trade for an agreement not to kill you."

"As I understand it, you require the power of Witchlock to be a threat to one such as myself."

"Not necessarily true, but I do plan to get Witchlock back as well."

His half-hearted smile taunted her. "How do you plan to take it from the Sterling witch who wields it?"

Veronika laughed heartily. "From what I have learned, she has tapped only a small percentage of Witchlock's power. In fact, I have managed to connect with her. Now she's in hiding, but she can't escape me. Once I have the girl you promised me, I will have the weapon I need to destroy Adrianna. When that happens, you will wish you had become my ally."

"I must admit, you've piqued my interest. Perhaps you should consider the two of us working together to develop the girl. Just look at what I did on my own with Ossian."

Veronika stroked Ossian's head as though he were a pet. "He is special. I will give you that, but he is wholly mine now." She waited to see if the druid would show his anger or if he could be managed.

Cathbad walked forward with his hands in his pockets. When he was within twenty-five yards, he sighed loudly. "Ossian is a great loss to me." He allowed another few silent seconds then said, "I agree to make this trade and become allies. I only hope you can back your words or I'll be givin' up a treasure for an empty hand."

"I *will* rule this land, and once we become allies, you will be at my side. Send me the girl."

He cocked his head with a sly look in his eyes. "Meet me in the middle and I will hand her to you, witch."

Ossian said to Veronika, "He will trust me even though I am your servant."

Veronika considered his words and said to Cathbad, "Bring the girl to the middle and I will send Ossian to retrieve her."

Cathbad gave Ossian a long consideration, then nodded. He removed his cape and swirled it once. When he lowered the cloth, Phoedra stood next to him, staring straight ahead.

Veronika took in the girl's closed eyes and pale complexion. "Is she alive?"

"Very. I have her in a calm state. She's a young girl, very high-strung. I did not want her to work herself up to the point of being sick. You might have accused me of bringin' you damaged goods."

Veronika had to admit that she would have done the same.

Ossian started toward Cathbad, and when he was halfway there, Daegan stepped out from the balcony of a building to the side where a mock king and queen would view the jousting.

Daegan demanded, "I am the dragon king of Treoir. The child is of the Beladors whom I rule. You were a fool to think I would allow you to keep her. Give the girl to me and I will allow you to live, Cathbad."

Ossian turned to Veronika. "That is the dragon king I told you about."

Calling Ossian back to her, Veronika said, "If you are so powerful, dragon, why do you not teleport her away?"

Sending a sly look to both parties, Cathbad warned, "I have Phoedra tethered by my majik. It will kill her if anyone tries to take her by force."

Veronika shouted at Daegan, "You can *not* have the child. She is mine and Cathbad is my ally." Looking at the druid, she said, "Is that not so?"

Cathbad called back, "It is so if you can kill the dragon and show us all who holds the power."

"I will kill you both," Daegan declared.

"Leave, dragon king, or I will destroy you." Veronika raised her hands and called up her ancestors, who formed a mighty circle of protection around her.

As Daegan turned to Veronika, he burst from his clothes, shifting into a massive dragon with red scales and wings. He was the image of nightmares with silver reptilian eyes and jaws wide enough to bite a person in half. He opened his wings and spewed fire up into the air.

She informed her ancestors, "We must not allow this dragon to win." To Daegan, she shouted, "You will be the first to die as a statement of my power and an example of how I will slay all who challenge me."

"Challenge accepted," the dragon answered in a deep voice. Taking to the air, Daegan swooped away.

"Is he leaving?" Ossian sounded nervous.

"Hardly," Veronika replied. "He's going high to gain speed. There he comes." She shouted to her ancestors, "*Protect our family!*"

Cathbad backed up, taking Phoedra with him. She floated above the ground.

Fire burst from the dragon, blazing down across the thirty-foot-wide circle of translucent ancestors Veronika stood within.

Ossian dove to the ground, wrapping his arms around his head.

When the dragon had passed overhead, her servant stood and spoke with wonder in his voice. "We live."

"Of course we do," Veronika told him, annoyed at his lack of faith.

The dragon ran another attack pass, but when he finished blowing a streak of flames and turned, flapping to gain air, Veronika raised her hands and shouted a very old Russian spell.

Power streaked up her arms and shot from her fingertips, twisting into a thick rope of energy that lassoed around the dragon's head.

He beat his wings, turning and fighting to fly away.

She held firm, yelling, "Give up. You're beaten."

A new burst of fire scorched over her circle. When it ceased, she still stood with her ancestors and Ossian.

She laughed and told the spirits of her family, "Lend me your power to take down this dragon."

Energy swelled around her, then funneled into her body. She leaned forward a little then arched back, yanking with all her might on the rope of energy.

The dragon's neck snapped forward, dragging his body down in such a way that it forced his wings to fold. He hit the ground hard with a loud boom, shaking the earth beneath her feet.

Dark smoke boiled from the dragon's snout, then subsided into a thin trail drifting away. His eyes remained shut. His huge chest gave one last exhale, becoming still.

Cathbad called out. "I must admit I did not think you could do it, Veronika. I know we will make great allies."

Veronika reveled in her glorious win.

She'd had no idea any dragons still existed, though she'd heard talk of this one while she had been locked away in VIPER.

Nonhumans and humans would sing of her great victory, but they would also bow down to her as soon as she gained Witchlock. That Sterling bitch who stole it could not run far enough.

Turning slowly, she gave a series of half-bows. "Thank you, family. I know you are tired. Rest and I will speak to you soon."

The ancestors faded away.

Ossian had not moved since the dragon came crashing down. His eyes bulged in shock. "You will rule this world, my queen."

"Yes, I will." Smiling, she gave her servant another indulgent pat. "Come, Ossian. You should look at the dragon up close to truly appreciate the battle you've witnessed." She strolled to where Daegan's huge head lay on its side, as tall as she was.

Putting the toe of her shoe on his nose, Veronika tapped. "Bad dragon."

Cathbad had moved up to the other side of the massive flying lizard. "That's quite a kill, Veronika. You ever faced off with a dragon before?"

"Actually, no, I didn't think any still existed. Until this one, I had believed the stories were all myths."

"No, they were true," Cathbad assured her. "I recall when this one's father ruled the land where he grew up. There were quite a few dragons at one time."

"Hmm. Well, he's dead now. If we face another one, you'll know I can handle it. I hope you bring at least half that much power to the table."

Giving her a charming smile, he said, "I might just surprise you." His smile fell away. He jerked his head back and forth, looking all around. "Is this a trick?"

Beladors emerged from the darkness.

CHAPTER 32

Quinn strode from the tree line as Belador warriors spread out wide around the area where Veronika posed next to the dragon. He glanced at Reese who followed close beside him. He'd asked Evalle and Storm to wait among the trees with more Beladors until he needed them.

Sparing a glance for the dragon heaped on the ground, Quinn had a moment of hesitation. Daegan had said not to worry, because he could handle Veronika, but not a muscle moved in that giant dragon body.

No one knew what Veronika was capable of when she accessed her ancestral realm.

Daegan had said to stick with the plan no matter what. They all had a duty.

Quinn's voice boomed, "Give me Phoedra or prepare to take your last breath." He'd changed into a pair of cargo pants and a T-shirt, now prepared to fight as he wielded a Belador sword.

Time to put it to good use.

Veronika said to Cathbad, "Bring the girl and come with me, druid."

Cathbad had Phoedra by the arm, but stayed where he had positioned himself with Phoedra, off to the side.

Quinn's heart tried to fight its way out of his chest when he took in Phoedra. His daughter. He wanted to snatch her away, but believed what Cathbad had said about her being majikally bound to him. She had better not be harmed.

When Cathbad failed to join her, Veronika's eyes lit with excitement as if she saw an opportunity anyhow. She asked

Quinn, "Where is Adrianna? I might consider trading the girl for that witch."

Quinn snarled, "I will not make any deal with you. Phoedra is mine." He shoved his gaze at Cathbad. "Hand her over now or face the consequences."

Veronika's gaze went to Cathbad. "Now it is time for you to show me *your* value, druid."

"I would be happy to do so if I believed you could back your word, but I fear you've overstated *your* value, Veronika."

She had an expression of total confusion as if she couldn't comprehend his meaning.

Cathbad lifted his hands, uttering a string of words as he backed away from Phoedra.

Quinn kept an eye on Veronika when he told Reese, "Go get Phoedra."

Reese rushed toward his daughter.

Veronika whipped her hand faster than the eye could follow. She struck a blast of energy like a lightning bolt that scorched the ground between Reese and Phoedra.

Reese jumped back at the last second.

Phoedra started shaking her head as if coming out of a foggy state. She took a look around and froze in place.

Twenty Beladors had fanned out in an arc behind Veronika, each holding up a kinetic shield, but Quinn had told them not to link. Veronika could knock them down like a string of bowling pins with one strike if they linked their powers.

Quinn had seen enough.

He lifted his hands and hit Veronika with a megaload of his power, knocking the bitch off her feet. She landed backward and literally flew upright, floating above the ground.

"Touch that girl and you die now," Quinn warned Veronika and anyone else, like Cathbad, who had pulled back only to the edge of the field. Stepping toward Veronika, he told Phoedra, "Go with Reese."

Phoedra stared at him, then looked up at Veronika floating in the air, then turned her gaze on the dragon.

Evalle came out of the tree line. "Reese?"

"I've got her." Reese lunged forward again.

When Veronika turned to strike at Reese and Phoedra again,

Quinn stepped in between and threw up a kinetic wall that sent Veronika's power bouncing back at her.

The energy slapped Veronika and burst across her body. She screamed, but Quinn doubted that one hit would seriously harm her.

His plan had been to minimize her targets until they had a clear advantage. He had plenty of Belador power here, but no one knew for sure what Veronika was capable of, which made her too dangerous to attack with all they had.

Ossian had been standing still, watching the byplay. "My queen?"

"Kill him, you fool," Veronika ordered, clearly talking about Quinn.

Ossian had a moment of looking kicked in the nuts, then nodded as if to himself. He rushed forward, stopping a stone's throw from Quinn, who still held a kinetic field in place. Evalle and Devon jumped in, adding their kinetic fields to Quinn's.

Reese had taken Phoedra to the trees where Storm had agreed to protect Quinn's daughter with a team of three Beladors until Quinn could get to her.

Ossian opened his arms and created an arch of power flying from hand to hand. The energy thundered and rumbled.

He controlled an electrical storm.

Quinn had no idea what Ossian could do with that, but before he could say anything, Ossian's face and body wobbled and blurred, then warped into ... Lionel Macaffey?

Lionel was a Belador who had gone missing six weeks ago after finishing guard duty at VIPER.

Evalle said, "Do you see what I see, Quinn?"

"Yes, I think we know what happened to Lionel." Quinn warned, "Evalle and Devon, that energy may break through."

Evalle said, "Don't even think that we're leaving you to fight alone."

"Nope," Devon agreed. "Whoa. His face just changed again. He looks like the one she called Ossian a minute ago."

Quinn said, "If we can't stop him, we can't stop Veronika."

Reese stepped up between all of them and ordered, "When I say go, give me an opening in your kinetic wall."

Quinn wanted to toss her over with Phoedra, but he took one

look at Reese and realized she would not be shoved aside. She had told him point blank that she made her own decisions. He had to respect her choices, just as she had to respect his.

He told Evalle and Devon, "You two keep your shields. I'll drop mine."

Evalle didn't like that one bit. "Are you serious, Quinn? That guy might kill you before she does whatever the hell she does. This isn't a demon fight."

Reese shouted at her, "I've got this!"

"You better," Evalle snarled right back.

Quinn might die from an overload of static energy between those two.

"Ready, Quinn?" Reese asked, sounding calm as she gripped the medallion in one hand, rolling the fingers of her free hand into a fist, then opening them. She did that twice.

"Just say when."

Stretching her power arm back, Reese kept her gaze on Ossian and said, "Now."

Quinn lowered his shield.

Ossian must have known immediately. He shoved his hands at Quinn. Explosive power shot away from him in a rolling storm of lightning popping in all directions.

Reese whipped her loaded hand forward at the same moment.

Her power spiraled out in a deadly lash of demon energy that clashed with Ossian's. She walked forward, pushing everything she had into the force she drove.

Quinn said, "*Stop!*"

"Can't."

She kept pouring power at Ossian, until he dropped to his knees under the pressure. They stood ten feet apart in a fierce version of power arm wrestling.

Veronika moved in the air as if to attack Reese.

Quinn lashed out with kinetic power, popping her sideways.

Reese made one more shove and the energy engulfed Ossian. He burst into flames and screamed. His face whipped back and forth through different changes until his body shriveled to the ground in a stinking mass of charred skin, muscle and bone.

When Quinn looked beyond the burned corpse, Veronika dropped to the ground with her hands on her hips. "You killed my polymorph. I was willing to accept the girl or Adrianna. Now I will take them both and you will all die."

Lifting her hands, Veronika said, "Come to me, family. I call to all of my ancestors. I beg of you to kill everyone except Phoedra!"

Hell, she'd called up a family reunion.

Howling from thousands of souls rocked the air, but the sound seemed muffled. Quinn glanced up to see spirits crawling all over an invisible dome like translucent roaches trying to get in.

Cathbad had agreed to hand over Phoedra and to build a ward over this site. He'd kept his part of the bargain made in the Tribunal, setting the ward as he'd backed away.

It had to have taken hours to create a ward capable of preventing Veronika's ancestors from entering this space.

Quinn would have felt bad for anyone else who looked as pained as Veronika did when her supernatural cavalry failed to show up.

She screeched so loudly his eardrums threatened to burst.

"You can not stop me!" Veronika wove her hands around and around each other, powering up to make another strike.

Daegan's voice boomed, "Give it up, Veronika."

Thank the gods Daegan had survived. Quinn would find out more later, but he was damned happy their dragon king lived.

She spun around in a blur and looked up at Daegan, whose dragon form now towered above her. "No!" she screeched. "You're dead!"

Adrianna walked out from behind Daegan with the Witchlock power spinning in a huge ball of white above her open palm. "No, *you're* dead."

The huge, red dragon chastised Veronika in a deep baritone, "Did you really think that puny whip of energy harmed me?"

Looking like the deranged witch she was, Veronika started screaming and sending an arc of energy shooting at Adrianna.

The Sterling witch whispered to her ball of white power and sent her own energy streaming to meet Veronika's. When the two hit, Veronika's energy burst like a fireworks display.

"I will take that from you," Veronika threatened.

"Not now. I found out how to block you from connecting to me, thanks to my friends in Treoir. You're done, Veronika."

Raising her hands, Veronika tossed what looked like a mother lode at Adrianna.

Quinn noted that Daegan didn't interfere.

When Quinn and Daegan had finished at the Tribunal, then met with Daegan's advisors, Adrianna had told everyone not to try to help if she engaged Veronika.

Adrianna walked straight into the power cloud Veronika created. She lifted her ball of Witchlock and shouted an order.

Veronika's power rumbled then boomed in an explosion of white and floated down as snow.

Quinn walked forward, telling Veronika, "You have been found guilty of committing an atrocious sin against Beladors and threatening our entire world. You will face sentencing by VIPER."

Looking beaten, Veronika was slow to acknowledge his words. When she turned her gaze to him, her eyes twinkled with an unholy light as she declared, "I will not die alone." She whipped her arm in an arc toward where Phoedra stood in the tree line.

Quinn dove into Veronika's mind. It was like jumping into a volcano ready to explode.

Screams and shouts filled the air around him but he was blind to anything except stopping that witch from killing his child. He fought her with strike after strike of his mental energy. Her natural defense surged hard, battling back.

His head would explode at any minute. He was locked too deeply to back out.

Then white light blinded him to everything else and he landed on the ground, staring up at a black sky.

CHAPTER 33

Reese slapped Quinn's cheeks. "Don't you dare give up now."

His eyes had rolled up so far she couldn't see anything but white.

Daegan walked up, now in his human form and dressed like a medieval warrior. "How is he?"

"He's going to be dead if he doesn't answer me," Reese said, trying not to show her panic.

Fingers curled around her wrist. "Stop beating me," Quinn ordered in a rough voice, blinking and squinting until he could hold his eyes open.

She stared at his beautiful blue gaze and felt her soul come back to life. She'd almost lost Quinn and Phoedra. "Don't do that crap again."

"What crap? Kill a crazy witch?" He lifted his head and Reese helped him sit up. "She is dead, right?"

Evalle walked up. "Yep. Dead, dead, deadski, as Beetlejuice would say. Looks like someone lit a cherry bomb behind Veronika's eyes."

Reese looked up, smiling. "I've watched that movie with Phoedra. She loves it."

Quinn lurched to his feet. "Where is she?"

"Phoedra is safe," Evalle assured Quinn. "She's over with Storm and he's using his native majik to keep her calm, which is a good idea. I don't think she's ever seen any of this supernatural stuff before."

Reese stood next to him. "She hasn't, but she's bright and intuitive, so she'll get there."

Daegan said, "Devon, would you take some warriors and dispose of those bodies? Use the same procedure we do for witches."

"You got it."

Reese fell into step with Quinn, who had started for Phoedra, but he stopped and turned back. "What about all the other missing children?"

Daegan answered, "Cathbad made good on his word. His warriors delivered them as agreed."

"That's wonderful. It's unfortunate that we owe him a favor, but—"

"*I* owe him the favor," Daegan clarified. "I have no issue with that as long as the kidnapping ends as well, which I believe it will. Just as we discussed, Cathbad stayed long enough to remove the ward when Veronika's ancestors dispersed as soon as she died."

Quinn agreed, "When Cathbad claimed that had all been Queen Maeve's doing and that he would not stop the attacks, I had my doubts. But he didn't light up like a red bulb in the Tribunal when he made those statements."

Daegan nodded. "There is still a price to be paid for those of ours she killed, and I will collect in full, but I wanted the children returned and to know the other families would be safe first."

"One question, Daegan. How did you survive Veronika's attack? It appeared you had been killed."

"As a dragon, I've always had the ability to go into a deep sleep that mimics death. I've used it only when I needed to heal a serious wound."

Quinn murmured, "Interesting."

Reese asked, "Are we really done with Veronika?"

Quinn appeared to ponder his answer. "Possibly. We were always worried about attacking because we had no idea what power she drew from her ancestral realm and whether she might be stronger after death."

"That was freaky."

"One way to describe it." He sighed. "To be honest, I think only time will tell." His gaze swept across the scene, taking in the field of warriors and the two dead bodies.

If Reese had to guess, she'd say he was struggling between

walking away to be with Phoedra and staying to supervise the rest of this operation as the Maistir.

Quinn told Daegan, "If you don't need me right now, I'd like some time with my daughter."

"Granted. Take all you need. I intend to continue spending time with our warriors for quite a while."

"Thank you."

Reese tried not to let her thoughts show on her face. She had a difficult decision to make in about twenty-five steps.

Quinn walked with her, putting an arm around her shoulder and whispering close to her ear. "I was terrified when you walked out to face Ossian. I don't want you doing that crap either."

"Somebody had to break up that party."

Two more steps and he said, "You heard Daegan. I'm free to get to know Phoedra. I'd like for you to stay and help us transition. In fact, I'd like you to stay, period."

Her heart thumped at a crazy pace.

What was she going to do?

When they stepped inside the tree line, Storm looked up from where he kept an eye on Phoedra.

Quinn said, "Thank you for watching over her. You can release her from your majik now."

Storm nodded, whispered something, and stepped away from Phoedra.

Until that happened, she'd been standing there staring forward with a relaxed look on her face. The minute Storm released whatever he had been doing to keep her calm, Phoedra turned into a panicked, hot mess.

She started crying and screamed, "*Reese!*"

Reese put a hand out to get Quinn to wait, and he did as she ran forward to hug Phoedra. The poor girl was shaking hard and not making sense. "What's going on? What, Reese? Did you ... I saw a dragon? No ... that's wrong. Cathbad said ... I don't ..."

Reese held tight as Phoedra cried and started hyperventilating.

People were running into the area, asking what was wrong. Someone used kinetics to lift a body. Phoedra saw it and started keening.

Reese turned to Quinn, who looked pained, unsure what to do

to help Phoedra. He took a step forward.

Grabbing her medallion with one hand and keeping her arm around Phoedra with the other, Reese said, "I'm sorry, Quinn."

His face fell, then the world shifted and blurred as she teleported away.

CHAPTER 34

When the teleporting ended, Reese looked around to see if this had worked out the way she'd hoped.

Yes. She and Phoedra were on the sugar-white sand of Daytona Beach in Florida. If she hadn't screwed up, it was sometime between Wednesday and Thursday in the middle of the night.

The sand glowed in the pitch dark, but she'd had few choices for teleporting somewhere safe to land in an open spot and she chose a place Phoedra had said many times she wanted to visit.

Phoedra wobbled, then looked up and turned to the waves gently rolling into the shore. "Is this Daytona? Oh, crap, this just gets more insane."

The girl had been close to hysterics when Reese had zapped them out of Atlanta, so she considered this an improvement.

"Can we sit here and talk, Snook?" Reese asked.

"Why not? Are we going to the moon next?"

"No, silly." Reese had just sat down when Phoedra sat in her lap, hooked her arms around her and cried her heart out some more. Reese ran her hand up and down Phoedra's back, soothing her and telling her it was all going to make sense soon, but she was safe.

At least Phoedra would be safe.

Reese had burned her only teleport to come here, but everyone was so focused on what they wanted and what they thought should happen, that no one was paying attention to Phoedra.

This little girl was tough, but she was still just a kid.

Screw Yáahl.

He'd jerked Reese around for years and hadn't told Phoedra anything. This child had grown up thinking she'd been abandoned.

Not Quinn's fault. The shock on his face as Reese had disappeared with his child had said it all.

He'd never forgive Reese.

She couldn't blame him even if she'd do it again for Phoedra. She'd have to find a way to live with Quinn's anger, but just thinking about giving him up hurt.

She still heard his last words. *I want you to stay.*

Everything she'd ever wanted had been right in front of her, but Phoedra needed her more at that moment. Phoedra had been deprived of so much for so long, then put through hell for the past twenty-four hours.

This child deserved a time-out from life in a quiet place with someone she knew and trusted. She needed a chance to catch her breath and to figure out what was happening.

Phoedra had no idea any of this supernatural world existed. She didn't know Yáahl and evidently Donella was one of his minions.

Maybe this was why he'd put Reese in Phoedra's path.

Had Yáahl known that at some point Phoedra would need an anchor in a violent world?

At this point, Reese was the only one who Phoedra would trust to tell her the truth about who she was and what her future meant.

When Phoedra finished sniffling and scooted off Reese's lap to sit beside her, Reese put an arm around her shoulders and pulled her in close.

"I want to explain all this. Are you ready?"

"I think so."

"First, I have to admit that I've been keeping a truth from you, but only for your protection. I belong to a world of people who have supernatural powers."

Phoedra lifted her head and Reese could barely see her face in the dim light from a dock down the way. "Cathbad said I was special. Do I have powers?"

Reese didn't know whether to thank Cathbad or hurt the man for holding Phoedra hostage, but it appeared he'd treated her fairly. "You are special. You will have powers and abilities as you mature. I think some might have shown up under duress when the kidnappers complained about you hurting their heads."

"Yeah." Phoedra curved her shoulders in, acting self-conscious. "I knew something was happening, but I'm not sure what I was doing."

Reese rubbed her arm. "I know, Snook. Once you understand what's going on and more about my world—your world too, now—you'll have a chance to train."

All of a sudden, Phoedra got that hero worship look in her eyes like she did when Reese showed her a new defensive move. "What all can you do?"

Reese mentally crossed her fingers and hoped she was doing this right. "I can zap a demon."

"Are there really demons?"

Reese hoped showing up out of the blue in Daytona would buy her time before any local demons found their way to her. "Yes, but don't worry. You're related to one of the most powerful preternatural groups in the world known as Beladors. An army of them showed up tonight to rescue you and save the world." Reese smiled, hoping to keep this on the lighter side, but that was asking a lot when she had to tell a girl she was not really human.

"Related? Do they know anything about my mother and father?"

"Yes. I know, too. But I only figured it out after you got kidnapped, so I promise I haven't been hiding that from you." Well, she had been pretty damn certain Kizira was Phoedra's mother after the psychic event, but there was no point in complicating this by getting picky on a timeline. The information was all that mattered.

"Tell me," Phoedra begged, her voice jumpy with excitement.

"Your mother has passed away," Reese began, because she wanted to get the bad news out of the way.

"That's what Madame Salina said."

"Eh, I guess," Reese allowed, debating on if she should warn Phoedra not to take too much of what Madame Salina said to heart. *Later.* She went on to explain who Kizira was, who the Medb were, and how *bad* they were. She wanted Phoedra to know that Cathbad was not just part of the Medb, but dangerous, so that the girl wouldn't let her defenses down around him in the future. Reese explained the Beladors the best she could and how they were actually enemies of the Medb, then she finally got to the point of Phoedra's father.

"Do you remember the man who walked up with me right before we left?"

"You mean right before you had Scotty beam us here?"

Reese smiled, happy to see shades of Phoedra coming back. "Yes. His name is Vladimir Quinn and he's the Belador Maistir over all of North America. He's also your father."

That stole the words from Phoedra, whose mouth moved silently.

Rushing ahead, Reese said, "He has faced every battle you can imagine to get to you. He never knew about you until Kizira told him on her deathbed, but she died before she could tell him how to find you. He offered his life in trade for you today, but in the end he was able to save you and stay alive. He wants very much to get to know you and to take care of you."

For the next few minutes, Phoedra stared out at an ocean that vanished into the black night. "What about Donella?"

"She was raising you for your guardian, but she clearly cares for you."

"Is she, uhm ... "

"Like us?" Reese filled in. Nearby flapping caught her ear. *Please don't let a seagull poop on us.*

"Uh huh," Phoedra said, encouraging Reese to explain.

"Yes, I think Donella is not entirely human, but I really don't know what she is. Maybe some form of earthly angel." That sounded ridiculous to Reese's ears, but no one had given her a bio on these players.

Blowing out a weary breath, Phoedra asked, "How is all this possible?"

Reese had heard a steady beat of wings and looked up. Even with the night as black as a tar pit, she made out a circle of crows zooming around them.

"Reese?"

Lowering her gaze, Reese said, "What?"

"I don't understand how all this is possible."

"Actually, at your age I didn't either. But once you've had some time to become familiar with it, I think you'll do just fine."

Phoedra looked up. "Are those crows?"

"Yes." Lifting the medallion, Reese said, "I know you're watching. You might as well show yourself."

"Who are you talking to?" Phoedra asked.

"Your guardian."

"Does he know where we are?"

"Yes, I do," Yáahl answered from behind them.

Reese didn't turn around. She gave him her normal Paula Deen greeting. "Hey, Yáahl."

Phoedra had twisted to look up at him, then turned back. "When did you get a Southern accent, Reese?"

"Yáahl is his name." She spelled it for Phoedra, then took a look at him all dressed up in a suit. If he didn't want Phoedra to know his identity, he shouldn't have appeared right now.

Reese asked him, "Why can't you just show up like that the other times?"

"Would that help Phoedra?"

"Guess not." Reese said, "Phoedra, this your guardian."

"Are you two ready to return home?" he asked.

Phoedra had that caught-in-the-headlights look.

Reese told Yáahl, "No. I think Phoedra has been yanked around enough."

"I have a commitment," Yáahl started.

Reese jumped up. "You did what you said you'd do, but Quinn is her father and he deserves to get to know her. She deserves a parent who loves her. Quinn has fought unbelievable things, deadly things, and crazy beings to protect her. He doesn't sit on the top of a mountain passing out decisions and letting his minions handle his dirty work."

Yáahl didn't argue with her, but he was clearly angry. He politely asked Phoedra, "Would you mind sitting there for a moment so I might have a private word with Reese?"

"Just don't leave me."

"I won't," Reese said before Yáahl could reply. She still had the medallion. She doubted he'd kill her in front of Phoedra, which meant she'd get in one good shot.

Reese followed him twenty feet away, downwind from Phoedra so their words would be carried away from the girl on the brisk breeze.

Still, she couldn't take her eyes off Phoedra.

"My minions will watch over her, Reese," Yáahl said.

She faced him. "That girl needs more than minions."

Ignoring her comment, he said, "Yet again you defy me. You did not return with her as you were instructed."

That was the final fucking straw.

"You know what, Yáahl? I'm not the person meddling in other people's lives. You are. I'm just the one stuck trying to fix the mess. I did what I thought was right for Phoedra. I even yanked her away from Quinn and left him panicked, because Phoedra needed a chance to process all of this with no one in her face. I did that for Phoedra. Not you. Not Quinn. Not Kizira. It's time people put *her* first. I can't live like this, Yáahl. Quinn's a good guy and I hated screwing him over."

The bane of her existence studied her a long moment, as if he could see all the way inside and found something she didn't want him to know.

She finally snapped, "What?"

"This man Quinn is more than a friend?"

Reese scoffed. "Don't change the topic. We're talking about Phoedra."

"Why are you fighting your attraction?"

"You don't know I'm attracted to him."

"You just admitted it."

Wind swatted hair in her face. She grabbed a handful and shoved it behind her ear. "I didn't say that, I was saying you can't know ..." She realized how it kept coming out and gave up. "Yes, I like Quinn. He's ... a very good man, but it doesn't matter what I feel for him. I'm a demon magnet with blood that kills babies. I am the last person he needs in his life. He's already been through hell and back with another messed-up woman. Now that you made me bare my soul, can we get back to Phoedra? What are you going to do? I want to know so that I can have time to explain it to her."

"What about you?"

"Me? Really? I've given up on ever getting my powers back, because you give me impossible tasks."

Yáahl tapped his chin. "Are you saying you've realized you can live a full life without your powers?"

She slapped her forehead. "Yes. If that's what you've been waiting to hear then this is me admitting that you win. I'm not hunting demons and I have things to live for, Phoedra being one. I want to stay around her so she has a friend since she's just found out Donella was not a real foster mother."

"On the contrary, Donella was an excellent one." He sounded insulted.

"I didn't say she wasn't a great person for raising Phoedra, only that Phoedra knows Donella was doing a duty. There's a big difference between someone who fosters because they want the child and someone who just does a good job of keeping them alive."

His silence bothered her.

A blue fog of energy formed next to them. It wavered in the air. Yáahl angled his head as if he were listening to someone. After a moment, he said, "Kizira wants me to make good on our agreement."

"Kizira?" Reese said in a low hiss, leaning forward to hide her words from Phoedra. "Where was she when Phoedra was being dragged around by kidnappers?"

"She should not be here at all. That she took a spirit form when you saw her in San Diego, probably cost her all the power she could muster, since her ashes were salted and scattered. She's hanging on to this plane by threads."

Reese straightened and looked at the blue energy trembling as if it were straining to do something. That had been one powerful woman. "Tell her I'm sorry she isn't getting to raise her daughter and that she has a lovely child."

When Yáahl seemed to hesitate, Reese added, "Please."

He gave her a small nod and stood still for a moment. "Kizira says to tell you thank you and that Quinn deserves some happiness in his life."

What was Reese supposed to say to that? "He does."

Slowly the blue fog shrank until it disappeared.

Reese asked, "Is she gone?"

"Yes. She trusts that Phoedra will be well cared for."

Reese still had to convince the raven god to allow Phoedra to be with Quinn. "Look, Yáahl, I think Phoedra needs to be with her father. Quinn is sincere about wanting to take on that role and he almost died saving her. He has the entire Belador force and a dragon to protect her. Quinn has an enormous capacity to love." Reese hurt saying that because she'd blown any chance she had of being the recipient of Quinn's love. "Kizira placed her child in your care and she told Quinn to find Phoedra. He did."

"With your help."

"Yes, I helped, but that isn't the point. Letting Phoedra get to know Quinn is the right thing to do. You can't ask for much more dedication to a child than Quinn will shower on her and he's an honorable man."

"He is? So he would care for a child of his no matter the circumstances?"

"Didn't I just say that? Yes."

"That's good to know."

Talking to his crows was easier. Reese said, "Great. Let's go tell her she can live with her father."

"I never agreed to that."

CHAPTER 35

A Frisbee flew past Quinn and he spun around, heart racing.

Just a guy with his Labrador enjoying Piedmont Park.

Sun shone over the recently trimmed grass field. People lounged on blankets, talking and catching rays. Small children tottered near their mamas. Dogs chased balls and played everywhere he looked.

Quinn shook his head at being so lame.

What did he think he'd find here today that he hadn't found yesterday?

Sure, he'd told Reese this would be a good place for her dog, Gibbons, but that didn't mean she was in this city or that she would ever come here.

Three days ago, as he'd stood waiting to meet his child for the first time, he'd been shocked when he stared at the empty spot Reese had left behind when she teleported away with Phoedra.

He'd received a message a minute later.

A crow had delivered it.

The note had read:

Phoedra is safe with Reese, who will be in touch very soon. Thank you for keeping your daughter safe. Kizira asked me to protect her child and keep Phoedra from the nonhuman world for as long as possible. I had hoped to continue that duty for a few more years, but recent circumstances have changed everything. Reese presented a strong case for you to take over guarding and caring for your child. She'll explain more when you see her. Don't break their hearts, or I shall return.

Phoedra's Guardian

That guardian had it all wrong.

Reese was the one who had crushed Quinn's heart. He'd been ready to make a place for her in his life. He'd trusted her.

She'd betrayed him when she vanished with Phoedra.

Would he never learn anything about women?

Quinn strolled along, lost in thought until he heard a big dog making deep woof sounds. He looked up and thought he saw a mirage.

There came Reese and Phoedra walking toward him, towed forward by a leash attached to a huge beast covered in shaggy hair.

That bloody dog had a beard.

His heart paused, waiting to beat.

Phoedra had Kizira's eyes and black hair, although the pink stripe in it had to be an artificial addition. Reese's wild, reddish-brown hair blew softly around her face.

Her beautiful eyes were rimmed in sadness.

He probably looked no happier, but he would put all that behind him to show his daughter how much he wanted her. Phoedra had control of the mutt lunging forward.

Reese had dressed similarly to Phoedra. She had on a red sleeveless, button-down blouse tucked into a pair of jean shorts that showed off her sexy legs.

He could not go there.

Trust went two ways. She clearly didn't trust him or she wouldn't have left that evening without telling him in advance. She'd known all along that she had the capacity to teleport. There had been no hesitation when she lifted her medallion and vanished. During the flight to New Orleans, he hadn't pressed her about how she'd planned to return Phoedra home once she found her. He'd assumed that when Reese said she *had a plan*, that her plan was pretty much flying by the seat of her pants.

He should have known better.

Reese started the awkward conversation, "Hi, Quinn. Evalle said you would be here."

After three days of asking himself how he could have been tricked so easily, he wanted to unload some of the anger he'd been carrying around.

But his heart had started back up the minute Reese spoke. He also couldn't be angry when he looked at the beautiful young lady who was his daughter.

He hadn't felt this off-balance in his entire adult life. "Hello, Phoedra. I'm ..."

"Reese told me about you and my mother, Kizira. It was a lot to take in, especially with all the majik and stuff."

He smiled. "I can only imagine. I'm sorry you spent so many years not knowing. I would have come for you if I'd known."

Phoedra's innocent eyes shimmered. "Really? I mean, Reese told me that, but I guess I needed to hear it from you."

The longing in her voice squeezed his heart. He'd make sure his child knew from here on just how thrilled he was to have her as his daughter. "Of course. I would never leave a child of mine to fend for herself or to think she isn't loved. All I ask is that if you give me a chance, I'll show you just how much I do love you."

Tears welled up in Phoedra's eyes and spilled over.

Then she shocked Quinn by handing Gibbons's leash to Reese, then walking up to her father and wrapping her little arms around his waist.

Quinn could never describe the feeling of holding his child for the first time. He'd never considered having children, but from the moment he found out about Phoedra, he'd experienced a fierce need to protect her and care for her.

There would be an adjustment for both of them, but he relished this chance at getting to know her and only hoped he didn't screw up being a father.

When he looked over at Reese, his heart hummed with happiness just to see her there, but it stuttered for a second.

What about Reese?

What would happen when he took Phoedra? How could he just walk away and never see her again?

On the other hand, how could he trust her when she kept so many secrets from him? She was still keeping secrets. She knew who Phoedra's guardian was and he doubted that she'd give him the name.

Evalle would be telling him to allow Reese a chance to explain.

He could do that much, but only if she didn't disappear again.

Reese watched Phoedra hug him, her eyes shiny. Her smile was so melancholy.

He nearly reached out to her, the urge to make things better for her so strong he barely resisted.

What was it about the woman that made Quinn want to pick up a sword and battle dragons?

Or demons, in her case.

Reese cleared her throat. "I want to explain about leaving suddenly. I did have a reason."

"It's fine. She's back." Quinn struggled for the right words and those sure as hell weren't the ones. But his emotions were bottled up so thickly in his throat he couldn't sort out his thoughts.

Pulling Phoedra around to stand next to him with his arm around her shoulders, Quinn asked Reese, "What I mean to say is that we could discuss that later. How long are you here for?"

Reese looked at Phoedra, who ducked her head. Reese said, "I've moved here."

He shouldn't get excited, but hadn't he asked her to stay?

She'd hurt him when she left, but she had brought his daughter back to him. Okay, the truth. He wanted Reese to be here more than he could say.

Maybe she did have a good reason for what she did. When they got a chance to talk alone, he'd hear her out.

He smiled, determined to try to work through this with her. "That's nice to hear."

"I'm glad you think so, because I've been given temporary custody of Phoedra. She'll be living with me."

"What? You have to be joking."

Phoedra pulled away from him and Quinn regretted his angry tone. "I'm sorry, Phoedra. I know she's your friend, but I'm surprised since I'm your father."

Phoedra looked uncomfortable. "I know, but it's just that, uh, I've known Reese a long time."

Hell of a way to start with Phoedra by upsetting her. Damn it, this was exactly what Quinn meant about Reese keeping things from him. Who was the guardian behind all of this?

Reese's eyes flashed with her own anger, but she softened her tone. "Quinn, please listen. We all agree that Phoedra is your child and she's looking forward to finding out more about you and getting to know you, but the only way I could bring her back in the middle of all that goes on in the preternatural world in Atlanta was by agreeing to be her temporary guardian. She has a lot to learn. This way she'll get to know you, the Beladors, everyone. You just said yourself that you couldn't imagine how difficult this is for Phoedra. We have an apartment in town where you can visit any time you want to see ... her. I'm not standing in the way of you two developing a relationship. I'm here to facilitate that."

Phoedra had been watching and crossed her arms, looking ready to jump to Reese's defense. "Reese is the reason I'm here. She demanded that I be allowed to live near you and that when I say I'm ready I can make the choice to live with you."

Quinn asked, "Who, exactly, is holding the power over you two?"

Reese and Phoedra exchanged loaded glances, but said nothing.

"I want the truth. I think I deserve it."

Reese muttered, "Why is this crap never easy?" Raking a hand across her wavy hair as the light breeze toyed with it, she said, "He is someone Kizira went to when she was pregnant. She asked for sanctuary for Phoedra. He is the reason I was sent here to protect Kizira's body the first time you met me. He is the reason I was able to follow Phoedra right after she was kidnapped and taken to Tulsa. He has been her guardian since birth and it took a lot of arguing to get this concession from him. He made this deal with Phoedra, with her welfare in mind, so it's up to him to provide any additional details, including his identity. In fact, he said he got in touch with you right after we left that night."

"He had a crow deliver a message."

Reese and Phoedra looked at each other and laughed. "That's him."

Quinn had been willing to give trust another try, but now he realized Kizira, Phoedra and Reese trusted some other man, one with powers, more than Quinn.

Kizira had trusted this guardian more than Quinn, too.

That sucker punched him. "Is this the same person who has

prevented you from tapping your powers, Reese?"

"Yes. But I have them back now." Reese fought not to grin even more. Her eyes danced with happiness.

Quinn had bones to pick with her, but he was damned glad she had those powers back for her benefit, and now for Phoedra's.

Evidently he was going to get to visit his child.

He'd been through too many things in his life not to roll with unexpected situations when they popped up, but he would have his way on one thing. "I will abide by all of your rules," he started.

"Oh, thank you. I really want this to work, Quinn," Reese said, sounding as if she thought they were in agreement.

"However, I will not accept my daughter living below a standard I consider acceptable."

Reese got that stubborn look. "We have a nice apartment picked out. It's close to this park. Gibbons likes it, too."

Gibbons? Apparently aka the hairy beast, which had pulled loose from Reese and was now slobbering all over a very happy Phoedra.

While the dog had her attention, Quinn stepped up to speak privately with Reese. "There are no words to thank you for all you've done in watching over my daughter."

Her eyes sharpened with suspicion, which meant she read more coming from Quinn and would be correct.

"That does not excuse the many times you have withheld the truth or rearranged it to suit your purposes. I will be in Phoedra's life and I plan to convince her to move in with me very soon." He struggled between a desire to make his point and wanting to pull Reese into his arms and kiss the hurt look out of her eyes. He'd put it there with his cool tone, but in the last two days he'd been through hell, beating himself to pieces over trusting yet another woman who'd fooled him.

It didn't feel good.

Evalle would say it sucked. Her description was better.

First he got involved with Kizira only to find out afterwards that she was royalty in his enemy's court and then not until recently that their union had produced a child he'd never known existed.

Now, he'd fallen for another woman who couldn't tell him the truth about her past or who she answered to currently. The same person—a man who clearly was not a human—who held some sort of control over his daughter.

But Reese wasn't saying another word no matter how much he pressed her.

At some point in a man's life he had to admit that he was the one allowing himself to be manipulated.

No more.

Every time he looked at Reese, he saw a future that could be amazing if not for the twist of lies between them. Even if they straightened all that out, it wasn't just *his* issues that needed getting over. She had some reason for not being honest with him. It might be due to a past relationship, but that didn't mean he should be paying the price for another man's actions.

Being forced to see her on a regular basis as he got to know Phoedra would continue to shred his heart even more if he couldn't find his way through all of this.

Reese held his stare, saying nothing in her own defense.

Damn. Now he wanted to defend her.

His hand lifted on its own until he realized he was about to touch her. He lowered his arm to his side, determined to get the truth from her before he opened himself up again.

He'd give her a chance to show him whether she could meet him halfway or if he'd just been gullible this whole time.

Trey reached Quinn telepathically. *Are you somewhere you can break away to meet with Daegan?*

Yes. Give me a minute and I'll contact you back.

Quinn said, "I've been called away for Belador business."

"Go."

She was pissed, but he wasn't sure what she wanted from him at this point. He'd begged her not to disappear without a word, and she'd done it anyhow. "Do we understand each other?"

"Oh, yes, your lordship," Reese snipped. "I heard you loud and clear, but you hear me. You will not rule our lives. You will give me plenty of notice when you plan to come by or want Phoedra to visit you. This is the first time she and I will both have freedom. No one will be dictating to me, or *her,* anymore. I shouldn't have to say this, but I will keep Phoedra safe with my very life and I will help her adjust. You do your part and we'll be fine."

"We'll talk more later."

"I don't see the point in any future conversations between you and me except to arrange for visiting Phoedra," Reese snapped.

"You will when we talk."

"Don't hold your breath. I know your rules. You know mine. Don't screw this up. I went to bat for you, but I'm not handing her over until I'm sure it's in her best interest."

"Are you trying to say I can't take care of Phoedra?"

Reese's lips thinned. "I'll make it easier for you to grasp. I won't bless her moving in with you until I think that's where she'll be *happier*. You can dazzle her with your money and surround her with preternatural bodyguards, but that does not a home and family make. Good luck. Say goodbye, because we're headed back for our favorite movie night."

Favorite movie night. He had no idea what Phoedra's favorite anything was.

Reese had blasted him between the eyes with that one and he probably deserved it for arguing when Reese gained the upper hand without even saying the real words.

You don't know how to be a father.

Turning from her, he spoke to Phoedra and hugged her again, assuring her he would see her tomorrow and they'd take it a day at a time.

Walking toward the closest street to this side of the park, he sent a text and his car pulled up as he reached the curb.

After circling back, he had the car follow Reese and Phoedra to their apartment, which at least had front door security, but he didn't leave until he had arranged Beladors from a security firm he owned to stand guard all night.

Tomorrow, those two were moving.

He couldn't wait to see Reese's face when he informed her.

His gut forced him to admit the truth. He couldn't wait to see his daughter again ... *and* Reese. Dropping his head back against the seat, he thought about those hours he'd spent making love to Reese in the Keith's domain.

That had been the happiest time of his life until he'd held Phoedra a moment ago.

How was he going to spend this much time around Phoedra and pretend that he didn't want Reese with every fiber of his being?

Because he did.

Reese felt flush all over.

Damn Quinn's sexy hide. She knew he'd be angry about her teleporting away with Phoedra, but she hadn't anticipated how much all her half-truths and flat-out lies had weighed against her when it came time to meet again.

He felt betrayed and she could understand, but that didn't soften the blow to her heart.

Phoedra called out, "I'm making pimento cheese sandwiches. Sound good?"

Reese shouted, "Be there in a minute."

She dashed to the bathroom and barely made it before she threw up. The brand-new carpet in this apartment had some weird chemical smell, which was not sitting well with her. Clearly, she was more of an it's-been-through-fifty-renters carpet person.

It wasn't just her.

Gibbons had been feeling puny right after Yáahl had teleported him and Reese's belongings, along with Phoedra's, to this apartment. He'd allowed Phoedra time to talk with Donella before all that had happened.

Kids were resilient, but Reese intended to make sure this one had an easier path starting now.

Reese bent over the toilet and heaved again.

Maybe it was the teleporting. Reese had been teleported three times and shoved through a bolthole, all in the last few days.

That had to be it.

Still, she couldn't face pimento cheese right now, which was strange since she normally loved those sandwiches. She'd explain to Phoedra and eat some soup with crackers.

Had to be the carpet and teleporting, right?

She couldn't be truly sick with the demon energy still inside her, but evidently that didn't prevent supernatural travel and sharp chemical odors from souring her stomach.

The only other option for her would be pregnancy, which

wasn't possible. Quinn had used condoms all three times and she'd been way outside the window of fertility. She'd kept an eye on her cycle for ten years, even during the most recent months—okay, years—she'd spent entirely alone.

"*Re-eese!*"

"I'm on the way," she called back. She rubbed her stomach and chuckled at the big bad demon killer being taken down by carpet.

CHAPTER 36

Cathbad held his temper when he wanted to destroy the queen's throne room, along with her in it. "I warned you not to put Ossian at risk."

Queen Maeve had the wit about her to foster an apologetic expression he didn't believe for one second. She began, "I didn't intend for him to be harmed. I had hoped to bring us Veronika's power. It would have made us invincible."

"Do you really think Veronika would have come to you? You are too old to be that naïve." No, she wasn't naïve, but the reincarnation *had* corrupted her mind. "That witch wanted to rule alone. I knew it and so did everyone else with any significant power."

"I admit I may have misjudged her."

"Misjudged? That's how you excuse sendin' Ossian to have his majik churned to the point he had to be in constant pain? I saw him. He was hurtin' and he had been a loyal follower. He was an amazin' weapon and our best intelligence gatherer. First you force us to break ties with the coalition, then you destroy my polymorph. I poured everythin' I could into him and he turned out perfect. Then you manipulated him, because you couldn't compel him."

"Let's not quarrel over this," she said, waving off the significance of what she'd done. "We'll make another one. I'll help you."

Quinn had been right.

Maeve was far worse than merely irrational and losing occasional control. She'd reached a special level of crazy.

"I need some time to myself," Cathbad announced.

She whipped around in a blur of silk and sparkles. "What are you saying?"

"I just need to get away and deal with my anger. I'm grievin' the loss of Ossian. I know you don't understand that, but he meant a lot to me."

She released a sound of quiet disgust. "Go then. I have plenty to keep me busy."

"If you mean all the Belador children you put bounties on, that's stopped and they have all been returned to their families."

"Have you lost your mind? I gave up a load of Noirre gaining those assets. What were you thinking to squander them?"

"I was thinkin' to save your life, because they were gatherin' an army of deities to invade TÅµr Medb and drag you back to make an example of you," he shouted, cracking the floor in all directions from where he stood. "The dragon was furious about your touchin' Belador children. The Tribunal went mad when Veronika escaped and they found out you were behind her breakout."

"They can't prove anything," she argued.

"That's not a concern to them. You see, they found out you were tryin' to team up with Veronika. You threatened the very existence of TÅµr Medb and all the witches and warlocks down in the human world who've been followin' your reckless orders. If you start somethin' while I'm gone, good luck to you. I'm not steppin' in to fix it again."

With that, Cathbad teleported away, whirling through space as he seethed over how much he wanted to make her pay for Ossian.

When the teleporting ended, he stood in shin-deep snow, but he now wore thick fur boots, rugged pants and a wool shirt, with a fur cape. He would not be out in this for long, though.

Turning around, he took a moment to enjoy the vista of snow-capped mountains as far as he could see.

He'd missed this.

Two thousand years was too long.

Wind and rain had altered some spots, but the mountain range had changed little since the day he'd walked away. He opened his mind to the tranquility he loved about this place and slowly let his pain slide away. After he'd allowed enough time to put his mind at peace over the loss of Ossian, he turned and waded through fresh snow to a large boulder. With a flip of his hand, the boulder made a grinding sound as it moved away from the mouth of the cave.

Inside, he tossed flames to torches that quickly caught and illuminated his way deep inside. He could have teleported in, but he hadn't enjoyed a quiet walk in many years. The tunnel descended slowly, curving back and forth, then into a long arc, gradually straightening until it opened into a massive room.

An ice palace.

Sparkling crystals hung from the ceiling like ice daggers prepared to attack anyone below. A throne of ice and sapphires perched on a raised chunk of ice ten feet square and one foot thick. Ornate trunks, filled with gold in every form from jewelry to coins to serving pieces and furnishings, had been piled three stories high against the far wall.

Exactly the way he'd left it.

The middle of the cavern was a wide-open space a hundred feet across and a hundred feet high with a pool of water seventy feet across and three times as deep.

Pulling a very old rune stone shaped as a square with rounded edges from his pocket, he turned the carved side to face the center of the cave and began bringing the elements together.

"As sun rises and falls, I ask of you the eyes to see."

Light glowed through the chamber.

"As the force of time changes all, I ask of you the power to be."

Thunder rolled through the mountain.

"As the breath of life touches all, I ask of you to set one free."

Air swirled and rushed around the fur cloaking him. The room's temperature dropped another twenty degrees below freezing.

Ice began to form on top of the pool.

He stood firm, waiting for the elements to answer him with a yes or a no.

The ground beneath him shifted and shuddered once.

Again.

He would stand here for days if the elements required such of him, but his senses told him he would not have to wait that long for a decision.

A whirring sound started below ground. The water began spinning slowly. The layer of ice cracked and buckled as the swirl picked up speed and spun until the center dipped as it was sucked into the vortex.

If he'd misjudged his power or the elements ...

Out of the pool, a force exploded upward, sending a wall of water shooting out in all directions.

Cathbad held his hand up, creating an invisible shield to avoid being drowned or washed away.

A roar of fire blasted giant icicles from the ceiling, which went flying everywhere.

Had he not been prepared, he'd have been impaled by one of them.

Swooping down in a ferocious dive, then landing gracefully at the last second to tower above him, a magnificent dragon covered in luminescent white and pale-blue scales glared at Cathbad.

He removed his protective shield. "Hello, my sweet. I promised I'd return."

The End.

Watch for TREOIR DRAGON HOARD (book 10) in 2018.

Thank you for reading this series. Posting a review is the easiest way to help readers and authors. If you have a moment to post a review (any length) at the e-retailer where you purchased BELADOR COSAINT, I'd really appreciate it.

If you'd like to stay up on all Dianna's news, visit her website – www.AuthorDiannaLove.com - and sign up for her newsletter. You'll be notified as soon as a new Belador story is available (you'll only receive an email when there is news to share or when special deals are offered to Dianna Love's Reader Community).

NOTE: We NEVER share your contact information.

To contact Dianna – email her assistant –
Cassondra@authordiannalove.com
Websites: AuthorDiannaLove.com and Beladors.com
Facebook – "Dianna Love Fan Page"
Twitter @DiannaLove
"Dianna Love Reader Community" Facebook group page
(You're invited)

Love Paranormal Romance?
Dianna has a new shifter series with unusual world building, which launches with **GRAY WOLF MATE.**
Visit www.AuthorDiannaLove.com for more on this series.

Reviews on Belador books:

"…non-stop tense action, filled with twists, betrayals, danger, and a beautiful sensual romance. As always with Dianna Love, I was on the edge of my seat, unable to pull myself away."
~~Barb, The Reading Cafe

"…shocking developments and a whopper of an ending... and I may have exclaimed aloud more than once…Bottom line: I really kind of loved it."
~~Jen, top 500 Reviewer

"DEMON STORM leaves you breathless on countless occasions."
~~Amelia Richard, SingleTitles

"...Its been a very long time since I've felt this passionate about getting the next installment in a series. Even J. K. Rowling's Harry Potter books."
~~Bryonna Nobles, Demons, Dreams and Dragon Wings

The Belador series is an ongoing story line. You may want to read the books in order. Available in ebook/print/audio.

*Be sure to visit www.**AuthorDiannaLove.com**
for the best prices:

Blood Trinity
Alterant
The Curse
Rise Of The Gryphon
Demon Storm
Witchlock
Rogue Belador
Dragon King Of Treoir
Belador Cosaint
Treoir Dragon Hoard (2018)
*Tristan's Escape (*Belador novella occurs between Witchlock and Rogue Belador timelines)*

BLOOD TRINITY – Belador Book 1

Atlanta has become the battlefield between human and demon.

As an outcast among her own people, Evalle Kincaid has walked the line between human and beast her whole life as a half-blood Belador. An Alterant. Her true origins unknown, she searches to learn more about her past before it kills her, but when a demon claims a young woman in a terrifying attack and there's no one else to blame, Evalle comes under suspicion.

The one person who can help her is Storm, the sexy new agent brought in to catch her in a lie, just one of his gifts besides being a Skinwalker. On a deadly quest for her own survival, Evalle is forced to work with the mysterious stranger who has the power to unravel her world. Through the sordid underbelly of an alternate Atlanta where nothing is as it seems to the front lines of the city where former allies now hunt her, Evalle must prove her innocence or pay the ultimate price. But saving herself is the least of her problems if she doesn't stop the coming apocalypse. The clock is ticking and Atlanta is about to ignite.

"BLOOD TRINITY is an ingenious urban fantasy ... Book One in the Belador series will enthrall you during every compellingly entertaining scene." **Amelia Richards, Single Titles**

"...a well written book that will take you out of your everyday life and transport you to an exciting new world ..." **Heated Steve**

ALTERANT: Belador Book 2

Evalle must hunt her own kind...or die with them.

In this explosive new world of betrayals and shaky alliances, as the only Alterant not incarcerated, Evalle faces an impossible task — recapture three dangerous, escaped creatures before they slaughter more humans...or her.

When words uttered in the heat of combat are twisted against her, Evalle is blamed for the prison break of three dangerous Alterants and forced to recapture the escapees. Deals with gods and goddesses are tricky at best, and now the lives of all Beladors, and the safety of innocent humans, rides on Evalle's success. Her Skinwalker partner, Storm, is determined to plant all four of his black jaguar paws in the middle of her world, but Evalle has no time for a love life. Not when a Tribunal sends her to the last place she wants to show her face.

The only person she can ask for help is the one man who wants to see her dead.

"There are SO many things in this series that I want to learn more about; there's no way I could list them all." **Lily, Romance Junkies Reviews**

THE CURSE: Belador book 3

Troll powered gang wars explode in cemeteries and no one in Atlanta is safe.

Demonic Svart Trolls have invaded Atlanta and Evalle suddenly has little hope of fulfilling a promise with the freedom of an entire race hanging in the balance, even if she had more than two days. She takes a leap of faith, seeking help from Isak, the Black Ops specialist who recently put Evalle in his cross hairs and has a personal vendetta against Alterants who killed his best friend.

Bloody troll-led gang wars force Evalle into unwittingly exposing a secret that endangers all she holds dear, and complicates her already tumultuous love life with the mysterious

Skinwalker, Storm. But it's when the entire Medb coven comes after her that Evalle is forced to make a game-changing decision with no time left on the clock.

"Evalle, continues to be one of my favorite female warriors in paranormal/urban fantasy... I loved The Curse... This was a great story from start to finish, super fun, lots of action, couples to root for, and a fantastic heroine." **Barb, The Reading Café**

RISE OF THE GRYPHON: Belador Book 4

If dying is the cost of protecting those you love ... bring it.

Evalle has a chance to find out her true origin, and give all Alterants a place in the world. To do so, she'll have to take down the Belador traitor and bring home a captured friend, which means infiltrating the dangerous Medb coven. To do that, she'll have to turn her back on her vows and enter a vicious game to the death. What she does discover about Alterants is not good, especially for the Beladors.

Her best friends, Tzader and Quinn, face unthinkable choices, as relationships with the women they love grow twisted. With time ticking down on a decision that will compel allies to become deadly enemies, Evalle turns to Storm and takes a major step in their relationship, but the witchdoctor he's been hunting now stalks Evalle. Now Evalle is forced to embrace her destiny . . . but at what price?

"Longtime fans of the Belador series will have much to celebrate in the fearless Evalle Kincaid's fourth outing...with such heart and investment, each scene has an intensity that will quicken the pulse and capture the imagination..." **RT Book Reviews**

DEMON STORM: Belador book 5

We all have demons... some are more real than others.

With Treoir Island in shambles after a Medb attack that left the survival of the missing Belador warrior queen in question and Belador powers compromised, there is one hope for her return and their future – Evalle Kincaid, whose recent transformation has turned her into an even more formidable warrior. First she has to locate Storm, the Skinwalker she's bonded with who she believes can find the Belador queen, but Storm stalks the witch doctor who's threatening Evalle's life. When he finally corners the witch doctor, she throws Storm a curve that may cost him everything, including Evalle. The hunter becomes the hunted, and Evalle must face her greatest nightmare to save Storm and the Beladors or watch the future of mankind fall to deadly preternatural predators.

DEMON STORM includes a **BONUS SHORT STORY -** DEADLY FIXATION, from the Belador world.

"There is so much action in this book I feel like I've burned calories just reading it." **D Antonio**

"...nonstop adventures overflowing with danger and heartfelt emotions. DEMON STORM leaves you breathless on countless occasions."
~~**Amelia Richard, Single Titles**

WITCHLOCK: Belador Book 6

Witchlock vanished in the 13th century ... or did it?

If Atlanta falls, Witchlock will sweep the country in a bloodbath.

After finally earning her place among the Beladors, Evalle is navigating the ups and downs of her new life with Storm when she's sucked into a power play between her Belador tribe and the Medb coven. Both groups claim possession of the Alterant gryphons, especially Evalle, the gryphon leader. But an influx of demons and dark witches into Atlanta threatens to unleash war between covens, pitting allies against each other as a legendary majik known as Witchlock invades the city and attacks powerful beings. Evalle has one hope for stopping the invasion, but the cost may be her sanity and having to choose which friend to save.

"Evalle and friends are back in another high energy, pulse pounding adventure...Fans of Rachel Caine's Weather Warden series will enjoy this series. I surely do." **In My Humble Opinion Blogspot**

ROGUE BELADOR: Belador Book 7

Immortals fear little ... except a secret in the wrong hands.

While searching for a way to save Brina of Treoir's failing memories, Tzader Burke discovers someone who can help her if he is willing to sneak into the heart of his enemy's stronghold—TÅµr Medb. He'll do anything to protect the woman he loves from becoming a mindless empty shell, but his decision could be the catalyst for an apocalyptic war. The deeper he digs for the truth, the more lies he uncovers that shake the very foundation of being a Belador and the future of his clan.

With battles raging on every front, a secret is exposed that two immortal powers have spent thousands of years keeping buried. Tzader and his team have no choice but to fight for what they believe in, because the world as they know it is never going to be the same again.

"When it comes to urban fantasy, Dianna Love is a master." **Always Reviewing**.

DRAGON KING OF TREOIR: Belador Book 8

The Treoir dragon holds the fate of the Beladors in one hand ... and his own in the other.

The Beladors finally have a true leader in Daegan, their new dragon king, but life is far from secure now that they've inherited his enemies. As their Maistir, Vladimir Quinn played a risky role in freeing the dragon from the lair of their enemy, the Medb. Quinn now faces a heavy price for his part. The Medb queen is out for blood. Vigilante killings erupt among Atlanta's secret preternatural community and all fingers point to the Beladors. The dragon king has his first real test as a ruler when he has to choose between protecting his people and entering a hostile realm full of deities capable of killing a dragon. But as a two-thousand-year-old warrior, Daegan has never shied away from any battle. Quinn, Evalle, Storm and friends race to discover who is trying to turn the entire VIPER coalition against the Beladors before war breaks out. With the clock also ticking down for Quinn, who has been ordered to hand over Kizira's body to the Medb queen, Daegan reveals an even greater reason the Beladors have to prevent the queen from any chance to use necromancy on that body than secrets Quinn protects.

Freedom is never free. Not when the powerful gods and goddesses poised to decide Quinn's fate see an opportunity to also destroy a threat to their existence – the last dragon shifter.

"Once again, Dianna Love gives us another fantastic story that keeps us glued to our seat, unable to put the book down."~~**The Reading Café**

BELADOR COSAINT: Belador Book 9

Belador Maistir Vladimir Quinn and his team are hunting preternatural predators targeting innocent humans in Atlanta. A powerful entity behind the brutal attacks is determined to force their dragon king out into the open by threatening Belador families and exposing the preternatural world to humans. When Quinn's daughter is kidnapped, he has no idea where to look. He could use the help of fiery Reese O' Rinn and her remote viewing ability, but he has even less chance of locating Reese, who vanished into thin air the last time they met. When the VIPER coalition refuses to aid the Beladors, their dragon king invokes the ancient rule of cosaint to protect his people, but will that backfire on Quinn, the dragon and the Beladors?

OTHER BOOKS BY DIANNA:

Complete Slye Temp romantic thriller Series
Last Chance To Run (free e-book for limited time)
Nowhere Safe
Honeymoon To Die For
Kiss The Enemy
Deceptive Treasures
Stolen Vengeance
Fatal Promise
*This series is complete, but watch for HAMR
BROTHERHOOD, the new spinoff series. It will include some
Slye Temp characters.

Micah Caida young adult Trilogy
Time Trap (ebook free e-book for limited time)
Time Return
Time Lock

To read excerpts, go to http://www.MicahCaida.com

(Micah Caida is the collaboration of NYT bestseller Dianna Love
and USA Today bestseller Mary Buckham)

To buy books and read more excerpts, go to
http://www.MicahCaida.com

TEENS – Visit www.RedMoonTrilogy.com to read Time
Trap for free just by just clicking on this website link.

AUTHOR'S BIO

New York Times bestseller Dianna Love once dangled over a hundred feet in the air to create unusual marketing projects for Fortune 500 companies. She now writes high-octane romantic thrillers, young adult and urban fantasy. Fans of the bestselling Belador urban fantasy series will be thrilled to know more books are coming after Belador Cosaint plus Dianna is launching a new paranormal romance series – League of Gallize Shifters. Her Slye Temp sexy romantic thriller series wrapped up with Gage and Sabrina's book–Fatal Promise–but Dianna has plans for HAMR BROTHERHOOD, a spinoff romantic suspense series coming soon. Look for her books in print, e-book and audio (most). On the rare occasions Dianna is out of her writing cave, she tours the country on her BMW motorcycle searching for new story locations. Dianna lives in the Atlanta, GA area with her husband, who is a motorcycle instructor, and with a tank full of unruly saltwater critters.

Visit her website at Dianna Love or Join her **Dianna Love Reader Community** (group page) on Facebook and get in on the fun!

A WORD FROM DIANNA…

Thank you for reading *Belador Cosaint*. This series has lived in my head and my heart for a long time. I'm often asked, "How many more Belador books will there be?" I believe a series should end when it has reached the last story arc. All I'll say for now is that the end is not in sight. I have a lot more to share with you about the Belador world.

No book happens without my amazing husband, Karl. He's my rock day and night. Everything we face, we do together. He is my life.

A special thank you to Jennifer Cazares and Sherry Arnold for being very early super readers who caught a number of small things missed by all of us in multiple editing passes. Your help insures a smooth read for everyone.

I know you often see me mention Cassondra, who does a terrific job of helping me turn out the best book I can in addition to being my assistant. She and her husband, Steve, have been a huge support throughout the majority of my writing career. They're also dear friends. Judy Carney steps in when I hit the point where I need multiple power readers to catch edits and bumps to insure you can enjoy your read. I've known Joyce Ann McLaughlin for along time and love how she helps not just me but other writers by being a super sharp beta reader, plus she is my audio editor when the wonderful Stephen R. Thorne narrates each book. Fans chose him and I'm thrilled they did!

A super big thanks also to Kimber Mirabella and Sharon Livingston Griffiths, who are always willing to read any time I need it. A special shout out to Candace Fox who does so many things to help me with guest visits on our Reader Community

Facebook page and supporting my books in too many ways to list. Thanks also to all of my awesome early review team who just keeps on rocking! My deep appreciation to Leiha Mann's support and all she does to help me promote my books.

An extra thanks to Xiamara Parathenopaeus, of S Squared Productions, who surprises me all the time with beautiful promotional creations.

The incredible Kim Killion has once again created a cover I love, as she has for all my books, and Jennifer Litteken uses her special mojo to turn my pages into book format. Much appreciation to both of you.

Hugs and love to Karen Marie Moning, a wonderful and talented woman I have the good fortune to hold as a friend. She's generous of heart and spirit.

I want to also thank the considerate people I run into when researching areas of Atlanta and Tulsa, Oklahoma this time. It's amazing how much help strangers are willing to offer in even a one-minute conversation. Tulsa is a great town. Also, thank you to my secret resources (I promised not to share your name, but you do deserve appreciation).

Thank you again to my peeps on the Dianna Love Reader Group on Facebook. You make every day wonderful.

Dianna

Made in the USA
Columbia, SC
03 October 2017